BY PIERCE BROWN

Red Rising

Golden Son

GOLDEN SON

GOLDEN SON

Pierce Brown

DEL REY

NEW YORK

Copyright © 2015 by Pierce Brown

Chart on pages viii and ix copyright 2015 © by Joel Daniel Phillips

Published in the United States by Del Rey, an imprint of Random House, a division of Random House LLC, a Penguin Random House Company, New York.

DEL REY and the HOUSE colophon are registered trademarks of Random House LLC.

Library of Congress Cataloging-in-Publication Data

Brown, Pierce
Golden son / Pierce Brown.
p. cm.—(The Red Rising trilogy ; bk. 2)
ISBN 978-0-345-53981-6 (hardback) — ISBN 978-0-345-53982-3 (ebook)
1. Government, Resistance to—Fiction. I. Title.
PS3602.R7226G65 2015
813'.6—dc23   2014031015

Printed in the United States of America on acid-free paper

www.delreybooks.com

2 4 6 8 9 7 5 3 1

First Edition

Book design by Caroline Cunningham

To mother,

who taught me to speak

GOLD
The fiercely intelligent rulers of humanity.

SILVER
Innovators, financiers, and businessmen.

WHITE
Priests and priestesses who oversee the ritual functions of Society.

COPPER
Administrators, lawyers, and bureaucrats.

BLUE
Pilots and astronavigators bred to crew starships.

YELLOW
Experts in human and natural sciences. Doctors, psychologists, and scientists.

GREEΠ
The programmers and developers of technology.

VIOLET
The creative class of artists, musicians, and performers.

ORΛΠGE
Provide systems support upon star ships and all manner of mechanical enterprises.

GRΛY
Police and military personnel.

BROWΠ
Servants in homes, businesses, and social institutions.

OBSIDIΛΠ
A monstrous race bred only for war.

PIΠK
Unparalleled in beauty, they are bred and trained for the physical arts of pleasure.

RED
Unskilled manual laborers conditioned to brutal environs.

ON THE FOUNDATION OF THE COLORS

When the first colonists ventured forth from Earth
to make their home on the moon, they created
a hierarchy for labor. In time, they
improved this hierarchy through
genetic and surgical manipulation
of their fellow man. The result
was a color-coded Society
of perfect efficiency,
one dominated by a
superior breed of
humanity, the
Golds.

DRAMATIS PERSONÆ

House Augustus and Allies

NERO AU AUGUSTUS   ArchGovernor of Mars, head of House Augustus, father to Virginia and Adrius

VIRGINIA AU AUGUSTUS/MUSTANG   daughter of Nero, twin sister to Adrius

ADRIUS AU AUGUSTUS/JACKAL   son of ArchGovernor, heir to House Augustus, twin brother to Virginia

PLINY AU VELOCITOR   chief Politico of House Augustus

DARROW AU ANDROMEDUS/REAPER   ArchPrimus of the Institute of Mars, lancer of House Augustus

TACTUS AU RATH   lancer of House Augustus

ROQUE AU FABII   lancer of House Augustus

VICTRA AU JULII   lancer of House Augustus, half sister to Antonia, daughter of Agrippina

KAVAX AU TELEMANUS   head of House Telemanus, ally of House Augustus, father to Daxo and Pax

DAXO AU TELEMANU   heir and son of Kavax, brother to Pax

House Bellona

TIBERIUS AU BELLONA   head of House Bellona

CASSIUS AU BELLONA   heir to House Bellona, son of Tiberius, lancer of House Bellona

KARNUS AU BELLONA son of Tiberius, elder brother of Cassius, lancer of House Bellona

KELLAN AU BELLONA Praetor, cousin of Cassius, nephew of Tiberius

Notable Golds

OCTAVIA AU LUNE reigning Sovereign of the Society

LYSANDER AU LUNE grandson of Octavia, heir to House Lune

AJA AU GRIMMUS the Sovereign's chief bodyguard

MOIRA AU GRIMMUS the Sovereign's chief Politico

LORN AU ARCOS former Rage Knight, head of House Arcos

FITCHNER AU BARCA former Proctor Mars, father of Sevro

SEVRO AU BARCA/GOBLIN lead Howler, son of Fitchner

AGRIPPINA AU JULII head of House Julii, mother to Victra and Antonia

ANTONIA AU SEVERUS-JULII former House Mars, half sister to Victra, daughter of Agrippina

Sons of Ares

ARES Terrorist Leader, color unknown

DANCER Ares' lieutenant, a Red

HARMONY Dancer's lieutenant, a Red

MICKEY Carver, a Violet

EVEY former slave of Mickey, a Pink

Once upon a time, a man came from the sky and killed my wife. Beside him now, I walk on a mountain that floats over our world. Snow falls. Battlements of white stone and shimmering glass yawn out of the rock.

Around us swirls a chaos of greed. All the great Golds of Mars descend upon the Institute to lay claim to the best and brightest of our year. Their ships swarm the morning sky, cutting over a world of snow and smoking castles for Olympus, which I stormed only hours before.

"Take a last look," he tells me as we near his shuttle. "All that came before was but a whisper of our world. When you leave this mountain, all bonds are broken, all oaths dust. You are not prepared. No one ever is."

Across the crowd, I see Cassius with his father and siblings as they make their way to their shuttle. Their eyes burn at us over the white, and I remember the sound of his brother's heart as it beat its last. A rough hand with bony fingers lays claim to my shoulder, clutching possessively.

Augustus stares at his enemies.

"Bellonas do not forgive or forget. They are many. But they cannot harm you." His cold eyes peer down at me, his fresh prize. "For you belong to me, Darrow, and I protect what is mine."

As do I.

For seven hundred years, my people have been enslaved without voice, without hope. Now I am their sword. And I do not forgive. I do not forget. So let him lead me onto his shuttle. Let him think he owns me. Let him welcome me into his house, so I might burn it down.

But then his daughter takes my hand, and I feel all the lies fall heavy on my shoulders. They say a kingdom divided against itself cannot stand. They made no mention of the heart.

PART I

||||||||||||||||||||||||||||||||

BOW

Hic sunt leones. *"Here be lions."*

—*Nero au Augustus*

1

||||||||||||||||||||||

WARLORDS

My silence thunders. I stand on the bridge of my starship, arm broken and held in a gelcast, ion burns still raw on my neck. I'm bloodydamn tired. My razor coils around my good right arm like a cold metal snake. Before me, space opens, vast and terrible. Small fragments of light prick the darkness, and primordial shadows move to block those stars on the fringes of my vision. Asteroids. They float slowly around my man-of-war, *Quietus,* as I search the blackness for my quarry.

"Win," my master told me. "Win as my children cannot, and you will bring honor to the name Augustus. Win at the Academy and you earn yourself a fleet." He likes dramatic repetition. It suits most statesmen.

He'd have me win for him, but I'd win for the Red girl with a dream bigger than she ever could be. I'd win so that he dies, and her message burns across the ages. Small order.

I am twenty. Tall and broad in the shoulders. My uniform, all sable, now wrinkled. Hair long and eyes Golden, bloodshot. Mustang once said I have a sharp face, with cheeks and nose seemingly carved from angry marble. I avoid mirrors myself. Better to forget the mask I wear, the mask that bears the angled scar of the Golds who rule the worlds from Mercury to Pluto. I am of the Peerless Scarred. Cruelest and brightest of all humankind. But I miss the kindest of them. The one who asked me to stay as I bid her and Mars goodbye on her balcony almost a year ago. Mustang. I gave her a horse-crested gold ring as a parting gift, and she gave me a razor. Fitting.

The taste of her tears grows stale in memory. I have not heard from her since I left Mars. Worse, I have not heard from the Sons of Ares since I won at Mars's Institute more than two years ago. Dancer said he would contact me once I graduated, but I have been cast adrift among a sea of Golden faces.

This is so far from the future I imagined for myself as a boy. So far from the future I wanted to make for my people when I let the Sons carve me. I thought I would change the worlds. What young fool doesn't? Instead, I have been swallowed by the machine of this vast empire as it rumbles inexorably on.

At the Institute, they trained us to survive and conquer. Here at the Academy they taught us war. Now they test our fluency. I lead a fleet of warships against other Golds. We fight with dummy munitions and launch raiding parties from ship to ship in the way of Gold astral combat. No reason to break a ship that costs the gross yearly output of twenty cities when you can send leechCraft packed with Obsidians, Golds, and Grays to seize her vital organs and make her your prize.

Amid lessons of astral combat, our teachers hammered in the maxims of their race. Only the strong survive. Only the brilliant rule. And then they left and let us fend for ourselves, jumping asteroid to asteroid, searching for supplies, bases, hunting our fellow students till only two fleets remain.

I'm still playing games. This is just the deadliest yet.

"It's a trap," Roque says from my elbow. His hair is long, like mine, and his face soft as a woman's and placid as a philosopher's. Killing in space is different from killing on land. Roque is a prodigy at it. There's poetry to it, he says. Poetry to the motion of the spheres and the ships that sail between. His face fits with the Blues who crew these vessels—airy men and women who drift like wayward spirits through the metal halls, all logic and strict order.

"But it's not so elegant a trap as Karnus might think," he continues. "He knows we're eager to end the game, so he will wait on the other side. Force us into a choke point and release his missiles. Tried and true since the dawn of time."

Roque carefully points to the space between two huge asteroids, a narrow corridor we must travel if we wish to continue following Karnus's wounded ship.

"Everything's a damn trap." Tactus au Rath, rangy and careless, yawns. He leans his dangerous frame against the viewport and shoots a stim up his nose from the ring on his finger. He tosses the spent cartridge to the floor. "Karnus knows he's lost. He's just torturing us. Leading us on a little merry chase so we can't sleep. The selfish prick."

"You're such a little Pixie, always yapping and whining," Victra au Julii sneers from her place against the viewport. Her jagged hair hangs just past ears pierced with jade. Impetuous and cruel, but neither to a fault, she disdains makeup in favor of the scars she's earned through her twenty-seven years. There are many.

Her eyes are heavy, deeply set. Her sensual mouth wide, with lips shaped to purr insults. She looks more like her famous mother than her younger half sister, Antonia; but in her capacity for general mayhem she far outstrips both.

"Traps mean nothing," she declares. "His fleet has been dashed. He has but one ship. We've seven. How about we just bust his mouth?"

"*Darrow* has seven," Roque reminds her.

"Your pardon?" she asks, annoyed at the correction.

"Seven of Darrow's ships remain. You called them ours. They are not *ours*. He is Primus."

"Pedantic poet strikes again. The point is the same, my goodman."

"That we should be rash instead of prudent?" Roque asks.

"That it is seven against one. It would be embarrassing to let this drag out any longer. So, let's squish the Bellona thug like a cockroach with our sizable boot, fly back to base, take our just rewards from old Augustus, and go *play*." She twists her heel for emphasis.

"Here, here," Tactus agrees. "My kingdom for a gram of demon-Dust."

"That your fifth stimshot today, Tactus?" Roque asks.

"Yes! Thank you for noticing, Mommy dearest! But I grow weary of this military crank. I believe I desire Pearl clubs and copious amounts of respectable drugs."

"You're going to burn out."

Tactus slaps his thigh. "Live fast. Die young. While you're a boring old raisin, I'll be a glorious memory of finer times and decadent days."

Roque shakes his head. "One day, my wayward friend, you're going to find someone you love who makes you laugh at the silly person you once were. You'll have children. You'll have an estate. And somehow you'll learn there are more important things than drugs and Pinks."

"By Jove." Tactus stares at him in utter horror. "That sounds resolutely miserable."

I peer at the tactical display, ignoring their banter.

The quarry we chase is Karnus au Bellona, the older brother of my former friend, Cassius au Bellona, and the boy I killed in the Passage, Julian au Bellona. Of that curly-haired family, Cassius is the favorite son. Julian was the kindest. And Karnus? My broken arm stands testament—he's the monster they let out of their basement to kill things.

Since the Institute, my celebrity has grown. So when news reached the Violet gossip circuit that the ArchGovernor was finally sending me to further my studies, Karnus au Bellona and a few handpicked cousins were dispatched by Cassius's mother to "study" as well. The family wants my heart on a plate. Quite literally. Only Augustus's badge holds them back. To attack me is to attack him.

In the end, I could give a bloody piss about their vendetta or my master's bloodfeud with their house. I want the fleet so I can use it for the Sons of Ares. What a mess I could cause. I've made a study of supply lines, sensor stations, battlegroups, data hubs—all the pressure points that might cause the Society to stagger.

"Darrow . . ." Roque comes closer. "*Guard your hubris. Remember Pax*. Pride kills."

"I want it to be a trap," I tell Roque. "Let Karnus turn and face us."

He tilts his head. "You've set your own trap for him."

"Now, what makes you say that?"

"You might have told us. I could have—"

"Karnus falls today, brother. That is the simple fact of the matter."

"Of course. I only want to help. You know that."

"I know." I stifle a yawn and let my eyes sweep the bridgepits behind and below me. Blues of many shades toil there, working the systems that run my ship. They speak more slowly than any other Color save Obsidian, favoring digital communication. They are older than I, graduates of the Midnight School, all. Beyond them, near the back of the bridge, Gray marines and several Obsidians stand sentinel. I clap Roque on the shoulder. "It's time."

"Sailors," I call to the Blues in the pit. "Sharpen your wits. This is the final nail in the Bellona coffin. We put this bastard into the ether and I promise the greatest gift in my power to give—a week of solid sleep. Prime?"

A few of the Grays near the back of the bridge laugh. The Blues just rap their knuckles on their instruments. I'd give half my substantial bank account, compliments of the ArchGovernor, to see one of those pale airbrains crack a smile.

"Enough delay," I announce. "Gunners to positions. Roque, cluster the destroyers. Victra, attend targeting. Tactus, defense deployment. We're ending this now." I look over at my wispy helmBlue. He stands central in the pit beneath my command platform amid fifty others. The snaking digiTats that mark the Blues' bald heads and spidery hands glow subtle shades of cerulean and silver as they sync with the ship's computers. Their eyes go distant as optic nerves revert to the digital world. They speak only out of courtesy to us. "Helmsman, engines to sixty percent."

"Aye, *dominus.*" He glances at the tactical display, a globular holo floating above his head, voice like a machine. "Mind, the concentration of metal in the asteroids presents difficulty in assessing spectro readings. We're a mite blind. A fleet could hide on the other side of the asteroids."

"He doesn't have a fleet. Into the breach," I say. The ship's engines rumble. I nod to Roque and say, *"Hic sunt leones."* The words of our master, Nero au Augustus, ArchGovernor of Mars, thirteenth of his name. My warlords echo the phrase.

Here be lions.

2

||||||||||||||||||||||||

THE BREACH

On the tactical readout, the six nimble destroyers move around my remaining man-of-war. Eerie silence from the Blue crew as the functions of war take over. On the plane through which their minds now drift, words are slower than icebergs. My lieutenants monitor my fleet. At any other time, they'd be on their personal destroyers or leading men in leechCraft, but at the moment of victory, I want my fellows near. Yet even when my lieutenants stand here at my side, I feel that separation, that deep gulf between their world and mine.

"Missile signatures," says the comBlue. The bridge does not burst into action. No warning lights panic the crew. No shouts break the stillness. Blues are icy specimens, raised from birth in communal Sects that teach them to embrace logic and enact their function with cold efficiency. It's often said they're more computers than men.

The dark space beyond my viewport blooms fresh with a thick veil of microexplosions. Our flak bursts in a great screen of dull white clouds. Incoming missiles explode as the flak bursts detonate the missiles' payloads prematurely. One gets through and a destroyer on our far wing ripples from the simulated nuclear blast. Men would pour from her. Gases would seep out. Explosions might puncture holes in the metal hull and bring burning oxygen rupturing forth like blood from a whale, only to be swallowed in a blink by the black. But this is a wargame, and they do not give us real nukes. The deadliest weapons here are the students.

Another ship falls victim as railgun salvos rip through the flak.

"Darrow . . ." Victra worries.

I stand absently thumbing the place Eo's ring once graced.

Victra turns to me. "Darrow . . . he's chewing us to pieces, if you haven't noticed."

"Lady has a point, Reap," Tactus echoes, face glowing blue from the tactical display. "Whatever you have in store, don't be shy about it."

"Coms, tell Ripper and Talon squadrons to engage the enemy."

I watch the tactical display as the squadrons I dispatched a half hour prior swoop around either side of the asteroids and descend on Karnus's flank. From this distance, they are impossible to see with the naked eye, but they pulse gold on the display.

"Congratulations, my friend," Roque whispers before it is even done. There's a strange reverence in his voice, any earlier frustration now gone. "With this, everything will change." He touches my shoulder. "Everything."

I watch my trap close, feeling the imminent victory drain the tension from my shoulders. The Grays of my bridge take a step forward. Even the Obsidians lean to watch the displays as Karnus's ship registers my squadrons' signatures. He tries to flee, blasting his engines to escape what's coming. But the angles conspire against him. My squadrons loose missiles before Karnus can deploy a flak screen or bring his own missiles to bear. Thirty simulated nuclear explosions wrack his last ship. There is no point to capturing his ship at this point in the game, and so the Blue fighter pilots relish a little overkill.

And like that, I have won.

My bridge erupts with shouts from Grays and the Orange technicians. The Blues wrap their knuckles vigorously. The Obsidians, at odds with this hi-tech world, make no sound. My personal valet, Theodora, smiles to her younger charges at the bridge's valet station. A former Rose courtesan well past prime age, she's heard her fair share of secrets and serves as my social advisor.

Across the ship, from engines to kitchens, the victory transmits through holo screens. This is not just my victory. Each man and woman shares it in their own way. That is the scheme of the Society. To prosper, your superior must prosper. As I found a patron in Augustus, so must the lowColors find their own in me. It breeds a loyalty of necessity to Golds that the Color system itself cannot create by mere dictation.

Now my star will rise, and all aboard will rise with it.

Power and promise are celebrity in this culture. Not long ago, when the ArchGovernor announced he would sponsor my studies at the Academy, the HC channels blazed with speculation. Could someone so young, someone from such a piteous family, win? Look what I did at the Institute. I broke the game. I conquered the Proctors, killed one and bound the others like children. But was that a mere flash in the night? Now those prattling bastards have their answer.

"Helmsman, set course for the Academy. We've laurels to claim," I announce to cheers. *Laurel.* The word itself echoes through my past, making bitter my mouth. Despite my smile, I feel no great joy at this victory. Just grim satisfaction.

One more step, Eo. One more step forward.

"*Praetor* Darrow au Andromedus." Tactus plays with the title. "The Bellona will shit themselves. I wonder if I can leverage this into a command, or do you think I must join your fleet? Can never tell. Gorydamn bureaucracy is so tedious. Coppers to grease. Golds to lobby. My brothers will want to throw us a party, naturally." He nudges me. "At a Brothers Rath party, even you might finally get bedded."

"As if he'd touch your friends." Victra squeezes my hand, fingers lingering as though she wore a gown instead of armor. "Loath as I am to say it, Antonia was right about you."

I feel Roque flinch, and remember the sound of Antonia cutting Lea's throat as she tried to lure me from hiding at the Institute. I had stayed in the shadows, listening to my small friend fall wetly to the mossy ground. Roque had loved Lea in his own fast way.

"I've told you before not to mention your sister's name in our presence," I say to Victra, her face souring at the curt dismissal.

I turn back to Roque.

"As Praetor, I do believe I have authority to stock my fleet with personnel of my choosing. Perhaps we should bring back some old faces. Sevro from Pluto, the Howlers from wherever the hell they got shipped off to, and maybe . . . Quinn from Ganymede?"

Roque flushes in the cheeks at the mention of Quinn's name.

Personally, I wish for Sevro the most. Neither of us is particularly diligent at keeping in touch over the holoNet, especially me, because I haven't had access to it since the Academy began. Anyway, all he's partial to sending is holograms of uniquely perverted unicorns and video clips of him reading puns. Pluto, if anything, has made him stranger. And perhaps more lonely.

"Dominus." The helmBlue's voice draws me to the display.

"What's wrong?" I ask.

His eyes are glazed. Distant, jacked into the ship's sensors, seeing the raw data of the display I stare at. "Not clear, *dominus.* Sensor distortion. Ghosting."

On the large central display, the asteroids are there in blue. We're gold. Enemies red. There should be none left. Yet a red dot throbs there now. Roque and Victra walk toward it. Roque motions his hand and the data transfer to his datapad. A smaller holo globe floats in front of him. He enlarges the image and cycles through analytic filters.

"Radiation?" Victra hazards. "Debris?"

"The asteroid's ore could cause a mirror refraction from our signal," Roque says. "Couldn't be software. . . . It's gone."

The red dot flickers away, but the tension has spread through the bridge. All stare at the display. Nothing. There's no one else out here except my ships and Karnus's defeated flagship. Unless . . .

Roque turns to me, face drawn, terrified.

"Flee," he manages just as the red signal burns back to life.

"Full power to engines," I roar. "Thirty degrees plus our midline."

"Launch remaining missiles at the surface of the asteroid," Tactus commands.

Too late.

Victra gasps, and I see with my naked eyes what our instruments struggled to detect. One shadowed destroyer emerges from a hollow in the asteroid. A ship I thought we defeated three days ago. Its engines were off as it lay in wait. Its front half is torn and black from damage. Now its engines blast at full power. And its trajectory takes it directly toward my ship.

It's going to ram us.

"Evac suits and pods!" I shout. Someone's screaming for us to brace for impact. I rush to the side of the bridge where my command escape pod is built into the wall. It opens at my word. Tactus, Roque, and Victra sprint into its confines. I hold back, shouting at the Blues to hurry and unsync. For all their logic, they'll die for their ships.

I range about the bridge, screaming at them to activate their escape hatch. The helmBlue does, pressing a button that causes a hole to dilate in the floor of the pit. One by one, they unsync and are sucked down the gravity tube into their escape pods.

"Theodora!" I shout, seeing her prying at a young Blue who still clutches his operations display with white-knuckled fear. "Get in the gorydamn pod!" She doesn't listen. Nor does the Blue let go. I start toward them just as the proximity sensor lets loose one final warning blast.

All slows.

Bridge lights throb red.

I jump for Theodora, wrapping my arms around her.

And the destroyer hits my man-of-war at her midline.

Clutching Theodora to my chest, I'm thrown thirty meters across my bridge, slamming into a metal wall. White pain rips across my left arm along the seams of the mending break. I'm slapped with darkness. Lights dance there, first like stars, then as weaving lines of sand disturbed by wind.

Red light seeps through my eyelids. A gentle hand pulls at my clothing.

I open my eyes. I'm wrapped around a dented electrical column as the ship shudders, groaning like an ancient, dying beast sinking in the deep. The column trembles violently against my stomach as the destroyer finishes shearing through our middle. Gutting us with slow cruelty.

Someone's shouting my name. Sound fades back into being.

Lights bathe the bridge, alternating shades of murderous red. Warning sirens. The ship's swan song. Theodora's delicate old hands pull at me, like a bird pulling at a fallen statue. I'm bleeding from my forehead. My nose is broken. I wipe the stinging blood from my eyes and roll onto my back. A broken display sparks beside me. It has my blood on it. Did it fall on me? A bar lies beside it, and my eyes drift to Theodora. She pried it off. But she's so small. Her hands cup my face.

"Get up. *Dominus,* if you want to live, you have to get up." The old woman's hands tremble from fear. "Please, get up."

Groaning, I pull myself to my feet. My command escape pod is gone. In the collision, it must have launched. Either that or they left me behind. So too has the Blue escape pod jettisoned away. The frightened Blue has become a stain on a bulkhead. Theodora can't tear her eyes away from the sight.

"There's another pod in my quarters," I mutter. Then I see why Theodora winces. Not from fear, but pain. Her leg is shattered, splayed off to the side like a length of wet, cracked chalk. They don't make Pinks to last through this. "I won't make it, *dominus.* Go, now."

I bend to a knee and throw her over the shoulder of my good arm. She whimpers horribly as her leg shifts under her. I feel her teeth rattle. And I run. I run through the broken bridge toward the wound that is killing my ship, through the bridge level's hallways into a scene of chaos. People swarm the main halls, abandoning their posts and functions as they race to escape pods and the troop carriers in the forward hangar. People who fought for me—electricians, janitors, soldiers, cooks, valets. They'll never make it to safety. Many change course when they see me. They tumble forward, leaning against me, panicked and crazed in their mania to find safety. They pull at me, screaming, pleading. I push them off, losing a small part of my heart as each falls behind. I can't save them. I can't. An Orange grabs Theodora's good leg and a Gray sergeant hits him in the forehead till he drops like a stone to the ground.

"Clear a path," the thick Gray bellows. She whips her scorcher out of her tactical holster and shoots it into the air. Another Gray, re-membering himself, or perhaps thinking I'm his ticket out of this deathtrap, joins her in parting the chaos. Soon two more carve a path at gunpoint.

With their help, I make it to my suite. The door hisses open at my DNA's touch and we move through. The Grays back in after us, train-ing their scorchers at the thirty desperate souls who ring the entrance. The door hisses as if to close, but an Obsidian pushes through the crowd and jams herself into the doorframe, preventing the door from closing. An Orange joins her. Then a low-ranking Blue. Without hes-itation, the Gray sergeant shoots the Obsidian in the head. Her com-panions gun down the Blue and Orange and shove them off the doorframe so it can close. I tear my eyes away from the blood on the ground to lay Theodora on one of my couches.

"*Dominus,* how much room is there in the escape pod?" the Gray sergeant asks me as I head to the pod's entry lock. Her hair is buzzed in military fashion. A tattoo on her tan neck peeks from under her collar. My hands fly over the control prism, entering the password with a series of hand motions.

"Four seats. You get two. Decide among yourselves."

There's six of us.

"Two?" the female sergeant asks coldly.

"But the Pink's a slave!" one of the Grays hisses.

"Not worth shit," says another.

"She's *my* slave," I growl. "Do as I say."

"Slag that." Then I feel the silence as much as hear it, and I know one of them has pulled a gun on me. I turn, slowly. The stocky old Gray is not a fool. He's backed out of my reach. I've no armor, only my razor. I might be able to kill him. The others ask what the hell he thinks he's doing.

"I'm a free man, *dominus.* I should get to go," the Gray says, voice trembling. "I have a family. It is my right to go." He looks to his fel-lows, bathed in the nasty red of the emergency lights. "She's just a whore. A jumped-up whore."

"Marcel, put the gun down," says the dark-skinned corporal. His eyes are heavy for his friend. "Remember your vows. We'll draw lots."

"It's not fair! She can't even have children!"

"And what would your children think of you now?" I ask.

Marcel's eyes fill with tears. The scorcher quivers in his thick hand. Then a gunshot. His body stiffens and crumples lifelessly to the deck as the bullet from the sergeant's scorcher carries through his head to slam into the metal bulkhead.

"We do it by rank," the sergeant says, holstering her weapon.

Were I still the man Eo knew, I would have stood frozen in horror. But that man is gone. I mourn his passing every day. Forgetting more and more of who I was, what dreams I held, what things I loved. The sadness now is numb. And I carry on despite the shadow it casts over me.

The escape pod opens, magnetic lock thudding back. The door hisses upward. I pick Theodora from the couch and strap her into one of the seats. The straps are nearly too big, made for Golds. Then something deep and horrible roars in the belly of my ship. Half a kilometer away, our torpedo stores detonate.

Gone is the artificial gravity. Gone are the stable walls. It's an insidious sensation. Everything spins. I slam into the escape pod's floor. Ceiling? I don't know. Pressure vents out of the ship. Someone vomits. I smell it rather than hear it. I shout at the Grays to get in the pod. Only one stays behind now, face drawn and quiet, as the sergeant and a corporal pull themselves into the escape pod. They strap in across from me. I activate the launch function and salute the Gray who stays behind. He salutes back, proud and loyal despite the quiet in him as he faces his last moment of life, eyes distant and thinking of some young love, some path not taken, perhaps wondering why he was not born Gold.

Then the door closes and he is gone from my world.

I'm slammed into my seat as the escape pod shoots away from the dying ship. Ripping through debris. Then we're weightless again and drifting away from trouble as inertial dampeners kick in. Out our viewport I see my flagship burping plumes of blue and red flame. Processed helium-3, which powers both ships, ignites near my man-of-war's engines, causing a chain-effect explosion that rips the ship apart. Suddenly I realize it wasn't debris I felt against my escape pod as I left the ship. It was people. My crew. Hundreds of lowColors spilled into space.

The Grays sit opposite me.

"He had three girls," the dark-skinned corporal says, shuddering as the adrenaline fades away. "Two years and he was out with a pension. And you popped him in the head."

"After my report, coward won't even scrape a death pension," the sergeant sneers.

The corporal blinks at her. "You cold bitch."

Their words fade, overcome by the beating of blood in my ears. This is my fault. I broke the rules at the Institute. I changed the paradigm and thought they wouldn't adapt. That they wouldn't change their strategy for me.

And now I have lost so many lives, I may never know the tally.

More people just died in a blink than during a whole year of the Institute, their deaths opening a black hole in my stomach.

Roque and Victra hail me over the coms. They will have tracked my datapad and know I am safe. I barely hear them. Anger, thick and evil, swirls inside me, making my hands shake, my heart slam.

Somehow, Karnus's ship continues through space after bisecting my command, damaged but not broken. I stand in my pod, unbuckling the seat's restraints. At the far end of the escape pod lies a spitTube with a preloaded starShell—a mechanized suit meant to make a man a human torpedo. It's designed to launch Golds to asteroids or planets, because the pod wouldn't survive atmospheric reentry. But I'll use it for vengeance. I'll launch myself onto that Bellona bastard's bloodydamn bridge.

Theodora has not yet woken. I'm glad.

I tell the corporal to help me into the suit. Two minutes later, I'm in the metal carapace. Takes another two to argue with the computer over the calculations required for my trajectory to intersect with Karnus's so that I can smash through the bridge windows. I've never heard of anyone doing this. Never seen it even attempted. It's madness. But Karnus will pay.

I start my own countdown.

Three . . . The enemy ship passes arrogantly a hundred kilometers away. It is like a dark snake with a blue tail, a bridge in place of eyes. Between us, a hundred escape pods glimmer, so many rubies cast into the sun. *Two* . . . I pray that I will find the Vale if I do not survive this. *One.* My controls go dead and red flashes across my helmet. The Proctors override my computer and freeze my controls.

"NO!" I roar, watching Karnus's ship disappear into the black.

3

||||||||||||||||||||||||||

BLOOD AND PISS

Eight hundred and thirty-three men and women. Eight hundred and thirty-three killed for a game. I wish I never knew the tally. I repeat the number again and again as I sit in the passenger hold of the rescue ship sent to ferry me back to the Academy. My lieutenants sit, afraid to meet my gaze. Even Roque leaves me be.

The instructors disabled my craft before I could launch. They say they did it to spare me a fool's mistake. The gambit was rash, stupid, and unfitting a Gold Praetor. I stared blankly at them as they debriefed me via holo.

We reach the Academy in the ebbing day hours of my ship's time cycle. The place is a great domed metal port on the fringes of an asteroid field, ringed with docks for destroyers and men-of-war. Most are filled. Home to the Academy and mid-sector command, it is one of the hives of the Society's military for the midworlds of Mars, Jupiter, and Neptune, though it does serve other planetary forces when their orbits take them near. My fellow students will have been watching here in the dormitories. So too will have many Fleet officials and Peerless who flocked here for the final weeks of the game for parties and viewing.

None will mention the cost of life demanded by Karnus's victory. But the defeat will set back my mission. The Sons of Ares have spies. They have hackers and courtesans to steal secrets. What they did not have was a fleet. Nor will they now.

No one greets my lieutenants or me at the dock.

Reds and Browns bustle about to the orders of two Violets and a Copper, who make preparations for Karnus's Victory in the grand antechamber. The blue and silver of House Bellona trim the cavernous metal halls. The eagle crest of his family covers the walls. They have white rose petals for him. Red rose petals are reserved for Triumphs, true victories where Gold blood is shed. The blood of eight hundred thirty-three lowColors doesn't count. That's a clerical issue.

My lieutenants slept as we traveled back to the Can. I did not. Tactus and Victra stumble now ahead of me, walking silently as if still wrapped in slumber. Despite the heaviness in my shoulders, I don't yearn for sleep. Regret lies behind my bloodshot eyes. If I sleep, I know I'll see the faces of those I left to die in the ship's hallways. I know I'll see Eo. I can't face her today.

The Academy smells of antiseptic and flowers. The rose petals sit in bins off to the side. Ducts above recycle our breaths and purify the air, making a steady hum. Fluorescents piss pale light down from the ceiling, as if to remind us that this is not a kind place for children or fantasies. The light, like the men and women here, is harsh and cold.

Roque stays at my side as we walk, though his aspect is deathly. I tell him to get some sleep. He's earned it.

"And what have you earned?" he asks. "Not a day of sulking. Not a day of self-flagellation. Of all the lancers, you are second. *Second!* Brother, why not take pride in that?"

"Not now, Roque."

"Come now," he continues. "It's not victory that makes a man. It's his defeats. You think our ancestors never lost? You don't need to huff and puff about this and make yourself one of those Greek clichés. Drop the hubris. It was just a game."

"You think I give a shit about the game?" I wheel on him. "People are dead."

"They chose lives of service to the fleet. They knew the danger and died for a cause."

"What cause?"

"To keep our Society strong."

I stare at him. Could my friend, my kind friend, be so blind? What choice did these people have? They were conscripted. I shake my head. "You don't understand a thing, do you?"

"Of course I don't understand. You never let anyone in. Not me. Not Sevro. Look how you treated Mustang. You drive friends away as though they were enemies."

If he only knew.

I find the garden abandoned. It sits at the top of the Can, a large vestibule of glass, earth, and greenery designed as a retreat for fluorescent-weary soldiers. Stunted trees sway in a simulated breeze. I take off my shoes, peel off my socks, and sigh as the grass goes between my toes.

Lamps above the trees make a false sun. I lay beneath them till, with a groan, I pull myself up toward the small hot spring that lies in the center of the glade. Bruises, most faded, stain my body like little ponds of blue and purple ringed with yellowing sands. The water soothes my aches. I'm thinner than I should be, but strung tight as piano wire. Were my arm not broken, I'd say I was healthier than at the Institute. Fighting on Academy bacon and eggs beats the shit out of the half-raw goat meat of that place.

I find the haemanthus blossom by the side of the pool. It took life where no water laps. It is indigenous to Mars, like me, so I do not pick it. I buried Eo in a place like this. Buried her in the fake forest above Lykos mine, where I last made love to her. We were scrawny, innocent things then. How could so frail a girl have such a spirit, such a dream as freedom, when so many strong souls toiled and kept their heads down for fear of looking up?

I shouted at Roque that I did not care about the defeat. Yet I do, and there's guilt for caring about that when so many lives should demand all my sorrow. But before today, victory made me full, because with every victory, I've come closer to making Eo's dream real. Now defeat has robbed me of that. I failed her today.

As if knowing my thoughts, my datapad tickles my arm. Augustus calls. I peel the hair-thin display off and close my eyes.

His words echo in memory. "Even if you lose, even if you cannot take the victory for yourself, do not allow a Bellona triumph. Another fleet under their control will tip the scales of power."

So much for that. I float in the water, drifting in and out of sleep till my fingers wrinkle and I grow bored. I am not meant for these quiet moments. I pull myself from the water to dress. I can't keep Augustus waiting for long. Time to face the old lion. Then sleep, maybe. I'll have to stand and watch the damn Victory for Karnus, but after that I'll be away from this ugly place and headed back to Mars, and maybe Mustang.

But as I turn to leave the pool, I find my clothes are gone, as is my razor.

Then I sense them.

Hearing their military boots behind me. Their loud, excited breaths. Four of them, I guess. I pick a stone from the ground. No. I turn and find seven blocking the one entrance into the garden. All Golds of House Bellona. All my blood enemies.

Karnus comes with the Bellona, fresh from his ship. His face is as haggard as mine, his shoulders maybe half again as broad. He towers over me—an Obsidian in every way but birth and mind. That laughing mouth of his grins with uncommon intelligence. He rubs a hand over his dimpled chin, muscled forearms looking like they're carved from smoothed riverwood. There's something terrifying about being in the presence of someone so large that you can feel the vibrations of their voice in your bones.

"Looks like we caught the Augustus lion away from his pride. 'Lo, *Reaper*."

"*Goliath*," I mutter, using his call sign.

Goliath the breaker. Goliath the son killer. Goliath the savage. Mustang says he once broke the spine of a fancy Luneborn Gold over his knee after the brat thought to splash a drink in his face at a Pearl club. His mother then bribed the Judiciar to let him off with a fine.

The list of fines he's paid for murder stretches longer than my arm. Grays, Pinks, even a Violet. But his true reputation comes from killing Claudius au Augustus, the ArchGovernor's favorite son and heir. Mustang's brother.

Karnus's cousins orbit around him. All Bellona. All born under the blue and silver sigil of the conquering eagle. Brothers, sisters, cousins to Cassius. Their hair is curly and thick, faces all beauty. Their influence stretches across the Society. As does the reputation of their arms.

One is much older than I, shorter but more powerfully built, like a tree stump with blond moss covering his head. He is a man in his thirties. Kellan, I remember now. A full Legate, a knight of the Society. And he came here with his brothers and cousins for me. Arrogance drips off that one. He feigns a yawn as he plays these schoolyard games.

Fear thunders into my chest.

I find it difficult to breathe. Yet I smile, fingers grazing the datapad's com functions behind my back.

"Seven Bellona," I chuckle. "What need have you of seven, Karnus?"

"You had seven ships against my one," Karnus says. "I've come to continue our game." He cocks his head. "Did you think it ended with your ship dying?"

"The game is over," I say. "You won."

"Did I win, *Reaper*?" Karnus asks.

"At the cost of eight hundred and thirty-three people."

"Whining because you lost?" asks Cagney. She's the smallest of his cousins, a twentysomething lancer to Karnus's father. She's the one cradling my razor, the one Mustang gave me. She swishes it through the air. "I think I'll keep this. I don't think I've even heard of you using it. Not that I judge. Razors are tricky. The perils of an uneducated upbringing, I fear."

"Go stick your fist up your cousin," I sneer. "Must be a reason you curly-haired shits all look alike."

"Must we listen to him bark, Karnus?" Cagney whines.

"I taught Julian to fish, *Reaper*," Kellan, the Legate, says suddenly.

"As a boy, he didn't like it because he thought it hurt the fish too much. Thought it was cruel. That's the boy your master had you kill. That is the measure of *his* cruelty. So how grand do you feel? How brave do you fashion yourself?"

"I did not want to kill him."

"Oh, but we want to kill you," Karnus rumbles. He nods to his cousins. Two of the Bellona break branches off the trees and toss them to their kin. They have razors, but apparently, they want to take their time.

"If you kill me, there will be consequences," I say. "This is not a sanctioned duel, and I am Peerless. I am protected by the Compact. This will be murder. The Olympic Knights will hunt you. Try you. Execute you."

"Who said anything of murder?" Karnus asks.

"You belong to Cassius," Cagney's foxlike face splits with a smile.

"Today, you are protected by Augustus," Karnus says. "His chosen boy. To kill you would mean war. But no one goes to war over a little beating."

Cagney favors her left leg. Knee injury. A cousin of hers leans on his heels. Frightened of me. The big one, Karnus, squares up, meaning he doesn't give a piss about whatever damage I can deal. Kellan smiles and stands relaxed. I hate those sort of men. Hard to judge. I calculate my chances. Then I remember my broken arm, my injured ribs, and the contusion over my eye, and cut those chances in half.

I'm scared. They cannot kill me, I cannot kill them. Not here. Not now. All of us know how this dance will end. But dance we do.

Karnus snaps his fingers and they rush toward me all at once. I throw the stone into Cagney's face. She goes down. I rush at Karnus, howling like a mad wolf, slipping past his first blow, and rage a flurry of strikes into his nerve centers, driving my elbow into his right bicep, rupturing tissue. He rocks back, and I press into him, using his bulk to shield me from the others and their sticks. I strip a stick away from one of the Bellona cousins, leveling her with an elbow to her temple. Then I turn, spinning the stick toward Karnus's face. But it's blocked. Something hits the back of my head. Wood shatters. Splinters dig into the scalp. I don't stumble. Not until Karnus hits me so hard in my face with his elbow that a tooth pops out.

They don't take turns coming one by one. They surround me and they punish me with the efficiency of their deadly art, *kravat*. They aim for nerves, organs. I manage to stand, hit a few of my assailants. But I'm not long on my feet. Someone jams their stick into my skin, impacting the subcostal nerve. I drip down to the ground like melting wax and Karnus kicks me in the head.

I bite through half my tongue.

Warmth fills my mouth.

The ground is the softest thing I feel.

Choking on salt.

Blood and air spray out of my mouth as Karnus puts his foot on my stomach, then throat. He laughs. "In the words of Lorn au Arcos, if you must only wound the man, you better kill his pride."

I gurgle for breath.

Cagney replaces Karnus, sitting on my chest, knees pinning down my arms. I suck down air. She smiles in my face and looks at my hairline, lips parted with excitement of dominating another person. She twists my hair into her grip. Her hot breath smells like spearmint. "What have we here?" she asks, pulling my datapad from its place on my arm. "Dammit. He hailed the Augustans. I'd rather not fight that Julii bitch without my armor."

"Then stop dawdling," Karnus growls. "Do it."

"Shh," she whispers as I try to speak, tracing a knife over my lips, pushing it into my mouth till the brittle metal clacks against my teeth. "That's a good little bitch."

Roughly, she saws off my hair.

"Nice and quiet. Good Reaper. Good."

Blood stings my eyes as Karnus shoves Cagney off my chest, grabs me and hoists me off the ground with his left hand. He flexes his right arm, cursing about his ruined bicep. He can't pull it back to swing a punch, so instead he grins toothily at me and head-butts me once in the chest just at the sternum. My world rocks. There's a crackle. The sound of twigs over a fire. I wheeze out bubbling, inhuman sounds. Karnus head-butts me again and tosses my aching body to the ground.

I feel warmth splash over me and the smell of piss claw into my nostrils. They laugh and Karnus breathes into my ear.

"Mother bid me to tell you: a pauper can never be a prince. Every time you look in the mirror, remember what we did to you. Remember you breathe because we let you. Remember your heart will one day be on our table. Rise so high, in mud you lie."

4

||||||||||||||||||||||||

FALLEN

I stand before my master, but he does not care.

The office walls are of paneled wood, and on the floor lies an ancient rug his iron ancestor took from a palace of Earth after the fall of the Indian Empire, one of the last great nations to stand against Gold. What dread those natural-born humans must have felt to see the Conquerors falling from the sky. Man perfected, but bringing chains instead of hope.

I stand in front of Augustus's desk, a bare thing of wood and iron, just before the seven-hundred-year-old bloodstain where the final Indian emperor had his head parted from his body by a sleek Gold killer.

Idly, Nero au Augustus strokes the lion that lies beside his desk. They look like twin statues. Behind them is space. A viewport peers into the blackness, where the ships of the Scepter Armada lie like giant golems in terrible slumber. We pass them on the last leg of our three-week voyage from Mars.

Augustus peers at his desk as a stream of data runs over the wood.

It seems so long ago that he took me on a tour of Mars to show me our domains—from the latfundias where highReds toil over crops to the great polar reaches where Obsidians live in medieval isolation. He favored me then, bringing me close, teaching me the things his father taught him. I was his favorite, second only to Leto. Now he is a stranger, and I, an embarrassment.

It's been two months since the day Karnus beat me at the Academy. Though my hair has grown back and my broken bones have mended, my reputation has not. And because of that, my tenure in ArchGovernor Augustus's employ is tenuous, at best. My enemies grow by the day. But these new ones prefer whispers to razors.

More and more do I believe the Sons of Ares chose the wrong man. I am not made for the cold war of politics. Not made for subtlety. Hell, I'd hide a boy in the gut of a horse any day, but I wouldn't know how to bribe someone properly if my life depended on it.

A gentle, warm voice made for half-truths drifts through the Arch-Governor's office. "Three refineries. Two nightclubs. And two Gray police outposts. All bombed since we left Mars. Seven attacks, my liege. Fifty-nine Gold fatalities."

Pliny. Slender as a salamander, with skin as smooth as a Pink's. The Politico is no Peerless Scarred, never even went to the Institute. His glittering eyes peer out from eyelashes that would put peacock plumage to shame. Muted lipstick coats thin lips. His hair is coiled and scented. His body thin but muscular in a pleasing but utterly facile way beneath a too-tight embroidered silk tunic. A child could beat the living hell out of this beautiful kitten of a man. Yet he's ended families with a rumor here, a joke there. His power is of a different breed. Where I am kinetic energy, he is potential.

I've heard he's also responsible for ruining my reputation. Tactus even hinted that Pliny might have put Karnus up to the violence in the garden, or at the very least, arranged a holoCam to record my proud moment.

Beside Pliny stands the fourth man in the room, Leto. He's a bright lancer ten years my senior with braided hair and a half-moon grin. He's also a poet with the razor, a younger Lorn au Arcos, according to some. It's likely he'll inherit Augustus's estate instead of the Arch-Governor's blood heirs—Mustang and the Jackal. Truth be told, I rather like the man.

"The Sons of Ares grow too bold," Augustus mutters.

"Yes, my liege." Pliny squints. "If it is indeed they who perpetrate the acts."

"What other ant bites us?"

"None that we know of. But there are spiders, ticks, rats in the worlds. The bombings are crude for Ares, indiscriminate, uncharacteristically violent. Discontiguous from the pattern of technological sabotage and propaganda in his profile. Ares is not capricious, so I struggle believing these acts originate from him."

Augustus frowns. "Then what do you suggest?"

"Perhaps there is another terrorist group, my liege. With eighteen billion souls on the census, I hardly think one man has a monopoly on terrorism. Perhaps even a criminal syndicate. I've been creating a database I can share. . . ."

Pliny is right. The terror attacks that have plagued Mars and other planets make little sense. Dancer spoke of justice, not revenge. These attacks are petty and gruesome—the bombing of barracks, fashion outlets, bazaars, highColor coffee shops, and restaurants. Ares would never condone them. They draw too many eyes for too little result, daring the Golds to act, to crush the Sons.

I've sent messages to Dancer via the holoBox. Nothing. Just silence. Could he be dead? Or has Ares abandoned me for this new strategy of bombing?

Pliny yawns. "Perhaps Ares has changed his tactics. He's a deuced one."

"If Ares is a man," Leto says.

"Interesting." Augustus swivels abruptly. "What makes you think Ares isn't a man?"

"Why do we assume Ares is a man? He could be a woman. Could be a group of individuals for all we know, which would go a long way toward explaining the discordant nature of these new attacks." Leto turns to me, eyes inclusive. "Darrow, what do you think?"

"Don't befuddle Darrow with complex questions!" Pliny crows defensively. "Make it a yes or no so he can understand." Pliny flashes me the most pitying of smiles and squeezes my shoulder in sympathy.

"Behind his lepid smiles, he's an honest, simple beast. You should know that."

I stand there and take it.

He turns away. "In any manner, Leto, you're forgetting we designed Red culture to be highly patriarchal. Their identity as a people centers around the collection of resources to propagate the embryonic terraforming of Mars. Physically strenuous, grueling tasks performed by *men*. Tasks we don't let their women perform, even if they are capable, pursuant to the Stratification Protocol. So, you see, it can't be a woman, because no roughneck Ruster would follow a man or a woman who has never ridden a clawDrill."

Leto smiles cleverly. "*If* Ares is a Red."

Pliny and Augustus both laugh. "Maybe he's a deranged Violet who's taken his acting to a new stage," Pliny offers.

"Or a Copper cambist beleaguered by filing provincial tax returns," Leto adds.

"No! An Obsidian who, dare I say, has finally forsaken his terror of technology and developed the skills to use a holoCamera?" Pliny slaps his leg. "I'd give away one of my Roses just to see—"

"My goodmen. Enough." Augustus cuts him off, tapping his finger on the desk. Pliny and Leto share a grin and turn back to Augustus. "Your recommendation, Pliny?"

"Of course." Pliny clears his throat. "Unlike their propaganda and cyber attacks, the brutality is quite simple to counter. Ares or not, issue a reply. Our kill teams are prepared for tactical strikes on several terrorist training grounds beneath Mars's surface. We should strike now. If we wait, I fear the Sovereign's Praetorians will take matters into their own hands. Luneborn don't understand Mars. They'll slag it up."

"A fool pulls the leaves. A brute chops the trunk. A sage digs the roots." Augustus pauses. "Something Lorn au Arcos once said to my father. It's engraved on the Hall of Blades in New Thebes. Striking training grounds will do nothing except fill the holoNet with pretty explosions. I tire of political plays. Our strategy must change. With every bombing, the Sovereign grows wearier of my administration."

"You govern *Mars*," Leto says. "Not Venus or Earth. Ours is not a placid planet. What does she expect?"

"Results."

"What do you have in mind, my liege?" Pliny asks.

"I intend to poison the Sons of Ares's roots. I want suicide bombers, not Grays. Find the ugliest, nastiest Reds on Mars, hold their families hostage, and threaten to kill their sons and daughters if the fathers do not do as we command. Focus the suicide bombers on surface areas with high youth density as well as two choice mines. No women bombers. I want social divide. Women against violence."

How little life costs here. Just words in the air.

"Urban areas too," he continues. "Not just Browns and Red miners and agriculturalists. I want dead Blue and Green children in schools or arcades next to Sons of Ares glyphs. Then we'll see if other Colors still sing that girl's gorydamn song."

My heart dips a beat. Eo's song spread further than she dreamed, reaching the holoNet and ripping across the Solar System, shared over a billion times thanks to anarchist hacker groups. Time and again, I fear I'll be recognized. Perhaps some Gold will search through the records to find that Eo's husband's name was also Darrow. But even I hardly recognize that skeletal, pale boy. And as for names? There are no true records for lowRed names. I had a number designation given to me by some officious Copper administrator. L17L6363. And L17L6363 was hanged from his neck until dead, whereupon his body was stolen by an unknown perpetrator and presumably buried in the deep mines.

"You plan to alienate Red from the other Colors, then alienate the Sons from Red." Pliny smiles. "My liege, sometimes I wonder why you even need me."

"Do not patronize me, Pliny. It's beneath the both of us."

Pliny bows. "Indeed. Apologies, my liege."

Augustus looks back to Leto. "You're squirming like a pup."

"I worry this will make matters worse." Leto frowns to himself. "Presently the Sons are a nuisance, yes. But hardly our chief plight. If we do this, we could be pouring fuel on the flames. And worse, we'd be as guilty as the Sons themselves. Terrorists."

"There is no guilt." Pliny peers idly at a stream of data on his datapad. "Not when you're the judge."

Leto isn't satisfied. "My liege, our imperative to rule exists because we are fit to best guide mankind. We are Plato's philosopher kings. Our cause is order. We provide stability. The Sons are anarchists. Their cause is chaos. We should use *that* as our weapon. Not Grays in the night. Bombers among children."

"We should aspire to a higher purpose?" Pliny asks.

"Yes! Perhaps fashion a media campaign against the Sons. Darrow, wouldn't you agree?"

Again, I do not answer. Not until the ArchGovernor acknowledges my presence. He does not value impudence or impropriety unless it benefits him.

"Idealism." Pliny sighs. "Admirable in the young, if misguided."

"Take care in talking down to *me*, Politico," Leto growls, scanning Pliny's smirking face for the absent Peerless scar. "Your plan should be less brutal, ArchGovernor. That is my point."

"Brutality." Augustus lets the word hang in the air. "It is neither evil nor good. It is simply an adjective of a thing, an action in this case. What you must parse is the nature of the action. Is it evil or good to stop terrorists who bomb innocents?"

"Good. I suppose."

"Then what do our methods matter so long as we harm fewer innocents than they would harm if we continue to allow them to exist?" Augustus folds his long-fingered hands. "But at the core, this is no philosophical issue. It is a political one. The Sons of Ares are not the threat. Not at all. All they are is a weapon for our political enemies, namely the Bellona, to use as an excuse to claim I cannot control Mars.

"The curlyhairs already seek to strip me of the Governorship. As you know, the Sovereign has sole power to remove me from the position, even without a vote from the Senate. If she wishes, she can give Mars to another house—Bellona, our allies the Julii, even a non-Martian house. None of these entities would run Mars as effectively as I. And when Mars is run effectively, all benefit—low and high. I am not a despot. But a father must cuff the ears of his children if they make an attempt to set fire to his house; if I must kill a few thousand for the greater good, for helium-3 to flow, and for the citizens of this planet to continue to live in a world untorn by war, then I will.

"Which brings us to Darrow au Andromedus." Now his cold eyes turn on me, fresh from ordering the deaths of a thousand innocents, and I cannot help but flinch as a dark hate rises inside me. I bow my head in polite deference.

"My liege. You summoned me?"

"I did. And your purpose here shall be brief. You were a gambit when I took you from the Institute and put you in my employ. You know this?"

"Yes."

"I thought your merit to be sufficient, and I found your rivalry with Cassius au Bellona amusing in a schoolyard way. But the bloodfeud declared between you has become"—he spares a glance at Pliny—"burdensome to my interests, both economically and politically. Substantial revenues have been lost due to tariff increases to the Core, where Bellona supporters lie. Houses waver in their commitment to honoring deals made years ago at the trade table. So, as an act of reconciliation to these aggrieved parties, I have decided to sell your contract to another house."

I shudder inside.

"My liege . . . ," I try to interject. This cannot happen. If he strips me of my place, nearly three years of work will have been for nothing. "If I may—"

"You may not." He opens a drawer and idly tosses a slab of meat to his lion. The lion waits for Augustus to snap his fingers before eating. "The decision was made a month ago. There is no use bandying words with me. I'm not Quicksilver negotiating the price of lithium futures. Pliny . . ."

"The particulars are rather simple, Darrow. So they shall be easy to grasp." Pliny hasn't taken his eyes from me. "The ArchGovernor has been overly kind in giving you the fair warning in case of termination, as stipulated in your contract."

"My contract says I'm to be given six months' fair warning."

"If you'll recall section eight, subsection C, clause four, you're to be given six months' fair warning *unless* you fail to act in a manner befitting a lancer of the esteemed House Augustus."

"Is this a joke?" I look to Leto and Augustus.

"Do you see us laughing?" Pliny asks primly. "No? Not even a scoff or chortle?"

"Of all the lancers, I came in second at the Academy! You couldn't even make it through the Institute."

"Oh, it's not *that*! You did well . . . enough."

"Then what?"

"It is your constant presence on HC talk shows."

"I've never gone on the HC! I don't even watch it!"

"Oh, please. You relish your own celebrity. Even though they mock you, you bathe in the limelight and cloak this house with shame. We know your datapad search histories. We see you preening at yourself on the HC as though it were your personal mirror. The stories run on you and the ArchGovernor's daughter—"

"Mustang is in court on Luna!"

"Which you likely encouraged. Did you ask her to join the Sovereign's court? Is it part of your plan to divide daughter from father?"

"You're spinning horseshit, Pliny."

"And you create a tawdry name for Augustus. You brawl with Bellona in baths set aside for refreshment and contemplation. This we cannot abide."

I don't even know what to say. He's making it up. There's enough in reality to make a case, but he lies just to spit in my eye, just to show that I am in his power.

Pliny continues. "The termination of the contract will occur in three days."

"Three days," I echo.

"Till then, you will accompany us to the surface of Luna and stay in the residence provided for the House Augustus for the Summit, though, as of this moment, you are no longer a lancer of this house. You do not represent the ArchGovernor and may not use his name to gain access to facilities nor curry favor with young ladies or young men, neither in boast, promise, or threat. Your house datapad will be confiscated. Your lancer ID codes have already been downgraded and you will cease and desist participation in all projects to which you were previously assigned."

"I've only been assigned construction projects."

Pliny's lips crawl into a reptilian smile. "Then this shall be an easy transition."

"To whom am I being sold?" I manage. Augustus doesn't look in my eyes as he abandons me. He pets his lion. You would guess I'm not even in the room. Leto stares at the ground. Ashamed. He's nobler than this charade, but Augustus wanted him here to watch, to learn how to amputate a rotten limb.

"You are not being sold, Darrow. Despite your birth, I would have expected you to understand your place. We are not Pinks or Obsidians to be sold as slaves. Your *services* are being *traded* at auction," Pliny says.

"It's the same gory thing," I hiss. "You're abandoning me. Whoever buys my *services* cannot protect me from the Bellona. Those curlyhair bastards will hunt me down and kill me. The only reason they didn't two months ago was because—"

"Because you were an Augustan representative?" Pliny asks. "But the ArchGovernor does not owe you anything, Darrow. Is that the misapprehension you suffer? In fact, you owe him! Protecting you costs us money. It costs us opportunities, contracts, trade. And that cost has proven too dear. We must be seen to promote peace with the Bellona. The Sovereign wants *peace*. You? You're a source of friction, a chafing burr in our proverbial saddle, and an instrument of war. So now we melt our sword into a plowshare."

"But not before you use it to lop off my head."

"Darrow, do not beg." Pliny sighs. "Show some resolve, young man. Your time here has expired, yes, but you've got pluck. You've got the vigor of a young man. Now, straighten that spine of yours and leave with the dignity of a Gold who knows he tried his best." His eyes laugh at me. "That means leave this office. *Now*, my goodman, before Leto throws you out on your preposterously toned buttocks."

I stare at the ArchGovernor.

"Is this what you take me for? Some sniveling child to be pushed into a corner?"

"Darrow, it'd be best if—" Leto begins.

"It is you who have pushed us into a corner," Pliny answers, putting a hand on my shoulder. "If you're worried you won't receive a severance package, you will. Enough money to—"

"The last time one of the ArchGovernor's lackeys touched me, I buried a knife in his cerebellum. Six times." I look at his hand as he quickly withdraws it. I square my shoulders. "I do not answer to a scarless Pixie whelp. I am a Peerless Scarred. ArchPrimus of the 542nd class of the Institute of Mars. I answer to the ArchGovernor alone."

I take a step toward Augustus, causing Leto to take a protective angle. The length of my temper is well remembered. "You put Julian au Bellona in the Passage with me, my liege." My eyes burn down at him. "I killed him there for *you*. I warred against Karnus for *you*. I kept my mouth, the mouths of my men, sealed after you tried to buy your son victory at the Institute." Leto flinches at that. "I altered the recordings. I proved myself better than your blood heirs. Now, my liege, you say I'm a *liability*."

"You are a Peerless Scarred," the ArchGovernor agrees, examining data on his desk. "But you are of little substance. Your family is dead. They left you with no lands, no holdings of resources or industry, no position in government. All was seized as their debts came due, including their honor. What scraps you have been given by your betters, cherish. What favor you curried, remember."

"I thought you favored deeds, not titles. My liege, Mustang has left you. Do not make the mistake of severing me from you as well."

Finally he raises his head to look at me. Eyes belonging to some creature beyond man—a distant, callous calculation fueled by monstrous, inhuman pride. A pride that goes beyond him and stretches back to man's first feeble steps into black space. It is the pride of a dozen generations of fathers and grandfathers and sisters and brothers, all distilled now into a single brilliant, perfect vessel that bears no failure, abides no flaws.

"My enemies embarrassed you. So they embarrassed me, Darrow. You told me you would win. But then you lost. And that changes everything."

5

||||||||||||||||||||||||

ABANDONED

I will soon die.

That is the thought I carry with me as our shuttle coasts away from Augustus's flagship and flits through the Scepter Armada. I sit among the lancers, but I am not one of them. They know. Appropriately, they do not speak to me. Whatever bond they could make does not matter. I have no political capital. I overhear Tactus being offered a wager to see how long I'll last outside of Augustus's protection. One lancer says three days. Tactus argues ferociously against the number, showing the true extent of the loyalty I earned from him at the Institute.

"Ten days," he declares. "At least ten days."

It was he who launched the escape pod without me. I always knew his friendship was conditional. Yet still the wound gnaws deep, carving in me a loneliness I can't express. A loneliness that I've always felt among these Golds, but tricked myself into forgetting. I am not one of them. So I sit there in silence, staring out the window as we pass the gathered fleet and wait for Luna to appear.

My contract ends on the final evening of the Summit, where all ruling families gather on Luna to deal with matters pressing and frivolous. That is the three-day window I have to improve my stock, to make others think that I am undervalued by the ArchGovernor and ripe for recruitment. But no matter my value, I am marred. Someone had me, then threw me away. Who would want such a used thing?

This is my fate. Despite my Golden face and talents, I am a *commodity*. It makes me want to tear my bloodydamn Sigils out. If I'm to be a slave, I should at least look a slave.

To make matters worse, there's the price on my head. Not officially, of course. That is illegal, because I am not an enemy of the state. Yet my enemy is far worse. Far crueler than any government. She is the woman who sent Karnus and Cagney to the Academy.

They say every night since I stole Julian's life in the Passage, his mother, Julia au Bellona, has sat at the long table of her family's high-hall upon the slopes of Olympus Mons and lifted the semicircular lid of the silver tray brought to her by the Pink manservants. Every night, the tray remains empty. And every night she sighs in sadness, peering down the table at her large family only to repeat the same vindictive words: "It is clear I am unloved. If I were loved, there would be a heart here to sate my hunger for vengeance. If I were loved, my boy's murderer would no longer draw breath. If I were loved, my family would honor their brother. But I am not. He is not. They do not. What have I done to deserve such a hateful family?" Then the grand Bellona family will watch their matriarch uncoil from her chair, her body withering from hunger, nursing instead on hate and vengeance, and they will remain silent as she leaves the room, more wraith than woman.

What has kept my heart from her plate is the ArchGovernor's arms, money, and name. Politics, the very thing I hate, has kept the breath in me. But in three days, that aegis will be a shadow of memory, and all that will protect me are the lessons my teachers have given me.

"It'll be a duel," one of the lancers says. Then louder. "Can't turn that down and keep his honor for long. Not if Cassius himself offers it."

"Old Reaper has a few tricks up his sleeve," Tactus says. "You might not have been there, but he didn't kill Apollo with his smile."

"Used a razor, didn't you, Darrow?" another lancer asks, tone mocking. "Haven't seen you on the fencing grounds of late."

"You've never seen him there," says another. "The Pixie avoids what he's not good at, eh?"

Roque stirs angrily beside me. I put a hand on his forearm and turn slowly to regard the offending lancer. Victra sits behind him, idly watching the scene.

"I don't fence," I say.

"Don't? Or can't?" someone asks with a laugh.

"Leave him be. Razormasters are expensive," Tactus notes with a sly grin.

"Is that how it is, Tactus?" I ask.

He makes a face. "Oh, *come now.* Just having a go at you. So gory-damn serious. You used to be more playful."

Roque says something to make Tactus scowl and turn away, but I don't hear. I've sunken into memory, where this Golden game once seemed so easy. What has changed? Mustang.

"You're more than this," she whispered as I left her for the Academy. Tears swelled in her eyes, though her voice did not waver. *"You don't have to be a killer. You don't have to court war."*

"What other choice do I have?" I asked.

"Me. I'm the other choice. Stay for me. Stay for what might be. At the Institute, you made followers of boys and girls who have never known loyalty. If you go to the Academy, you abandon that to be my father's warlord. That's not what you are. That is not the man I . . ." She did not turn, but her face changed as her sentence trailed away, lips drawing a hard line.

Love? Was that what we built in the year after the Institute?

If so, the word stuck in her throat, because she knew, as I knew, that I had not given her all of me. I had not shared all that I am. Greedily, I kept secrets. And how could someone like her, someone with so much self-worth, bare herself and throw her heart at a man who gave so little in return? So she closed her golden eyes, shoved the razor into my hands, and told me to go.

I don't fault her. She chose politics, governance—peace, which is what she thinks her people need. I chose the blade, because it is what my people need. It fills me with a strange emptiness knowing that I was enough for her when I was never enough for Eo. Roque was right. I pushed her away.

I didn't push Sevro away. I asked him to be stationed with me, then suddenly he was reassigned to Pluto like many of the Howlers, relegated to protecting far construction operations from petty pirate raids. I now suspect Pliny's hand in that.

My path has never felt lonelier.

"You'll not be abandoned," Roque says, leaning in close. "Other families will want you for themselves. Don't let Tactus in your head. The Bellona won't make a move against you."

"Of course they won't," I lie. He can still sense my fear.

"Violence isn't allowed in the Citadel, Darrow. Especially bloodfeuds. Even duels are outlawed unless consent is given by the Sovereign herself. Simply stay on Citadel grounds till you've a new house, and all will be well. Bide your time, do what you must, and in a year, the ArchGovernor will feel like a fool when you've risen under the tutelage of another. There is more than one path to the top. Always remember that, brother."

He grips my shoulder.

"You know I would ask my mother and father to bid for you . . . but they won't go against Augustus."

"I know." They could spend the millions on the contract and not even notice the loss, but Roque's mother has not sat a Senator for twenty years because of her charity. Her lot is thrown in with Augustus's contingent in the Senate. What he wills, she supports.

"I'll be fine. You're right," I say as Luna appears in the window, hushing the aides, and filling me with dread. The city moon of Earth. Orbiting satellites and installations encircle it like a steel angel's halo wrapped around a ball of amber held to the sun. "I'll be fine."

6

|||||||||||||||||||||||||

ICARUS

We land near the Citadel. Sticky, polluted wind bends the towering trees near our landing pad. Perspiration quickly beads along the top of my high collar. Already I do not like this ugly place. Despite the fact that we land here on Citadel grounds, which are far from the nearest cities and surrounded by forests and lakes, Luna's air cloys and sticks to the lungs.

On the horizon, just past the spiked spires of the Citadel's western campus, Earth hovers, swollen and blue, reminding me that I am so far from home. The gravity here is less than Mars's, only one-sixth Earth's, and makes me feel unsettled and clumsy. I seem to float when I walk. And even though coordination quickly returns, my body suffers its own lightness with strange feelings of claustrophobia.

Another vessel lands to the north.

"Looks like Bellona silver," Roque says quietly, squinting against the sunset.

I chuckle.

He glances back at me. "What?"

"Just imagining having a pulseRocket right about now."

"Well, that's just . . . lovely of you." He walks along. I follow, eyes lingering on the vessel. "I do love the sunsets of Luna. Like we're in Homer's world. Sky a hot shade of fresh-forged bronze."

Above, the alien sky melts into night with the long setting of the sun. For two weeks, the daylight will disappear from this part of the moon. Two weeks of night. Luxury yachts cruise through this strange day's end, while nimble Blue-piloted ripWings soar past on patrol like bats glued together from shattered ebony.

The one-sixth gravity lets these Luneborn build to their heart's desire. And build they do. Beyond the Citadel grounds, the horizon is fenced with towers and cityscape. RungPaths wind everywhere so that citizens can pull themselves through the air with ease. The network of rungs stretch between high towers as would ivy, linking the heavens with the hells of the lowDistricts. Along them, thousands of men and women crawl like ants on vines, while Gray patrol skiffs buzz around the thoroughfares.

The household of Augustus is assigned a villa nestled within thirty acres of pines on Citadel grounds. It's a pretty thing among other pretty things in this stately place. There are gardens, paths, fountains carved with little winged boys of stone. All that sort of frivolity.

"Fancy a session of *kravat*?" I ask Roque, nodding to the training facility beside the villa. "My mind's running away with itself."

"I can't." Roque winces, stepping out of the way of our fellow lancers and their attendants who file into the villa. "I have to attend the conference on Capitalism in the Governed Age."

"If you wanted a nap, I'm sure they have beds in the villa."

"You joking? Regulus ag Sun is giving the keynote."

I whistle. "Quicksilver himself. So you're going to learn how to make diamonds out of gravel? You hear the rumor about him owning the contracts of two Olympic Knights?"

"It's not rumor. Least according to Mother. Reminds me of what Augustus said to the Sovereign at her coronation. 'A man is never too young to kill, never too wise, never too strong, but he can damn well be too rich.'"

"Arcos said that."

"No, I'm sure it was Augustus."

I shake my head. "Check your facts, brother. Lorn au Arcos said it, and the Sovereign turned to reply, 'You forget, Rage Knight, I am a woman.'"

Arcos is as much myth as man, at least to my generation. Reclusive now, he was the Sword of Mars and the Rage Knight for over sixty years. Peerless Knights across the Society have offered him the deeds to moons if he would but tutor them for a week in his form of *kravat*, the Willow Way. It was he who sent me the knifeRing that killed Apollo and then offered me a place in his house. I rejected it then, choosing Augustus over the old man.

"'You forget, I am a woman,'" Roque repeats. He cherishes these stories of their empire the way I cherished stories of the Reaper and the Vale. "When I get back, let's talk. Not the usual banter."

"You mean you won't yammer on about a childhood crush, drink too much wine, wax poetic about the shape of Quinn's smile and the beauty of Etruscan grave sites before falling asleep?" I ask.

His cheeks flush, but he puts a hand over his heart. "On my honor."

"Then bring a bottle of foolishly expensive wine, and we can talk."

"I'll bring three."

I watch him leave, eyes colder than my smile.

Several of the other lancers attend the conference with Roque. The rest make themselves comfortable as Augustus's Gray security teams comb the grounds. Obsidian bodyguards trail Golds like shadows. Pinks sway gracefully into the villa in a constant stream, ordered from the Citadel's Garden by members of the ArchGovernor's household staff who find themselves bored from travel and seek a little merriment.

A Pink Citadel steward guides me to my room. I laugh when I arrive. "Perhaps there has been a mistake," I say, looking around the small room with its adjoining washroom and closet. "I'm not a broom."

"I don't under—"

"He's not a broom, so he won't fit in this closet," Theodora says, standing in the doorway behind us. "It is beneath his station." She looks around, pert nose sniffing disdainfully. "These would not even suit as closet to *my* clothes on Mars."

"This is the Citadel. Not Mars." The steward's pink eyes survey the lines on Theodora's aged face. "There is less room for useless things."

Theodora smiles sweetly and gestures to the rose-quartz tree pinned to the man's breast. "I say! Is that the black poplar of Garden Dryope?"

"Your first time seeing it, I would guess," he says haughtily before turning to me. "I don't know how they raised your Pinks in Mars's Gardens, *dominus,* but on Luna your slave should do her best to look less affected."

"Of course. How rude of me," Theodora apologizes. "I merely thought you would know Matron Carena."

The steward pauses. "Matron Carena . . ."

"We were girls together in the Gardens. Tell her Theodora says hello and would call on her if time is found."

"You're a Rose." His face goes sheet white.

"*Was.* All petals wilt. Oh, but do tell me your name. I would so like to commend you to her for your hospitality."

He mumbles something quite inaudible and departs, bowing lower to Theodora than to me.

"Was that fun?" I ask.

"Always nice to flex a little muscle. Even if everything else is starting to droop."

"Seems my career ends where yours began." I chuckle morbidly and walk over to the holoDisplay sitting near the bed.

"I wouldn't," she says.

I bite my bottom lip, our signal for spying devices.

"Well, of course, that. But the holoNet is . . . not where you want to be right now."

"What are they saying about me?"

"They're wondering where you'll be buried."

I haven't time to reply before knuckles rap against the frame of my room's doorway.

"Dominus, Lady Julii requests your presence."

|||||||||||

I follow Victra's Pink to her room's private terrace. Her bath alone is larger than my bed.

"It's not fair," a voice says from behind the ivory-white trunk of a lavender tree. I turn to see Victra playing with the thorns of a shrub. "You being cut loose like a Gray mercenary."

"Since when have you been concerned with what's fair, Victra?"

"Must you always fence with me?" she asks. "Come sit." Even with the scars that distinguish her from her sister, her long form and luminous face is without true fault. She sits smoking some designer burner that smells like a sunset over a logged forest. She's heavier of bone than Antonia, taller, and seems to have been melted into being, like a spearhead cooling into angular shape. Her eyes flash with annoyance. "I'm as far from an enemy as you have, Darrow."

"So what are you? A friend?"

"A man in your position could use friends, no?"

"I'd rather have a dozen Stained bodyguards."

"Who has the money for that?" she laughs.

I raise an eyebrow. "You do."

"Well, they couldn't protect you from yourself."

"I'm a bit more worried about Bellona razors."

"Worry? Is that what I saw on your face as we descended?" She lets a merry sigh escape her lips. "Curious. See, I thought it was dread. Terror. All the truly unsettling things. Because you know this moon will be your grave."

"I thought we weren't fencing anymore," I say.

"You're right. It's just I find you very odd. Or, at least I find your choice in friends to be odd." She is sitting in front of me on the lip of the fountain. Her heels scrape against the aged stone. "You've always kept me at arm's length while bringing Tactus and Roque close. I understand Roque, even if he is as soft as butter. But Tactus? It's like flossing with a viper and expecting not to get bitten. Is it because he was your man at the Institute that you think he's your friend?"

"Friend?" I laugh at the idea. "After Tactus told me how his brothers broke his favorite violin when he was a boy, I had Theodora spend half my bank account on a Stradivarius violin from Quicksilver's auction house. Tactus didn't thank me. It was as if I'd handed him a stone. He asked what it was for. I said, 'For you to play.' He asked why. 'Because we're friends.' He looked back down at it and walked away. Two weeks later, I discovered he took it and sold it and used the money for Pinks and drugs. He is not my friend."

"He's what his brothers made him to be," she notes, hesitating as if reluctant to share her information with me. "When do you think he's ever received something without someone wanting something in return? You made him uncomfortable."

"Why do you think I'm wary with you?" I lean closer. "It's because *you* always want something, Victra. Just like your sister."

"Ah. I thought it might be Antonia. She's always ruining things. Ever since the shewolf gnawed her way out of Mother's womb and stole human clothes. Good that I was born first, else she might have strangled me in my crib. And she's only my half sister anyway. Different fathers. Mother never saw much point in monogamy. You know Antonia even goes by Severus instead of Julii just to take a piss on Mother. Cantankerous brat. And I get saddled with her moral baggage. Ridiculous."

Victra plays with the many jade rings on her fingers. I find them odd, contrasting with the Spartan severity of her scarred face. But Victra has always been a woman of contrasts.

"Why are you talking with me, Victra? I can't do anything for you. I have no station. I have no command. I have no money. And I have no reputation. All the things you value."

"Oh . . . I value other things too, darling. But you do have a reputation, all right. Pliny's made sure of that."

"So he did play a part in the gossip. Thought Tactus was just running his mouth."

"A part? Darrow, he's been at war with you since the moment you kneeled to Augustus." She laughs. "Before then, even. He counseled Augustus to kill you then and there, or at least try you for the murder of Apollo. Didn't you know?" She shakes her head at my blank stare. "The fact that you're just now realizing this shows just how ill-equipped you are to play his game. And because of that, you're going to be killed. That's why I'm speaking with you. I'd rather you found an alternative instead of sulking in your beastly quarters. Otherwise, Cassius au Bellona is going to come and he's going to take a knife and dig right here . . ." She caresses my chest with a long-nailed finger, etching the outline of my heart. ". . . and give his mother her first real meal in years."

"Then what is your suggestion?"

"You stop being such a little bitch." She smiles up at me and holds out a dataSlip. Grudgingly, I take the edge of the thin metal slip, but she holds on, pulling me toward the edge of the fountain, between her legs. Her lips part, her tongue playing along the top as her eyes trace my face, up and up to my eyes, where they try to spark a fire. But there's none there; with a feline sigh, she lets the dataSlip go. I run it over my personal datapad and an advertisement for a tavern appears on my display.

"This isn't on Citadel grounds," I say.

"So?"

"So, if I leave, it's open season on my head."

"Then don't advertise your leaving."

I take a step back. "How much are they paying you?"

"You think this is a setup!"

"Is it?"

"No."

"How do I know you're telling the truth?"

"Most people can't afford the truth. I can."

"Oh, that's right. I forgot. You never lie."

"I am of the *gens Julii*." She stands slowly, anger uncoiling like a razor. "My family trades in commerce enough to buy continents. Who could afford to purchase my honor? *If* . . . one day I become your enemy, I will tell you. And I will tell you why."

"Everyone's honest till they're caught in a lie."

Her laugh is husky and makes me feel small and boyish, reminding me she's seven years older than I. "Then stay, Reaper. Trust in chance. Trust in *friends*. Hide here till someone buys your contract, and pray they didn't do it just to serve you up to the Bellona like a suckling pig."

I weigh the odds and extend a hand to help her up. "Well, when you put it that way . . ."

"Colonel Valentin?" Victra asks the shorter of the two Grays who wait for us on the ramp of the shuttle. It's a shit can. One of the ugliest fliers I've ever seen. Like the front half of a hammerhead shark. I eye the taller of the Grays warily.

"Yes, *domina,*" Valentin says, nodding his cinderblock head with the rigid precision of a man risen through the ranks. "You are sure you were not followed?"

"Certain as death," Victra says.

"We should depart fastlike, then."

I follow Victra into the shuttle, scanning the grounds behind us. We wore ghostCloaks as soon as we departed Augustus's villa. A dozen hidden hallways and six old gravLifts later, we arrived in a dusty, seldom-used section of the Citadel's launch pads. Theodora left us there. She wanted to come, but I won't take her where we're going.

A Gray scans Victra and me for bugs as we board the ship.

The ship's ramp slides closed behind us. Twelve craggy Grays fill the small passenger hold of the shuttle. They're not the dashing sort. Just craftsmen of a dark trade.

Though there are averages, Colors are diverse in composition due to human genetics and the differing ecosystems throughout the Society. The Grays of Venus are often darker and more compact than those of Mars, but families move and mix and breed. The talent levels in each Color are even more variable than appearance. Most Grays aren't destined for anything more than patrolling shopping centers and city streets. Some go to the armies. Some to the mines. But then there are the Grays who were born a special breed of wicked and clever and have been trained all their lives to hunt the Gold enemies of their Gold masters. Like these in the shuttle with us. They call them lurchers—after the mutt dogs of Earth crossbred for uncommon stealth, cunning, and speed, all for one purpose: killing things bigger than they are.

"We're bound for Lost City and it's just the twelve of you?" I ask.

I know they're enough. I just don't like Grays. So I push their buttons.

They eye me with the quiet reserve of a family meeting a stranger on the road. Valentin's the father. He's built like a squat block of dirty ice carved by a rusted blade, and his sun-blasted face is dark and set with quick eyes. His lieutenant, Sun-hwa, leans toward us, tough and gnarled as an olive tree.

Both are Earthborn by the looks of their continentally ethnic features. These Grays wear no triangular badge of the Society's Legion on their civilian street clothes. Means they've served their mandatory twenty years.

"We're tasked with your protection, *dominus*," says Valentin as Sun-hwa loads an exotic circular weapon on the inside of her left wrist. Looks plasma based. "My team has prepared a secure route. Estimated traveling time: twenty-four minutes."

"If Pliny finds out where I'm going, or if the Bellona know I'm out of the Citadel . . ."

"The lurchers know the situation," Victra says.

"I don't see a Gold badge. Mercenaries?"

"Means we are good enough to live this long, *dominus*," Valentin says flatly. "We've prepared for all eventualities. Contingency plans and support have been organized."

"How much support?"

"Enough. We're just the transporters, *dominus*." His mouth twitches into a smile and I take his word for it. "Bigger problem than the Bellona is third parties thinking an opportunity's just stumbled their way. Where we're going, there will be a hell of a lot of third parties, *dominus*. Shit complicates our ROI. Sun-hwa?"

"Wear this." Sun-hwa tosses me a bag of plain clothing. Her voice drones on in a monotone drawl. "You're tall can't do shitall about that but we'll do a quick dye job with this this and this." She tosses Victra another bag. "For you. Boss thought you'd dress too fancy."

Victra laughs at that.

"Muzzles off, boys," Valentin barks as the ship trembles and rises in the air. "We're live." Thumpers and burners prime in practiced hands. Staccato sound of steel on steel. Like metal knuckles cracking as magnetic rounds go into chambers. The lurchers conceal weapons in hidden holsters over tight scarabSkin armor. Three wear illegal wrist weapons. I eye the contraband as I slip into my scarabSkin. It drinks in the light, a strange pupil-like black. More the absence of color than anything else. Better than the duroArmor we had at the Institute, it'll stop some blades and the occasional projectile weapon like the common scorcher.

The ship shudders as its main engines overtake the vertical thrusters.

"Talon and Minotaur, be advised. Icarus is on the move," Valentin rasps into his com. "Repeat. Icarus is on the move."

7

||||||||||||||||||||||||

THE AFTERBIRTH

On Luna, there is no dark. No true dark, at least. Lights of a million shades swim together, glossing over the moon's jagged, cracking steel skin of cityscape. Snaking public trams and air thoroughfares, flashing communication centers, bustling restaurants, and austere police stations weave into the metal dermis of the city like blood capillaries, nerve endings, sweat glands, and hair follicles.

We fall away from Gold districts, forsaking the high reaches of the city where stately shuttles and gravBoots ferry Golds to opera houses atop kilometers-high towers. We dive down past the wealthy Silver and Copper districts, wending our way through rungPaths and aerial trains, through the midDistricts where the Yellows, Greens, Blues, and Violets reside, past the lowDistrict where Grays and Oranges make their homes.

Down and down we go to the gutters of the city where the roots of this colossal steel jungle burrow into the ground. Myriad lowColors ride public transportation from factories to their windowless apartments, some no larger than one meter by three. Only room enough for a bed. Cars rattle out exhaust in clogged beacon-lit boulevards. The deeper we go, the fewer the lights, the dirtier the buildings, the stranger the animals, but the more brilliant the graffiti. I glimpse Gray police standing over arrested Brown vandals who covered an apartment complex with the image of a hanging girl. My wife. Ten stories tall, hair burning, rendered in digital paint. My chest constricts as we pass, cracking the walls I've built around her memory. I've seen her hanged a thousand times now as her martyrdom spreads across the worlds, city by city. Yet each time, it strikes me like a physical blow, nerve endings shivering in my chest, heart beating fast, neck tight just under the jaw. How cruel a life, that the sight of my dead wife means hope.

No matter our reputations, no enemy would seek us here. No ears to listen. No eyes to see. This is a place of gang killings, robberies, turf battles, drug trade. That my new friend wants such human privacy, privacy not even a jamField can really offer in the Citadel and the High City, means much. It worries me. Means the rules are void. But Victra was right and Roque was not. Patience will do me nothing. I must take a risk.

The team of lurchers has secured an abandoned garage. They provide security for the shuttle while Valentin's team escorts me from the garage into the bustle of the dirty street outside. Refuse and water make bogs out of alleys. Humid air is thick with the sweet musk of rot and the charred soot of burning garbage. Hawkers cry out wares from cracked sidewalks, clogged with Reds, Browns, Grays, and Oranges of all species—urchin, invalid, working class, gangers, tweakers, mothers, fathers, beggars, cripples, children. The lost.

Eo would say this is the hell they've built their heaven upon. And she'd be right. Gazing up, I see more than half a kilometer of tenement buildings before the polluted haze makes a ceiling for the human jungle. Clotheslines and electrical lines crisscross overhead like vines. This sight is hopeless. What is there to change here but everything?

We're to meet at the Lost Wee Den. It is a large, tall tavern with a flickering red sign covered in pithy graffiti. Fifteen levels, all open and looking down on a central drinking hall of tables and booths filled with some two hundred customers. I can smell the piss in the metal booths, which sag from use. Bottles rattle and glasses clink as swill is slammed back. Indigo and pink lights flicker on the fifteenth floor, where they've dancers and private rooms for customers. I pass with Valentin through two bouncers with biomod hands—one Obsidian with skin pale as bleached marble and arms thicker than mine, the other a dark-skinned Gray with a scorcher muzzle built into his arm.

The rest of my Grays filter in behind me in staggered intervals. Some wearing contacts, pretending to be other Colors. One even wearing a fleshMask to look pretty as a Pink. Can't even tell it's digital till you put a magnet near it. They look like they belong here. I doubt I do, despite the Obsidian dye job they've done to me.

The Sigils on my hands are covered with Obsidian prosthetics. My hair is white, eyes black. Skin made paler with cosmetics. Victra and I are too large to pass for any other Color. Fortunately, Obsidians, though rarer than the other lowColors, are not out of place down here. I follow Valentin to a table in an alcove near the back of the hall where a young man lounges behind a pack of mercenaries and a single Obsidian. A deep silence fills me as I watch the Obsidian stand and leave the table to sit at an adjacent one. Others eye him too before remembering themselves and looking down at their drinks—like water birds as a crocodile glides past. The Obsidian is a foot taller than I. And the whole of his face is tattooed with a skull. *Stained.*

So much for a low profile.

"Better to reign in hell than serve in heaven?" I ask the reclining man.

"Reaper! Even Milton knew Lucifer was a petty son of a bitch." He smiles enigmatically and waves to the chair across from him. "Do stop towering over me."

He's not even wearing a disguise. I look over at Victra. "Thought it was going to be a new friend."

"Well, you two have never been *friends* before. That'd be the new part. You boys have fun now."

"You're not staying?" I ask.

"I showed you the door. You have to walk through it." She squeezes my butt playfully and sways out. The Jackal watches her leave, leaning slightly to get a better view.

"Didn't think you cared about women."

"I could be dead and I'd still appreciate her. But I don't have to tell you that. Alone in space for months on end. Ship all to yourself. Whatever was there to do?"

I sit across from him. He offers me a bottle of greenish liquor.

I shake my head. "I drink to forget about men like you."

"Ha! An Arcosian insult, if I'm not mistaken. One of Lorn's best. Though there's enough to choose from." He leans back. Enigmatic in his dullness. Face plain. Eyes like smooth, worn coins. Hair the color of desert sand. Lone hand twirling a silver stylus with the quickness of an insect skittering over blasted ground, crack to crack. "The Jackal of Augustus and the Reaper of Mars, together again, at long last. How we have fallen."

"You chose the venue," I say as he sets his stylus behind his ear and takes a chicken leg from a platter on the table. He strips the skin with his teeth.

"Does it unnerve you?"

"Why would it? We both know how fond you are of the dark."

He suddenly laughs, a whining high-pitched bark, like a dog being stabbed. "So much pride to you, Darrow au Andromedus. Family all dead. Disgraced, penniless things. So average that your parents didn't even try to introduce you to Society. No friends remaining. No one who knew you before you slipped into the Institute, so unassuming-like. But how you rose when given a chance."

"Well, at least you still like to talk," I mutter.

"And you still like to make enemies."

"Everyone has a hobby." I examine the stump where his right hand should be. "Desperate for attention? You're the only Gold alive that wouldn't bother getting a new hand."

"I wonder why you provoke me still when your reputation is shattered. Your bank accounts emptied." I shift in my seat. "Oh, yes. You didn't know? Pliny is thorough when he cuts a man's hamstrings. He emptied all your funds. So really there's very little to you. But here you sit, at the bottom of a moon. Alone. With me, with mine. Throwing insults."

"These are yours?" I ask, glancing at the lowColors around us. "I would have thought they'd disgust you."

"Who said you have to like your children?" the Jackal asks pleasantly. "They are a product of our Golden loins." He gnaws on the chicken leg, cracking the bone with his teeth before discarding it. "Do you know what I have been doing with my time?"

"Wanking off in the bushes?"

"Alas, no. My defeat at your hands set me back. I'm not afraid to say it. You hurt me and my plans. My sister also wounded me. Gagging me? Binding me naked and throwing me at your feet? That stung, especially when all the grand lords and ladies of our fine Peerless caste got a chuckle at my expense."

"We both know you don't feel pain, Adrius."

"Oh, call me the Jackal. Hearing 'Adrius' from your lips is like hearing a cat bark." He shivers, but leans delightedly forward in his seat when a Brown woman with thick arms and tattoos webbing her pale, pockmarked skin slips from the kitchens carrying three steaming bowls. She sets them before us. "Thank you!" he says, taking two for himself.

I eye the bowl suspiciously.

"I'm not a poisoner," he says. "I could poison my father anytime I want, but I don't. Do you know why?"

"Because you've not gotten what you need out of him."

"And that is?"

"His approval."

The Jackal watches me through the steam of his bowl. "Quite. I have been offered a great deal of apprenticeships. They offer it to my father's name, not to me. They despise me because I ate students. But it's such hypocrisy. What else was I to do? We're told to win, and I did my best. And then they criticize. Act noble, as though they didn't commit murder themselves. Madness."

He shakes his head with a little sigh. "Yes, I could have gone to study war at the Academy like you. I could have studied politics at the Politico School on Luna. I might have been a decent Judiciar if I could stomach Venus. But I will rise without their hypocrisy. Without their schools."

"I've heard the rumors. Any true?"

"Most." He pulls more noodles out of the bowl, spreading red pepper sauce over them. "I am a businessman now, Darrow. I buy things.

I own things. I create. Of course I'm seen as a money-grubbing Silver by those pretentious Peerless jackasses. But I am not one of the fading lords of twentieth-century Europe. I understand there is power in being practical, in owning things. People. Ideas. Infrastructure. So much more important than money. So much more insidious than"—he makes a funny motion with his hand—"*spaceships* and *razors*. Tell me, does a ship matter if you can't supply and transport the food to feed its crew? I above all others know the importance of food."

"You own this place, don't you?" I ask.

"In a manner." He smiles with too much teeth. "I feel I must be blunt with you. We were nearly eighteen when we left the Institute. We are now twenty. I have been two years in exile, and now I wish to return home."

"To socialize with Peerless jackasses?" I laugh. "If you have been paying attention at all, you'll know I don't have your father's ear."

"Paying attention . . ." He shares a glance with Victra and leans forward. "Reaper. I am the attention. Do you know how much of the communications industry I have acquired?"

"No."

"Good. That means I'm doing it properly. I've acquired more than twenty percent. With my silent partner, I own nearly thirty. You're wondering why? Certainly families like Victra's do not consider themselves dirtied by business. After all, the Julii have partaken in trade for centuries. But media is different for us. Slimy. Leave that to Quicksilver and his ilk. So why would someone with my lineage dirty his hands with it? Well, I want you to imagine media as a pipeline to a city in the desert." He waves around. "Our metaphorical desert. I can provide only thirty percent of the content of what comes through that pipeline, but I can affect one hundred percent of it. My water contaminates the rest. That is the nature of media. Do I want this city in the desert to hallucinate? Do I want its inhabitants to writhe in pain? Do I want them to rise up?" He sets his chopsticks down. "It all starts with what I want."

"And what do you want?" I ask.

"Your head," he says.

Our eyes meet like two iron rods colliding, sending stinging reverberations through the body. A palpable discomfort even being near him, much less meeting those dead gold orbs. He's so young. My age, but there's a childishness to him, a curiosity despite the ancient cast of his eyes, that makes him feel like a perversity. It's not that I feel cruelty and evil radiating from him. It's the feeling that crept over me when Mustang told me how, as a boy, he killed a baby lion because he wanted to see its insides to understand how it worked.

"You have a weird sense of humor."

"I know. But I'm so glad you get my jokes. So many prickly Peerless these days. Duels! Honor! Blood! All because they're bored. *There's no one left to fight.* So gorydamn tedious."

"I believe you were making a point."

"Ah, yes." The Jackal runs his hand through his slicked-back hair, like I've seen his father do. "I brought you here because Pliny is an enemy of mine. He's made my life very difficult. Even penetrated my harem. Do you know how many spies of his I've had to kill? I went through so many servants. I'm not trying to make you feel sorry for me," he says quickly.

"I was on the verge of it."

"Understanding my plight, however, is how you will help me best. As of now, Pliny controls my father's favor. Like a snake hissing in his ear. Leto is his design, did you know that?" I didn't. "He found the darling boy, knew he would win my father's cold heart because he would remind Father of my dead brother, Claudius. So Pliny cultivated him, trained him, and convinced my father to adopt him as a ward with aims of making him the heir. Then you come waltzing into our lives and disrupt Pliny's plan. It took two years to dispatch you, but patiently, he did. Just as he did me. Now Leto will be my father's heir, and Pliny will be Leto's master."

That hits me hard. I knew Pliny was dangerous. Perhaps I never really knew just how dangerous.

"So what's your plan?" I glance around the room. "Going to take back your father's favor with plebeians and pitchforks?"

"As any Gold with a decent education would know, there's a certain crime syndicate that runs things in Lost City. A vast criminal enterprise that, if you trace it all the to the tip-top, is under the influence of the office of the Sovereign of our little Society. Octavia au Lune may seem the paragon of Gold virtue. But she's got a fetish for the dirty stuff—assassinations, organizing workers' strikes in her own ArchGovernors' domains, rigging appointments. Her handling of Lost City is no different.

"She and her Furies handpicked the crime family leadership; these three individuals are her creatures. But here's the juicy kink. I've found certain members of that same organization who are . . . restless."

I frown. "They don't like Lune?"

"She's an onerous bitch. One who has spat in my father's eye and cozied up to the Bellona. But no. My champions don't think on that plane. They are lowColors, *Darrow*. They're restless to be atop the shitpile."

"Why Lost City?" I ask. "What does it matter?"

"It is merely a piece of the puzzle. I'm going to help these ambitious lowColors move up, for a price. When they are in power, they are going to kill off a menace that plagues the Society: Ares and his Sons."

8

IIIIIIIIIIIIIIIIIIIIIIII

SCEPTER & SWORD

I go cold inside. "The Sons of Ares? I wasn't aware they were so dire a threat."

"They're not yet, but they will be," he says. "The Sovereign knows it. So does my father, even if it is not in vogue to say it aloud. The Society has faced terrorist cells before. Throw enough lurcher teams at them and they are dispatched easily enough. But the Sons are different.

"They are not a rat biting our heels, but a termite colony slowly gnawing our foundation as quietly as possible till they've done such work that our house crumbles around us. My father has given Pliny the task of eliminating the Sons. But Pliny has been failing. He will continue to fail because the Sons of Ares are clever, and because my media adores giving them attention. But when they become a thing so dreadful to the Society, to the Sovereign, to my father, that the very machine of governance grinds to a halt, I will step forward and say, 'I will cure this disease in three weeks.' And then I will, with my media, with the syndicates systematically killing all the Sons, and with you gloriously beheading Ares himself."

"You want a figurehead."

"I am not glamorous. I do not inspire. You are like one of the Old Conquerors. Charismatic and virtuous. When they look at you, they see none of the soft decadence of our meager time, none of the political poison that has saturated Luna since Lune's family rose to power. They will look at you and see a cleansing knife, a new dawn for a Second Golden Age."

Like father, like son. Both targeting the Sons of Ares in similar ways. It's chilling thinking of the war that will rage between crime syndicate throat-cutters and Ares's agents. It will destroy the Sons.

"The Sons of Ares are only the beginning. A leverage point. You want to rule."

"What other ambition is there?"

"But not just Mars . . ."

"Just because I'm small doesn't mean my dreams have to be. I want it all. And to get it, I'm willing to do anything. Even share."

"Perhaps you are not aware of what happened two months ago," I say. "Stop a Gold anywhere and ask. They'll tell you what the Bellona family did to the Reaper of Mars. I have no reputation. The only thing I inspire is laughter."

"Cassius was shamed," the Jackal says in irritation. "He was pissed on. Beaten at the Institute. Embarrassed. Now he's the deadliest dueler on Luna. He fought any that would contest his worth. And now he's the Sovereign's favorite new pet. Did you know the old crow is making him an Olympic Knight? Lorn au Arcos and Venetia au Rein both retired this year. That means the posts of Rage Knight and Morning Knight are open."

"She'd make him one of the twelve?"

"He is a piece on her board." The Jackal leans forward. "But I tire of playing pawn to my elders."

"As do I. Makes me feel like a Pink," I say.

"Then let us rise together. I the scepter, you the sword."

"You won't share. It's not in your nature."

"I do what I need to do. No more. No less. And I need a warlord. I'll be Odysseus. You be Achilles."

"Achilles dies in the end."

"Then learn from his mistakes."

"It's a good idea." I pause at his spreading smile. "With one problem. You are a sociopath, Adrius. You don't only do what you need to do. You wear whatever face you need, whatever emotion you desire like a glove. How could I ever trust you? You killed Pax." I let the words hang in the air. "You killed my friend, your sister's protector."

"Pax and I had never met before. All I saw was an obstacle in my path. Of course I knew of the Telemanuses, but after Claudius got his brains splattered everywhere, Father split Mustang and me up to protect us. Put me in even greater isolation than her. I was his *heir*. I had no friends, only tutors. He ruined my youth. And then he discarded me as he discarded you, because we lost. You and I mirror each other."

A fight breaks out in the level above us. A scorcher cracks. Bouncers rush upward, cradling their own weapons. Most of the patrons sit undisturbed.

"What of your sister?" I ask hesitantly, knowing deep down that I have no other options left but this one.

"Do you want to know how she fares?" he asks plainly. "Who shares her bed? I can give you whatever answers you want. My eyes are everywhere."

"I don't want that." I shake my head, trying to banish the dark idea of someone sharing her bed. Of her finding joy in someone else, even if she deserves to. Even stranger is thinking the Jackal knows these things. "Is she involved in this?"

"No," the Jackal says with a heavy laugh. "You know she's with Lune now. It's hilarious, really. Who would have thought that of the two of us, she'd be the prodigal twin? Well, *more* prodigal."

"She cannot be hurt," I say. "If she is, I will cut off your head."

"That's aggressive. But you have a deal. So you are with me."

"I've been with you since I got into the shuttle. You know I have no other options. And I know no other person would ever summon me *here*. The variables could only lead to this end." And why should they not?

I took his hand, he took a friend. All he has done is bite and claw for his own survival. Watching him now, so small and plain in a world of gods, it's almost as if he's the hero nobly struggling against a father who rejected him, against a Society that laughs at his size, his weakness, and scorns him as a cannibal even though it was they who told him to do whatever he had to do to win. In an odd way he *is* like me. He could have had his hand repaired, but he chose not to, wearing it as a badge of honor instead of shame.

So I'll go along with this. Then, in the end, maybe I'll kill him. For Pax.

His face splits into a grand smile. "I'm so pleased, Darrow. So pleased. And, to be honest, a bit relieved."

"But what is next?" I ask. "You must need something from me now."

"A Gold by the name of Fencor au Drusilla has learned of my . . . dealings with the syndicates. He is trying to blackmail me. I need you to kill him."

Of course. "When?"

"Not for a week or so. The real purpose of killing him will be to gain favor with one of the Sovereign's cousins who was slighted by Fencor. With Fencor's death, you'll fall into the cousin's . . . favor."

I choke down a laugh. "You'll have me play the role of a Pixie gallant, flitting about court, bedding ladies?" Mustang will think I'm doing it to spite her.

The Jackal's eyes sparkle with mischief. "Who said anything about ladies?"

"*Oh,*" I say, realizing what he means. "Oh, that's . . . complicated. Tactus might be better for this. . . ."

The Jackal chuckles at my surprise. "Oh, you'll do just fine. But all this is worry for another day. For now, relax. I'll purchase your contract through a second party as soon as it goes up for auction."

"The Bellona will try to buy it."

"I have a backer. We'll outspend them."

"Victra?"

"No. She's more of a broker in this. What you have to understand about Victra is she's not . . . how do you say . . . *partisan.* She just loves stirring the pot. The backer you'll meet soon enough."

"That won't work," I say. "I want to meet him now. I'm not your puppet. I share everything I know, you share everything you know."

"But I know so much more. *Fine.*" He leans forward. "You'll meet him tonight. It's not that I don't trust you. I just think it appropriate that he introduces himself."

"Fine enough. I want to bring the Howlers back. And Sevro."

"Done. You'll also need to select a blademaster, someone to tutor you with the razor. We'll need you to kill a few people publicly in the future."

"I know how to use a razor," I say.

"Not what I've heard. Come now, there's no shame in it. I have a few names. It's a pity Arcos isn't tutoring. These days I might actually have the funds to afford Stoneside and his Willow Way. . . ."

His words trail off and his eyes drift from me, pulled to the slinking form of a woman who cuts through the smoke and drab of the tavern like an ember falling through fog. I can smell the almond on her skin, the citrus of her lips as she nears our table, graceful and stirring as the air of Venus's Summer Coast. Bones fragile, avian. She wears a black shift that covers her skin except her bare shoulders.

Then I catch her eyes and I almost fall out of my chair. It's a shot to the heart. My pulse patters. It's her. The girl with wings who could never fly. But now . . . she's fled from Mickey, it seems. Wings gone, ripened into womanhood. But why is Evey here? Did the Sons send her? I can barely keep my composure. She hasn't recognized me.

"I didn't know Roses to grow so deep among the weeds," the Jackal says to her.

Her laughter drifts like the beating of a butterfly's wings. She traces the bottom edge of the worn table and shrugs minutely.

"Common men can't afford uncommon things. But my mistress heard uncommon men were in Lost City and sent me as an . . . ambassador."

"Ah . . ." The Jackal leans back, appraising her. "You're a syndicate girl. One of Vebonna's?" Off her nod, the Jackal looks at me and mistakes my expression of surprise for one of desire. "Take her upstairs, Darrow. On me. A welcoming gift. Let me know if you want to buy her. We can discuss business tomorrow."

At the word "Darrow," Evey's composure buckles for a blink. She steps back and I hear her breath pattern change. And when her eyes meet mine, I know she sees through the Obsidian disguise and glimpses the Red underneath all these lies. However, the surprise there means she's not here for me. She's here for the Jackal, but why? Is she with the Sons? Or did Mickey finally sell his prize to this Vebonna gangster?

"I don't do slaves," Evey says to the Jackal, pointing to my Obsidian sigils.

"You'll find there's more to this one than meets the eye."

"*Dominus, I—*"

He grabs her hand, twisting her pinky horribly. "Shut up and do as you're told, girl. Or we'll take what you won't give." He flashes a great smile and releases her. She holds her hand, trembling. It doesn't take much to wound a Pink.

I stand. "I believe I'll take it from here, my friend."

"I'm sure you will!"

I wave the bodyguards away who try to accompany me.

I follow Evey up the handrungs leading to the fourth floor, earning hoots from some of the patrons. My eyes catch one of the holoCans above the bar. Images of a bombing ripple in three dimensions. It looks to be at a café. A Gold café. My eyes widen as the extent of the devastation is shown. Was it the Sons?

Another bombing flashes across a different screen. And another. And another till dozens of bombings flood the screens throughout the tavern. All heads turn to watch, silence yawning through the vast tavern. Evey's hand tightens around mine, and I know it was the Sons who committed the bombings. They sent her. But why Luna? Why the Jackal? Why haven't they contacted me?

"Hurry," she says as we reach the fifteenth floor, pulling me through the pink lights, past the dancers and hungry patrons to the last door at the end of a narrow corridor. I follow her inside the dark room and immediately smell the acrid tang of scorcher oil. Air shifts behind me as a man in a ghostCloak creeps forward. It takes considerable effort to resist the impulse to kill him.

"He's one of ours," Evey snaps. She turns on the light. Six Reds in heavy military tech decloak. They wear demonHelms with high-grade optics. "Call in the skimmer."

"He's not Adrius au Augustus," one of them growls.

"He's a bloody Obsidian."

"Strange-looking one." One of the Reds with the optics jumps back, scorcher priming. "Bone density is Gold!"

"Stop!" Evey shouts. "He's a friend. Harmony has been looking for him."

Not Ares or Dancer?

"You weren't here for me," I say, eyeing their weapons. "You were hunting."

She turns to me. "I'll explain later, but we have to go."

"What did you do?" I ask as one of the Reds pulls out a plasma-Torch and cuts a hole in the wall, opening the room up to the stink of the city. Moist air rushes in and lights flood the room as a small drop-ship descends, opening its side hatches parallel to the improvised door.

"Darrow, there's no time."

I grab her. "Evey, why are you here?"

Her eyes flash with triumph. "Adrius au Augustus has murdered fifteen of our brothers and sisters. I was sent to capture or kill him. I chose the latter. In twenty seconds, he'll be ash."

I rip one of the Reds' datapads off his arm and prime my concealed gravBoots. Evey shouts at me. The boots whine mournfully as they lift me into the air. I rip back the way we came, rupturing through the door instead of opening it, flying down the hallway like a bat out of hell. I smash past a dancer, careen over two Orange customers, and turn a razor-tight right angle down over the railing toward the Jackal's table as he finishes his liquor. His Stained marks me, as do the Grays. Too slow.

On the screens, over the bombings, the static crackles and a blood-red helm burns.

"Reap what you sow," Ares's voice growls from a dozen speakers.

The table melts under the Jackal's hand. Consumed by the bomb Evey planted. The Stained throws the Jackal away from the table like a doll and curls his titanic body around the mushrooming energy. His mouth moves in a death whisper, *"Skirnir al fal njir."*

9

||||||||||||||||||||||

THE DARKNESS

The energy blossoms outward from the Stained liquid to the eye, evaporating his body and spreading over the floor like spilled mercury before darkening, slipping back to the origin, sucking men and chairs and bottles toward it like a black hole before detonating with a deep, nightmare roar. I snag the Jackal up by his jacket and fly through the wall, slamming shoulder first as, behind us, glass, wood, metal, eardrums, and men rupture.

My boots fail. We fly across the street and slam into the building opposite, cracking concrete and falling to the ground as the Lost Wee Den shrinks inward like a grape becoming a raisin becoming dust. She exhales a death rattle of fire and ash before sagging to ruin.

Beneath me, the Jackal's unconscious, his legs badly burned. I vomit as I try to stand, my skeleton creaking like the trunk of a young tree after its first hard winter wind. I stumble up only to fall back to the ground, emptying my stomach a second time. Pain in my skull. Nose dripping blood. Ears trickling with it. Eyeballs throbbing from the explosion. Shoulder dislocated. I gain my knees, wedge my shoulder against the wall and roll the joint back in, quivering out breath as it pops into place. The feeling of needles tickles my fingers. I wipe the sick off my hands and wobble finally to my feet. I pick up the Jackal and squint into the smoke.

I hear nothing but the wailing of stereocilia. Like screaming sparrows in my inner ear, throbbing. I shake away the lights that dance across my vision. Smoke swallows me. People flow past, water around a rock, rushing to help those trapped. They'll find only death, only ash. Sonic booms puncture the night. The Jackal's support teams roar down from the city above. And as they land to take him out of this hell, the sparrows in my ears fade, devoured by the crackling of flames and the crying of the wounded.

I stand in front of an abandoned factory, four hundred kilometers from the Citadel, deep in the Old Industrial Sector. Newer factories have been built atop this one, burying it beneath a fresh skin of industry like a deep blackhead. Grime skins the place. Carnivorous moss. Rust-filled water. I'd have thought it a dead end if I didn't know my quarry so well.

The datapad I took from the Red survived the explosion. I left the Jackal for his support teams and slipped farther down the street, where I stole a Gray police craft. After wiping the datapad's tracking device, I hacked into the datapad coordinates history.

I knock hard on the locked door to the factory's main level. Nothing. They must be shitting themselves. So I kneel on the ground, hands behind my head, and wait. After a few minutes, the door creaks open. Darkness inside. Then several figures slip forward. They bind my hands, cover my head with a bag, and push me into the factory.

After taking me down an old hydraulic elevator, they guide me steadily toward the sound of music. Brahms's Piano Concerto no. 2. Computers hum. Welding torches flare bright enough to glow through the bag's fabric.

"Here, get off him, you brutes," snaps a familiar voice.

"Careful, clown," rumbles some Red.

"Babble at me all you want, you rusty baboon, he's worth more than ten thousand of you inbred rough—"

"Dalo, get out," Evey says softly. "Now."

Boots thud away. "Can I stop pretending now?" I ask.

"By all means," Mickey says.

I snap the cuffs they used to bind my wrists behind my back, and strip off the bag that covers my head. The concrete and metal laboratory is clean, quiet but for the soothing music. A faint haze floats in the air from Mickey's water pipe in the corner. I tower over him and Evey. She can't contain herself.

No longer the seductress Rose from the tavern, she throws herself into me like a little girl greeting a long-lost uncle. Her hands linger on my waist as she eventually pulls back and stares up into my Gold eyes with her pink ones. Despite her giggling, she's all sensuality and beauty, with willowy arms and a slow, intimate smile that echoes none of the grief killing nearly two hundred people should mark her with. The winged girl has become a carrion bird and she doesn't seem to have noticed. I wonder if she'd smile so broadly if she had to kill all those people with a knife. How easy we make mass murder.

"I could recognize you anywhere," she says. "When I saw you at the table . . . my heart skipped a beat. Especially in that ridiculous Obsidian makeup. Darrow, what's wrong?"

She yelps when I pick her up by the front of her jacket and shove her against the wall.

"You just killed two hundred people." I shake my head, sore and heavy with the weight of what's happened. "How could you, Evey?" I shake her, seeing again the crew of my ship venting into space. Seeing all the dead I've left in my path. Feeling Julian's pulse fade to nothing.

"Darrow, darling—" Mickey tries.

"Shut up, Mickey."

"Yes. All right."

"Reds. Pinks. LowColors. Your own people. Like they were nothing." My hands tremble.

"I was following orders, *Darrow*," she says. "Adrius has been investigating us. He had to be taken out."

So with all his scheming, he'd been noticed. Tears brim in Evey's eyes. I don't recoil from them. Who gives a shit about how she feels after what she's just done? But I release her, letting her slide pathetically down the wall, hoping she might show some glimmer of regret that would make me think those tears are for the people she killed and not for herself, not because she's scared of me.

"This isn't how I wanted it to be," she says, wiping her eyes. "When you saw me again."

I stare down at her, confused. "What happened to you?"

"She had a different teacher than you," Mickey says. "I took her wings off and Harmony gave her claws."

I turn to Mickey. "What the hell is going on?"

"It would take a year to explain." He crosses his arms and examines me. "But let us first say, you've been missed, my darling prince. Second, please do not link my morality to that lost soul. I agree. Evey is a little monster." He glares past me at Evey as she stands. "Maybe now you'll see yourself for what you are." His sneer fades, quick eyes scanning me toe to head. "Third, you look divine, my boy. Absolutely divine."

His eyes dance over my face. His mouth opens, closes, tripping over itself it has so much to say. Sharp of face, oily of hair, he slides forward like a blade on ice. All angles. Skin wrapped around slender bones. Was he so thin when last I saw him? Or does he simply not have his cosmetics? No. His blinks are slow. Languid. He's tired. Older. And seemingly beaten down. A queer air of vulnerability in the way his shoulders hunch and his eyes dart around, as if expecting to be hit at any moment.

"I asked you a question, Mickey," I say.

"I can't think about the forest! I'm still examining the tree! It's astounding how your body flourished. Simply astounding, my darling. You've actually grown larger. How fare your pain receptors? Did the hair follicles ever grow irritated as I was concerned? What about the muscle contraction; do you find it above the average of your peers? Pupil dilation fast enough? All I heard for months was talk of you on the HC. They could not show the Institute, of course. But there were videos leaked on the holoNet. Such videos—you killing a Peerless Scarred. Taking some strange fortress in the sky, like a champion of old!"

Even they swallow the myths of the Conquerors, the noble champions of old. He grips my shoulder desperately, his hand weaker than I remember. "Tell me about your life. What the Academy is like. Tell me everything. Are you still lovers with that delectable Virginia au Augustus?" He frowns suddenly. "Oh, of course you're not. She's with—"

"Mickey." I grip him. "Calm down."

He laughs so hard he coughs, turning from me to wipe his eyes. "Just good to see a friendly face. They don't allow me kind company these days. None at all. Monstrous, really."

"Shut up, Mickey," Evey snaps.

His eyes slip to Evey, who now stands far from my reach, fingering the burner holstered on her hip as though it would protect her from me.

"Why are you on Luna? What is going on?" I ask. "Have you joined the Sons?"

"Much has happened," Mickey murmurs. "I'm not here by—"

"He works for us, now, Darrow," Evey interrupts coldly. "Whether he likes it or not. We took his little skin den apart. Used the funds he made from selling flesh to buy transport here and equip an army. We're striking back, Darrow. Finally."

"One Pink terrorist and a handful of Reds playing with guns," I say without looking at her. "Is that your army?"

"We drew blood from the Golds today, Darrow. If you don't respect me, respect that. I killed the son of Mars's ArchGovernor. What have you done that makes you think you can come here and spit on what we've done?"

"You didn't kill him," I say.

She looks blankly at me. "Don't be ridiculous."

I stare back, angry.

"But how . . . The bomb . . . ," she says. "You're lying."

"I got him out in time."

"Why?"

"Because my mission is complicated. I need him. Where is Dancer? Who is in charge here? Mickey—"

"I am," says another voice from my past, one with an accent like my wife's, except this voice is poisoned and bitter with anger. I turn to see Harmony at the door. Half her face still blasted with that terrible scar. The other half is cold and cruel, older than I remember.

"Harmony," I say mildly. The years have done nothing to warm us to each other. "It's good to see you. I need to debrief. There's so much to say." I can't even think where to begin. Then I notice the glance she gives Evey. "Harmony, where is Dancer?"

"Dancer is dead, Darrow."

Later, Harmony sits with me in front of Mickey's desk in an office of cheap, angular furniture and jars filled with hybrid organs floating in preservative gas. Mickey sits behind the desk, fidgeting with that old platonic puzzlecube of his. He sees me looking at it and he winks. He's gotten better. Evey leans against a barrel of chemicals. I sit, utterly lost. Dancer had a plan for me. He had a plan for all this. He's not supposed to be dead. He can't be.

"It was Dancer's last wish for Mickey to carve us a new army. One that will rival the Golds in speed and strength. We've taken our greatest men and women and put them to the carving. They cannot survive a Gold procedure like the one you endured, but some manage to brave this new program." She waves out the glass where a hundred coffin-like tubes splay across the floor. Inside each, Reds of a new breed. "Soon we'll have a hundred soldiers who can cut Gold deeper than any before."

As if a hundred would be enough to fight the Gold war machine. My Howlers and I could likely shred any unit these terrorists put together. And we're not even the deadliest Golds.

She gestures with a new arm, having lost the one of flesh and bone to an Obsidian, when raiding an armory for weapons. It's a limb of metal now. Fluid and strong, with illegal blackmarket sockets for weaponry. Good workmanship, but nothing compared with Mickey's carving. Of course she'd never let him work on her.

"So Mickey is a prisoner?" I ask.

"Slave, more like," Mickey grunts with a small smile. "They don't even give me wine."

"Shut up, Mickey," Evey snaps.

"Evey." Harmony fixes the young woman with a tolerant stare before regarding Mickey. "Remember what we talked about, eh? Mind your tongue."

Mickey flinches, eyes darting down to her left hand. There is an empty holster on her belt. Something Mickey is scared of. Harmony is behaving for me.

"You afraid he's going to say how you beat him?"

She shrugs, dismissing my judgment. "Mickey sold girls and boys. Can't enslave a slaver. Far as I see it, he's bloodydamn lucky not to have a bullet in his brain. Could hire a Carver to give him horns and wings and a tail so he'd look like the monster he is. But I haven't. Have I, Mickey?"

"No."

"No?"

"No, *domina.*"

The word makes me recoil in disgust.

"Dancer always respected him," I say. "I respect him, despite all his . . . eccentricities."

"He bought people. Sold them," Evey says.

"We've all sinned," I say. "Especially you, now."

"Told you he'd be bloodydamn holier than thou. Acting like he doesn't compromise his morality day in, day out. Finding excuses for wicked bastards like our Mickey here." Harmony smirks to Evey, sharing a private joke. "That sort of attitude is all fine up there, Darrow. But you'll learn we don't compromise here anymore. That's the past."

"Then Dancer is truly dead."

"Dancer was a good man." She's silent for too short a moment for it to count as respectful. "But good men tend to die first. Half a year back, he hired a Gray mercenary team to hit a communications hub so we could steal data. I said we should kill them once the job was done. Dancer said . . . what was it again? . . . 'We aren't devils.' But after the Gray captain collected his pay, he pissed off to the local Society Police headquarters and offered them Dancer's location. Bloodydamn lurcher squad put Dancer and two hundred Sons in the dirt in two minutes. Never again. If they kill one of us, we kill a hundred of them. And we don't trust Grays. We don't pay Violets. They've lived off our toil for ages. We only trust Reds."

Evey shifts uncomfortably.

"There was another Red at the Institute," I say after a moment. "Titus. Was he one of yours?" I glance toward Mickey.

"Don't look at me," Mickey says.

"How did you know Titus was a Red?" Harmony asks quickly. "Did he tell you?"

"He . . . let it slip. Small mannerisms. No one else noticed."

"Then you found each other?" she asks, not smiling, but sighing free a weight she's long carried. "He was a good lad. I'm sure you became friends?"

"He never discovered me. Did you carve him, Mickey?"

With Harmony's blessing, he answers. "No, darling. You were my first. My only." He winks. "I consulted on his carving. But an associate of mine did his procedure based on the successes you and I pioneered."

"Dancer found you," Harmony says. "I found Titus. Though his name was Arlus when we pulled him from Thebos mines. He didn't care about keeping it."

It's fitting that Harmony would find Titus. Birds of a feather.

"What happened to him?" she asks. "We know he died."

What happened to him? I let a Gold put him in the bloody ground.

I look stonily at the three of them, thankful they cannot read my thoughts. They know nothing. I can barely conceive of what they must think of me. They've such small perspectives on what I've done, on what I've become. I thought there was a plan, a long, large reason for all my toil. But there was nothing. I know that now. Even Dancer was just waiting to see what happened. Hoping.

I expected to be welcomed back with open arms. I expected an army waiting. A grand plan. For Ares to take off his infamous helm and dazzle me with his brilliance and prove all my faith warranted. Hell, all I wanted was to find them again so I would not feel alone. But I feel more alone than ever sitting here in a concrete room with these three pale people on rickety plastic chairs.

"A Gold named Cassius au Bellona killed him," I say.

"Was it a good death?"

"By now, you should know there's no such thing."

"Cassius. The same one you have a bloodfeud with. Is that why?" Evey asks eagerly. "Is that why the Bellona want to kill you?"

I run a hand through my hair. "No. I killed Cassius's brother. It's one of the reasons they hate me."

"Blood for blood," Evey murmurs like she knows what the hell she's talking about.

"We hit them hard today, Darrow. Twelve blasts across Luna and Mars. Dancer and Titus have been avenged," Harmony says. "And we'll hit them harder in the days to come. This cell is just one of many."

She waves her hand at the desk and scenes rise as the holoDisplay comes to life. Violet news anchors drone on about the carnage.

"Am I supposed to be impressed?" I ask. "You're as bad as them. You know that, yes? Never mind the strategy of it. Never mind you're taunting a sleeping dragon. Evey herself killed over a hundred low-Colors just hours ago."

"There weren't Reds," Harmony says, and then adds, in an amazingly insincere afterthought, "or Pinks."

"Yes, there were!"

"Then their sacrifice will be remembered," Harmony says solemnly.

"*Vox clamantis in deserto,*" I exclaim.

Mickey sits quiet, but he allows himself a small smile.

"Trying to impress us with your Gold fancy talk?" Harmony asks.

"He feels like a voice crying out in the desert. Shouting all in vain," Mickey explains. "It's simple Latin."

"So you know what's what," Harmony says. "Become a Gold and suddenly you have all the answers."

"Wasn't that the point of me becoming a Gold? So we could see how they think?"

"No. It was to position you to strike at their jugular." She balls her fist and strikes the palm of her metal hand in emphasis. "Don't act like you were born better than I. Remember, I know what you are inside. Just a scared boy who tried to kill himself when he was too weak to save his wife from hanging."

I sit speechless.

"Harmony, he's just trying to help," Evey says softly. "I know it must be hard, Darrow. You've spent years with them. But we have to hurt them. See, that's all they understand. Pain. Pain is how they control us."

She continues slowly.

"The first day I served a Gold was the greatest pleasure I felt in all my life. I can't explain it to you. It was like meeting God. Now I know that it wasn't pleasure I felt. It was the absence of pain.

"That is how they train Pinks to live a life of slavery, Darrow. They raise us in the Gardens with implants in our bodies that fill our lives with pain. They call the device Cupid's Kiss—the burn along the spine, the ache in the head. It never stops. Not even when you close your eyes. Not when you cry. It only stops when you obey. They take the Kiss away eventually. When we're twelve. But . . . you can't know what it's like, the fear that it'll come back, Darrow."

Evey plays with her nails. "Gold needs to feel pain. They need to *fear* it. And they need to learn they may not hurt us without consequences. That's what Harmony means."

And I thought the Golds were broken. We're all just wounded souls stumbling about in the dark, desperately trying to stitch ourselves together, hoping to fill the holes they ripped in us. Eo kept me from this end. Without her, I'd be like them. Lost.

"It's not about hurting them, Evey," I say. "It's about beating them, Eo taught me that, Dancer too. We're swinging at the apples when we should be digging at the roots. What will bombing them do? What will assassination accomplish? We need to undermine their Society as a whole, erode their way of life, not *this*."

"You've lost sight of your mission, Darrow," Harmony says.

"You say that to me?" I ask. "How could you possibly understand what I've seen?"

"Exactly. What you've seen. Dine with the masters and forget the slaves. You can afford to live a life of theories. What about what I've seen? We're down in the shit. We're dying. And what are you doing?

Philosophizing. Living the plush life. Bedding Pinks. I had to *listen* as Dancer died. I had to hear the bloodydamn screams rattle over the coms as the lurchers came to kill. And I could do nothing to save them. If you had lived through that, you would know fire can only be fought with fire."

I know where these words lead. They gave me a hole in my gut. Put me weeping in the mud, Cassius standing over me. That is how this will end.

"You may have lost all you love, Harmony. I'm sorry for that. But my family is still in a mine. They will not suffer because you are angry. My wife's dream was about a better world. Not a bloodier one." I stand. "Now, I want to talk to Ares."

Silence lies heavy upon the room.

"Give us a moment." Harmony looks at Mickey and Evey. She watches Mickey stand reluctantly. He pauses, as if to say something to me, but, feeling Harmony's eyes on him, thinks better of it.

"Good luck, my darling," he says simply, patting my shoulder.

"Let me stay," Evey says, drawing close to Harmony. "I can help with him."

Harmony touches her hip. "Ares wouldn't allow it."

"After what I did today . . . don't you trust me? I'm not like the rest."

"I trust you, as much as any Red. But this is something I can't share with you." She kisses Evey softly on the lips. "Go."

Evey pauses at the door, looking back at me. "We're not your enemies, Darrow. You have to know that."

The door clicks shut behind her and we're left alone in Mickey's office.

"Does she know?" I ask.

"Know what?"

"That you sent her on a suicide mission."

"No. She's not like us. She trusts."

"And you'd sacrifice her?"

"I'd sacrifice any of us to kill a Peerless Scarred. All we get are worthless Pixies and Bronzies. I want the real tyrants."

"You're using her worse than Mickey ever did."

"She has a choice," Harmony mutters.

"Does she?"

"Enough." Harmony sits and gestures for me to do the same. "Dancer may be dead, but Ares has a plan for you."

"No. No. I'm done listening to his plans through others. I've sacrificed three years of my life for him. I want to see his face."

"Impossible."

"Then I'm done."

"How can you be done, eh? You're trapped. You bloodywell can't go home to Lykos, can you? One way out. Buckle tight and stay the course."

Her words strike hard. I can't go back. The loneliness in that is inexpressible. Where is my home? Where will I go even if this all ends with Gold falling to ashes?

"You won't meet Ares. Even I've never even seen his face, Helldiver."

"You haven't? You've worked for him almost as long as Dancer. Years. How can you of all people trust him?"

"Because he put the first gun in my hand. He wore his helmet and pushed a mark IV scorcher with a full ion clip into my palm."

"Is Ares a man?" I ask.

"Who cares?" She pulls up a holoDisplay. The electrons swirl in the air, coalescing into a series of maps. I recognize the topography. Mars. Venus. Luna, I think. Dozens of red dots blink throughout blueprints of cities, dockyards, and a dozen other vital organs. Bombs, I realize. Harmony looks tiredly at the map. "This is Ares's plan. Four hundred bombings. Six hundred assaults on weapons depots, government facilities, electric companies, communications grids. It is the sum of the Sons of Ares. Years of planning. Years of scraping up resources."

I had no idea we could carry out such action. I stare at the map in awe.

"The bombings today were meant to provoke a response. Get them all hot and bothered. We want them mobilizing. If they mobilize, they condense. Easiest to burn pitvipers when they are packed tight."

"When will this take place?"

"Three nights from now."

"Three nights," I repeat. "At the conclusion of the Summit. He can't want me to do th—"

"He does. Three nights from now, the Summit finishes up nice with a gala. Wine, Pinks, silks, whatever the hell you Goldbrows do. All the bloodydamn Governors, all the Senators, Praetors, Imperators, Judiciars from across the Society will be here. A Solar System of monsters brought by the power of the Sovereign to one place. It'll be ten more years before we see this. There's no way for the Sons to get in, but you can go where we can't. You can strike the blow that we cannot."

I feel the words coming like a train down a tunnel.

"When they have all gathered nice and tightlike. When the Sovereign stands to give her speech, you kill the Goldbrow bastards with a radium bomb we hide on you. Mickey and a crew of gizmos built the tech. Once we see the bomb has detonated via the dataRecorder we'll plant on you, we unleash hell across the system. Burn them out."

This is the sum of all I've done?

"There has to be another way."

"There were always two plans, Helldiver. This, and you. Ares and Dancer said you were our hope, our chance at another path. They boasted like boys that you could destroy Gold from inside. But you failed, like I said you would. You're gonna claim blood is on Evey's hands. Well, it's on yours too."

"You don't even know the blood I have on my hands, Harmony. I'm not some bloodydamn saint. But Evey's attack was a crime."

"The only crime is if we lose."

I shatter. "There's more at play here than you understand. We cannot face Gold. No matter the blow we strike, they will eradicate us like this." I snap my fingers.

"So you won't do it."

"No, I won't do it, Harmony."

"Then the war begins without your help," she says. "We had two Sons ready to try to enter the gala. They are not Gold, so bets are higher they'll get caught and cut to ribbons in a Praetorian torture cell before completing their mission. Means the leaders of Gold will live on, and our tiny chances of winning this shitstorm shrink, because you don't trust Ares."

"Slag this. Ares should have told me this himself if he wanted my help!"

"How? He is on Mars preparing the revolution. There is no way to communicate. They monitor everything. How could he contact you without exposing your cover?" She leans forward, lower teeth exposed ferally. "Tell me, Darrow. Do you even know how much they've stolen from you?"

It's something in her tone. "What do you mean?"

"Here's what I mean." She jams a series of orders into the holo-Cube and an image appears of Lykos mines. My blood goes cold. "The recording of Eo's death, the one we pirated and broadcast . . ."

My heart thuds in my throat.

"It wasn't complete." She presses play and the room around us becomes the mine. We're a part of the three-dimensional holo. It's the raw footage, not the stuff on the newsreels, not the stuff I've seen a hundred times. It shows the hanging without a soundtrack.

I hear my own cries of pain as the Grays beat the boy I used to be. Weeping in the crowd. The awkward silence of unedited footage. My mother hangs her head and Uncle Narol spits in the dust. Kieran, my brother, covers his children's eyes. Feet shuffle. Dio, Eo's sister, stumbles up the metal scaffold. Shoes scraping over rust. Sobbing. Then Dio leans toward my wife. Eo stands small, so pale and thin, little more than the smoke of the burning girl I remember. Her lips move. Again, I don't hear it, just as I didn't hear it that day. Suddenly Dio sobs uncontrollably and clings to Eo. What was said?

"Use the equipment. That's what it's there for, eh?"

I've wondered it a thousand times but never had access to this footage. I never knew how I'd find it without raising suspicion. And the thought scared me, as it scares me now—what was I not strong enough to hear? What could Dio bear that I could not?

In the news footage that was pirated, they don't even show Dio. But here, with the raw footage, I can rewind. I do so. I can amplify the sound. I do so. I watch it happen again: My mother hangs her head. Narol spits. Kieran covers the children's eyes. Feet shuffle. Dio goes up the scaffold. All the sound is magnified. I sort out the white noise with the controls, and I hear what my wife said to Dio.

"In our bedroom, there is a crib I made. Hide it before Darrow returns."

"A crib . . . ," Dio murmurs.

"He must never know. It would break him."

"Don't say it, Eo. Don't."

"I am with child."

10

||||||||||||||||||||||

BROKEN

I break.

Sitting in a void. Staring at my hands. The hands that could not save my wife, my child. She was right. I wasn't strong enough to bear the truth of her second sacrifice. Eo could have lived. Eo could have given us the child we always wanted. But she thought that future wasn't worth her silence. I wasn't worth it. . . .

I feel something deep in my chest, a hollow cold ache. Like blackness has opened in the pit of my soul even as my body tightens and coils around grief. I weigh a million pounds. Shoulders slump. Chest compresses. My fingers clutch together. Funny to think these hands have been with me this whole time. They touched her lips. They helped pull her ankles. They buried her in the soil. But they didn't just bury her, did they?

No. They buried another life. One unborn. Our child, dead before it lived. And I never even knew. I mourned without knowing the greatest injustice. I failed them both. The amplified video replays again.

"I am with child," she tells Dio on the scaffold. *"I am with child."*

I replay it a dozen times, feeling myself shrink into a corridor of grief.

The Golds didn't just kill her. They killed what I've always wanted to be—a husband and a father. If only I had stopped her. If only I had not pouted like a child when we lost the Laurel, she wouldn't have thought to take me to the garden. If only I had the strength to pretend losing the Laurel didn't bother me.

All the family I could have had. A wife. Sons. Daughters. Grandchildren. They've been slaughtered before they ever were. Eo will never hold our daughter. She will never kiss our son to sleep and smile over at me as his little hands clutch my finger. I'm all that's left of that family that could have been. A dark shadow of the man I was meant to be.

The rage rises. We had a chance, and it is gone. Everything I wanted is gone, because of me and because of *them*. Their laws. Their injustice. Their cruelty. They made a woman choose death for her and her unborn child over a life of slavery. All that for power. All that so they can keep their perfect little world.

"You were not strong enough then," Harmony says. "Are you strong enough now, Helldiver?" I look at her, tears blurring my sight. Her hard eyes soften for me. "I had children, once. Radiation ate their insides, and they didn't even give them pain meds. Didn't even fix the leak. Said there weren't enough resources. My husband just sat there and watched them die. In the end, the same thing took him. He was a good man. But good men die. To free them, to protect them, we must be savages. So give me evil. Give me darkness. Make me the bloodydamn devil if we can bring even the faintest ray of light."

I stand and wrap my arms around her as I'm reminded of the true horrors our kind face. Had I really forgotten? I am a child of hell, and I've spent too long in their heaven.

"Whatever Ares wants, I'll do it."

"Pliny sent the bitch," the Jackal hisses as the Yellow physicians slowly remove the burned skin from his arm and reapply new growth cultures. "It wasn't Sons of Ares. They wouldn't kill that many low-Colors. It's against profile. Pliny probably. Or the Sovereign's Praetorians using cover."

The lights of passing ships glow through the glass. He curses and shouts at his servants to black out the windows. Grays brought me here to his private skyscraper instead of the Citadel, as I requested. The place crawls with mercenaries. He prefers Grays to Obsidians, except apparently that Stained. I'm the only other Gold, which shows the extent of the Jackal's trust. His name would certainly bring enough hangers-on to fill a city, but he's comfortable in his isolation. Like me.

"Could it have been Victra?" I ask. "She didn't stay. . . ."

"She's already proven her loyalty. She wouldn't use a bomb. And she's in love with you. It wasn't her."

"In love with me?" I ask, startled.

"You're blind as a Blue." He snorts but says no more about it. "Our alliance must remain a secret until we're off this damn moon, which means you were not in that tavern. If Pliny knew the extent of our plans, he would have been more thorough. I believe he was only targeting me. So you will return to the Citadel. Pretend as if nothing has happened. I will continue my plan with the syndicate lords, then purchase your contract at the end of the Summit."

At which point, their world will change.

I turn to leave him, but his voice arrests me at the door. "You saved my life. Only one other person has ever done that. Thank you, Darrow."

"Tell your new skin to grow faster. You won't want to miss the closing gala."

The next three days pass in a haze, my mind on Eo and what we lost. I cannot find escape from the grief. It plagues me even as I work myself to death in the estate's gymnasium. I do not indulge in small talk. I pull back from my friends. None of this matters. Not to me. Life fades in the presence of pain. Theodora notices, and tries her best to relieve my dourness, even suggesting I distract myself with Roses from the Citadel's Garden.

"Better you, *dominus,* than some rough man from the Gas Giants," she says.

News of the bombings sweeps through the Citadel, dominating the news. The Society plays it well—broadcasting their aid relief. Sending out instructions on how to handle a potential crisis. Yellow psychologists analyze Ares on-screen, conclude that a latent sexual trauma in his youth makes him lash out to seize control of his world again. Violet actors and entertainers raise money for those families who have lost loved ones. Quicksilver himself volunteers three percent of his personal fortune to relief efforts. Obsidian and Gray commandos attack asteroid bases where Sons of Ares "train." Gray antiterrorist agents hold press conferences saying they have apprehended those responsible, likely some Reds they pulled out of a mine or Luna's slums.

It's a farce and the Golds play it so well. They hide from the cameras and make this seem a fight of all the Colors against Red terrorists. This is not Gold's fight. It belongs to all of Society. Moreover, Society is winning because our sacrifice and obedience allow the righteous to prosper. Bloodydamn horseshit.

Yet still, blame must be placed. So the ArchGovernor is pulled away to face inquiries regarding his handling of the situation. How have the Sons spread from Mars to Luna? they will ask. The Gold hornets' nest has been stirred, as I said it would be, but still the gala continues. I watch the Golds play their games of intrigue, diplomacy, spiriting off to galas and conferences and summits, untouched by the dirty games with terrorists. They are protected, shielded from horror.

It would bother me, but they are shadows to me now. As though they've already fallen into some distant memory.

I touch the bomb on my chest in regret. It is of Mickey's make. A copy of the pegasus I wore at the Institute, which contained Eo's hair and now lies secreted away with my other personal effects. All I need do is twist its head and it becomes the bomb. The ring they gave me will activate it.

I draw away from friends, from Victra. She's asked Roque what is wrong with me. I know he will answer that I'm like the wind, a creature of vagary and moods. Or something like that. He draws closer to me, visiting my rooms when I've gone to bed, attempting to spar with me in the gymnasium. But I cannot smile with him or listen to his soft voice read poems or discuss philosophy or even share jokes. I can't let myself feel for him, because I know he will soon be dead. I try to kill him in my heart before I kill him in the flesh.

Can I add him to the list of those I've already sent to the grave?

I finally find my answer the night of the gala, when Theodora brings me my pressed clothing from the laundry. She doesn't say anything that reminds me of Roque. Doesn't offer pithy wisdom. Instead, she does something I've never seen from her. She makes a mistake. While setting my uniform down on a chair, she knocks over a glass of wine on a nearby table. The wine splashes over the sleeve of my white uniform. What flashes through her eyes chills me—terror. The sort a deer might have when staring at an oncoming aircar. She streams out apologies as though I would hit her if she did not. It takes her a moment to compose herself, for the flash of panic to dissipate. When it does, she sits there on the floor, dabbing at the uniform in silence.

I don't know what to do. I stand there awkwardly for a moment before putting a hand on her shoulder to tell her all's well. That's when she begins to cry in great heaving sobs that rack her small shoulders. She flinches from my touch and composes herself, telling me I'll have to wear black instead of white. She may not know what is about to happen, but she can feel it in me, in the air.

While the other lancers play with one another, take microabrasion baths, and consult with stylists to prepare themselves for the gala, I lace up my thick military boots with trembling fingers. I've never been good at saving my friends. It seems I always drag them into harm's way. Sevro, I believe, is still alive only because of the distance between us. Fitchner was always afraid I'd kill his son. Said my life's strand was so strong that it frayed all those around it. Now, seeing Theodora like that . . . it reminds me how fragile and complicated we really are. I don't know why she cried. Some past trauma? Some sense of what's to come? Not knowing reminds me of the depth to the people around me. I am speechless, cold, but Roque is warm . . . he would have known what to say.

I knock on his door several minutes before Augustus's entourage is set to depart the villa for the gala. There is no answer. I open the door and find my friend sitting on his bed, holding an ancient book gently by its spine. His smooth features ripple into a smile when he sees it is me.

"I thought you were Tactus come to beg me to shoot some stims before the gala. He always thinks because I'm reading, I'm not doing anything. There is no greater plague to an introvert than the extroverted. Especially that beast. He will run himself into the ground one of these days."

I force a chuckle. "At least he's sincere about his vices."

"Have you met his brothers yet?" Roque asks. I shake my head. "They make Tactus look like a lamb."

"Goryhell," I swear. I lean against the door's frame. "That bad?"

"The brothers Rath? They are terrible. Terribly rich. Terribly talented. And their chief virtue lies in their ability to sin. They're prodigies at it." Roque grins conspiratorially. "If you believe rumors—and I love rumors, remind me of Byron and Wilde—Tactus's brothers opened a brothel in Agea when they were fourteen. Classy affair till they started arranging more . . . customized experiences."

"Then what happened?"

"Ruined daughters, sons. Insults. Duels. Dead heirs. Debt. Poison." He shrugs. "It's the Rath family. What do you expect from those blackguards? It's why everyone was so surprised Tactus had taken up with an Iron Gold like you," he clarifies. "You know his brothers mock him for being in your shadow. It's why he's always so sarcastic. He wants to be like you, but he can't. So he resorts to his usual defenses." He frowns. "Sometimes I feel like you understand all of us better than we understand ourselves. Then other times, it's like you couldn't care less." Roque tilts his head at me when I say nothing. "What is it?"

"Nothing."

"You're never one for nothing." He sets his book down on his chest and pats the edge of the bed, drawing me into the room. "Sit, please."

"I came because I wanted to apologize," I say very slowly, sitting on the edge of the bed. "I've been distant these last months, particularly these last days. I don't think I was fair to you. Not when you've been my most loyal friend. Well, you and Sevro, but he won't stop sending me strange pictures over the net."

"More unicorns?"

I laugh. "I think he has a problem."

Roque pats my hand. "Thank you. But you're like a hound apologizing for wagging its tail. You're always distant, Darrow. You don't have to apologize for how you are, not to me."

"More distant, perhaps?"

"Perhaps," he agrees, allowing it. "We all have our own tides inside. They go in. Out." He shrugs. "Not really ours to control. The things, people, that orbit us do that, at least more than we'd like to admit." After watching me a moment, he furrows his brow in thought. "Is this about Mustang? I know it was hard for you to leave her, no matter what you said at the time. You should seek her out while we're here. I know you miss her. Admit it."

"I don't."

"Liar, liar, cheeks afire."

"I've told you a hundred times, we're not talking about her."

"Fine. Fine. Then you're worried, aren't you? About the auction?" He pauses, smiling and watching me. "You shouldn't. I've settled that matter. I'm going to bid on you."

"Roque, you don't have the money."

"Do you know how badly a Pixie would pay to get a Peerless with my pedigree and connections in their debt? Millions. I could even go to Quicksilver if I need. He loans to Golds all the time. Point is, I'll have the money, even if my parents won't help me. So never you worry, brother." He pokes me with his foot. "House Mars has to mean something, eh?"

"Thank you," I say, stuttering out the words, unable to really grasp what he's done. And why? It puts his neck out. It endangers him and crosses his parents. "No one else has even mentioned the auction to me."

"They're afraid your bad luck is contagious. You know how it is." He pauses, waiting because he knows me so well. "There's something else. Isn't there?"

I shake my head. "Do you . . ." My words fail me. "Do you ever feel lost?" The question hangs between us, intimate, awkward only on my end. He doesn't scoff as Tactus and Fitchner would, or scratch his balls like Sevro, or chuckle like Cassius might have, or purr as Victra would. I'm not sure what Mustang might have done. But Roque, despite his Color and all the things that make him different, slowly slides a marker into the book and sets it on the nightstand beside the four-poster, taking his time and allowing an answer to evolve between us. Movements thoughtful and organic, like Dancer's were before he died. There's a stillness in him, vast and majestic, the same stillness I remember in my father.

"Quinn once told me a story." He waits for me to moan a grievance at the mention of a story, and when I don't, his tone sinks into deeper gravity. "Once, in the days of Old Earth, there were two pigeons who were greatly in love. In those days, they raised such animals to carry messages across great distances. These two were born in the same cage, raised by the same man, and sold on the same day to different men on the eve of a great war.

"The pigeons suffered apart from each other, each incomplete without their lover. Far and wide their masters took them, and the pigeons feared they would never again find each other, for they began to see how vast the world was, and how terrible the things in it. For months and months, they carried messages for their masters, flying over battle lines, through the air over men who killed one another for land. When the war ended, the pigeons were set free by their masters. But neither knew where to go, neither knew what to do, so each flew home. And there they found each other again, as they were always destined to return home and find, instead of the past, their future."

He folds his hands gently, a teacher arriving at his point. "So do I feel lost? Always. When Lea died at the Institute . . ." His lips slip gently downward. ". . . I was in a dark woods, blind and lost as Dante before Virgil. But Quinn helped me. Her voice calling me out of misery. She became my home. As she puts it, 'Home isn't where you're from, it's where you find light when all grows dark.'" He grasps the top of my hand. "Find your home, Darrow. It may not be in the past. But find it, and you'll never be lost again."

I've always thought of Lykos as my home. Of Eo as my home. Perhaps that's where I'm going now. To see her. To die and find home again in the Vale with my wife. But if that's true, why am I not full? Why does the hollowness grow inside me the closer I draw to her?

"It's time to go," I say, rising from the bed.

"As sure as I am your friend"—Roque begins to rise as well—"you will recover from this. We are not our station in life. We are us—the sum of what we've done, what we want to do, and the people who we keep close. You're my dearest friend, Darrow. Mind that. No matter what transpires, I will protect you as surely as you would protect me if ever I needed it."

I surprise him by clasping his hand and holding it for a moment.

"You're a good man, Roque. Far too good for your Color."

"Thank you." He squints at me as I release his hand and he straightens the wrinkles in his uniform. "But whatever do you mean by that?"

"I think we could have been brothers," I say. "Were this a different life."

"Why do we need another life?" Then he sees the automatic syringe in my left hand. His hands are too slow to stop me, but his eyes are quick enough to widen in trusting fear, like a loyal dog's as he's put slowly to sleep in its master's lap. He doesn't understand, but he knows there's a reason, yet still comes the fear, the betrayal that breaks my heart into a thousand pieces.

The syringe pierces Roque's neck and he sinks slowly down onto the bed, eyes drifting closed. When he wakes, everyone he has worked with and for over these past two years will be dead. He will remember what I did to him after he said I was his closest friend. He will know that I knew what was going to happen at the gala. And even if I don't die tonight, even if they do not discover I was the bomber by other merits, saving Roque's life means I will be found out. There is no going back.

11

||||||||||||||||||||||

RED

Tonight, I kill two thousand of humanity's great. Yet I walk with them now, untouched by decadence and condescension as never before. Pliny's arrogance raises none of my blood. Victra's immodest dress does not disconcert me, not even when she slips her arm in mine after Tactus offers her his. She whispers in my ear how silly she is for forgetting her undergarments. I laugh like it's a merry joke, trying to mask the coldness that's taken me over.

This is static.

"I suppose Darrow deserves some consolation before he leaves," Tactus says with a sigh. "Have you seen Roque, my goodman?"

"Said he was feeling ill."

"That's very Roque of him. Likely coiled around a book. I should fetch him."

"If he wanted to come, he would come," I say.

"*I* want him to come," Tactus replies. He shrugs at the other lancers who jockey for position close to our master.

"If you need him so badly, go fetch him," I say, tactically.

He flinches. "I *need* no one on my arm. But if I didn't know better, I'd think you're still bitter about the whole escape-pod affair."

"You mean when you launched it without him?" Victra asks. "Why would that ever bother him?" Even now that betrayal stings me.

"I thought he was dead! It was simple calculation." He bumps my shoulder with his fist and nods to Victra. "You understand. Had to watch out for the lady here."

"She is a delicate little flower," I say, pulling her away.

"Woe for the lone god of the sea," Tactus hums melodically. *"His friends, like mine, abandoned he!"*

Victra adjusts the gold pauldron on her shoulder, which winds its way down her arm in a series of golden cuffs. "That darling boy is so vain he could make a thunderstorm be about him." She notices my lack of care. "The bidding won't begin till after the gala." She nods to a landing aircar. "Well, I was wondering when he'd show."

The Jackal exits the car, skin faintly pink only in patches. His Yellows did him well. He bows faintly to his father, ignoring the murmurs of the aides.

"Father," he says, "I thought it fitting if the Family Augustus arrived at the gala with at least one of your children. We must present a united front, after all."

"Adrius." Augustus eyes his son for something to criticize. "I wasn't aware you enjoyed banquets these days. I'm not sure the fare will be to your liking."

The Jackal laughs theatrically. "Perhaps that is why my invitation was not delivered! Or was it the furor over the terrorist attacks? No matter. I am here now, and ever eager to attend your side." The Jackal falls in, smiling broadly to all, knowing his father will never escalate family quarrels in public. He offers me a particularly sinister sneer, one others see and shrink away from. All stage. "Shall we?"

I mind myself and say little as I follow with Victra at the end of the long procession that snakes its way through labyrinthine marble halls from our villa to the Citadel Gardens some two kilometers distant. The Sovereign's tower juts from the floor of the garden there, a grand, two-kilometer-high sword piercing a groomed garden thick with rose trees and streams.

Water runs through the garden in a thousand winding paths. Babbling brooks with colored fish lead to quiet lagoons where carved

Pink mermaids swim under flowering trees crawling with monkey-cats. Rangy tigerlynx lounge below the boughs. Violets wander through these bright woods, flitting here and there like summer moths, their violins echoing in eerie concert. It is a picture of Bacchus's night gardens without the obscene sexuality the Greeks found so hilarious—Pixies would chuckle at that smut, but Peerless do not. At least, not in public.

We glimpse other processions through the trees. See their standards, great flashing things of moving fabric and metal. Our red and gold lion crest roars in silent challenge. A raven on a field of silver marks the passing of the Family Falthe over a cobblestone bridge. We eye their lord and his lancers warily. As a matter of course, all carry razors, but other tech is forbidden—no datapads, no gravBoots, no armor. This is a classical affair.

The tower yawns above us. Purple, red, and green mosses climb the base of the great structure with vines of a thousand hues, wrapping the glass and stone like the fingers of greedy bachelors around the wrist of a rich widow. Six great lifts bear families skyward to the top of the tower.

Beautiful Pink servants and Brown footmen service the lift, all in white. Gold triangles of the Society decorate their livery.

The lift is flat, marble with gravthrusters. It sits in the middle of a clearing where green grass flutters in the wind. Several Coppers rush forward to talk with Pliny, who, as Politico, speaks on behalf of the ArchGovernor. There seems to be some confusion. The Falthe family files into the lift ahead of us.

"This is a social trap," Augustus mutters back to his favorite ward. Leto draws closer. "The fools. See how they feign accident. Soon they will tell us we must use the lift with the Falthes, when instead they should grovel to have us go before them."

"Could it not be an accident?" Leto asks.

"Not on Luna." Augustus crosses his arms. "Everything is politics."

"The winds shift."

"They've been shifting for some time now," Augustus murmurs. His sharp face surveys his aides, as if making an accounting of the razors we carry. Some wear them coiled at their sides. Others wear them around their forearms like I do with my borrowed blade. Tactus and Victra each use them as sashes.

"I want three lancers attending the ArchGovernor at all times," Leto announces quietly. We nod, the pack tightening. "No drinking."

Tactus moans in protest.

Expressionless, the Jackal watches Leto give orders.

Pliny returns from speaking with the Citadel staff. Sure enough, we're to share the lift with the Falthes. But something more menacing fills the air. Our Obsidians and Grays are to be left behind. "All families are to proceed to the gala without attendants," he says. "No bodyguards."

Murmurs go through our ranks.

"Then we won't go," the Jackal says.

"Don't be a fool," Augustus replies.

"Your son is right," Leto says. "Nero, the danger—"

"Some invitations are more dangerous to decline than to accept. Alfrún, Jopho." Augustus makes a cutting motion to his Stained. The two men nod silently and join the others to the side. Genuine emotion—worry—fills their eerie eyes as we join the Falthes on the lift and ascend. The head of the Falthe house smiles. His station improves.

The gala upon the roof of the Sovereign's tower is modeled as a winter fairyland. Snow falls from invisible clouds. It dusts the spearlike pines of man-made forests and frosts my short hair with snowflakes that taste like cinnamon and orange. Breath billows in front of me.

The ArchGovernor's appearance is noted with trumpet calls. Tactus and some of the younger lancers cut the Falthes off, obstructing their path so Augustus can enter the gala first. A body of pale gold and bloody red, we move into a grand landscape of evergreens. The pride of Gold culture awaits us. A terrible sea of faces that have seen things the first men could never even dream. You can see glimmers of our shared past at the Institute. The charmers of Apollo. The killers of Mars. The beauties of Venus.

Beneath the spire, the Citadel sprawls, and beyond those grounds glisten the cities with all their million lights. You would never guess that beneath that sea of twinkling jewels lurks a second city of filth and poverty. Worlds within worlds.

"Try not to lose your head," Victra whispers to me, raking a clawed hand through my hair before going to speak with friends of hers from Earth.

I walk toward our table. Great chandeliers hover overhead on small gravthrusters. Light sparkles. Dresses move like liquid around perfect human forms. The Pinks serve delicacies and spirits on plates and in goblets of ice and glass.

Hundreds of long tables spread concentrically around a frozen lake at the center of the winter land. The Pinks wear skates to serve here. Beneath the ice, shapes move. Not sexualized perversities as one would find entertaining Pixies and lowColors. But mystical creatures with long tails and scales that glitter like the stars. In another life, it would have been Mickey's dream to have a creature commissioned for this feast. I smile to myself. I suppose, in a way, he already has.

The tables are neither named nor numbered. Instead, we find our place as we see a great lion seated upon the center of our table, nearly motionless. Each family's table is so claimed by their sigil. There are griffins and eagles, ice fists and huge iron swords. The lion purrs contentedly as Tactus steals a serving tray of appetizers from a Pink and sets it between the beast's massive paws. "Eat, beast! Eat!" he cries.

Pliny finds me. His hair is bound behind him in a tight, complicated braid. His clothing, for once, is as severe as his pointed nose, like he means to impress the Peerless about him with his hawkish features and sparse accoutrements. "I'll be introducing you to several interested parties later in the evening. When I signal for you, I expect you to join me." He looks around distractedly, seeking important persons for his own aims. "Till then, cause no trouble and mind your manners."

"No trouble." I take out my pegasus pendant. "On my family's honor."

"Yes," he says without looking. "And what a noble family it is."

I gaze around the gala. Hundreds mill about already, with more arriving by the minute. How long should I wait? It is difficult to hold on to the rage that made me embrace this decision. They killed my wife. They killed my child. But no matter the anger I summon by re-minding myself, I cannot burn away the fear that I steer the rebellion toward a cliff.

This will not be for Eo's dream. It will be for the satisfaction of those living. To sate their lust for vengeance rather than honoring those who have already sacrificed everything. And it will be irrevers-ible. But so is the course that has been set.

So many doubts. Is this me being a coward? Rationalizing inac-tion?

I'm thinking too much. That makes a bad soldier. And that is what I am. A soldier for Ares. He gave me this body. I should trust him now. So I take the pegasus and slap it on the underside of Augustus's table, just near the table's end.

"A toast?" someone says. I turn and find myself face-to-face with Antonia. I've not seen her since the Institute, when Sevro pulled her down from the cross she was nailed to by the Jackal. I flinch away, mind flashing to the night she cut Lea's throat, all to draw me out of the dark.

"I thought you were on Venus studying politics," I say.

"We've graduated," she replies. "I did enjoy your *christening*. Watched it several times with my friends. Odious scent, urine." She sniffs me. "Hard to get out."

Nature was cruel to make her so terribly beautiful. Full lips, legs nearly as long as mine, skin smooth as river stone, and hair like spun golden yarn from that storybook about the princess of cinders. All a mask for the wretched creature beneath. "I can tell you missed me while I was away." She hands me a goblet of wine. "So let us toast to a good reunion."

It makes little sense to me that we live in a world where she can stand here weaving her evil webs when my wife is dead, when kind Golds like Lea and Pax have been ground to ash and shot into the sun.

"Fitchner once said something to me, Antonia. It seems appropri-ate now." I raise my goblet in a polite toast.

"Oh, Fitchner," she sighs, her breasts rising aggressively from her too-tight golden dress. "The bronze rodent has been making a name for himself here. Whatever did he say?"

" 'A man can never miss chlamydia.' " I dump the wine out in front of her and push past. She grabs my arm and pulls me back to her, bringing me close enough that I feel the heat of her breath. "They're coming," she says. "The Bellona are coming for you. You should run now." She looks at my razor. "Unless you think you're good enough with that to beat Cassius in a duel?" She releases me. "Good luck, Darrow. I will miss having an ape at the ball. More than Mustang will, at least."

I pay no attention to her words and wander away, willing more houses to fill the gala so that I may end this soon. A host of Praetors, Quaestors, Judiciars, Governors, Senators, family heads, house leaders, traders, two Olympic Knights, and a thousand others come to bid my master a good evening. These older men talk of Outrider attacks on Uranus and Ariel, a foolish rumor of a new Rage Knight already gaining the armor, mysterious Sons of Ares bases on Triton, and a resurgent strain of plague on one of Earth's dark continents. Light fare.

Many others take my master aside, as though a hundred eyes did not watch their every move, and with voices like syrup, tell him of whispers in the night, of shifting winds and dangerous tides. The metaphors mix. The point is the same. Augustus has fallen out of favor with the Sovereign the same way I have fallen out of favor with him.

The ships flitting above in the night sky are as distant from the conversation as I. My attention has fallen upon the Sovereign herself. How strange a thing, to see the woman just there beyond the dance floor, at the raised podium, speaking with other house lords and men who rule the lives of billions. So close, so human and frail.

Octavia au Lune stands with her coterie of women, the three Furies—sisters she trusts above all others. For her part, the Sovereign is more handsome than beautiful, face impassive as a mountain's. Her silence is her power. I see her speech is seldom, but she listens; always, she listens to words as the mountain listens to the whispering and screaming of wind through its crags, around its peaks.

I see a man standing alone near a tree. He's near as thick around as its trunk. A hand dwarfs his small goblet, and he wears the mark of a sword with wings, a Praetor with a fleet. I approach him. He sees me coming and smiles.

"Darrow au Andromedus," Karnus growls.

I snap my fingers at a passing Pink. Taking two of the wine goblets from his ice tray, I pass one to Karnus. "I thought that before you come to kill me, we might as well share a drink."

"There's a sport." He downs his own drink and takes the one I offer him. He eyes me over the glass. "You're not a poisoner, are you?"

"I'm not so subtle."

"Equal company, then. All these snakes about . . ." He grins like a crocodile, dark Gold eyes tracing the men and women. The wine is gone in a moment. "It's strangely decadent tonight."

"I hear Quicksilver arranged the festivities," I say.

"Only on Luna would they let a Silver pretend he's a Gold." Karnus grunts. "I hate this moon." He takes a delicacy off a passing tray. "Food's too heavy. Everything else too light. Though I hear the sixth course will be something to die for."

Noting his strange tone, I cross my arms and watch the party. It's a strange comfort being around this hateful man. Neither one of us has to pretend to like the other. No masks here, at least not as much as usual.

He chuckles deeply. "Julian would have liked this fancy fare. He was a simpering, vile child."

I turn to examine the killer. "Cassius said only pretty things about him."

"*Cassius.*" He snorts out something like a laugh. "Cassius once wounded a bird with a slingshot. Came to me crying, because he knew he had to kill it to put it out of its misery, but he couldn't. I dropped a rock on it for him. Just like you did." He smirks. "I should thank you for sweeping away the genetic chaff."

"Julian was your brother, man."

"He pissed the bed as a boy. Pissed the bed. Always tried hiding the sheets by giving them to the laundrywomen himself. Like we didn't own the laundrywomen. He was a boy who did not deserve his mother's favor or his father's name." He grabs another glass of wine from a passing Pink. "They try to make it tragedy, but it isn't. It's natural law."

"Julian was more a man than you are, Karnus."

Karnus laughs in delight. "Oh, do explain that one."

"In a world of killers, it takes more to be kind than to be wicked. But men like you and me, we're just passing time before death reaches down for us."

"Which will be soon for you." He nods to my razor. "Pity you weren't raised in our house. We learn the blade before we learn to read. My father had us make our blades, had us name them and sleep beside them. You might have stood a chance then."

"Wonder what you would have been if he had taught you something else."

"I am what I am," Karnus says, taking another drink. "And they sent me after you, me of all the sons and daughters, because I am the best at what I am."

I watch him for a moment. "Why?"

"Why what?"

"You have everything, Karnus. Wealth. Power. Seven brothers and sisters. How many cousins? Nieces? Nephews? A father and mother who love you, yet . . . you are here, drinking alone, killing my friends. Setting the purpose of your life to ending *me. Why?*"

"Because you wronged my family. No one wrongs the Bellona and lives."

"So it's pride."

"It's always pride."

"Pride is just a shout into the wind."

He shakes his head, voice deepening. "I will die. You will die. We will all die and the universe will carry on without care. All that we have is that shout into the wind—how we live. How we go. And how we stand before we fall." He leans forward. "So you see, pride is the only thing." His eyes leave mine and look across the room. "Pride, and women."

I follow his eyes and I see her then.

She wears black amid a sea of gold, white, and reds. Like a dark specter, she glides in out of the lift near the edge of the fake forest. She rolls her flashing eyes, twists her smirking mouth at the heads that turn in her direction to stare at her funereal gown. Black. A color to show disdain for all the merry Golds about. Black like the color of the military uniform I now wear. I'm reminded of the warmth of her flesh, the mischief in her voice, the smell at the nape of her neck, the kindness of her heart. I stare so hard I almost miss her escort.

I wish I had missed him.

It is Cassius.

He of the bloodydamn golden curls is with the girl who nursed me to health in the winter, who helped me remember Eo's dream. His hand on her waist. His lips whispering into her ear. As surely as Cassius au Bellona put a sword in my stomach, he now sticks a dagger in my heart.

His hair thick and lustrous. His chin cleft, hands steady. Shoulders powerful, made for war. Face made for the hearts of court. And he wears the rising sun of the Morning Knight. The rumors are true. It rips through the party. The Sovereign has made him one of the twelve. Despite the fact that I won the Institute, he's risen higher, tearing through the Dueling Circuit on Luna like an ancestor possessed. I've watched him on the HC, watched him stalk around the Bleeding Place as another Gold lies near death.

But here, now, he dazzles, charms. Face split with a white smile. In his Golden body he has all I have and more. He is faster on his feet than I. As tall. More handsome. Wealthier. He has a better laugh and people think him kinder. Yet he has none of my burdens. Why too does he deserve this girl, who makes all but Eo pale in comparison? Does she not know how petty he is? How cruel his heart can be?

I cannot go to her, not even when I draw close enough to hear her laugh. If she saw me, I think I would shatter. Would there be guilt in her eyes? Awkwardness? Am I a shadow over her happiness? Will she even care that I see her with him? Or will she think me pathetic for approaching her?

It aches, not that I suspect Mustang is being petty in seeking my enemy, but because I know she is not petty. If she is with Cassius, it is because she cares for him. It aches deeper than I thought it would.

"And so you see . . ." Karnus's hand falls heavily on my shoulder. ". . . you will not be missed."

Tightness spreads through my chest as my shoulders carve a path out of the gala. I take a smaller lift down, away from these people who know only how to hurt. Away into the woods where I find a bridge that spans a fast-flowing stream. I lean over the polished railing, gasping for air, each breath a statement.

I do not need Mustang.

I do not need any of these greedy creatures.

I'm done with their games of power.

Done with trying to go it on my own.

I was not good enough to be a husband.

Not good enough that my wife would let me be a father.

Not good enough to be a Gold.

Now I'm not good enough for Mustang.

I've failed to do what I set out to do.

Failed to rise.

But I won't fail now. Not now.

I take the ring the sons gave me. Hand trembling. Nerves stampeding. I want to retch, there's so much wrong inside of me. I take the cold ring to my lips. Say the words and the corrupt perish. Say "Break the chains" and Victra vanishes. Cassius evaporates. Augustus melts. Karnus dissolves. Mustang dies. Across the Solar System, bombs ripple and Red rises to an uncertain future. Trust in Ares. Just trust he knows what he is doing.

Break the chains.

I try to say the words, Eo's last before she hanged. But they do not come. Force it out. Dammit. Make my mouth work. But it won't. It can't, because inside I know that this is wrong. It isn't the violence. It isn't compassion for the people I would kill. It's anger.

Killing them proves nothing. It solves nothing.

How could this be Ares's plan?

Eo said if I rose, others would follow. But I've not yet risen. I've not yet done as she asked of me. I am not an example. I am an assassin. I do not have an excuse to give up. To hand over her dream to others. Ares never knew Eo. He never saw the spark in her. I did. Before I draw my last breath, I must build the world she wanted to raise our child in. That was her dream. That was why she sacrificed, so others would not have to. And I will not let others decide my fate. Not now. I do not trust in Ares if it means I must reject Eo.

Not if it means I must sacrifice my trust in myself.

I wipe the tears from my face, anger replaced by purpose. There must be another way. A better way. I have seen the cracks in their Society, and I know what I must do. I know what the Golds most fear. And it has nothing to do with Reds rising. It has nothing to do with bombs or plots or revolution. What terrifies the Golds is simple, cruel, and as old as mankind itself.

Civil war.

PART II

||||||||||||||||||||||||||||||||||||

BREAK

If you're a fox, play the hare.
If you're a hare, play the fox.

—Lorn au Arcos

12

||||||||||||||||||||||||

BLOOD FOR BLOOD

I stalk back into the gala.

The Golds have taken their seats and formalities have begun in earnest. I am not subtle as I duck beneath the table and scrounge around on the ground to find the pegasus pendant. I put it in my pocket. Straighten my jacket. Ignore the questioning glances and move boldly away from Augustus's table toward the object of my interest. Pliny hisses my name. I pass him by. He knows nothing of what I have in store.

I weave through the tables that seat the noble families, gathering eyes as a stone rolling down the mountain gathers snow. I feel them adding to my velocity. My gait is careless, my hands coiled with danger, like the muscles of a pitviper. Thousands watch me. Whispers form a cloak behind as they realize my target; he sits at his long table surrounded by his family members—a perfect Golden man attentively listening to his Sovereign speak. She preaches of unity. Order and tradition are paramount. No one rises yet to challenge me. Perhaps they don't understand. Or perhaps they feel the force of me now and dare not rise.

The Bellona notice the whispers now, and they turn, almost as one, a family of fifty and more, to see me—a martial man, all in black. Young, untested in war. Unblooded beyond the halls of the Institute and the asteroids of the Academy. Some have reasoned me mad. Some have called me brave. Tonight, I'm both. The weight is gone. All the pressure I let crush me as I worried about expectations, as I gentle-footed around making a decision. All velocity, I tell myself. Don't freeze. Don't stop. Never stop.

The Sovereign's voice falters now.

Too late to go back. I dive in.

Smile.

And the gala goes dead silent as I spring thirty feet in the low grav-ity and land hard on the Bellona table. Dishes crack. Servers scatter. Bellonas fall back. Some shout at me. Some do not move even as their wine spills. The Sovereign watches, struck by curiosity, her Furies stir-ring at her side. Pliny looks about to die. He's gripping his knees in panic. Beside him, the Jackal is as strange and unreadable as a lonely desert creature.

I did not wear dress shoes tonight. My boots are thick and heavy. They crack the porcelain as I trod along the Bellona table, shattering dishes of pudding and squishing tender steaks. My blood pumps through me. Intoxicating. I lift my voice.

"I'll have your attention." I crush a plate of peas underfoot. "You *may* know me." There's nervous laughter. Of course they know me. They know everyone of worth, though mine is more of rumor than substance. I see the Furies whispering to the Sovereign. See Tactus grinning his ass off. Karnus leans forward anxiously. Victra's smiling at the Jackal. Even see Antonia nudging a tall, serene Gold. I avoid looking at Mustang. Pliny gibbers in Augustus's ear. Augustus raises a hand to shut him up. "Do I have your attention?" I ask.

Yes. I do.

"Boy, sit down!" someone shouts.

"Make him," Tactus replies drunkenly. "No? That's what I *sur-mised*!"

"For those of you who do not know, I am a lancer of the House of Augustus, for another hour or so." They laugh. "I am the one they call the Reaper of Mars, who struck down a full Peerless Knight, who stormed Olympus and made slaves of my Proctors. My name is Darrow au Andromedus, and I have been wronged.

"We Peerless Scarred come from Golden ancestors. From conquerors with spines of iron. Honorable men, honorable women. But before you today, I see a family that is dishonorable. A family with spines made of chalk. A corrupt and fraudulent family of liars and cowards that conspires to steal my master's Governorship, illegally."

I crush a serving plate with my boots. Who knows if they conspire to do it or not? It sounds good. It seems like they conspire. And it's the mask I need them to wear. Karnus replies beautifully by whipping out his razor and surging toward me. His father, the Imperator, waves him back. Praetor Kellan looks about to grab my feet and jerk me down where Cagney would no doubt cut my throat with my own razor. The younger girls of their family think me a demon. A demon that killed their cousin, brother. They have no idea what I really am. But perhaps Lady Bellona does. Cadaverous in her grief, she sits surrounded by her brood like a withered lioness. They look to her as much as to her husband. The last thing I note is the trembling of her long right hand, as though it aches for a knife with which to cut me.

"Twice I have been wronged by this family. Once in the mud of the Institute. Again at the Academy by that one . . . and this one . . . and that one." I point out all those who beat me in the gardens. I see Cassius now near the head of the table, just by his father and mother. Mustang sits beside him. Her face a mask. Disappointed? Upset? Bored? When she quirks an eyebrow at me, I meet her eyes, walk toward her and set my foot on the edge of the wine decanter that sits in front of Cassius. All eyes focus there, like light falling into a black hole. Pausing time, space. Bending all forward. Breaths catch. "All courts of Golden law permit a man to defend his honor against any force that would desecrate it unjustly. From the old lands of Earth to the icy bowels of Pluto, the right of challenge exists for any man and any woman. My name, gentle lords and ladies, is Darrow au Andromedus. My honor has been pissed upon. And I demand satisfaction."

I tip the wine over onto Cassius's lap.

He explodes up at me. Golds all over the grand party burst up from their seats in a great roar. Tactus rushes from our table, joined with

Leto, Victra, all of the aides and bannermen of the vassals to my ArchGovernor—the Corvos, the Julii, the Voloxes, the huge Telemanuses, Pax's family. Razors snap into hands. Curses splinter the winter air. Aja, the largest and darkest of the Furies, leans down from the Sovereign's table and bellows, *"Stop this madness!"*

It's only begun.

My hands shake like they used to in the mine. Now, as then, serpents surround me.

You could never hear them, the pitvipers. Could rarely see them. Black as pupils, they slither in the shadows till they strike. But there's a fear that comes when they near. A fear separate from the rumbling of the drill. Separate from the throbbing, nauseating heat that builds in your balls as you carve through a million tons of rock and all the friction radiates up, making a bog of piss and sweat inside your suit. It's fearing the coming of death. Like a shadow has passed across your soul.

That fear fills me now as these Peerless stand around me, a mass of serpentine gold. Whispering. Hissing. Deadly as sin.

Snow on the ground crunches under my heavy boots. I bend down as the Sovereign speaks. She tells of honor and tradition. How martial duels mark the greatness of our race, so she makes an exception for the day. We may duel beyond the gaming grounds. This bloodfeud must be put to rest here, now, in front of the august of our race. So confident is she in her newest Olympic Knight. But why wouldn't she be? He's killed me before.

"Unlike the cowards of old, we settle flesh to flesh. Bone to bone. Blood to blood. Vendettas die in the Bleeding Place *virtute et armis,*" the Sovereign recites.

By valor and arms. No doubt she has already spoken to her advisors. They will say I am outmatched, that Cassius is the better swordsman. It never would have gone this far if she hadn't been assured a beneficial outcome.

"As it was with our ancestors, it is now and again to the death," she declares. "Are there any contentions?"

I hoped for this.

Neither Cassius nor I say a thing. Mustang steps forward to object, but the Fury, Aja, shakes her head, stopping her.

"Then today, *res, non verba*." Actions, not words.

I speak with my master before stepping into the center of the circle that now forms as Browns cart away the tables from the snowy plain. Pliny hovers beside Augustus. As do Leto, Tactus, Victra, and the great Praetors of Mars. So many famous faces, so many warriors and politicians. The Jackal stands farther away, shorter than the rest, impassive, speaking to no one. I wonder what he would say to me were there fewer ears to hear. He does not look angry. Perhaps he's learned to trust in my plans. He nods his head, as if reading my thoughts. We are still allied.

"Is this spectacle for me? For vanity? For love?" Augustus asks as I stand before him. His eyes dig into me, trying to find meaning. I can't help but glance over at Mustang. Even now, she draws me from my task.

"You're so young," he nearly whispers. "What they tell you in the storybooks is wrong; love does not survive things like this. Not the love of my daughter, at least." He pauses, reflecting. "Her soul is like her mother's."

"I don't do it for love, my liege."

"No?"

"No." I bow my head to him and remember Matteo's highLingo. "The duty of the son is the father's glory. Is it not?" I fall to a knee.

"You are not my son."

"No. The Bellona killed him, stole him from you. Your firstborn son, Claudius, was all a man could hope for—a son better and wiser than his father. So let me make you a present of *their* favorite son's head. Enough quibbling. Enough of their politics. Blood for blood."

"My liege, Julian was one thing. But Cassius . . . ," Pliny tries.

Augustus ignores him.

"I weep for your blessing," I say again, pressing my master. "How long will you keep the Sovereign's favor? A month? A year? Two? Soon she will replace you with the Bellona. Look how she favors Cassius. Look how she steals your child. Look how the other goes the way of a Silver. Your heirs are depleted. Your time as ArchGovernor will end. Let it. For you are not a man fit to be ArchGovernor of Mars. You are a man fit to be king of it."

His eyes flash. "We have no kings."

"Because none have dared craft themselves a crown," I say. "Let this be the first step. Spit in the Sovereign's eye. Make me the sword of your family."

I pull a knife from my boot and make a quick cut beneath my eye. The blood falls like teardrops. This is an old blessing, from the iron ancestors, the Conquerors. And it will chill those who see it—a relic of a bygone, harder age. It is a Mars blessing. One of iron and blood. Of the raging ships that burned the famed Britannic Armada above Earth's North Pole, and dashed the fastkillers from the land of the Rising Sun amid the asteroid belt. My master's eyes ignite like dormant coals breathed upon, slowly, then all at once.

I have him.

"I give my blessing freely. What you do, do in my honor." He leans toward me. "Rise, goldenborn. Rise, ironmade." Augustus touches his finger to the blood and then presses the mark beneath his own eye. "Rise, Man of Mars, and take with you my wrath."

I rise to whispers. This is no simple squabble now between boys. It is the battle of houses. Champion against champion.

"*Hic sunt leones,*" he says, tilting his head—part challenge, part benediction. What a vain swine of a man. He knows my desperation to stay in his good graces. He knows he stands playing with matches on a powder keg. Yet his eyes glitter lustfully, hungering for blood and the promise of power as I hunger for air.

"*Hic sunt leones,*" I echo.

I pace back to the center of the circle, nodding to Tactus and Victra. They touch the handles of their razors, as do the other aides. Our pack mentality is keen. "Prime luck," Tactus says.

High above, ships swim quietly through the long-night. Trees sway in the breeze. Cities sparkle in the distance. Earth hovers like a swollen moon as I unravel my razor from my forearm.

Mustang comes to me as Cassius's mother kisses his forehead.

"So you're a pawn now?" she asks quickly.

"And you're a trophy?"

She flinches before her lips curl into a slight sneer. "You say that to me? I don't even recognize you."

"Nor I you, Virginia. Serving the Sovereign now?"

But I do recognize her, despite the terrible gulf that now makes her feel more stranger than friend. The tightness in my chest is of her making. So too is the awkward tension in my hands as they yearn to touch her, yearn to hold her and tell her this is all a false guise. I'm not a pawn to her father. I'm more than that. All this is for good. Just not *their* good.

"'Virginia.'" She cocks her head at me, smiling sadly as she spares a glance for the two thousand waiting Peerless. "You know, I've wondered over these last years . . . I suppose I should have wondered from the start, but you cut such a rare character—it was distracting. But I'll ask now." Her bright eyes cut through me, searching, judging. "Are you insane?"

I look over at Cassius. "Are you?"

"Jealousy? That's ripe." She leans in with a harsh whisper. "Shame you don't respect me enough to suppose that I have my own plan. You think I'm here because my aching loins thrust me into Bellona arms. Please. I'm no bitch in heat. I protect my family by any means necessary. Who do you protect but yourself?"

"You betray your family by being with him." I have no false answer that may parallel the truth. I must suffer being a villain in her eyes. Yet I can't meet them. "Cassius is a wicked man."

"Grow up, Darrow." She looks like she's going to say something deeper, but she just shakes her head and, turning, says, "He's going to kill you. I'll try to convince Octavia to end it early." Her words fail her at first. "I wish you hadn't come to this moon."

She leaves me, giving Cassius a squeeze on the hand before joining the Sovereign's entourage on the raised dais.

"Alone at last, my old friend," Cassius says, slashing me with a smile.

Once we were like brothers. We shared food and raced that first day at the Institute. Stormed House Minerva together. How he laughed when I stole their cook and Sevro their standard. We galloped over the plains that night underneath the light of twin moons. I remember the woe in his eyes when they captured Quinn. When my kin, Titus, beat him and pissed on him. How I felt the tears welling then, when we were like brothers, before it all fell apart.

The cinnamon-and-orange-flavored snow still falls. It settles in his curly hair. On his broad shoulders. It was in the snow that he last fought me. Buried rusty steel into my lower gut and left me dying in my own filth. I have not forgotten how he twisted that blade to make sure the wound did not close.

His blade is ebony now.

It curls in front of him, over a meter of narrow sword when solid. More than two meters of lashing razor whip when loosed with the toggle on the handle, which sends a chemical impulse through the blade's molecular structure. Golden marks line the blade, telling the lineage of his family. Their conquests. The Triumphs thrown in their honor. Old, arrogant, powerful. My blade is naked, absent of embellishment.

"So, I've taken what's yours," he says, walking closer and nodding to Mustang.

I laugh, "She was never mine. And she's certainly not yours."

The White arrives, hustling forward in his robes. Head bald. Back crooked.

"But I've had her in ways you haven't." His voice lowers so only we might hear, "I wonder, do you lie alone at night, thinking of the pleasures I give her? Does it vex you that I know how she kisses? How she sighs when you touch her neck just so?"

I don't answer.

"That she moans my name instead of yours?" He doesn't laugh. He may loathe what he says, but he'd say anything to hurt me. In most ways, he's not a bad man. He's just *my* bad man. "In fact, she moaned as I went inside her this morning."

"What would Julian say if he could see you now?" I ask.

"He'd echo mother and beg me to kill you."

"Or would he weep at the devil you've become?"

He uncoils his razor and ignites his aegis. My own aegis hums as I activate it—an ion-blue transparent energy shield that bows slightly outward from my left glove, one foot long by two feet wide. Snow melts when I sweep the aegis near the ground. A corona of haze forms around the blue light.

"We're all devils." His sudden laugh floats up like a silk ribbon carried away with the breeze. "This was always your problem, Darrow. You have an inflated view of yourself. You think you have some sort of morality tucked away. You think you are better than us, when really you are less. Forever playing games you cannot master against people you cannot match."

"I matched Julian well enough."

"*Bastard.*" His face contorts, and he lashes forward, bellowing wordlessly, knocking me back before the White can give the benediction. They shout for us to stop, but as the razors scream, the shouts fade away and all eyes widen as man-killing metal wails through slow-falling snow. He uses the tenets of *kravat*. Four seconds of precise, kinetic violence, retreat. Assess. Engage.

We are the only sound in this strange place. The odd, high-pitched keen of an arching whip. The thrum of the solid blade. The crack as aegises on left arms spark white when blades slash into them. The crunch of snow and the creaking of leather.

Despite his anger, Cassius is perfect in his form. His feet shuffle, never crossing; his hips swivel as he lunges in the compact salvos. His breath comes measured, paced. He lashes his whip forward in a sweep, then hardens the blade and swings it up, aiming for my groin. His movements flicker fast. Trained. Honed by masters and Swords of the Society. It's easy to see why he has devastated his opponents since childhood, why he gutted me at the Institute. Because his enemies fight like him, but slower. I don't fight like them. I learned that lesson.

Now he will learn his.

"You've been practicing. You can match six moves a set," he says, drawing back. He darts forward, feinting high and sweeping low to claim my ankles. "But you're still a novice." He sends a flurry of seven blows at me, almost skewering me through the right shoulder. I recognize the engagement pattern, but am still a fraction off his speed. I barely escape, throwing myself out of the way of a thrust at the last moment. Two more sets of seven come in quick succession. I barely escape the last, falling to a knee, panting, looking around at the gathered guests.

"Do you hear that?" he asks. I hear nothing but the wind and the throbbing of my heart. "That is the sound of dying alone. No one to weep. No one to care."

"Arcos will care," I whisper.

He stiffens. "What did you say?"

"Lorn au Arcos will care if his last student dies," I say, dropping the falsely ragged breath, straightening proudly. Cassius stares at me as if he's seen a ghost. He hesitates. So too do those who hear what I say. "While you ate, I trained. While you drank, I trained. While you sought pleasure, I trained from the weeks after the Institute to the days before the Academy."

"Lorn au Arcos doesn't accept students," Cassius hisses. "Not for thirty years."

"He made an exception."

"Liar."

"Oh?" I laugh. "Did you think I came here to be killed? Did you think yourself entitled to my life? No, Cassius. I came here to cut you down before your parents."

He steps backward, eyes dancing to his father, to Karnus. I cock my head at him. "Come now, brother. Don't you want to see how well I can really fight?"

He pauses and I charge him like some night carnivore, shoulders hunched with primeval economy, quiet as the dark itself.

Lorn's words come back to me. *A fool pulls the leaves. A brute chops the trunk. A sage digs the roots.* And so I peel apart his legs, sending set after set into him. Not for the four seconds the Golds teach. But for seven. Then six, alternating, then breaking the pattern. Twelve moves a set.

His defense is precise. And if I fought as he taught me to fight, I would die to him. But I was taught to move by my uncle, and to kill by a legend. I rage and spin, leaving my feet and striking down, beating him as a great hurricane slapping and smashing and hammering him back. And when he attacks, I bow to the side until such time that I can break him, as Lorn au Arcos trained me to do. Move in a circle. Never retreat backward. No attack opens when a man allows himself to be pushed backward. Use their force to create new angles. Flow around him. The *Willow Way*. Pretty, fluid, like a spring song in defense, then lashing and horrible as the branches of a willow in deep winter as glacial winds scream down from the mountains.

Inside me, Red meets Gold.

My blade flashes between whip and curved slingBlade. It crashes into his sword, and the aegis on his left side crackles from the force of my blows. Cassius falters. He's a prizefighter getting pummeled by a back-alley brawler.

I'm laughing. Laughing madly and the crowd around is cheering in shock, some screaming when I hit Cassius's aegis so hard it overloads. Sparks hiss from the unit on his arm. I rip open a wound there, one on his elbow, his kneecap, his ankle. I flick the blade up and slash his face. I stop and move backward fluidly, posing with whip as it slithers into a curved slingBlade. Those who watch this will never forget.

Women are screaming for Cassius. Lovers he has had in his youth, who now watch the man they grew with, the man who bedded them, left them with false promises, and made them think they'd just lost the strongest of a generation. They watch as another man turns him into a throbbing mess of blood.

I embarrass him. But it's all for a purpose. All to make that simmering hatred between Bellona and Augustus boil over into war.

I pace about the circle like a caged lion till I come in front of Imperator Bellona.

"Your son is going to die," I say savagely, a foot away from his face.

He's thick. Square-jawed, kindly, with a pointed beard. His eyes shimmer with the promise of tears. He says nothing. He is a noble man, and he will follow the honorable path, even if it means watching his favorite son die.

Even in the midst of my rage, I feel the shame. Feel the horror of being the man who comes from the dark to savage a family. "Will you just watch?" I shout at the Bellona. Imperator Bellona's wife is not so noble. She seethes, glancing at the Sovereign accusatorily. I see what she wants.

I go back at Cassius. They will have to watch and do nothing, as I watched Eo.

"Lady Bellona, are you noble enough to watch your Cassius die? Watch as he disappears from the world?" Her lips curl. She whispers to Karnus, to Cagney. "Is that the strength of House Bellona? Do you watch like sheep as the wolf comes among the fold?"

I make a grand show of it for the hot-blooded ones. Cassius tries to fight. He stumbles as I cut his kneecap, falling into the snow before scrambling desperately to his feet. His blood makes a shadow in the snow. This is how slowly he killed Titus. He's panicked, glancing at his family, knowing it will be the last time he sees them. They have no Vale. This life is their heaven. Despite everything, it is a sad sight and I pity him.

Cagney, urged on by Lady Bellona, has already taken a step forward, her sharp, pretty face riven with rage. I just need to hurt her strong cousin Cassius a little more. But Imperator Bellona jerks her back with a stern hand. He glares darkly at Augustus, then peers around the assembly.

"No Bellona shall interfere. On my honor."

Yet his wife does not agree. She aims one more pointed glance at the Sovereign, and the Sovereign raises a hand. "Hold!" she calls. "Hold, Andromedus!"

I'm actually stunned by the interruption.

All look to the Sovereign's dais. Cassius pants for breath. She can't be so stupid. Can she? The interruption confirms the rumors for me, for everyone. The Sovereign reveals her favoritism. She's chosen the Bellona family. They will supplant the Augustuses on Mars. Cassius would have been important to that plan. Now, because of her miscalculation, he's about to die and her plan is going to be squabbed. Still, I had no idea she'd do as she's about to do. It is so stupid. So short-sighted. Her pride has made her a fool.

"There has been an addendum to the rules. Since the White was unable to give the customary benediction, the contest will be to death *or* yielding," she declares, glancing at Cassius's mother. "Those are the limits to the duel. So many of our prized children are lost at our schools. No need to waste these two prime men on account of school-yard pranks."

"My Sovereign," Augustus calls, greedy for his bloody prize, "the law is clear. Once a contest is declared, the rules may not be altered by man or woman."

"You cite laws. That's a pleasant irony, coming from you, Nero."

There are snickers from the crowd, which tell me rumors of his involvement with rigging the Institute for the Jackal are very much in fashion.

"My Sovereign, we stand with Augustus in this matter," booms a voice. Daxo au Telemanus steps forward. Pax's elder brother, tall as my friend was, but less beastly. More a pine tree than a great boulder of a man. Like his father, Kavax, his head is bald, but engraved with Golden angels. A mischievous sparkle dances in sleepy eyes nestled under great swirling eyebrows.

"Hardly a surprise," snarls Cassius's mother.

"Perfidy!" Kavax, Daxo's father, roars. He alternates stroking his forked red beard and the large pet fox he cradles in his left arm. "This reeks of perfidy and favoritism. My temper is slow. But I find myself offended. Offended!"

"Careful, Kavax," Octavia says icily, "some things cannot be unsaid."

"Why else would he say them?" Daxo asks, glancing at the families from the Gas Giants, where he knows he will find allies in this debate. "But I believe he would counsel you now, my Sovereign: even your words cannot change law. Your father discovered this by your own hand, no?"

The Sovereign's Furies step forward menacingly. For her part, the Sovereign allows herself only the strictest of smiles. "But, young Telemanus, you fail to remember, my word *is* law."

This is something you do not do. A Gold may rule other Golds. But declare your rule at your own peril. The Sovereign has been so long on the Morning Throne that she has forgotten this. Her words are not law. They now become a challenge.

One I accept with open arms.

She knows the words a mistake when she meets my eyes and we both realize in that moment there is one move I can make that she cannot counter.

"You will not steal what is mine," I growl.

I wheel on Cassius. He brings up his blade. He never let me yield in the mud of the Institute. He knows I will not let him yield now. His face goes pale as I charge. He's thinking of all he's about to lose. How very precious his life is. A Gold to the end. Others shout at me to stop, screaming that it is unfair.

This is the definition of fairness.

They would have let me die.

He lunges for my throat. It's a feint. He whips his razor down to wrap around my leg. He expects me to recoil. I charge straight at him, inside the arch of his swing, jump over his head in the low gravity, then swing my whip backward without looking. My whip coils around his extended right arm. I press the button that makes the razor contract, and with the sound of a frozen tree branch cracking in winter, I claim the sword arm of Cassius au Bellona.

It's equal parts silence and screams. I do not turn, not for a long moment. When I do, I find Cassius still standing, teetering, not long for this world. No one else moves as Cassius falls. His father looks at the ground, silent.

"I said stop!" the Sovereign shouts. Two Furies jump from the dais, landing with their blades dancing into hand.

"Finish it," Augustus commands.

I stalk toward Cassius. He spits at me, lips trembling. Contemptuous even now. I raise my blade. Then a hand settles around my wrist. Not an iron grip. A soft one. Warm against my skin. Delicate.

"You've won, Darrow," Mustang says quietly, coming around in front of me so her eyes meet mine. The Furies pause outside the circle. "Don't lose yourself to this."

I could not imagine Eo watching me from the Vale. In this hell, I've lost my faith. Mustang brings it sweeping back. Eo may watch me, or she may not. Only one thing is certain. Mustang watches me now, and what I see in her eyes is enough to let my hand fall to my side. It's then she smiles, as if seeing me again for the first time in years.

"There you are."

"*Kill him!*" screams Cassius's mother. "Kill him now!"

"No!" roars Imperator Bellona. Too late.

Mustang's eyes widen.

I turn in time to see the circle dissolve, crumbling inward as though it were made of sand. Not altogether, but tentatively. One Bellona sprints at me in silence, low, deadly. Another follows. Then Tactus comes from the Augustus group. Then another lancer. I hear my friend's war howl. A second echoes. There's more than just one Gold present who was in my army.

Cagney au Bellona is first to me. My stolen blade rasps toward my neck. I duck, but I would have lost my head had Mustang not thrown up her own blade to deflect the slash. Sparks sting my face, and Tactus takes Cagney from the side, cutting her clean in half.

Screams.

The Bleeding Place collapses entirely. Golds of Bellona and Augustus sprint to protect their fellows. Others flee. Karnus slashes at Tactus—too much for my friend. I rush to his aid, saving him till Victra and others come between Karnus and us. Mustang is lost in the fray. I search frantically for her. A blade flashes at my head.

Shouts boom as the Sovereign calls for peace. But it is beyond her. A woman screams at Cagney's ruined body. Dozens of men and women, all with blades, slash into one another. Tactus tosses me the razor Cagney stole. Then he takes a blade through the shoulder defending me again. I spin to my friend's aid and hack the arm off the Bellona man as he pulls his blade out of Tactus. I jerk my friend toward me. Slashing a path clear. A blade scratches my forearm. I glimpse Mustang in the chaos, covering Cassius's wounded body. I don't know if the Bellona will kill her. They let her sit at the table. Still, I don't know. I rush toward her, throwing my weight into the bodies between us. Tactus helps.

I smash into a woman. Antonia. Her eyes light up as she brings a knife up to my stomach, but Victra, her sister, punches her in the face and Tactus starts kicking her in the head as she falls. Victra offers me a laughing smile until Karnus jerks her down by her hair. He's fought off as Leto enters the fray, turning back the tide with the precise thrusts of his rainbow razor. The Telemanuses join him, father and son decimating the Golds who come before them with razors half the size of my body.

"Tactus, on me!" I shout.

Tactus is bleeding, but he's up and howling madly like he's still fighting beside Sevro. Together, we jump high in this easy gravity. He knows I go for Mustang. But the Bellona are too thick. Razors too deadly.

"Mustang!" I shout, fending two Bellonas off. Slash away one's face and punch another in the throat with my aegis. Another joins them. And another, till there's a thick Bellona bullwark blocking my path.

"Protect the ArchGovernor!" Mustang shouts at me, voice more composed than my own, making me feel an idiot obsessed with chivalry. Of course she does not need me to save her. "Protect my father!" And though I can't see her among the throng, I obey.

I let Tactus jerk me away by the collar toward our retreating line, which is being assailed from the side. Someone else roars for us to protect Augustus. Others scream to defend Imperator Bellona and Cassius. Many family lords have been carried away by armed cadres of family members, who back out of the chaos with their blades at the ready. They flee the spire, using the lifts to take them from the place, as gravBoots were forbidden. It's nearly deserted. The Sovereign's Praetorians—purple-and-black-clad Obsidians and Golds—cluster around and fly her from the ruined gala. Razors and pulseBlades fill calloused hands. Grays come led by Golds in Praetorian purple to disperse us. They wear riot gear and their scorchers shoot painballs and scatterwaves at the battling families, scattering the Golds like summer flies.

"AUGUSTUS!" huge Karnus screams as he rushes from the Bellona ranks through the scatterwaves like a madman. He knocks someone down with his shoulder, shatters a lancer's face with his aegis, and charges headlong at Augustus, hoping to kill his family's rival in one fell swoop. "AUGUSTUS!"

Leto, our best swordsman and Augustus's ward, intercepts him in front of the ArchGovernor.

"*Hic sunt leones!*" he calls to the sky.

Leto moves like the sea, fluid and terrible in his grace. He crashes Karnus back and is about to open him along the belly when suddenly he falters. Freezes mid-swing. Karnus stumbles back, then straightens, perhaps confused that he is still alive. He cocks his head at Leto, who reaches for his thigh, as though stung.

Leto sinks slowly to a knee, arms sluggish. His long hair tumbles over his face, then he seems to freeze in place, suddenly motionless in the center of the chaos. Sad eyes glow with the engine plume of a passing ship as it coasts peacefully into the horizon. He is beautiful in that moment before Karnus chops off his head.

"*Leto!*" Augustus roars.

His eyes widen and he pushes against the Telemanus men, who bear him away. I glimpse the Jackal tucking his silver stylus into his sleeve, the one he spun on his fingers as he proposed our secret alliance.

We lock eyes.

He grins toothily.

And I know I've made a deal with the devil.

13

||||||||||||||||||||||

MAD DOGS

We flee the top of the spire. I had to leave Mustang behind. She knows what she is doing. Somehow I had managed to forget that. She always knows what she's bloody doing.

"They won't hurt her," Augustus says to me, and I believe it's the first time I've seen emotion on his face. No. The second time. When he screamed for Leto, it was as if he'd lost a son. He looks that way now, face slack and older by twenty years. He lost his eldest son. He lost his second wife, the mother of his children. Now he loses the man he adopted to replace that son, and he fears for the woman who reminds him of that wife.

If they do hurt her, it's on me.

I've set things in motion. For once, it couldn't have gone better. Blood trickles down my hands, sheeting between the fingers, pooling around the cuticles in a horseshoe. Knuckles flex white where there is no blood. It disgusts me, but this is what my hands were made for.

We flee the place of winter and trees, having drenched it red. Many carry our wounded, nearly a dozen in number. Seven dead. Barely twenty unscathed in the entire entourage. Others are missing. Matchless Leto is gone, Pliny's aide was cut apart, and one of our Praetors took a blade in her neck from Kellan au Bellona.

I carry the Praetor in my arms and try to staunch the bleeding as we take the lift down the spire. Hard chance. Victra presses a piece of her dress against the wound.

I'd give anything for a pair of gravBoots. We cluster tight around our lord. Razors out. Blood soaks my arm to the elbow. Sweat dribbles down my face and ribs. Red drops splatter at our cadre's feet against the lift's floor, dripping from hands, wounds, blades. Yet there are white smiles slashing the faces around me.

I'm hot in my uniform, so I undo the top buttons. Tactus bleeds beside me. His wound goes through his left shoulder. Clean thrust.

"It's just blood," he tells Victra, who worries over him.

"It's a hole in you."

"Not a strange thing." He smiles at her waistline. "Goryhell. You've a hole in you, and you don't see me complaining. *Sheeeeeeowww.*" He yelps as she jams a bandage from her dress onto his wound. He laughs in pain a second more, then looks at me and shakes his head, eyes wild and happy. "Training with Lorn au Arcos, man. You sneaky ponce."

He saved me from Cagney. I nod and bump bloody fists, past slights and wagers on my life temporarily forgotten.

Many of the other Golds, the Praetors, the knights, the martial men and women in particular—and we have more in proportion to our Politicos and economists than most houses—wipe their brows, leaving ruddy smears. These are the sort of Golds who would tell you the problem with being a Gold is that everyone is already conquered. Means no one worth fighting. No one to use all that training and all that power against. Well, I just gave them a fresh taste of battle. And even though their Governor's ward is dead, even though their chief Praetor bleeds out on my shoulder and Mustang is in enemy hands, they want to play. And making corpses is the game of the day.

Old and young look at me hungrily. Waiting to be fed.

This is what it's like being the alpha, the Primus. The others look to you for guidance. They can smell the tangy odor of blood on you before it's even there. Age doesn't matter. Experience doesn't matter. All that matters is that I provide these sick sons of bitches with fresh kills.

Children cry around us, startling me. Such fragile things on a night like this. The sons and daughters of Augustus's youngest sister. Their father strokes their hair to calm them. Snorting, his wife bends and slaps each child across the face till they cease their whining. "Be brave."

Our Obsidians and Grays are not waiting for us on the ground. They've been taken somewhere. Neither are the Sovereign's Obsidians or her Golds coming through the air. Which means she hasn't yet decided what to do. Just as I thought. She can't slaughter us. For a house to wipe out another house is one thing, but for the great leader to do it with the power and funds entrusted to her by the Senate? It's happened before, and that Sovereign was beheaded by his daughter. The daughter who now sits on the throne.

Oh, she must hate me for this.

Below the lift, lights glow along the cobbled paths that cut through the huge forest of flower trees. The musicians no longer play. Instead, we hear shouts and screams and long periods of terrifying silence. Golds run beneath. Fleeing to the stone halls past the forest, where they can access their ships, fly home. Only, some aren't fleeing. They are hunting.

Something has happened I did not expect. Other family feuds find satisfaction tonight. It felt the same at the Institute when the other students realized it wasn't a game. That there weren't rules. An eerie feeling, a notion that devils roam the grounds instead of men. Who knows what anyone will do now that the rules are gone?

There are four hunters in the distance. A pack of three men and one young woman dash silently through the forest. They hop a brook. Running with all the vigor of the hungry. All the ambition of youth. From House Falthe, it seems. I recognize raisin-eyed Lilath, the girl the Jackal sent to deliver the holo of me killing Julian to Cassius. With her is Cipio, the stout young man who once aided Antonia in and out of the bedroom.

We watch them in silence as our lift descends. Carrying death, the lean pack streaks through the trees toward an unsuspecting line of House Thorne family members, all in dresses and suits of red and white; too late they head frantically for the stone halls. Their standard is the rose. It falls as the killers burst from the trees. A family dies. Scary how quiet and fast it is with razors. Different from my duel. I took my time. They don't. I see a boy of ten cut apart. There's no mercy for Gold children. They are not seen as innocent. They're enemy seeds. Destroy them or fight them years from now. A woman in a ball gown slashes back, manages to kill one of the Falthes before being cut down. Two children run. One is caught. The other escapes. She's the only one.

Then the Falthe lancers dance. Taking large, exaggerated stomps. They turn in different directions, grinding their toes into the dark ground. Only they aren't dancing.

"Goryhell," Tactus curses, and rubs his face.

"The children . . . ," Victra whispers.

Augustus says nothing, face resolute as stone.

"The Thornes have fifteen children." Tears bead in Victra's eyes, surprising me.

"Monsters," the Jackal whispers, sending chills up my spine, because his acting is so damn good. He couldn't give a piss.

Children. Would Eo have sung if she'd known this was the chorus? We all carry burdens. And as the killers slip away from the murdered family, I know my burden will crush me under its weight one day. Just not today.

"Data jammer deployed," says Daxo au Telemanus. He flashes me the datapad on his wrist. "Datapads are dead. They don't want us contacting our ships in orbit."

Augustus looks at his blank datapad and says that soon the other families will be summoning their Obsidian, Gold, and Gray attendants. We must be off planet and back in a position of strength before the tide turns against us.

"You made this chaos, Darrow. Deliver me from it." He leans toward me and feels the pulse of the Praetor I carry. "Get rid of her. She'll be dead in a minute." He wipes his hands. "The children weigh us down enough already."

The Praetor murmurs something to me as I set her on the floor of the lift. I don't know what she says. When I die, I will say nothing because I know the Vale waits on the other side. What waits for this warrior? Only darkness. I didn't even understand her last words; we discard her like a broken sword. I close her eyes with my bloody fingers, leaving long, fading marks. Victra squeezes my shoulder, noting the respect I give.

Standing, I give my orders to the lancers and the other men of war. There are fifteen I would consider good killers. Some my age, others well into old age. Yet not one contradicts me. Not even Pliny. The Telemanuses in particular seem eager to follow. Each holds my gaze longer than necessary, nodding deeper than mere formality.

"I hope no one is bored." They laugh. "We'll have company if another family decides they may earn favor with the Bellona or the Sovereign by taking the ArchGovernor's head," I say. "We must kill that company, and carve our way to the hangars. Telemanus, you and your son are now the ArchGovernor's shadows. Attend nothing else. Do you understand?" They nod their massive heads. *"Hic sunt leones."*

"Hic sunt leones."

When the lift reaches ground, forty men and women wait for us. Family Norvo of Triton and Family Codovan of Jupiter's moons.

"Unfortunate odds," Tactus sighs.

"Cordovan and Norvo are ours," Augustus replies. "Bought and paid for."

"Rapscallion! Codovan, you rapscallion!" Kavax thunders. "I thought you were a Bellona man!"

"So did they!" Augustus expected something like this.

I take command of the new Golds. Again, I thought someone would object. They just stand watching me, waiting for my orders. All these Praetors, all these politicians and sinewy men and women of war. I hold back a chuckle. Amazing the power you have when you're bloody up to the sleeves and none of it is your own.

We escort the ArchGovernor out of the forest. Three times we're assailed, but I have Tactus take Augustus's cloak and lead some of the attackers on a wild-goose chase. Rose petals of a thousand shades fall from the trees as Golds fight beneath them. They're all red in the end.

The gang of three from House Falthe try to ambush Tactus as he returns to the main body. He wheels on them and with little help lays all but Lilath low. She scampers off as he kills Cipio and stomps on the dead man. *"Babykillers,"* he spits over and over, till Victra pulls him away. I watch for the Jackal. Every moment I expect a dart in the back, to die as Leto did. But the Jackal merely follows, as does his father. No one saw what he did to Leto. Or if they did, their fear silences them.

When we reach the stone halls beyond the forest, finally crossing a white limestone bridge, the rules of the Society seem to return. Low-Colors skitter out of our way as we, now seventy strong, storm through the halls to the hangars to leave this moon. But when we reach our hangar, we find that our ship is gone. We rush to the landing pads lined with trees and grass. All the family ships are missing. Society ripWings patrol the sky.

We question a shaking Orange. Tactus holds him up by his collar. He shudders as he looks at us seventy bloody souls. He's never spoken to a Gold before, much less ones like us. Victra knocks Tactus's hand away and speaks quietly to the Orange.

"He says the ships were required to return home two hours ago."

"First they don't let Obsidians into the gala, now this," Tactus mutters.

"That means the Sovereign planned something," says the Jackal. "A something that was never allowed to blossom. She removed our Obsidians, our ships, to isolate the houses from their sources of power," he explains, eyeing the Telemanuses warily. "Marooning us. What do you suppose she had up her little sleeves, Father?"

Augustus ignores his son, looking to the sky.

"Mothermercy," Victra curses.

"Gather yourselves!" Kavax bellows to his warriors.

"Piss on my face." Tactus goes pale beside me.

I look up and see doom coming. *"Praetorians!"* Seventy razors curl out and we fan apart in case they have energy weapons.

"Darrow. You're with me," Augustus says.

The enemy is little more than black dots in the night sky. But our eyes are keen. The dark bastards streak from the night clouds and impact the ground like fallen devils, always in their threes.

Thumpthumpthump. Thumpthumpthump. Thumpthumpthump.

They land between the trees on the grass, blocking our way back to the Citadel. Obsidian Praetorians and Gold knight-captains. The Praetorian Obsidians are titanic, like golems pulled from the stone of some mountain. Crueler by far than those we used at the Academy. No armor like theirs in all the worlds. Dark purple inlaid with black, like coral curling over their titan bodies. They stand in tight squad formation, loyal and bound to one another as they are to their faith.

Thumpthumpthump till there are ninety-nine. *Thump.* Their Golden commander lands last, on a knee. He rises, tall helmet a laughing wolfskull. His cape of gold, emblazoned with the pyramid of the Society, kicks sideways in the wind. An Olympic Knight. There are twelve in the Solar System, sworn to protect the Compact of the Society against all who'd defy it. This is the Rage Knight, the post Lorn filled for sixty years till he left for Europa. They represent what the Golds see as the dominant themes of man, the same as our school houses. A man slighter than myself wears the armor. So the Sovereign's already filled Lorn's former post.

"Declare yourself, knight!" I shout.

The knight allows his helm to melt back into his armor. His flaxen hair falls over an ugly hatchet face. Wet from sweat, lined with age and stress. I bark out a laugh when he smiles out that sideslash of a mouth. I draw stares. Now they'll only think me madder. The Rage Knight falls from the sky, and I laugh in his face.

He cackles. "Don't you recognize me, you little shiteater?"

"Fitchner, you look uglier than I remember!"

"Fitchner?" Tactus snorts. "How nostalgic."

"Hello, boyo." Fitchner laughs at seeing Tactus in the ArchGovernor's cloak. "Nice cape, but you're not *ArchGovernor Augustus.*" Fitchner clucks his tongue and sets his hands on his hips. "ArchGovernor! ArchGovernor! Darling, where the devil are you?"

The ArchGovernor rolls his eyes and steps past me. "Proctor Mars."

"There's the darling! And that's an old title, didn't you know?"

"I see you have a new helmet."

"It is pretty, isn't it? The ladies love it. Can't remember when I was laid so much by Golden stock." Fitchner moves his hips suggestively. "It was such a bother getting it. Thought there'd never be an end to the duels and tests! We did it in front of the Sovereign, boyo. Each man, each woman, making their case. Everyone who thought the post should be theirs. Time and again. But fortune favors the nasty!"

"How . . . ," I wonder aloud. "You beat *everyone*?"

"Hardly," my ArchGovernor sneers. "It goes to the great warriors." He strafes Fitchner with his eyes. "Which you are not, Fitchner. What did you promise the Sovereign for your new helmet? I'm sure the price was high."

"Oh, I rode Darrow's star when he beat your boy. Hello, Jackal, you little rugrat. Then there was a gorydamn contest and, well, you can ask Tactus's eldest brother and Proctor Jupiter about the specifics. . . ." He strikes a pose. "I'm more than meets the eye, eh?"

"So you don't have a new master with the new helmet?" Augustus asks.

"Master? Pfah!" Fitchner comically puffs up his chest. "Olympic Knights have no master but our conscience. We defend the Society's Compact, subservient only to duty."

"Once. Now you are the Sovereign's servants," Daxo declares.

"As are we all, my dear Telemanus," Fitchner replies. "Great admirer of your brother and your family, by the by. Wonderful warhammer you carried at that tournament on Thebos. Gorydamn scary lineage. I've always meant to ask, which of your ancestors screwed the rhinoceros?"

Daxo raises his eyebrows in delicate offense. Kavax grumbles like Pax might have.

"Sorry. Was it a grizzly instead?" Fitchner grunts another laugh. "A joke. Keen? We're all servants, though, eh? Gorydamn slaves to the one with the scepter."

"I assume, then, your loyalty to Mars is gone and cannot be . . . remembered?" Augustus asks. "Since you're a servant."

Fitchner claps his gloved hands together. "Mars? Mars? What is Mars but a gorydamn hunk of rock? It's done nothing for me."

"Mars is home, Fitchner." Augustus waves to those around us. "The Sovereign bid you to find us. Well, here we are—kin from your own planet. Will you join your loyalty to us? Or will you give us up?"

"Oh, you are a jokester, Augustus! A prime jokester. My loyalties are to the Compact and to myself, as yours are to yourself, my liege. Not to a rock. Not to false kin. So do not waste your breath. Now, I've been told to place you and your kin under house arrest. You recall we set aside a prime villa for your pleasure? It'd be dandyfine if you could scamper on back there. Enjoy our hospitality. Your Sovereign insists."

"You forget yourself," Augustus hisses.

"I forget much. Where I put my pants. Who I've kissed. Who I've killed." Fitchner touches his arms, his belly, his face. "But forget myself? *Never!*" He points to the Obsidians around him. "And I've certainly not forgotten my dogs."

"And where are mine? Where is Alfrún?"

"I killed your Stained mutts. Both of them." Fitchner smiles. "They were barking, Augustus. Barking so loudly."

Rage burns across Augustus's face.

"I hope they weren't expensive, boyo," Fitchner says with a smile.

"You speak as though we are familiars, *Bronzie.*"

"We are familiar."

"As though we were equal. We are not equal. I am a descendant of the Conquerors, of the Iron Golds! I am the lord of a planet. What are you? A—"

"I'm a man with a stunFist." He shoots Augustus in the chest. Augustus crumples backward as his Praetors gasp. "That'll show him to not wear his armor to galas. Now!" Fitchner smiles. "Who can I reason with?"

"Me." The Jackal takes a step forward. "I am heir to this house."

"Hmm . . . pass! You're creepy."

He shoots the Jackal in the chest with the stunFist.

"Foolishness! Enough foolishness." Kavax steps forward, pushing his son back. "Speak with me or Darrow. It's plain enough, your intentions."

"Indeed. Darrow. You shall come with me."

"Like hell," Victra sneers, stepping in front of me.

Fitchner rolls his eyes. "Telemanus, you and your son take the ArchGovernor back to his villa and then return to your own. Matters must be sorted." Fitchner gazes quietly at the bald Gold. His words now scrape out like raw iron on slate. "This is not a request, *Telemanus.*"

Telemanus looks to me. "My boy trusted this one. So shall I."

"I need your assurance my friends will not be hurt," I say to Fitchner.

He looks at Victra. "They won't be."

"Convince me."

He sighs, bored.

"The Sovereign can't gorywell execute an entire house absent a trial for treason. Can she? That violates the Compact. And you know how that would make us Olympic Knights feel, not to mention the other houses. Remember how her father met his end. But if you resist, well, that's another matter entirely." Fitchner flips a piece of gum into his mouth. "Do you resist?"

"Not today," I say.

14

||||||||||||||||||||||||

THE SOVEREIGN

"Once upon a time, there was a family of strong wills," she says, voice slow and measured as a pendulum. "They did not love one another. But together they presided over a farm. And on that farm, there were hounds, and bitches, and dairy cows, and hens, and cocks, and sheep, and mules, and horses. The family kept the beasts in line. And the beasts kept them rich, fat, and happy. Now, the beasts obeyed because they knew the family was strong, and to disobey was to suffer their united wrath. But one day, when one of the brothers struck his brother over the eye, a cock said to a hen, 'Darling, matronly hen, what would *really* happen if you stopped laying eggs for them?'"

Her eyes burn into mine. Neither of us look away. Silence in the sparse suite, except the sound of rain at the windows of her skyscraper. We're among the clouds. Ships pass in the haze outside like silent, glowing sharks. The leather creaks as she leans forward and steeples her long fingers, which are painted red, a lone splash of color. Then her lips curl in condescension, accenting each syllable as though I were an Agea street child only just learning her language.

"In so many ways you remind me of my father."

The one she beheaded.

That's when she fixes me with the most enigmatic smile I may ever have seen. Mischief dances in her eyes, subdued and quiet beneath the cold trappings of power. Somewhere inside is the nine-year-old girl who infamously started a riot by throwing diamonds from an aircar.

I stand before her. She sits on a couch by a fire. Everything is Spartan. Hard. Cold. A Gold woman of iron and stone. All this drabness as if to say she needs not luxury or wealth, just power.

Her face is creased but not faded by time. A hundred years, or so I hear, not cracked by the pressures of office. If anything, pressure has made her like those diamonds she scattered. Unbreakable. Ageless. And she will be without age for some time longer, if the Carvers continue their cellular rejuvenation therapy.

That is the problem. She will cling to power far too long. A king reigns and then he dies. That is the way of it. That is how the young justify obeying their elders—knowing it will one day be their turn. But when their elders do not leave? When she rules for forty years, and may rule for a hundred more? What then?

She is the answer to that question. This is not a woman who inherited the Morning Throne. This is a woman who took it from a ruler who had not the courtesy to die in a timely fashion. For forty years others have tried to take it from her. Yet here she sits. Timeless as those fabled diamonds.

"Why did you disobey me?" she asks.

"Because I could."

"Explain."

"Nepotism shrivels under the light of the sun. When you changed your mind to protect Cassius, the crowd rejected your moral and legal authority. Not to mention, you contradicted yourself. That in itself is weakness. So I exploited it, knowing I could get what I wanted without consequence."

Aja, the Sovereign's favorite killer, broods in a chair near the window—a powerful panther of a woman with skin duskier than her siblings', and eyes with slitted pupils. She is one of the Olympic Knights, the Protean Knight to be technic. She was Lorn's last student before me. Though he didn't teach her everything. Her armor is gold and midnight blue and writhes with sea serpents.

A young boy enters quietly from another room to sit beside Aja. I recognize him immediately. The Sovereign's only grandson, Lysander. No older than eight, but so very composed. Regal in his quiet, thin as a scarf. But his eyes. His eyes are beyond gold. Almost a yellow crystal, so bright they could nearly be said to shine. Aja watches me appraise the boy. She takes him onto her lap protectively and bares her teeth, their whiteness fiercely bright against her dark skin. Like a great cat playfully saying hello. And for the first time I can remember, I glance away from a threat. The shame burns hot and sudden in me. I might as well have kneeled to her.

"But there are always consequences," the Sovereign says. "I'm curious. What did you want out of that duel?"

"The same as Cassius au Bellona. The heart of my enemy."

"Do you hate him so much?"

"No. But my survival instinct is . . . enthusiastic. Cassius, as far as I am concerned, is a stupid boy crippled by his upbringing. His stock is limited. He talks of honor but he stoops to ignoble things."

"So it wasn't for Virginia?" she asks. "It wasn't to claim her hand or sate your jealous rage?"

"I'm angry, but I'm not petty," I snap. "Besides, Virginia isn't the sort of woman who would stand for such things. If I did it for her, I would have lost her."

"You have lost her," Aja growls from the side.

"Yes. I realize she has a new home, Aja. Easy to see."

"Do you lash out at me, my goodman?" Aja touches her razor.

"My goodlady, I do but lash out." I smile slowly at her.

"She'll gut you like a pig, boyo," Fitchner says quickly. "Don't give a piss if Lorn taught you how to wipe your ass. Think twice on who you insult here. The true blades of the Society do not duel for sport. So mind your gorydamn tongue."

I touch my razor.

He snorts. "If you were a threat, do you think they'd let you keep that?"

I nod to Aja. "Another time, perhaps." I turn back to the Sovereign, straightening. "Perhaps we should discuss why you are holding my house under military guard. Are we under arrest? Am I?"

"Do you see shackles?"

I look at Aja. "Yes."

The Sovereign laughs. "You're here because I want you to be."

An idea comes to me. I try not to smile. "My liege, I should like to apologize," I say loudly. They wait for me to continue. "My manners have always been . . . provincial. And so I find the manner of my actions nearly always distracts from their purpose. The base fact is, Cassius deserved worse than what I supplied. That I disobeyed you was not meant as insult by myself or the ArchGovernor. Were he not unconscious on account of your dog"—I glance at Fitchner—"I wager he would do what needed to be done to make amends."

"Make amends," she repeats. "For . . ."

"For the disturbance."

She looks to Aja. "Disturbance, he says. Dropping a dish is a disturbance, Andromedus. Helping yourself to another man's wife is a *disturbance*. Killing my guests and cutting off the arm of an Olympic Knight is not a disturbance. Do you know what it is?"

"Fun, my liege?"

She leans forward. "It is treason."

"And you know how we treat with treason," Aja says. "My father taught my sisters and me." Her father, the Ash Lord. Burner of Rhea. Lorn despises him.

"An apology from you is insufficient," the Sovereign says.

"Apology?" I ask.

The Sovereign is caught off guard by my tone.

"I said I should like to apologize. But the problem is, I cannot, because it should be you who apologizes to me."

Silence.

"You little whelp," Aja says, rising slowly.

The Sovereign stops her, words cutting clear and cold. "I did not apologize to my father when I took his head from his body. I did not apologize to my grandson when his mother's ship was destroyed by

Outriders. I did not apologize when I burned a moon. So why would I apologize to you?"

"Because you broke the law," I say.

"Perhaps you were not listening. I *am* the law."

"No. You're not."

"So you *are* a student of Lorn's after all. Did he tell you why he abandoned his post? His duty?" She looks at Lysander. "Why he abandoned his grandson?"

I did not know the boy was Lorn's grandson. My teacher's retirement makes sudden sense. He always spoke of Society's fading glory. How men have forgotten themselves mortal.

"Because he saw what you have become, my liege. You are no Empress. This is no empire, despite what you may think. We are the Society. We are bound by laws, by hierarchy. No person stands above the pyramid." I look to her killers. "Fitchner, Aja, you protect the Society. You ensure peace. You sail to the far reaches of the System to root out weeds of chaos. But above all else, what is the purpose of the twelve Olympic Knights?"

"Go on," Aja says to Fitchner. "Play into his mummer's farce. I will not."

Fitchner drawls out, "To preserve the Compact."

"To preserve the Compact," I say. "And the Compact states, '*A duel, once begun, cannot reach resolution until its terms are properly fulfilled.*' The terms were death. But Cassius is not dead. His arm will not suffice. I honor the iron ancestors and my rights stand inviolable. So give me what is mine. Give my the gorydamn head of Cassius au Bellona. Or reject the legacy of our people."

"No."

"Then we have nothing more to discuss. You may find me on Mars."

I turn on my heel and walk toward the door.

"The lion fades," the Sovereign calls. "Find a new home. Here."

I stop in my tracks. These people are so bloodydamn predictable. They all want what they can't have.

"Why?" I ask without turning.

"Because I can give you resources Augustus cannot. Because Virginia has already seen how true that is. You want to be with her, don't you?"

"Why would you want a man who so easily trades his allegiance?" I turn and look Fitchner dead in the eye. "Such a man is little more than a common whore."

"Augustus abandoned you before you abandoned him," the Sovereign says. "His daughter saw it even if you don't. *I* will not abandon you. Ask my Furies. Ask their father. Ask Fitchner. I give a chance to those who stand apart. Join me. Lead my legions and I will make you an Olympic Knight."

"I am an Aureate." I spit on the ground. "I am no trophy."

I stalk away.

"If I can't have you, no one can."

Then they come. Three Stained file through the door. Each a foot taller than I. Each garbed in purple and black and carrying pulseAxes and pulseBlades. Their faces hide behind bonelike masks. Eyes of killers grown in the arctic poles of Earth and Mars stare out at me. Glittering black, like oil. I pull my razor and take my battle stance. Their throat-sung war chant rumbles under their masks, like the funeral dirge for a dead god.

"Go on. Sing to your gods." I twirl my razor. "I'll send you to meet them."

"Reaper, please stop," Lysander calls loudly. I turn to find him walking toward me, hands splayed plaintively. His coat is simple and black. He stands half my height.

His voice floats. Trembles like a delicate bird's.

"I have watched all your videos, Reaper. Six, maybe seven times. Even the Academy. My tutors believe you are the closest man to the Iron Golds since Lorn au Arcos, the Stoneside."

That's when I realize why he looks so nervous. I almost laugh. I'm this little bastard's boyhood hero.

"We need not see you die tonight. Could you not find a home here as you found with Sevro? With Roque and Tactus, and Pax, the Howlers, and all your great warriors? We have warriors too. Noble ones.

You could lead them. But . . ." He steps back. "If you fight, then you die because you make the mistake of believing righteousness puts you beyond my grandmother's power."

"It does," I say.

"Reaper, there is no place beyond her power."

This is how it happens. They give them heroes. They raise them on lies and violence, and then they let them grow into monsters. What would he be without their guiding hand?

"He wanted to see you," the Sovereign says. "I told him legend never matches fact. Better not to meet your heroes."

"And what do you think?" I ask little Lysander.

"It all depends on your next choice," he says delicately.

"Join us, Darrow," Fitchner drawls. "This is the place for you now. Augustus is done."

Smiling inwardly, I relax my blade. Lysander clenches a fist happily. I pace with him back to his grandmother, playing along but not yet proclaiming any allegiance.

"You're always telling me to bow," I tell Fitchner as I pass.

He shrugs. "Because I don't want you to break, boyo."

"Lysander, fetch me my box," the Sovereign says. Happily, the boy rushes out of the room as I sit across from his grandmother. "I fear the Institute taught you the wrong lesson—that you can overcome anything if you but try. That is incorrect. In the real world, you must go along. You must cooperate and compromise. You cannot bend the worlds to your morals."

"Would you have noticed me had I not tried to?"

She smiles softly. "Likely not."

Lysander returns moments later, carrying a small wooden box. He hands it to his grandmother and waits patiently by her side, eating a tart that Aja hands him. The Sovereign sets the box on the table.

"You value trust. So do I. Let us play a game absent weapons, absent armor. No Praetorians. No lies. No falsity. Just us and our naked truths."

"Why?"

"If you win, you may request anything of me. If I win, I get the same."

"If I ask for the head of Cassius?"

"I will saw it off myself. Now open the box."

I lean forward. Chair creaking. Rain patters on the windows. Lysander smiles. Aja watches my hands. And Fitchner, like me, has no idea what's in the bloodydamn box.

I open it.

15

||||||||||||||||||||||||

TRUTH

It takes everything I am not to flee. What comes hissing from the box is pulled out of nightmare, pulled so perfectly out of the depths of my subconscious that I nearly think the Sovereign knows where I come from. Where I *truly* come from.

"The game is one of questions," she says. "Lysander, please do the honors." She hands her son a knife. The boy cuts the sleeve of my uniform to the elbow, rolling it back to expose my forearm. His hands are gentle. He smiles at me apologetically.

"Don't be afraid," he says. "Nothing bad will happen, so long as you don't lie."

The carved creatures from the box—two of them—stare at me with three blind eyes apiece. Part scorpion. Part pitviper. Part centipede. They move like liquid glass, organs, skeleton, visible through skin, chitinous mouths chattering and hissing at the same time as one slithers onto the table.

"No lies." I force a laugh. "That's a breezy order when you're a child."

"He never lies," Aja says proudly. "None of us do. Lies are rust on iron. A blemish on power."

Power they're so drunk on, they can't even remember how many lies they stand upon. *Tell my people you don't lie, you brutish bitch, and see what they do to you.*

"I call these Oracles," the Sovereign says. One of her rings ripples liquid, forming a shell over her finger, turning it into a talon, needle growing slowly at the end. With this needle, she pricks my wrist and says the words "Truth over all."

One Oracle slips forward, skittering onto my arm, coiling itself around my wrist. Its strange mouth seeks the blood, latching on like a leech. Its scorpion tail arches four inches upward, drifting back and forth like a cattail in summer wind. The Sovereign pricks her own wrist, repeats the oath, and the second Oracle slithers from the box.

"Zanzibar the Carver designed this especially for me in his Himalayan laboratories," she says. "The poison won't kill you. But I've cells filled with men who have played my game and lost. If there is a hell, what's in that stinger is as close to it as science has let us come."

My pulse quickens as I watch the tail sway.

"Sixty-five," Aja says of my pulse. "He was resting at twenty-nine beats per minute."

The Sovereign lifts her head at that. "As low as twenty-nine?"

"When are my ears wrong?"

"Calm yourself, Andromedus," the Sovereign says. "The Oracle is designed to measure truth. It's in fluctuations of temperature, chemicals in the blood, pulse of the heart."

"You don't have to play if you don't want, Darrow," Aja purrs. "You can go the easy way with the Praetorians. Death is not so bad."

I glare at the Sovereign. "Let's play."

"Would you assassinate me tonight if you could?"

"No."

We all watch the Oracle. Even I. After a moment, nothing happens. I swallow in relief. The Sovereign smiles.

"This game doesn't have an end," I mutter. "How do I even win?"

"You make me lie."

"How many times have you played this game?" I ask.

"Seventy-one. In the end, I've trusted only one other. Where does Augustus hide his unregistered electromagnetic weapons?"

"Asteroid depots, hidden armories throughout Mars's cities." I list the particulars. "And in the dais of his reception room." That surprises them. "Where are yours?"

She lists off sixty locations in fast order. She tells everything because she's never lost. She's never had to worry about the information walking out the door. Such confidence.

"What does that pegasus pendant mean to you?" she asks. "Is it from your father?"

I look down. It's spilled out of my shirt. "It means hope. Part of my father's legacy. Did you help Karnus at the Academy?"

"Yes. I gave him that ship he rammed you with. Did you really intend to launch yourself at his bridge?"

"Yes. Why did you bring Virginia into your inner circle?"

"The same reason you fell in love with her."

My pulse quickens. Aja smiles, hearing it.

"Virginia is special. And we both come from fathers who . . . left much to be desired. When I was a girl, I would have given anything to belong to a different family. But I was the daughter of the Sovereign. I gave her a gift no one could have given me.

"You see, I collect people I enjoy, Andromedus. I even enjoy Fitchner there. Many might see him as repugnant. Might think his heritage unseemly, but, like you, he is so very talented. When I asked him to play this game before becoming one of my Olympic Knights, you know what he said?"

"I can imagine."

"Fitchner . . ."

He shrugs his slumped shoulders. "Told you to stick the box up your cootch. I'm not an idiot."

"I think it was even more crass than that," Aja grumbles.

"My turn." The Sovereign examines her Rage Knight. "Did Fitchner violate his oath as a Proctor and cheat at the Mars Institute, as rumor would have me believe?"

"Yes," I say, watching the Oracle instead of my old Proctor. "He cheated like the rest." I know Fitchner would not have gained this post were she not sure of his loyalty to her and not Augustus, which means Fitchner must have come clean and supplied her with details of Augustus's ill dealings. I glance back at the man. "Though I don't know if he was paid like the others."

"He wasn't. Their mistake," the Sovereign says. "Gave us video evidence. Audio. Bank statements. Useful leverage against each Proctor."

Sevro must have given his father the video footage when I had him tinkering with it. Crafty little bastard. He actually does care about his father, after all. Augustus would kill them both if he knew about the duplicity.

I want to interrogate the Sovereign about military outposts. Supply lines. Operational imperatives and security measures. But I know that would appear strange. It would lead to her asking strange questions of her own. The Oracle tightens slightly on my arm, sucking out only tiny drops of blood at a time. I don't know how well this thing can sense untruths. But what do I do if she asks me where I was born? Who my father is? Why I rub dirt between my fingers before I fight? Shit. She could just ask me if I'm a Red. But how would she ever think to do that unless I gave her the sense that something was . . . off about me?

"Are any in my inner circle your spies?" I ask.

"Very clever. No. Where did you go with Victra au Julii three days ago? And what did you do?" the Sovereign asks.

"To Lost City." Somehow, the Oracle senses I'm holding back. Its stinger trembles with excitement. "To meet the Jackal—Augustus's son." It tightens further. "To form an alliance." Sweat beads on my collar and the Oracle relaxes, the answer sufficient. "Why do they call Lorn Stoneside?"

"He didn't tell you? It's not because he's tough as stone like they'd tell you now. It's because on campaign in the Moon Rebellion, he was famous for eating anything. And one day a Gray bet him he couldn't eat stones. Lorn doesn't back down. When did Lorn teach you?"

"Every morning before first light, between my graduation from the Institute and enrollment at the Academy."

"Incredible no one found out."

"How many Peerless Scarred are there?" I ask. "Census data is so hard to come by." The Board of Quality Control is monstrous in hoarding its high-level material.

"There are 132,689, for nearly 40 million Golds. Why did Lorn take you as a student?"

"Because he thinks we're the same sort of man. What are your two greatest fears?"

"Octavia . . . ," Aja warns.

"Shut up, Aja. All's fair." She looks over to Lysander and smiles. "My greatest fear is that my grandson will grow up to be like my father. The second is the inevitability of age. Why did you cry when you killed Julian au Bellona?"

"Because he was kinder than the world let him be. Did you arrange Virginia and Cassius's courtship?"

"No. It was her idea."

I'd held on to hope that it was something arranged, something she had to do.

"Why did you sing the Red ballad to Virginia at the Institute?"

"Because she forgot the words, and I think it the saddest song ever sung." I pause before my next question.

"You want to ask about Virginia again, don't you?" The corners of her lips twitch with pleasure as she plucks my pain. "Do you want to know if I'll give her to you if you join me? It's possible."

"She is not a thing to be given," I say.

She laughs, amused at my innocence. "If you say so."

"Where are the three Deep Space Command Centers?" I ask recklessly.

She gives me the coordinates without blinking. "How did you know the words to the Reaping Song?"

"I heard it as a boy. And I forget little."

"Where?"

"It's not your turn," I remind her. "Why are you asking me these questions?"

"Because one of my Furies has led me to suspect the Sons of Ares are perhaps something different than we imagined. Something more dangerous. Who is Ares?"

My heart thunders.

"I don't know." I watch the Oracle's tail. It doesn't move. "Who you do think Ares is?"

"Your master."

"Thirty-nine, forty-two, fifty-six . . . ," Aja says.

The Sovereign wags a long finger. "Strange. Your heart gives you away."

I clear my mind. Let it all fade. Imagine the mines. Remember the wind moving through them. Remember her hands on mine as we walked barefoot through cold dirt to the place where we first lay together in the hollow of an abandoned township. Her whispers. How she sang the lullaby my mother sang to my siblings and me.

"Fifty-five, forty-two, thirty-nine," Aja says.

"Is Augustus Ares?" she asks.

Relief floods me. "No. He's not Ares."

The door slams open behind me. We turn to see Mustang stalking into the room wearing the gold and white uniform of House Lune, complete with the family's crescent moon symbol. A datapad glows on her wrist. She bows to the Sovereign. "My liege."

"Virginia, you're still a mess," Aja drawls.

"Blame this dumb son of a bitch." Mustang nods to me. "Seventy-three dead. Two Earthborn families erased, neither of which had anything to do with Bellona or Augustus. Over two hundred wounded." She shakes her head. "I grounded all ships as you asked, Octavia. Praetorian command has initiated a no-fly zone in orbit. All family-owned capital ships have had their warrants revoked and are being pushed beyond the Rubicon Beacons till we give further notice. And Cassius still lives. He's with the Yellows. Citadel Carvers are preparing plans for replacing the arm."

The Sovereign thanks her and asks her to sit. "Darrow and I are getting to know each other. Are there any questions you think we should ask him?"

Mustang sits beside the Sovereign.

"My advice, my liege? Don't try to solve Darrow. He's a puzzle with missing pieces."

"That's rather offensive," I say, playfully. But her words sting.

"So you don't think we should keep him?"

"Cassius and his mother will—" Mustang starts.

"Will what?" the Sovereign interrupts. "I made Cassius an Olympic Knight. He will be grateful, and he will study his razor so this does not happen again." Her face softens and she touches Mustang's knee. "Are you all right, my dear?"

"I'm fine. Seems like I interrupted your game."

I can't tell which woman is playing the other. But with Karnus's words at the gala, and the knowledge that the ships were grounded before I even started the skirmish, I know the Sovereign had plans. And now I think I can piece together just what they were.

"One last question. I've been saving it for the end."

"Do ask, boy. We have no secrets here. But it must be the last. Agrippina au Julii has been kept waiting long enough." Aja opens the box so the Oracles may go back inside.

"Tonight, at the gala, during the sixth course of the meal, did you plan to allow the Bellona to assassinate ArchGovernor Augustus and all those who sat at his table?"

Aja freezes. Mustang slowly turns to look at the Sovereign, whose face shows no hints of dishonesty. The woman breathes easily and with a soft smile lies through her teeth. "No," she says. "I did not."

The Oracle's barbed tail strikes at her flesh.

16

||||||||||||||||||||||||

THE GAME

Fitchner's razor buzzes, and he chops away the tail faster than a bee beats its wings. It flops to the floor, transparent stinger hissing out poison. On the Sovereign's arm, the wounded creature screams. Wailing and writhing like a dying cat. The Sovereign rips it off and throws it at the wall. My own releases slowly, as if connected with the other. Mewing pathetically, it retreats to its box to hide in the darkness. I dab away the faint trail of blood it left on my forearm.

"So you do lie," I say with a wicked grin.

The Sovereign exhales a long sigh.

Mustang stands, enraged. "You promised you would not hurt them. You lied."

"Yes." Octavia rubs her temples. "A matter of necessity."

"You said there were no lies here," Mustang hisses. "That was a precondition of my allegiance to you. The *only* thing I asked for, and you planned to do it while I watched?"

"Sit." The Sovereign stands, drawing nose-to-nose with Mustang. "Sit down."

Mustang sits, breathing heavily. She won't look at me or the Sovereign. She's surrounded by betrayal. The Sovereign notes this, piecing together a new strategy as Mustang draws a gold ring from her pocket and rolls it compulsively through her fingers.

"Do you know why I need your family gone?" Octavia asks Mustang. She doesn't reply. "I asked you a question, Virginia. Put aside petulance and answer."

"He is a threat to peace," Mustang replies flatly, slipping the ring on her finger. "He disregards your orders. He does not obey financial directives. He delays helium-3 experts for political gain."

"If I tried removing him from power, what would happen?"

Mustang looks up at her. "He would rebel."

"So what am I to do? If he rebels while on Mars, it becomes his planet fortress. The monies it would take me to pry him out—to find him, to kill him, to reinstate order—is . . . incomprehensible. Ships. Men. Food. Munitions. Trade. Helium-3 shortages. The Society would not recover for years.

"We cannot afford an enemy like him. But we also cannot afford an ally to so publicly affront us. What if the Governors of the Gas Giants thought they were immune to my orders because we're lenient with your father? Because we let him manipulate helium prices or ignore Sovereign directives? Forty years ago, in the first year of my reign, the Moons of Saturn rebelled. The war did not end until I destroyed the moon, Rhea, outright. Fifty million dead. That is how stubborn our race is. They know how difficult it is for me to flex my hand billions of kilometers from the Core. But still they are afraid. So much of a ruler's reign is a figment of the people's imagination. My power isn't ships. Isn't Praetorians. My power is their fear. But they must have fresh reminders."

"And so my family is to be the reminder."

"Yes. Tell me that doesn't make sense."

Mustang stays quiet for a long moment. "It is the logical political move. But he's my father. . . ."

"Which is why I didn't tell you. Consider this."

She waves her hand and a holo ignites on the floor, rising to fill half the room. It's a riot. Buildings smoke. Grays mow down women and men with pulse weapons. She changes the image. A dozen more dance

GOLDEN SON | 147

across the room. A woman falls in front of me, dead. Hole in her skull. Smoking still.

I stare down at the sudden horror.

"Is this Mars?" I ask, fearing for my family.

"You would think so, wouldn't you?" The Sovereign traces a finger through the muzzle of a pulseRifle as it fires. "It's Venus."

"Venus?" Mustang whispers. "There are no Sons of Ares on Venus."

"Nor will there be after tonight. The flame spreads even to the Core. Two hours ago, multiple bombings racked this Society. My Politicos and Praetors and various high-level personnel throughout the empire have initiated Order Zero. No media will report this. Wherever there are flames, we make quarantine. We *will* snuff them out. Something your father did not do, Virginia. In fact, he allowed the Sons to thrive. To spread here."

I warned Harmony. I only hope the Sons aren't all lost.

The Sovereign crouches in front of Mustang. "Your father must die. He hanged the very woman the Sons of Ares used to start all this. His face burns across their propaganda. If he goes, if we strike them, then they fade. We will kill two birds with one stone. Arrange the transfer of power to Bellona, and Mars is at peace for the first time in my reign. All it costs is fifty lives. I know he is your father, but you came into my fold for a reason."

Looking at Mustang, I understand that reason now, and it breaks my heart.

She stands slowly, walking to the window as if fleeing the decision. She stares out at a ship passing in the distant fog. "When Mother was alive, he used to ride with me through the forest. We'd stop at this wildblossom clearing and lay in the red flowers, arms out, pretending we were angels. That man is dead. Do with the new one as you like."

17

||||||||||||||||||||||||||

WHAT THE STORM
BRINGS

The Obsidians escort me to new quarters, Fitchner trailing along behind, pacing jovially on the marble floors. When we reach my door, he takes my hand.

"Well played, boyo. Good reading on her—knowing she wants what she can't have. Gorydamn clever. Warms my heart to finally see you playing the game and winning, you little pisser." He slugs my shoulder. "Tomorrow, we'll go to market and buy you servants. Pinks. Blues. Obsidians of your very own. For now . . . I left you a present." He gestures into my room where a lithe Pink lies on the bed. "Enjoy."

"You don't know me at all. Do you?" He sighs and leans forward.

"This is the hand life has dealt you. It's not a bad hand. Imagine the things you can do as a personal emissary of the Sovereign. She makes your Governor look like a small-town slumlord. You have your girl. You have opportunity. Embrace your new life."

The door slams.

A new life, but is it worth the cost? I don't know what's happening with the Sons. That's something I can't affect. But he expects me to let Roque die? To let Tactus and Victra and Theodora perish to Praetorian death squads?

I walk around my suite, ignoring the Pink. Luna's night clouds sprawl as far as the eye can see beyond the huge bank of windows that comprises the suite's north wall. Buildings puncture the clouds like glittering spears.

I am trapped by opulence.

Rain continues to pour. The storms of Luna are enigmatic creatures. For a man of Mars, it is a slow rain. Lethargic. As though the drops tire of their own fall in this low gravity. But the winds that come are gales. There are no cracks in the Citadel's windows through which the wind can whistle. I miss the moans of my old castle on Mars. Miss the laments of the deepmines. Those moments when the drill cooled and I sat there touching my wedding band through my frysuit, thinking of how soon it would be that I had her lips to mine, her hands on my waist, her body drifting light as dust over my own.

But I cannot think only of the Red girl. When I see the moon, I think of the sun: Mustang burns in my thoughts. If Eo smelled of rust and soil, then the Golden girl is fire and autumn leaves.

Part of me wishes I would remember only Eo. That my mind belonged to her, so I could be like one of those knights of legend. A man so in love with one lost that he closes his heart to all others. But I am not that legend. In so many ways, I'm still a boy, lost and afraid, seeking warmth and love. When I feel dirt, I honor Eo. And when I see fire, I remember the warmth and flicker of the flames across Mustang's skin as we lay in our chamber of ice and snow.

I examine the empty room, which smells neither of leaves nor soil, but cardamom. The room is too vast for my taste. Too rich. There is ivory on the walls. A sauna. A massage parlor adjacent to a pleasure-Chamber. There's a commChair, a bed, a small swimming pool. These are my chambers now. I see on a dataFile that I've been given a fifty-million-credit stipend to choose my attendants. They left me an additional ten million to populate my harem. This is the price they pay me for betraying my friends. It is not enough.

My eyes now fall on the Pink who lies on my bed. Naked, covered only by a blanket. I threw it on her to mask her form, thinking of poor Evey when I first saw her. But the longer I look at this new girl, the harder it is to remember Evey, to remember Eo or Mustang. That's what Pinks are for, to help you forget. So effective they even make you forget their own sad plight. When she grows old, she'll be sold off from the Citadel staff to some high-class brothel. And a few more lines will form and she'll be sold down the ladder and down the ladder till she has nothing more to give. It happens to men. It happens to women. And, I'm beginning to realize, it happens to Golds.

The Pink asks me to join her. To let her soothe what ails me. I don't reply. I sit on the edge of the windowsill, my hands kneading my thighs, waiting. I don't have my razor. Obsidians guard the hall outside. The glass window won't break by any means I have at my disposal, but I do not worry. I sit watching the storm, feeling another brew inside myself.

With a hiss, the door opens. I turn, a smile already cracking my face.

"Mustang, I—"

Through the door slips a demure male Pink with white hair and eyes that'd break a thousand hearts in Lykos. It breaks mine now. I was wrong.

"Who are you?" I ask.

He sets a small onyx box down on my bed in front of the other Pink.

"Who is it from?" I demand.

"You'll see, *dominus,*" he says. Daintily, he extends a hand to the other Pink, who, confused, takes it and follows him from the room. The door closes. I'm just as confused as the Pink. I rush to the box, opening it, and find a small holoCube. I activate it.

Mustang's face appears, glowing. "Take cover," she says.

The power goes out and the door locks by default. The room is plunged into darkness. Lightning lashes through the clouds outside; thunder rumbles. And I hear something. A howling. It is not the wind.

Another flash of lightning and he appears, floating in the bitter storm like the ugliest angel ever shit out of heaven. A wolfpelt hangs from his shoulders, whips in the wind. His black metal helmet is that of a wolfshead, and he's armed to the bloody teeth.

Sevro has come, and he's brought friends.

Lightning. Thunder again and this time it illuminates his slash of a smile and the eight floating killers behind him. Nine Howlers in all. Small, cruel little devils waiting in the darkness, silhouetted by the crackling of the storm's electricity. Long-legged Quinn is there too.

I duck into the sauna as Sevro touches the glass with a pulseFist after setting up a jamField to absorb the sound. The glass ruptures inward. The distorted sound of the storm follows them as they thump down onto the carpeted marble floor. Wind whips at my bedsheets and tapestries. One by one they kneel—pudgy Pebble, cruel Harpy, spindly, open-faced Clown, and all the others.

"Friends. Get up!" I bellow. "You're already short enough."

They laugh and rise. Pebble and Clown rush forward and weld shut my metal door with plasma torches.

Water drips from Sevro's hook nose as he nods toward me, his helmet absorbed into his armor. Hair buzzed in the shape of dragons. Quiet, and so full of derision, he hefts a huge, heavy bag in his other hand. And when he walks, he moves with disdain for this low gravity. As though it were a thing for weaklings and fools.

"*Lord* Reaper. You look like a Pixie ponce in this lady-den." Sevro sweeps into a theatrical bow after he places the bag at my feet. "Perhaps that's why Mustang believed you were in dire need of your gory-damn pack."

"She brought you back from the Rim?"

"All of us," Quinn says. "We've been here several weeks on standby. She needed men she knew wouldn't be loyal to the Sovereign."

An insurance policy. I can't believe I ever doubted her.

In no world would Mustang help kill her father. I realized during my conversation with the Sovereign that it had to be why she's here in the first place—to infiltrate the Sovereign's family like I infiltrated the Golds. As she entered the Sovereign's suite, I remembered how before the duel she mentioned having her own plans. Now it finally clicks into place. They were both playing their own games, but I helped reveal the Sovereign's hand.

The Sovereign wasn't worried about me knowing anything, else why play the game? But as soon as Mustang entered the room, the paradigm altered. She should have concluded the game then and there. But her pride got the better of her.

As for Mustang, I knew she was with me as soon as she took the gold horse ring I gave her from her pocket and slipped it onto her finger. My heart leaped in that moment, and I knew she'd find our way out of this.

"Sevro." I smile and clasp his hand. "Our ArchGovernor is—"

"I know. Mustang briefed us."

"Come here, you tall devil." Quinn steps past the others and slips her thin arm around my waist and kisses my cheek. She smells like home. I have missed these people. The wind howls as it passes through our jamField. Sevro's bionic eye glitters unnaturally. Quinn has brought me gravBoots, ebony in color. I slip them on.

"Mustang might have brought us from the Rim. But we didn't come for her. We didn't come for Augustus. We came for you, Reaper," Sevro snarls. Quinn frowns as Sevro spits on the pretty carpet. "We saw what you did to Cassius. And we want what you're trying to make."

"And that is?" I ask, more than a little confused.

"What poor killers always want. War," he growls. "And all its spoils."

"What of your father? He has a high place now."

"Fitchner is a shiteater," he sneers. "He's made his bed. Let him sleep in it while we burn the house down."

"Well, if you want war, if you want spoils, we better move. The ArchGovernor's the one with an army."

Quinn nods. "And Roque's down there. And Tactus."

"Tactus," Sevro mutters, though I know the sneer on his face is for Roque. He watches Quinn, eyes sad for the smallest moment, before adjusting his armor.

"So what's the plan?" I ask, and take the razor Pebble offers me.

Sevro and Quinn look at each other and laugh. "Mustang's fetching a ship. She said you'd figure out the rest," Quinn says.

Just then the door behind me shudders and glows with a dilating pupil of red-hot metal, and I notice something. The bag that Sevro threw down. It moves.

Sevro smiles at me. I know that smile.

"Sevro?"

"Reaper."

"What did you do?"

"Mustang brought us a package. Let's just say"—Quinn grins at my shoulder—"it's not their cook."

I unzip the bag and gawk.

"Are you mad?" I ask him.

He just howls.

18

||||||||||||||||||||||

BLOODSTAINS

Father once told me that a Helldiver can never stop. You stop and the drill can jam. The fuel burns too quickly. The quota might be missed. You never stop, just shift drills if the friction gets too hot. Caution comes second. Use your inertia, your momentum. That is why we dance. Transfer movement into more movement. Uncle Narol always told me to stop. He was wrong. Blew so many drill bits because of him.

Then again, Narol lived longer than Father, so maybe he has a point.

My Howlers jump with me out the window and we don't stop when we dive into the black storm. We freefall, piercing the clouds without the use of our gravBoots. Like black rain screaming toward the ground. I'm first. I feel them behind me. *My* Howlers. The oxygen is thin at first. I hold my breath. My eyeballs nearly freeze in their sockets. Tears trickle out. My body shivers as the cold wind bites me.

We use our gravBoots now to cut across the Citadel. Skirt among the clouds to keep from sight. Villas beneath. Buildings, gardens, and parks. Barracks and statued plazas. A ripWing cuts through the sky.

We slide behind a spire and stick there like spiders till our scanners say he's passed. I shiver amid my armored friends. Then we float down again. A kilometer from the villa. Weed carries Sevro's present now. Slung around his back, it weighs him down a bit.

I land on the wall that surrounds the villa and separates it from the other compounds where the other notable families hunker in fear of what the night brings.

It's warmer now that we're lower to the ground. Howlers land around me, looking like gargoyles on the wall. Darkness claims the villa's grounds.

"We're early?" I wonder. No signs of fighting. But the lights are out.

"Or late," Sevro says, "if they were murdered in their beds."

"This is to look like a Bellona massacre. The Sovereign won't want to be implicated." But what does that even mean? The Bellona would come with Grays, Obsidians, Golds, and despite all their vaunted honor, they would destroy every last woman and child with any means at their disposal. You do not let your foot off the throat of an enemy and remain powerful, as they have, for hundreds of years.

The killing will be silent, though. The Sovereign may control the Citadel, but chaos would bring unwelcome eyes, unwelcome variables, and it would make her look weak. Better to have the act done. Better to say the Bellona did it and damn what anyone thinks. With the Augustans dead, what is the point in mourning them? That's how Golds think. But if they are alive having escaped assassination . . . well, that's another thing entirely.

"Quinn." I lean close so I can hear her whisper.

"Visual is too clear. If they have optics, they'll spot us up on the wall." She points to the roof. "We can make an incursion there. Sweep down level by level." I hear the worry in her voice.

"We'll get Roque," I say. "Promise." I pat her arm. "Sevro, how long till we have the shuttle?"

"Mustang is ten out."

I pop my neck and rub the rain between my fingers. *"Per aspera ad astra."*

"Through the thorns to the stars." Sevro snickers. "You fancy little fart. *Omnis vir lupus.*" Everyone a wolf. The Howlers flash smiles to one another, and we rip away from the wall.

We land on the roof. Silent and dark. Weed stays on the high wall with Mustang's present squirming in the bag. Predators, we stalk over clay tiles in through a window on the villa's seventh level, two at a time. The place is a complex. Dozens of rooms. Seven levels. Fountains running throughout. Baths. Basement. Steam rooms. Their infrared is worthless, then. Too much hot water going through pipes. It's quiet as a crypt in here.

We creep along, checking the bedrooms, flowing like water around one another as we did at the Institute. Sevro and Thistle ghost ahead, scouting. GravBoots deactivated so the hum can't be heard. There's not a soul to be seen. Every room empty, beds unmade, including the ArchGovernor's. The Augustans are not here. So where are they?

They've no military armaments besides some armor and razors and a few pulseFists. The bodyguards were wiped out before they even returned to the villa. Augustus and his entourage couldn't have climbed the walls. Perhaps they flew away on gravBoots? But they would have been spotted. Shot down. We only slipped in because we're unexpected.

"*Captured?*" Sevro asks.

No. For the Praetorians tonight, the only good Augustan is a dead one.

Pop.

We all look at one another. A jamField has just gone up. A big one. We're inside it. Likely, the whole villa complex is inside it. Something's about to happen. I glance out the window and see a shadow moving across the garden lawn. Three shadows in the rain. I duck and signal Sevro. Praetorians. GhostCloaks. My heart makes my rib cage rattle.

He moves to the window, about to jump out to try to kill them. I pull him back.

"*What the hell are you doing?*" I whisper.

He scowls. "I want to kill someone."

"Not yet, dammit. We're not an army."

No one on the seventh level. We go down a circular marble stairwell. Their oiled armor creaks softly, echoing down the cavernous stairwell. We can see the marble of the first level more than a hundred feet beneath, but no movement. The first blood is found on the sixth level, seeping from the steam room. Pull the door open, heart throbbing into my throat, ready to see mutilated Golds. It's a sadder sight.

More than twenty Pinks, Browns, and Violets thought to hide in this room. The Bellona and Praetorians found them. Killed them. It is a queer sight. Each death so clean. Jab wounds to the skull. Just shows how little chance these poor servants had. The Golds put them down like cattle. I search through them frantically, hoping not to find her. Praying. She's not here— Theodora must be with the rest of them.

A cold rage fills me. I feel it seep into the Howlers.

We find the first dead Gold at the stairwell down to the fifth floor. An old knight of my house. His death was not pretty. We find another dead man farther on by a gravLift. He fell as if defending the lift while others descended.

Out the window, I glimpse the Augustan lancer who mocked my skills with the razor only a day ago. She rushes from the house to the gardens. A shape coalesces out of the darkness. A Gold Praetorian with purple fringe to his black armor chases her down. Two Bellona Obsidians hem her in, forcing her to turn straight into her pursuer. He kills her with one swing. Nothing to be done. Her death is so fast. One moment she is panting, fearing, running. The next, both parts of her fall to the ground.

"These Praetorians don't play with their food," Sevro mutters. Quinn looks at me, her eyes tracing the absence of armor or a helmet. She offers her own. I ignore her.

"Darrow, we didn't come all this way to watch you die of a blow to the head."

"Get off it," I say to her. "Roque will write a thousand gory poems if you get so much as a bump on yours."

"Keep the helmet, Q," Sevro begs. "If only because I hate poems."

I let my borrowed razor slither into my palm and move through the level. At the door of each room, my blood races. I expect to find Roque's corpse. Expect to see Victra's mangled body.

Sevro holds up a hand at the fourth-floor stairwell and motions me forward. I slip toward him with Quinn and peer down. Dust rises up the circular stairwell. Beyond it, on the bottom-floor landing, shadows move. But there is no noise. Sevro bends and places a piece of debris on the edge of a banister, gesturing me to watch. The Howlers cluster around, staring at it, and I stiffen. Though there is no sound, the piece of debris rocks slightly.

Vibrations in the building.

Before Sevro and the others can stop me, I jump over the banister and rip down the center of the spiral stairwell with ten times the velocity this moon's gravity would allow. *Pop.* I enter the domain of a second jamField, and sounds of war rattle over me. Concussive blasts, yelling, burners hissing out bullets, pulse weapons warbling like demented ghosts. The moment before I land, I tweak my gravBoots, jerking myself to a powerful stop. I slap into the marble and swing my razor around my head in a violent loop. Four Praetorian Grays die. Eight thumps hitting the floor. Their ghostCloaks disintegrate like thin window frost against hot breath.

Bodies, strewn across the halls. Rubble. Fires. Grays and Obsidians chase down Augustan Golds. Six Grays overwhelm two Golds with railRifles, magnetic ammunition screaming into aegises till they overload and warp backward, consuming the Golds' left arms. Rounds slap into the pulseShields that cover their bodies, overloading the circuitry. The Grays slip forward with practiced precision and shoot the Golds point-blank in their helmeted heads. The best armor in the Solar System crumples inward and the man and woman are gone. The Grays turn in my direction, level their rifles, and my Howlers cascade down around me. Their black aegises throb against the vambraces that cover their left forearms. They block the incoming fire. Sevro slips from formation. Quinn follows. Ghosting, they flicker in and out of sight, moving as twin strands of smoke. Somehow they're among the Grays, then back by my side before the Grays fall.

More weaponfire slams into our formation, nearly taking my naked head off. I duck behind my armored fellows. Terror pumps through me. A Gray pops into the hall and fires a microShot at us. Thirty tiny bombs spread out like a swarm of hornets. Thistle and Rotback blast the swarm apart with their pulseFists. A sheet of blue fire billows through the hall. A second swarm of bombs howls after the first. Quinn shunts off the power to her gravFist and shoots at the swarm of bombs just before they hit. They reverse course, back the way they came, where they slap into the Gray squad and detonate.

We won't last in here. Nothing will, I decide, when three Bellona Obsidians lope into view, Karnus au Bellona following at their heels. Some of my friends will die on this level if we fight all who come against us. There's a better way. A smarter way.

"Sevro, make a hole!" I shout, pointing seven stories above us, up the center gap in the stairwell. He shoots his pulseFist upward and chunks of stone rain down around us, suspended by Quinn's gravFist. Sevro shoots again and water rains down through the hole, swirling in the gravity bubble Quinn created. I stand and yell, "On me!"

We ascend out of the chaos before the Praetorians fall on us. I come to a halt two hundred meters above the villa. Wind whips. I had no plan when I dove down to the first level. I thought only of my friends. Now I know the Howlers and I will be killed if we fight. I let my razor curl placidly around my arm. I instruct the Howlers to do the same and I roar into the darkness.

"AJA!" The Howlers close around me, nervous as we float exposed above the villa. The storm sends sheets of rain down on us. "AJA!"

A horde of Praetorians disengage their ghostCloaks near the hot springs and lagoon, where the infrared is thrown into chaos by the heat of the water. Two Praetorians rocket up from the garden, cutting through pine trees, one a Stained. He flies closer, leveling his ionFist at my head.

"Get that thing out of my gorydamn face, you Stained whelp. Don't you recognize your betters?" A Praetorian Gold joins him. I don't recognize the woman. Her serpent helm recoils into her purple-black armor, sleeker than the Obsidians'. Face sharp and ruthless as an axehead.

"*Varga*, heel," she snaps. The Stained lowers his weapon. His helmet slides into his own Praetorian armor, and I discover *Varga* is a she. An Obsidian a head shorter than I, with a tribal tattoo consuming her pale face. White hair flutters behind her. More scars on her face than I have on my entire body.

"Ebony dog," Sevro snaps. "I'll shoot her if she snarls again."

"Were you the squad in the stairwell?" The Gold glances over us, unsure of what to make of me or my Howlers. "You killed my Grays."

"Don't weep over Grays," I say. "They raised their hands against me."

"Why are you here?" She wipes the rain from her face. "The Sovereign confined you to your room for the night. Are you responsible for the power outage?"

"My business is the Sovereign's." She can't afford not to believe me.

She pauses a beat and I realize she has optics in her eyes. She checks a database. "Liar."

The Stained's weapon comes back up.

"You know who I am, Praetorian," I say with as much authority as I can muster. "You also know I'm not on your list to kill. I have immunity."

"Revoked."

"So take me to Aja."

"Aja isn't here."

"Don't lie to me."

Her optics flicker in her irises as she receives a digital command. "Follow me."

We land on white stones and follow the Praetorian through the trees toward the lagoon where the hot springs terminate.

"What are you doing?" Sevro whispers in my ear, eyeing Varga. He flips the woman the crux with his middle finger wrapped around the index.

"I'm using your leverage."

Aja stands in the garden, flanked by Bellona—two Gold, the rest Obsidian. Only the one Stained, Varga. The lagoon breathes tendrils of steam around the Protean Knight's shoulders. She watches the water impassively, like a child watching a campfire, waiting for a log to burn.

"Darrow?" Aja purrs without looking at me. "You're not in your room." She sizes up the Howlers. Recognizes them. "And you killed my men. Fitchner was wrong about you."

"I have something you'll want," I say sharply. "But call off your dogs."

"They tried to escape before we came, even with their gravBoots confiscated. Foolish attempt. They tried to contact the Julii, but they've been bought."

"Victra?" I ask. She betrayed us.

"Alive. With the rest. She'll be spared thanks to her mother's cooperation. Two Augustan ships made an effort to run our blockade in orbit. We shot them down. The Augustans are like cornered badgers."

"Lions," I remind her.

She flicks blood off her razor. "Not quite."

"Are any still alive?" I keep the panic from my voice and glance back at the villa.

"The prizes are."

I breathe a sigh of relief.

She lets her razor slither into her hand. It goes rigid and she turns my way. Slitted pupils drink in the light. "Your friends are in the lagoon. They hid there because our infrared is blinded by the pool's heat. A desperate last attempt. The air filtration systems on their helmets will have short-circuited from the EMP. So all they'll have is the air in their helmets. Not much of it either. They won't last fifteen minutes. Those who don't have helmets . . . perhaps six minutes. Soon they'll bob up, like apples." She smiles pleasantly. "I'm saving them for Karnus; he is inside finishing up the diversions. He's a pleasure to watch, isn't he?"

Hot rain clatters on our armor. The only sound.

"Why are you here, Andromedus, and not in your room?" Aja plays with her razor, slicing raindrops in half. "The Sovereign was very clear."

"I have something you'll want," I repeat.

"What I want is for Octavia to be obeyed. Fly back to your room, boy, and take a nice shower and fondle the Rose we left in your bed. Drain your anger or whatever this is into her. And leave your oath whole. Do not raise a finger against me. You have killed Grays only. That is easily forgotten, yes? Return, and she will think this only a flight of youth. Stay, and I will add your corpse and those of your Bronzie friends to the heap."

The Howlers bristle behind me.

"As you killed the servants?" I ask heatedly. "Like goats for slaughter."

Aja turns back to the pool. "It's time you left, Reaper."

"You're disgusting." I step closer to her. "All this power, and this is how you use it? Killing families in the middle of the gorydamn night. Base fact is, you're a disgrace. I hope you remember the pain you brought others when I stand over your corpse."

She turns on me in all her fury. Razor snapping out. Eyes gleaming. But she can't touch me. Not now. Not this night.

"Darrow," Sevro calls with a sudden, odd pleasantness to his voice.

"Yes, Sevro?"

"All that talk about *remembering*. Aren't you forgetting something right now?"

"I think he is," Quinn agrees. "Our wise . . ."

". . . but forgetful *Reaper*," finishes Clown in a very frivolous fashion.

"Hmmm. Apologies, Aja. I forgot what I even came here to tell you." I stand there looking flummoxed.

Quinn sighs. "The bag."

"Oh, yes! Thank you for reminding me, Sevro!" I cry theatrically. Aja doesn't know what the hell to make of this sudden banter. "Tell Weed to get down here."

Sevro speaks into his com and a moment later Weed disengages his ghostCloak and flies from the wall a kilometer distant. We watch him approach. Pebble whistles a merry tune, earning a scowl from Harpy and a chuckle from Sevro, who picks it up as well. The Praetorians think they are insane. Wolfpelts hanging from their backs. Black, custom armor. Wolf helmets. And no one over two meters except for Quinn and me. It's like a Violet traveling circus.

"What are you playing at?" Aja demands.

"Has no one ever bartered with you?" I ask, surprised. "More's the pity."

Weed lands in front of me and hands me the bag Sevro gave me as a present. Aja asks what is in the bag.

"Order your men in the villa to stop the killing, and I will tell you."

"I don't negotiate with boys," Aja says.

I nudge the bag lightly with my boot, showing Aja that whatever is inside is alive. She frowns and perhaps she begins to understand what it is. She speaks in her com for her men to stand down. "What's in the gorydamn bag?"

I open it up and pull out the heir to the Morning Throne like he's a freshly caught rabbit. Lysander's hands and feet are bound gently, and a silk scarf has been tied over his mouth to keep him from making noise. I untie it.

"Hello, Aja," he says.

Aja lunges at him. I pull him backward. "Ah! Ah!" I hold my razor to the boy's neck, letting it curl around, just as the affectionate Oracle wrapped itself around my wrist.

Aja freezes. Her Praetorians watch quietly—black helmets and purple capes making them shadows. The few Bellona take steps forward. Aja motions them back. "Next person that moves, I cut them down. How did they get you, Lysander? Your guards—"

"It was Mustang," he says. "Came to say hello. Cut open my window and gave me to the Howlers."

"Have you been hurt?"

"Your turn to speak is at an end, Aja," I interrupt. "You will let my Housemembers rise from the pool. You will let them board the shuttle I have inbound. You will tell the ripWings and fighters in the sky and space above Luna to let us pass. Or I will have my Howlers kill the boy."

"You promised to protect the Sovereign," Aja whispers. "And you do . . . *this*? He is a boy. He is helpless."

"It's part of the game," Lysander says very seriously. "You play it too, Aja. We're all on the board."

"You see, he's less helpless than the servants you slaughtered tonight," Quinn replies. "Less than those your father burned on Rhea. But he's one of yours. So of course you care."

"You would kill a family to ensure the safety of your Sovereign," I say coldly. "I would kill a child to ensure the safety of my friends. Speak again, and I take his left hand."

She knows I would kill the boy.

I know I would not. I'm not Karnus. Not Evey or Harmony, despite what I'd have these Golds think. So even if they called my bluff, I would balk. Anyway, the moment I kill him, they kill everyone I know. The murder would be in vain.

This is exactly why I build my reputation as a killer, to leverage in situations like these. If they knew my heart, they'd kill my friends one by one. This is a gamble.

I gamble on pride of two sorts. The first pride is that the Sovereign will not let me kill her only grandson, whom she trained from childhood to take her place when the time comes. The second sort of pride is that deep down, she will believe it no great loss if Augustus and his family escape today. She has the will and the means to hunt us to the ends of the System. Why call my bluff and risk having her grandson die? I know this because of how she killed her father—not outright, but only when she had the support of all his former followers, only when they asked her to rise up against the tall tyrant and rule in his stead.

A woman like her has patience. If the Sovereign told me to do my worst, if she shouted to kill the boy and suffer the consequences, that would be foolhardy. A blunt, brutish demonstration of power, as if saying 'Take my grandson, you cannot hurt *me*.' No, instead she will feign weakness, let me have this victory, and then bring eternal ruin on me and mine. Fair enough. We'll play that game another day.

A ship roars overhead. A stork—built to deploy men in starShells to drop points, but slower than molasses sliding uphill. The bay doors open two hundred meters up, as I instructed. So long as we have the boy, the ship's speed doesn't matter a lick. Of course Mustang planned that.

"We're going to fetch our people now, Aja. Let your men know they're to do nothing to impede us."

Aja just stares at me, watching like a taunted panther in a zoo, eyes silent, horrible, as if willing the bars between us to disappear.

"Sevro, Thistle, check the villa. See if anyone managed to survive." They shoot away. "Quinn, guard the boy. The rest of you, get the ArchGovernor and his retinue out of the pool.

"You'll want to call off the ripWings," I say to Aja. They blink in the darkness kilometers above. "Too much noise and this whole thing will turn into a nightmare for all of us. The Sovereign massacring a house . . . but the house escapes! What a dastardly testament to her hunger, her impotence. What a debacle that might cause." I smirk at her. "Why, I fear some houses might rally around the offended house. Some may fear they too will be snuffed out like candles in the night. What would happen to the poor *Pax Solaris* then?"

Quinn stays with me, fingers twitching toward her weapons as Aja obeys my commands. I keep my hand on the boy as the other Howlers splash into the water and emerge with members of House Augustus clinging to them, soaked and gasping for air—some in formal wear, some in armor, most without helmets. They were sharing oxygen, it seems.

Augustus holds on to Harpy's back. The Jackal holds on to Clown's arm. Pliny hangs on to his feet. Where are my friends?

The Howlers deposit the survivors into the bay of the hovering stork high above and return to fetch the rest. Victra is the next they bring out. She's helmetless and wounded on her neck. But she clings to her razor as though it were the thing carrying her aloft. Her eyes strafe the gathered Praetorians wrathfully, and when they find me, they spark against mine like bits of flint. Her anger falls away for a moment and I see a smile of joy, then it's gone and she shouts.

"I will remember you all with great joy!" She laughs madly. "Starting with you, Aja au Grimmus. I will make a coat of your hide."

She disappears into the belly of the craft overhead. Roque is the next one borne aloft. Theodora is with him. I say a quiet prayer of thanks. Quinn touches my shoulder and gives him a wave. His thin face bursts into a smile at the sight of her. He doesn't even notice me. Then he's gone too, landing in the back of the ship. Thistle soon joins us from the manor, helping along several survivors, including the Telemanuses and Tactus, who bleeds from a dozen holes in his gold armor. He put up a nasty fight.

"Darrow?" he cries. "You mad bastard!" He sees the Sovereign's son and cackles gleefully. "Oh, that's ripe. That's ripe. I owe you a drink, my goodman. . . ." His voice fades away as he slips higher in the sky, though he managed to throw his fingers into the crux and wave them in Aja's direction.

"Tactus," Lysander whispers. "He's taller than in holos."

"That's the last of them," Sevro says to me.

"Tell your master we of Mars do not bow so easily," I say to Aja.

The rain beats down between us. Dripping over her dark face, so her eerie eyes blaze in the night. She breaks the silence I imposed on her.

"That is what the Governor of Rhea said when my Ash Lord came to put down his rebellion." Her voice does not sound like her own. It's as though someone speaks through her. "He looked at the thin man I sent with the armada and he laughed and asked why he should bow to me, the bitch patricide of a dead tyrant."

The Sovereign is speaking in Aja's ear, through her com, with Aja repeating the words. My blood runs cold.

"The Governor of Rhea sat upon his Ice Throne in his famed Glass Palace and asked one of my servants, '*Who are you to breathe fear into a man such as I? I who have descended from the family that carved heaven from a place where once there was nothing but a hell of ice and stone. Who are you to make me bow?*' Then he struck the Ash Lord here under the eye with his scepter. '*Go home to Luna. Go home to the Core. The Outer Reach is for creatures of sterner spines.*' The Governor of Rhea did not bow. Now his moon is ash. His family is ash. He is ash. So run, Darrow au Andromedus. Run home to Mars, for my legions will follow you to the ends of this universe."

"I hope so," I say.

"You have one bargaining chip," the Sovereign, through Aja, reminds me. "My grandson is your safe passage. If he dies, I wipe your ship from the sky. Spend him wisely."

Why is she telling me something I already know?

"It's time to go, Darrow." Quinn leans into my shoulder. She sets a hand on my low back, as if to remind me I am not alone. I nod to her.

She covers my retreat as I rise upward with the boy, razor slithering around his neck.

Quinn eyes the Praetorians warily and rises to follow. I have one bargaining chip.

What did the Sovereign mean by that? Was she reminding me that I could spend it only once? Only kill Lysander if my back was to the wall? Then I see why as Aja looks at Quinn rising from the ground as a cat looks at a mouse.

"Aja, no!" Lysander yells.

"Quinn!" I shout.

In a flash, Aja lunges forward, quicker than any cat ever born. She grabs Quinn's hair. Frantically, Quinn brings her razor around to fend the giant woman off. But she's too slow. Aja slams her head into the ground with her left hand. Punches her temple. Armored fist on bone. Four times before I can even blink. Quinn's legs kick and twitch and she curls inward like a dying spider, contorting from seizures. Aja backs away, watching me with a smile.

19

||||||||||||||||||||||

STORK

They know I am rash. Quinn is bait. Aja is the hook. They'll take Lysander if I bite and attack Aja. They'll use the split second my razor is away from him to stun or kill me. I hear the weapons primed behind me, so I keep the razor to the little boy's throat. Tears distort my vision as I float there impotently. I shake my head as the agony wells. I can't leave her. Reversing my boots, I return to pick her from the ground. But before I can reach her, another Gold flashes past me, descending from above, this one without armor, to scoop her from the ground and bear her aloft.

The Jackal.

I shoot up and away, through the rain into the bay doors and land inside the stork. My boots clank on the metal deck and I kneel, shoving Lysander forward into the bay toward Sevro. The boy sprawls to his knees. Several dozen dripping Augustans stare at me. They turn their eyes to the boy. The Jackal follows, clutching Quinn awkwardly with one arm.

Our ship rises and the doors hiss closed behind us. Roque pushes through the others to see me, then his eyes go to the Jackal, to Quinn, strength slipping from him with each second. The Jackal sets Quinn gently on the ground and kicks off the ill-fitting gravBoots he borrowed from one of the Howlers.

Roque's mouth works. No sound comes out. "Is she . . . ," he murmurs finally.

"Are there any Yellows on board?" the Jackal asks me. I look to Harpy.

I point Harpy toward the main cabins. "Find Mustang. Ask her."
She sprints off.

"The medkit," the Jackal snaps, feeling Quinn's pulse. He checks her pupils. No one moves. "Now!" Roque stumbles up to find it. Pebble rips it off the wall and tosses him the kit. He brings it back to the Jackal. Mind turned to static, I stare down at Quinn as another seizure racks her body and an inhuman sound rattles from her nose and mouth. Roque's face is bloodless beside me. His hands reach helplessly for the girl he loves, as though his will alone can mend what was broken; but inside he knows he is powerless. He sinks to his knees.

The Jackal opens the medkit and riffles through its contents.

His single hand moves confidently over the devices inside till they find a silver bar no larger than my index finger. He snatches it and activates the device. It hums softly, emitting a faint blue light.

"I need someone's datapad. Mine was fried in the EMP." No one moves. "The girl will die. A gorydamn datapad. *Now.*"

I hand him mine. He doesn't look up at me, though he pauses a second when he sees my distinctive hands.

"Thank you for the rescue, Reaper," he says hastily.

"Thank your sister."

Lysander rises and comes to my side. He watches quietly, no tears in his eyes. Pebble and Clown sit on their heels. No one touches Roque, though they glance at him, hands clutched on knees or razors, whispering whatever prayers to luck Golds whisper.

The Jackal moves the silver magnetic resonance imager over Quinn's head, watching the hologram on my datapad. He curses.

"What is it?" Roque asks.

The Jackal hesitates. "Her brain is swelling. If we can't control the pressure, we have a problem." He fumbles with the medical equipment and unwinds a machine with a transparent cord. "That pressure will deprive the brain of proper blood flow. It will starve itself as the vessels tighten under the swelling."

"Is she going to die?" I ask.

"Not from swelling," the Jackal says. "Not if I can drain the fluid and release the pressure as it builds. But we'll need to get her head tilted so the blood can flow through the neck veins. Keep blood pressure steady. Get her a supply of O_2." He looks up, so thin and wet I'd think him a Red instead of a Gold were it not for the dusty hair. "Pebble, isn't it? Find her oxygen. A breathing mask will do so long as it doesn't cover her face past her forehead."

Pebble slips away.

A fresh seizure contorts Quinn's body. I look on helplessly and set my hand on Roque's shoulder. He flinches against the touch.

Harpy slides back into the room. "No slagging Yellows."

"Shit," Clown swears. "Shit. Shit. Shit. Shit." He kicks the wall.

The Jackal pauses, glances at Roque, then acts. He points to Clown, Harpy, and several Housemembers. "I need someone for each of her arms and her head. She's going to keep seizing, and for some reason, I suspect this is going to be a bumpy ride. We're going to move her out of this damn bay and hold her down for the surgery." He pulls her hair back into a ponytail, asks me to hold it, and pulls a small ionizer from the medkit. He squeezes it with his teeth over his hand, wincing as it destroys bacteria and dry skin follicles. "Clown, get her hair—all of it."

The Jackal stands and tosses the ionizer to Clown, who bends and is about to scan it over Quinn's golden hair when Roque takes it from his grasp. He hovers over Quinn, unable to move.

"What's her name?" the Jackal asks Roque.

"Quinn."

"Talk to her. Tell her a story."

Trembling slightly, Roque sniffs and speaks quietly to Quinn. *"Once, in the days of Old Earth, there were two pigeons who were greatly in love. . . ."* He toggles the ionizer and moves his hand. It is intimate. Like he's bathing her. Just the two of them in some far-off place. Long before she told stories by the campfires of the Institute. Long before the horror.

I smell hair burning as the Jackal stands and comes to me.

"What happened down there?" he asks. "Was it a pulseFist?"

I look at him in surprise. "You didn't see? Aja used her hands."

"Goryhell." His jaw tightens. Dull eyes taking in the scene. "How did we come to this?"

"Octavia was set on this path all along," I say quietly. "Before we even came to Mars, she intended to give the Bellona the ArchGovernorship. The gala was a trap."

"When did you discover this? Before or after the duel?"

"Before," I lie.

"Well played. Makes us seem the victim. I see Mustang failed in her task."

"Did your father send her to infiltrate Octavia's court?"

"No. I imagine it was her own idea. Draw close to the dragon . . ."

"The Julii are against us too."

He nods thoughtfully. "Makes sense. Politicos tried to take Victra from us before Karnus and Aja came."

"You don't seem worried."

"Victra is her mother's favorite daughter." He shakes his head, remembering something. "But she took three Obsidians on for me. Three. She's with us, body and mind."

I watch Roque finish removing Quinn's hair. "Will she live?" I ask quietly.

"She has bone fragments in her brain tissue. Even if we stop the swelling, she's hemorrhaging. Badly."

We look down at Quinn, her head bald now. Face peaceful. Only small contusions on the side of her skull. You'd never guess she was dying inside. Roque strokes her forehead so gently, whispering soft things.

"Can you save her?" I turn to the Jackal. "Is there a chance?"

"Not here. If you get us to a medBay, then yes, there's a prime chance."

Roque sings a soft song to her as they lift her body to move to another room. The song is one he made around the campfire as my army ate in the highlands. Quinn was with Cassius then, as it seems all women are at one time or another. But even then, I noticed her eyes meet Roque's. They are the messenger pigeons from his story, crossing again and again in the sky. How excited he was to be reunited with her.

I crack inside. I can still save her. I can fix this.

The Sovereign was right. I misunderstood my own bargaining power. What was I going to do? Kill her grandson if Aja killed Quinn? What if he killed Sevro, Mustang, Roque? I'm lucky she didn't hurt more of them.

I turn to see Sevro.

He stands quietly in his armor watching us, watching Roque hold the girl Sevro loves but has never told, the girl he could never have. The pain is raw and etched deep into the lines of his hawkish face. Impervious Sevro, immune to hurt, to sadness, to having his eye gouged out by Lilath, the Jackal's lieutenant; it all falls on him now. Quinn never called Sevro Goblin like the rest of us. Victra puts a hand on his shoulder, noticing the pain if not understanding why it's there. He shoves her hand off.

"I don't know you," he snarls.

Victra backs away. "Sorry."

"What are you waiting for, Reap?" he demands. "We're not off this rock yet." He jerks his head. I follow, asking Victra to bring the Sovereign's boy.

Sevro and I climb a ladder and meet Tactus in the narrow corridor that leads to the passenger hold and the flight cabin.

"Oy, goodman," Tactus calls, favoring his injured shoulder. Wet hair dangles over laughing eyes. His voice is loud, unmindful of Quinn's condition. "Next time you're planning something dramatic, tell us you're coming so we don't go pissing our pants."

I push past him. "Not now, Tactus."

"Ever the bore." He eyes Sevro. "Looky, looky. Goblin. If possible, you've shrunk even further, my goodman."

Sevro doesn't smile.

We enter the passenger hold, where the Augustans and Howlers buckle themselves into bucket seats in preparation for breaching the atmosphere. Tactus follows at our heels.

"Hello, psychos," Tactus calls to the Howlers. "Pleasure to see your diminutive forms yet again. Especially you, Pebble."

"Eat shit," Pebble says, looking up from helping buckle one of Augustus's young nephews into his seat.

Tactus leans into me when we're past the passenger hold. "Good friends to come and rescue you. Thought they were scattered to the Rim."

"Were," Sevro says.

"What brought you back?" Tactus asks. "The weather?"

Sevro says nothing.

Tactus laughs despite the numerous holes in his armor. "Just how you like 'em. Eh, Darrow? Friends who will risk life and limb to always be in your shadow?" He nudges me, a bit too playfully, leaving faint smears of his blood on me. We come to the flight cabin's closed door. Tactus winces as he bumps a bulkhead with his shoulder. Sevro trails behind.

"How's the shoulder?" I ask.

"Better than that girl's head back there. Quinn, wasn't it? The fast one from House Mars. Aja slagged her good. Pity. I'd have taken her for a—"

Sevro kicks Tactus in the balls from behind, foot going between legs hard enough to dent metal. He elbows him in the side of the head, sweeps his legs in swift *kravat* form. Three more strikes to the ears before Tactus hits the ground. Sevro puts one knee into Tactus's shoulder wound, a forearm against Tactus's throat, the other knee to Tactus's groin, and his free hand dangles a knife over Tactus's eyeball. "Talk about Quinn again, and I'll cut your balls off and jam them in your eye sockets."

"Brother always said . . . keep your eye . . . on the ball," Tactus gags out.

The metal cabin door hisses open. Augustus fills the frame. He stares down at the scene just as Victra brings Lysander forward from the aft of the ship.

"They're almost done, my liege," I say. I step over Tactus and Sevro to join the ArchGovernor in the cabin. Victra does the same, except she steps on Tactus, grinding her heels.

"Prime work," she says to Sevro.

"Slag off, cow."

"Who is the little one?" she asks me as we slip into the cabin and close the door.

I tell her.

"The Rage Knight's son? Nasty little man. I don't think he likes me."

"Don't take it personally."

The cockpit is larger than my room in the Citadel's villa. An array of lights ring the pilot and co-pilot chairs. Mustang sits to the left, a Blue pilot to the right. The Blue is jacked into the ship. A blue light glows under the dermis of her left temple. Mustang flies, right hand in a holographic control prism, speaking quickly with the Blue. Out the curved viewport, Earth hovers. Augustus, Pliny, and comically stooped Kavax au Telemanus discuss our options behind Mustang.

It is quiet.

"Well done, Darrow," Augustus says without looking back to me. "Though you could have chosen a better ship . . ."

Mustang interrupts. "What's going on back there? They said someone was hurt."

"Quinn is dying," I say. "We have to get her to a medBay, fastlike."

"Even when we hit orbit, we're thirty minutes out from our fleet," Mustang says.

"Fly faster."

The ship trembles as Mustang and the Blue push it hard.

"It was a good plan," Kavax says, beaming down at Mustang. "It was a good plan, Virginia, infiltrating the Sovereign's household. Just like when you were a girl. The time you and Pax hid in the shrubbery to listen to your father's counsel. Except Pax was bigger than the shrub!" He booms a laugh that startles the quiet Blue.

Mustang reaches back to squeeze his forearm, hand smaller than his elbow. He preens like a hound with a pheasant in its jaws, looking around to see if we all noticed her compliment. She's got a way with men bigger than bears.

The love on the man's face makes Augustus's own disinterest monstrous. And even worse, thinking about the Jackal killing this man's son makes me sick.

Mustang spares me the slightest glance, her hair bound behind her head, the memory of a smile still creasing the corners of her lips, and it's like I've been punched in the heart. There's no smile for me. And the horse ring no longer graces her finger.

There's silence for a long moment. Augustus turns to look at me. "I assume Octavia attempted to bring you into her fold as well?"

"She attempted."

"Slag herself. Bet you told her to go slag herself, eh, boy?" Kavax booms. He slaps my shoulder, knocking me into Victra. "Sorry." He's bent like a hothouse tree grown too tall for its roof. Water drips from his red forked beard. "Sorry," he repeats to Victra.

"Actually, Lord Telemanus, I thought her offer tempting. She manages to treat her lancers with respect. Unlike others."

Augustus wastes no time with banter. "We'll amend that. I owe you a debt, Darrow. Provided we make it to my fleet."

"You owe it to Mustang and the Howlers as much as me," I say.

"What is a Howler?" he asks.

"My friends in the black armor. Sevro's the leader."

"Sevro. That wretched little thing that was atop my lancer, yes?" The ArchGovernor raises an eyebrow. "Thought I recognized him. Fitchner's boy." His tone sits poorly with me. "The one that killed that Priam brat in the Passage."

"He's with us, my liege. Loyal as my own hands."

The door hisses open and Sevro and Tactus join us. We all turn to look. Sevro recoils slightly. "What?" he challenges.

Tactus scoots off to the side, away from Sevro.

"Does your loyalty lie with me or with your father, Sevro?" Augustus asks.

"What father? I'm a bastard's bastard." Sevro looks the ArchGovernor up and down skeptically. "And all due respect, my liege, I could give a cat's frozen piss about you too. Your daughter brought me from the Rim. My allegiance is to her. But above all it's to Reaper. That's it."

"Mind your manners, you little puppy," Kavax growls.

"You must be Pax's father. Sorry he went. He's a man I might have died for. But I see he got his good looks from his mother."

Kavax isn't sure if he's been insulted.

Augustus observes this. "Darrow, I owe you an apology. You were right. Loyalty, it seems, can extend beyond the Institute. Now . . . Lysander." Augustus glances out the shuttle's viewports. We rise steadily. He kneels to speak with the boy. "I've heard tell that you are an exceptional lad."

"I am, my liege," Lysander says as firmly as he can. "They test me regularly, and I train in all manners of studies. I rarely lose in chess. And when I do, I learn, as I ought."

"Do you now? I had a son like you, once, Lysander. But I'm sure you knew that."

"Adrius au Augustus," Lysander says, knowing the lineage.

"No." Augustus shakes his head. "No. My younger son isn't like you at all."

The boy frowns. "Then the elder. Claudius au Augustus?"

Mustang glances back.

"Yes." Augustus nods. "A kind, special boy with a lion's heart. Better than me. Kinder. A ruler." He spares a strange, meaningful glance at me. "You would have been friends."

Lysander tries to look dignified. "What happened to him?"

"They left that part out, eh? Well, a large young man from the House Bellona by the name of Karnus took liberties with a certain young woman my son was courting. My son took umbrage and challenged Karnus to a duel. In the end, when my boy was broken and bleeding, Karnus kneeled, cupped my son's head"—he puts one hand around Lysander's head—"and smashed it on the cobbled stones till it broke open and all his specialness dripped out." He pats the boy on the cheek. "Let's hope you never have to see such a thing."

"Is that your plan for me, my liege?" Lysander asks bravely.

"I'm only a monster when it is practical." Augustus smiles. "I don't think I will have to be this time. You see, we're just trying to get home. So long as your grandmother permits our passage, then you will be safe."

"Grandmother says you're a liar."

"Ironic. You will tell her we've treated you well, I hope."

"If I am well treated."

"Fair enough." Augustus touches the boy's shoulder and stands. "Victra. Take him to the passenger hold."

Victra glowers. Of course Augustus chooses the only woman but Mustang. Tactus notices her reaction and steps forward. "Might I, my liege? I've not seen my own brothers in some time. I wouldn't mind talking with the lad." Augustus nods as if to say he doesn't care. Victra thanks Tactus, surprised by his gesture. He winks at her, punches my shoulder, and pats Lysander roughly on the head, almost knocking him down. I'd hate to know his brothers.

"Come, tiny one. Tell me, have you ever been to a Pearl club?" he asks, leading him away. "The girls and boys there are spectacular. . . ."

The ponderous stork climbs higher and higher. In two minutes, we'll hit the edge of the atmosphere.

"They tried to kill me as I slept," Augustus murmurs. "She knows I will not forgive this."

"She'll come to Mars," I say.

"Is there no chance for amends to be made?" Pliny asks.

"Amends?" Mustang snarls. "Make amends with the woman who burned a moon, Pliny? Are you an idiot?"

"*Peace* will preserve your line, my liege. More than war. Set yourself against the Sovereign, and what hope can there be?" Pliny is no fool with rhetoric. "Her fleets are vast. Her monies endless. Your name, your honor, no matter how great, cannot stand beneath the weight of the Society. My liege, you raised me to your side because of my worth. Because you trusted my advice. Without you, I am nothing. Your care is all I value. So heed my advice now, if you still hold it in regard, and do not let this wound against the Sovereign fester. Do not let war come of this. Remember Rhea, yes, and how it burned. Preserve your honored family with peace, by any means."

Augustus raises his voice. "When the Sovereign pushed against me,

I bent like Gold should, with grace, with dignity. But now she cuts at me, and beneath the grace, beneath the aplomb, her knife will strike iron. We make for Mars, and for war."

"We're reaching the low atmosphere," Mustang says. "Hold on."

"What is that light?" Sevro asks. "The blinking one over the altimeter."

The Blue snaps an answer. "The cargo bay door is opening, *dominus*."

"The cargo bay . . ." I frown. "Can you override it?"

"No, *dominus*. I'm locked out."

Why would the cargo bay door be . . . ?

"He volunteered," Mustang says, voice panicked. "Tactus volunteered."

"No," I snarl, startling everyone but Mustang. We realized it at the same time. *"Sevro, Victra, on me!"* I wheel around and sprint out the cabin doors, head ducked as I move as fast as I can toward the back of the ship.

"Prepare for evasive action," I hear Mustang say back in the cabin.

"What's happening?" Pliny whines.

"TACTUS!" I bellow. Victra and Sevro run at my heels. The other Howlers and Housemembers call to me, confused as I sprint through the passenger bay.

Screwface unbuckles his crashbelt. "He went past with the boy."

"Down!" I say, shoving him in his seat. "Everyone stay seated!"

Tactus wouldn't. He couldn't. But why the hell not? Why would I ever assume he wouldn't do what's best for him? It's in his nature.

We slide down railings to the storage level, past the room where the Jackal operates on Quinn. I shove open the door to the cargo hold and am greeted by the howling of wind. The hatch hangs open to show darkness wounded by city lights far beneath. Clown and an Augustus lancer lie unconscious, bleeding. They slide slowly toward the open bay door. As for Tactus, he's nothing but a distant dot in the darkness. I cannot see him clearly, but I know what he has taken: Lysander.

"Sevro." I grip my friend's shoulder. "Stop!" He's seething. Looks like he wants to jump out the back of the ship and follow Tactus into the air. He can't. It's too late. Instead, we catch the two unconscious Golds before they slip down the open ramp. Victra shuts it at the control panel. The door hisses closed.

"He doesn't have any communications gear," Victra says breathlessly. "Not after the EMP."

"Doesn't need the gorydamn gear." Sevro points to Clown's naked feet. "The bastard has gravBoots. Soon as he hits the ripWing scanners, he'll be picked up."

I do the math. "We have two minutes till they send boarding parties."

20

||||||||||||||||||||||||||

HELLDIVER

I should have known what Tactus would do. He killed his first Primus, Tamara, in the Institute. He only ever followed strength. Only ever sought victory. I knew he was a beast, but I thought he was my beast. I thought I could trust him. No, I thought I could *change* him. I curse myself. Arrogant fool. I stalk back to the cockpit, where Augustus addresses the Blue pilot.

"Pilot, will you be able to take us clear?"

"No, *dominus*. Geomet models don't show a probability of escape." Her response is fittingly Blue—emotionally distant, efficient, and declarative. Her body is thin, faintly avian. Like she's made all of twigs, neck long, bald head slightly smaller. Eyes large and as uncannily azure as the digital tattoos of her skull. When she moves, it's as though she's submerged in water. Asteroid born, judging by her flat accent.

"What is the likely scenario?"

"They will destroy our engines with ripWing fire. Precipitating a hull breach that will kill all aboard. Alternatively, precipitating a leechCraft assault. Capturing all aboard."

"Or they'll just blast us from the gory sky," Sevro adds.

"Blue, deliver me to my ship and you will receive command of a frigate," Augustus offers.

"I would prefer a cruiser," she notes.

"A cruiser, then."

"Very well." The Blue adjusts several knobs. "I will fly well, but the paradigm must be altered before they engage our vessel, if we are to survive."

The stork climbs toward the edge of Luna's atmosphere. This ship is a big-bellied beast. Fat with storage room, because all they're meant to do is birth soldiers out of the tubes in their guts. Men like me would tear her apart in our ripWings. We used ships like this at the Academy to launch men in starShells at enemy asteroid bases.

Friction fire wreaths the ship.

"If the hull is breached, hold your breath, *dominii*," the pilot instructs. "We don't have sufficient survival helmets aboard."

Victra frowns. "Our lungs will explode if we do that."

"Then exhale," the Blue replies. "And have thirty secs of life while eardrums explode and blood vessels swell like inflated balloons. I will hold my breath."

Sevro looks back at me, wide-eyed. "I hate space."

"You hate everything."

We pop clear of Luna's atmosphere. The fire fades and we slip into open space, where the armada's capital ships glide like behemoths of Europa's deep sea. Gun turrets dot their hide like barnacles, and hangar bays slice their undersides like great gills. Commercial ships float slowly along the shipping lanes. RipWings and wasps go about their patrols. None pay heed to our presence except those that escort us from Luna. The Sovereign would not broadcast this. Time ticks away.

There is nowhere to flee. We thought to pass just under the guns of the Scepter Armada when we had Lysander. But now we'll have to run the gauntlet.

Our pilot is calm as metal.

She said the paradigm must change.

What can I do? Think. Think.

"We will open communications to one of the ships," Augustus says. "Bribe them into sheltering us. Every man has a price."

"We're jammed. Can't even broadcast," Mustang reminds him.

We're going to die. We all know it. Augustus doesn't panic or surrender resolve. I don't know how I thought he'd handle death. Maybe I hoped he would wail about and turn pale. But for all his faults, he is stalwart. After a moment, he sets a bony hand on Mustang's shoulder. She flinches, surprised.

"Whether missile or boarding craft come, die like Golds," Augustus says solemnly to us. Not because he wishes us to think him strong in his last moments, but because he believes in what he is—a superior being, a master of his human frailties. For him, death is merely the ultimate frailty. Humans whimper when they die. They claw for life even if there is no hope. He will not. Death is not grander than his pride.

Golds, in many ways, are so like Reds. Helldivers go to their deaths for their families, for the pride of their clan. They do not whimper when the mines collapse around them or when the pitvipers come from the shadows. They fall and their friends weep and sweep their bodies aside. But we have the Vale to look forward to; what have the Golds? When they perish, their flesh withers and their name and deeds linger till time sweeps them away. And that is all. If anyone should claw for life now, it should be the Aureate.

I claw because I carry the torch of something that must not die, must not go out. That is why I grab Sevro on the shoulder and, with a horrible, eerie laugh, tell the pilot to take us closer to the deadliest ship in orbit, one which now has angled itself to intercept us.

"Take us near the *Vanguard*," I repeat to the Blue.

"That would cause our chances of survival to decrease by—"

"Never tell me the odds, just do it," I command.

Everyone turns and looks at me. Not because I've said something strange but because they've been waiting to turn and look at me. They've all been silently praying I would marshal a plan. Even Augustus.

Eo said people would always look to me. She believed I had some quality, some essence that gave hope. I rarely feel it in myself. There is none in me now. Just dread. Inside I feel such a boy—angry, petulant, selfish, guilty, sad, alone—and yet they look to me. I almost break underneath their gaze, almost wither away and ask someone else to take the reins. I can't do it. I'm small. I'm just a liar in a carved body. But that dream must not be extinguished.

So I act and they watch.

"You gone space mad?" Victra asks. "When they realize we don't have the boy . . ."

"Draw an angle toward the *Vanguard*'s bridge," Mustang tells the Blue.

Augustus gives me a curt nod, guessing what I plan. "*Hic sunt leones.*"

"*Hic sunt leones,*" I echo, saving my last look for Mustang, not the man who hanged my wife. She doesn't notice. I leave the bridge with Sevro at a dead sprint. Something hits our ship. Her hull shudders. They know we don't have Lysander.

"Howlers! Get up!" I shout.

Harpy throws up her hands. "I thought you said—"

"UP!" I roar.

Red secondary lights bathe the launch bay in bloody hues as Sevro and I load ourselves into the cold starShells. It takes two Howlers each to help us slip into the robotic carapaces. I lie in the armor as Harpy buckles my feet into the stirrups and closes the armored legs over my meat and bones. The Howlers are fast in their movements even as the ship lurches with another near missile strike. A siren howls, reporting a hull breach. I try to slow my breath as Victra fits my head into the starShell's helmet.

"Good luck." She leans her face close. Before I can stop her, she presses her lips to mine. I do not recoil, not this close to death. I let her lips part and cling warm and comforting around mine. Then the human moment is over, and she's gone, lowering the massive visor of my helmet. My Howlers howl and hoot at the sight. I can't help but wish it was Mustang who sealed me in this tin can and kissed me goodbye; but then the digital display owns my vision and I disappear from my friends into the metal launch tube. I'm alone. And scared.

Focus.

I'm cocooned, belly-down, in the spitTube. This is where most would piss themselves, separated from friends, from the warmth of life. There's no gravity in the tube. It isn't pressurized. I hate the weightlessness of it.

I can't look up or my neck will break when they launch me. I can't move side to side. My starShell is latched into a thousand toothlike magnetic hooks. They click into place like tiny insects, chattering.

In moments they'll shoot me into space. My breath rasps. My heart rattles against my sternum. I drink in my body's terror and smile. They said this was suicide at the Academy when I wanted to launch myself. Maybe they were right.

But this is why I was made. To dive into hell.

I'm a beetle of a man in a carapace of metal, weapons, and engines that cost more than most ships. I've got a pulseCannon on my right arm. When I need it, it will bloom like a haemanthus blossom.

I think of the time Eo laid a haemanthus before my front door, the time I plucked one from the wall on the night that I was supposed to win the Laurel. How far away those warm days seem from this cold place, where petals are metal instead of soft like silk.

"We're getting pinned in. Boarding parties imminent," Mustang's voice comes over the com. *"Priming your launch."* The ship moans as another missile almost claims us. Our shields are shot. Just the rickety hull holding us together.

"Aim true," I say.

"Always. Darrow . . ." Her silence says a thousand things.

"I'm sorry," I tell her.

"Good luck."

"This is not fun," Sevro groans.

The ship's hydraulic system hisses and the metal teeth jerk me forward in the tube, loading me into the chamber. Inches before my head, the magnetic stream of the railgun hums dreadfully, daring me to glance its way.

They say that many Golds can't take this, that even Peerless can panic and scream and cry in the spitTube. I believe it. Pixies would have heart attacks right now. Some cannot even ride in a spaceship for fear of small places and the vastness of space. Soft-bellied fools. I was born in a home smaller than the cargo bay of this ship. I made my life at the end of a clawDrill that makes this tube look like a child's toy, all while sweating and pissing my soul away in a frysuit cobbled together from scrap.

Still there's the terror.

"Watch how a pitviper strikes, my son." Father once clutched me by my wrist and made me play this game. *"Watch it coil upward and upward till it reaches its crest. Don't move before then. Don't strike out with your slingBlade. If you do, then it'll get you. It'll kill you. Move just when it's coming down. Do that with the terror in life. Don't act till you're as scared as you'll get, then . . ."* He snapped his fingers.

I'm at that point when the music of the machines takes hold. The clicks and the clacks, the hisses and the hums reverberate through the hull. A countdown begins.

"Ready over there, Goblin?" I ask Sevro over the com.

"Cacatne ursus in silvis?"

Does a bear shit in the woods? The ship spins and shudders. More sirens howl.

"Latin, now?"

"Audentes fortuna juvat," Sevro chuckles.

"Fortune favors the bold? You deserve to die if that's really going to be the last thing you say in this life."

"Yes? Well, you may suck my—"

My heart sticks to its downward beat.

The metal teeth jerk me forward into the tube's magnetic stream. And it happens. Even through my suit, g-forces hit me like the backhand of the Obsidians' thunder god. My vision flickers black. Stomach rises into throat. Lungs constrict. Blood slows in my veins. I snap forward. Lights flicker in my eyes. I don't see the walls of the tube I'm shot through. I don't even see the ship that brought me here. I see Eo's face in the darkness. I black out. Bodies can't take this. Too fast.

Darkness.

Then the darkness has holes.

Stars.

There's no meantime. One second I'm on the ship, the next I'm ripping through the deep of space at ten times the speed of sound.

Many shit their suits at this point. It's not a fear thing. It's biology and physics. The human body can take only so much. Mickey the Carver made sure mine could take just a little bit more. I hope Sevro's can too.

I rip soundlessly through space. Trust that Sevro is near me. Can't see him, even on the sensors. All too fast. Toward the greatest ship in the Scepter Armada—the one we should avoid. It all happens in six seconds. Emergency missiles streak past us. The gunners see us now. Know what's happening. But we're not using thrusters, so the missiles can't lock. Flack can't detonate on so short a fuse. The unspent canisters fly past us, nearly hitting me. Our pilot took a perfect shot.

Railguns miss us. Projectiles flash past. Sevro is howling in the com. Their shields are down. They can't bring them up fast enough. It takes time. Iridescent blue flickers over their hull as the pulseShields power up. *Too late, you sons of bitches.*

Too bloodydamn late.

I can't think. I'm screaming inside. Laughing like the flames of a wildfire. Laughing because I know it is my madness that these logical warriors cannot fight.

The bridge is close. I spare a look up. See Golds inside roaring at one another. Rushing to their evacsuits or escape pods. Staring at us approach like Mustang did when my horses of House Mars crashed into her and Pax in a muddy field. Our rage is something unique. Something these Luneborn don't understand.

Blues scatter. Obsidians pull their weapons. Two Golds don breathmasks and unfurl razors, readying for the kill. The second before we hit, I shoot my pulseCannon. It thumps on the thick glass. I shoot again and again and again. Then I curl into a ball and smash into the thick bridge glass with the full velocity of my launch as well as a last-second burst from my thruster boots.

Out of me roars a madman's scream.

21

||||||||||||||||||||||

STAINS

I explode through the bridge like a ball of lead shot into a store of china and glass. I crash into displays and strategy desks before blasting through the reinforced metal of the bridge walls, through the steel of the hallways till at last I slam bodily into a bulkhead a hundred meters through and past the bridge. Dazed. Can't find Sevro. I call him over the com. He groans something about his ass. Maybe he did shit himself.

We can't hear it because of our helmets, but the ship is filled with howling as the vacuum of space sucks crewmembers to their deaths. It really doesn't suck them out through the shattered windows so much as the internal pressure of the ship pushes them out. Either way, Blues and Oranges and Golds fly screaming into space. The Obsidians go silently. Not that it matters. Space makes all silent in the end.

My left arm spits sparks. My pulseCannon is shredded. Inside the suit, my arm hurts like hell. I have a concussion. I puke inside my helmet. Fills it with a bitter stench, stings the nostrils. But I keep my feet, and my right arm works well enough. Viewshield is cracked. I stumble as I'm sucked toward the bridge too.

I crawl back through the holes I made in the walls. Make it to the bridge to find the place in chaos. Crewmembers hold on to anything to prevent themselves from being sucked into the cold darkness. A Gold girl flips past me and flies out the bulkhead. Finally, red lights flash. Emergency bulkheads slam shut all over this part of the ship to cut the pressure leak. One begins to close behind me, reinforcing a wall that I crashed through. I hold it up when I see Sevro coming. The metal groans against the robotic arm of my starShell. Sevro dives through just in time and the door slams shut. Bridge is locked down with us inside. Perfect.

The pressure wind dies behind us as durosteel slats slide over the demolished viewports. The ship's officers and crew pick themselves up from the ground, gasping for breath, but there is none. Oxygen and pressure are still being pumped back into the room. So those with breathing masks—the Golds, Obsidians, and Blues—watch placidly as the few Pink valets and Orange technicians on the bridge flop like fish, gasping for air that is not there. One Pink vomits blood, his lungs exploding in his chest because he tried to hold his breath. The Blues watch the deaths in horror. They have never seen men die. They are used to seeing blips on the scanners disappearing. Perhaps a distant ship exploding or gouting flame as it is boarded by Obsidians and Grays. Their understanding of the mortal coil is being adjusted.

The Obsidians and Golds don't react to the scene. Some of the Grays attempt to administer aid, but it is too late. By the time the pressure and oxygen levels are normalized, the lowColors are dead. I'll never forget those faces. I brought them this. How many families will weep because of what I did here?

In anger, I stomp my metal boot on the steel deck. Three times. And those who did nothing while their allies died turn to see Sevro and me in our killing suits.

Oh, how those Gold and Obsidian faces finally emote.

An Obsidian charges us with a forcePike. Sevro hits him once, crushing the huge man with a metal fist. The other four link together and attack us, keening one of their hideous war chants. Sevro meets them, delighted to finally be the biggest in the room. I engage a squad of Grays who scramble for their weapons.

This is the way it goes. We're men of metal fighting disorganized men of flesh. Like steel fists punching the inside of a watermelon. I've never killed men with so little regard. And it frightens me how easy I find it in war. There is no ambiguity here, no violation of moral creed. These people are warColors. They kill me or I kill them. It's simpler than the Passage. Simpler that I don't know them, that I don't know their brothers and sisters, that I use metal instead of my own flesh to drive them through death's dark door.

I am good at it, better by worlds than Sevro, and that terrifies me above all else.

I am the Reaper. Whatever doubts I had in myself fall away and I feel the stain creeping over my soul.

We do our best to save the Blues. The bridge is large, but there aren't many Obsidians or Grays with projectile and energy weapons. No reason for them here; no one has ever come through the viewports. Two female Golds with razors are the true menace. One is tall and broad. The other has a quick face that is pinched with desperation as she charges us. With their razors, they could cut even our suits in half, so Sevro blasts them from a distance with his pulseCannon, overloading their aegises and splashing the energy onto armor where it overloads the pulseShields and eats into the armor, melting the Golds. This is why they control technology. Humans, no matter their Color, are fragile as doves in the meat grinder of war.

My enemies dead, I turn now to the Blues in the pits. "Is there a captain?" I ask.

In my suit, I stand nearly a meter taller than them. They're still staring at the mess we made of the others. I must be a walking nightmare. Arm spitting sparks. Suit half ruined. Holding a terrible razor.

"I don't have all day to threaten and stomp. You are erudite men and women. This is not your ship. You merely occupy it for the Gold who commands it. I now command it. So. Is there a Blue captain about?"

The captain survived. He's a placid, clean-looking man, more limbs than torso, with a fresh gash on his face that pains him terribly. He trembles and sniffles, holding the wound as though his face would fall apart were his hands to leave it. Mother would have called him a shiteating ninnypriss. Eo would have taken a different tack, so I stand over him and speak quietly.

"You are safe," I say. "Do not attempt anything rash."

I pop my helmet. The sick drips out. I tell him he's to go to the corner and strip off his star badge of rank. Trembling, he doesn't get a chance to obey. Sevro lurches forward, takes his badge, and picks him up and moves him like a doll.

A long-faced, proud-shouldered woman with deep olive skin snorts at the demotion. Her gaze is peculiarly shrewd for a Blue. Bald, like the rest, with digital azure tattoos swirling not only along crown and temples, but over hands and neck.

Sevro lopes back to me.

"Sevro, stop pissing around."

"I like being big."

"I'm still bigger."

He tries flipping me the crux in his suit, but the mechanical fingers aren't so agile.

I give orders to the Blues in the tech pits that our friends in the stork are to be given access to one of the hangar bays. After settling themselves back into their stations, they obey. All here are loyal, because I have them under my power. But throughout the ship, who knows? They may be loyal to the Sovereign. Or they may only be loyal to the man who rules this ship. It'd be foolish to think they all operate under the same creed. I'll have to make them.

I watch the stork coast into a hangar bay on a display. She's barely held together by her bolts. Two leechCraft festoon her. My Howlers will have to fight off the squads of killers they contained. They might manage, but if the *Vanguard*'s Obsidians and Grays besiege them in the hangar, then all is lost.

Sounds come now from the bulkhead that connects the bridge with the rest of the ship. A deepspine hissing. The door glows red from heat, a small pupil in the center of the thick gray durosteel. Obsidians or Gray marines, no doubt led by some Gold, endeavor to reclaim the ship. Should take them a little while.

"Is there a holoCam in the hall?" I ask the Blues.

They hesitate. "*Blackspace,* you daft gasbags," curses the female Blue I noted before. She pushes another Blue out of the way and syncs her tattoos with the console. A holo appears on one of the screens, confirming my fear. Golds lead the party attempting to make their way onto the bridge.

"Show me the engine room, the life support nexuses, and the hangar bay," I demand. She does. Again, Golds lead parties of Gray marines and Obsidian slave-knights to secure the ship's vital systems. They'll try to wrest control of it away from me. Worse, they'll try to board or destroy the stork to kill or capture Mustang and my friends.

"Who wants this ship?" I ask severely. I stalk along the raised command podium, kicking aside a body in my way, and look down at the communications Blues in their pit. They dodge my gaze, two women no older than I. Faces pale and fresh, like morning snow, now stained with tear tracks and grime. Wide cerulean eyes raw-rimmed and shot with red. They've seen friends die today, and here I rage selfishly, acting as though this is my triumph. It's so easy to lose myself.

Never forget what I am, I remind myself. *Never forget.*

We're being hailed by a dozen ships and the Citadel ground command. What's happened? they want to know. TorchShips and destroyers coast warily toward us. I open a closed-circuit com channel to the whole of my ship.

"Attention, crew of the vessel formerly known as the *Vanguard,* hereafter known as the *Pax.*" I pause dramatically, knowing that any good song, any good dance, is a game of tension leading to a climax of sound and movement.

Sevro can't stop grinning boyishly at me. He looks like an imp in the huge suit, head so small with his helmet off. He makes a big motion with his hands to try to make me laugh. I shake my head at him. Now isn't the time.

"My name is Darrow au Andromedus, lancer of the Martian House Augustus, and I have claimed this vessel as a spoil of war. It is mine. This means, per Societal rules of naval warfare, that your lives are mine. I am sorry for that, because it means you will likely all die.

"Your lives have been dedicated to one vocation or another— electronics, astral navigation, gunnery, janitorial service, lighting and repair, martial combat. My vocation is conquest. They teach us it in schools. And in school, they instructed me on the proper method of invading, seizing, and possessing an enemy warship. After one has captured the bridge of an enemy-held vessel, the procedure taught to us is simple: vent the ship."

Sevro activates the hidden console secured in the back side of a navigation display, one only Golds can access. The Blues recoil in surprise. It is like going into a man's kitchen and showing him a nuclear bomb hidden under his sink. The console scans Sevro's golden Sigil and blinks gold. All he need do is push in a code, and the entire ship will open to space. Twenty thousand men and women will die.

"We made these ships so we could empty them. Why? Not because we distrust your loyalty—in fact we rely on that—but because there are still"—I look at the roster one of the Blues gives me—"sixty-one Golds on board. They are loyal to the Sovereign. I am her enemy. They will not obey me. They will sabotage the ship, attempt to take the bridge; they will rally you, abuse your loyalty, and lead you to certain death. Because of them and their hatred of me, you will never see your loved ones again.

"There is yet another complication. Beyond this hull, the Sovereign wonders what happened here. Soon she will realize the pride of her armada no longer belongs to her. It is mine. Her Praetors' ships will vomit out squadrons of leechCraft carrying legions of Obsidians and Gray marines. They will led by Gold knights who want my head, fully prepared to kill all in their path.

"If I vent you into space, there will be no one to stop them from killing me. So you see, you are my salvation, and I am yours. I will not sacrifice twenty thousand of you to kill sixty-one of my enemies. I chose this vessel above all others because of its crew. The best the Society can offer. To me you are not expendable. So what I ask of you is this: choose me as your commander and overwhelm those Golds who think you expendable.

"You have my permission, my warrant and the badge of the Arch-Governor of Mars, Nero au Augustus, to capture or kill your Gold commanders for me. Take their weapons and subdue them, then make fast the ship against the invaders who come to destroy us. Do it now. If you wait, they will kill you! I will know the first men and women to rise up. As your new master, I will reward you. The Arch-Governor will reward you. Do it now! For I have just opened every armory throughout the ship. Seize weapons, and neutralize the tyrants."

A heavy silence as the first sparks of revolution are struck.

Sevro comes close. "That was rousing."

"Too demokratic?" I whisper.

"I don't think autocratic demokracy counts." Sevro wrinkles his nose. "You did threaten to vent them into space."

"Threaten? I thought I implied it rather smoothly."

"Smooth as gravel, dipshit." Sevro cackles a bit too enthusiastically and slaps his leg with his mech hand, denting the metal there. He winces, then looks up at me, slightly embarrassed. "Slag off."

The door behind us begins to hiss. I turn to look at the glowing bulkhead. My enemies have brought a drill to assail me. My hands shake from the adrenaline. I feel the weight of dozens of blue eyes. The red of the door deepens, spreading. We haven't long.

My razor ripples into killing form, long and terrible. "Company soon," I say. I glance at Sevro, who has been distracted by one of the holo screens. I order the Blues to take shelter.

"They're doing it," Sevro murmurs. "Goryhell. Darrow, come look."

He cycles through live visuals of Oranges and Blues ransacking the armories. Some Grays help them. Others stand by, unsure of their prerogative even as others shoot at the tide of their fellow shipmates. But no bullets can hold back this tide. They take weapons, run sloppily through halls, swelling their ranks. The roughest lead—not Blues, but Orange hangar workers and mechanics, along with Grays . . . one I recognize. The middle-aged corporal on my ship at the Academy, the one who escaped with us. He directs a score of men and women into the stateroom of a Gold. They subdue him respectfully. That peaceful accord is not far spread.

Three powerful squads of Golds, leading Obsidians and Grays, marshal in the life support rooms, at the engines five kilometers back to the aft of the ship, and just outside the bridge door. Those outside the bridge door number four Golds and six Obsidians. Ten Grays load weapons behind them.

"We're still going to have company," I say.

They'll be coming through the door at any moment. Sparks spit from the inside of the bulkhead as their heat drill gets the better of the door. Metal drips inward, bubbling to the floor. The Blues shiver in terror, and Sevro and I square ourselves up and don our helmets, preparing for the new onslaught. Again the stench of my sick fills my nostrils. I tell the Blues to hide in the communications bay. They'll be safe there.

A com light suddenly blinks on a console near me. Instinctively, I answer. A voice like thunder sends tremors through my bones. There is no visual.

"Can you hear me?" it asks.

"I can." I glance over at Sevro. Whoever calls us is using a voice amplifier that sounds like the breaking of thunder. Sevro shrugs as if he hasn't a clue who it is. "Who is this?"

"Are you a god?"

A god? An eerie quiet settles in me. That is no voice amplifier. I should have known by the cold, sluggish accent. I choose my words carefully, remembering my lore. "I am Darrow au Andromedus of the Sunborn."

"You took the vessel and you are not yet Praetor? How?"

"I flew in through the bridge."

"Alone from the Abyss?"

"With a companion."

"I will come to meet you and your companion, godchild."

The Blues look to one another in terror. They mouth something. *Stained.* The heaviness of fear settles on my shoulders. Sevro and I peer around the bridge, as though the beast were hiding somewhere in the shadows. More of the door peels away, dripping inward like some glowing red, rotting fruit.

Then one of the Blues gasps and we glance back at the HC monitor to see the cameras in the halls outside the bridge door relaying a scene of horror. It—*he*—runs at them from behind as they prepare to make entry into the bridge—an Obsidian, but larger than any I've ever seen.

But it's not just his size. It's how he moves. A dread creature stitched from shadow and muscle and armor. Flowing, not running. Perverse. Like looking at a blade or a weapon made flesh. This is a creature that dogs would flee. That cats would hiss at. One that should never exist on any level above the first tier of hell.

He smashes into the kill squad from behind with two pulsing white ionBlades that extend out of his armor three feet from his hands. The Grays he simply runs through, crushing them into the walls with his shoulders, splintering their bones. Then he starts the real killing. It's so savage I have to look away.

The heat drill continues melting the door of its own accord. And in its center forms a hole. Through it I can see men and women dying. Blood sizzles on the overheated metal.

When the Stained is done, he's bleeding from a dozen wounds, and there's only one Gold left. She stabs him with a razor, piercing his dark armor through the breastplate. He twists his body, locking the blade in, and then clutching it when she lets the blade relax back into a whip. Then he grabs her by her helmet, her golden armor glittering under the hall's lights. She tries to escape, tries to scramble away, but like a lion with a hyena in its jaws, he need simply squeeze. When she is gone, he lays her gently on the ground, tender now that he's brought her a good death. Sevro involuntarily steps back from the door.

"Mothermercy . . ."

The Stained stands on the other side, the door between us slowly melting from the center. When the hole in the door is the size of a torso, he removes his helmet. A hairless, pale face stares as me. Eyes black. Wind-weathered cheeks armored with calluses like the hide of a rhinoceros. Head bald except for a meter-long white shock of hair that hangs to his mid-back.

We lock eyes and he addresses me.

"**Godchild Andromedus, I am Ragnar Volarus, the Stained first-born of my mother, Alia Snowsparrow of the Valkyrie Spires north of the Dragon's Spine, south of the Fallen City, where the Winged Horror flies, brother of Sefi the Quiet, breaker of Tanos, which once stood by the water, and I make you an offering of stains.**"

He splays out his gigantic bloodstained hands and then reaches through the door with his right hand. His ionBlades retract into his armor. The razor still juts out of his ribs.

I'm pissing my bloodydamn suit.

"Well, frag me blind," Sevro mutters. "Do it, Darrow. Before it changes its mind."

Taking my helmet off, I step forward. I want this one.

"Ragnar Volarus. Well met. I see you wear no badge. Do you have a master?"

"I bore the mark of the Ash Lord, and was to be presented as a gift with this great vessel to the Family Julii. But you took this vessel, and so you have taken me."

The Julii? A gift for their betrayal of Augustus, no doubt.

And did he just use a bureaucratic loophole to justify killing his master's men? If there's irony in his voice, I can't find it. But why would he do that? Do those black eyes of his know me? Stained cannot use tech other than military matériel. He could never have seen me before, yet his hand remains, waiting to grip mine.

"Why do you do this?" I ask. "Is it the Julii?"

"They trade my kind." I had forgotten. It is Julii ships that carry Obsidian slaves across the abyss. They know to fear the speared sun of Victra's family crest.

He is not practiced at hiding his hate. It is cold as the ice the man was born into.

"Will you accept these stains, godchild?" he asks, leaning forward, voice plaintive, a strange worry creasing the corners of his mouth. Golds did this after the Dark Revolt, the only uprising to ever threaten their reign. We took their history, took their technology, wiped out a generation, and gave their race the poles of planets, the religion of the Norse, and told them we were their gods. A few hundred years later, I stand looking up at one of their most terrifying sons, and wonder how he can think of me as a god.

"I accept these stains in my name, Ragnar Volarus." Terrified, I reach forward and, with superheated metal surrounding our arms, clasp hands, nearly equal in size, though mine is sheathed in metal. I take the blood that his hand spreads to mine and wipe it over my exposed brow. "I accept their burden and their weight."

"Thank you, Sunborn. Thank you. I will serve on the honor of my mother and her mother before her."

"I have friends aboard the stork in hangar bay three. Save them, Ragnar, and I will owe you a debt."

Yellow teeth are revealed as he smiles, and from him undulates a war chant deeper than the ocean at storm. It fills the halls with dread. Fills me with joy and fear and primal curiosity. What did I just gain?

22

||||||||||||||||||||||||||

FIRE BLOSSOM

My body trembles in the aftermath of the giant's departure. Steadying myself, I turn back to the Blues, who stand transfixed, unsure of whether to look to me or the HC displays or the scanners that show the Sovereign's men-of-war encircling us. "You have nothing to fear here," I say. "The captain of this ship was demoted because he left his viewports open. Foolishly. Rank does not excuse mistakes. I wish for a new captain. We haven't much time. So I will decide in sixty seconds."

The proud-shouldered Blue comes forward past her fellows. At first, I thought the tattoos on her hands featured floral lines. Then I note a stream of mathematical notations: the Larmor formula. Maxwell's equations in curved-space time. Wheeler-Feynman absorber theory. And a hundred others that even I don't recognize.

"Give me the badge and I'll carve you a hole back to Mars, boy." Her voice has no inflection. It is flat. Precise and lazy all at once. Emotion bled out of it till only the letters and sounds of the words remain like equations in the air. "I swear it on my life."

" 'Boy'?" I ask.

"You're half my age. Shall I call you 'lord boy'? Or will you be offended?"

Sevro raises an eyebrow, flummoxed at the Blue's bland audacity.

"Forgive her, *dominus*," another Blue says smoothly. "She is an ensign with—"

I hold up a hand. "What's your name, Blue?"

"Orion Xe Aquarii."

"That's a boy's name," Sevro says.

"Is it? I hadn't noticed." Blues can be sarcastic? "My Sect intended for me to be a man. I surprised them."

"What Sect?" Sevro asks.

"She has no Sect. She was appropriated by the Copernican Sect, but dismissed shortly thereafter, for obvious reasons," that officious Blue interrupts again. "She's a Docker."

Orion flinches. She swivels on the other Blue. Her voice does not rise. "And what are you but a pedantic little gasp of a fart, Pelus? Hm?"

"You see," Pelus explains placidly, "she is a Docker. Emotional metrics are unmanageable. Not her fault. She is a product of her *greasy* environment."

"Bolly that," she says, stepping forward quickly.

She punches Pelus in the face. He wails, falling backward like he's never been hit before. Likely because he hasn't. Why would a Blue hit another Blue? They're test takers, math makers, star charters. Not fighters.

"I like the rude one," Sevro says.

"Wait, *dominus*! I desire the ship!" Another Blue slides forward, staring at Pelus on the ground. "I . . . I deserve it. Orion is no more than a . . . a . . . laggard! Her mastery of astrophysics leaves much to be desired, to say little of her understanding of extraplanetary mass kinetics. She didn't even attend the Observatory."

Another Blue pushes forward.

"Forget Arnus! He's a dodderhead at astrophysics and his assumptions in theoretical calculus are imprudent at best! I was second in command of this vessel for six months under the Ash Lord. I served upon it while it was in its dry berth. Logic supports the maneuver to place me as your captain, *dominus*."

The armada's ships continue to hail us over the coms. Men-of-war slide closer. Inside their bellies, brave men and women will be donning suits of armor; they'll board leechCraft and shoot into space to land on my hull, burrow their way through, praying that they will make it home to have a meal made by their mother, their spouse. All that while my Blues shove and push to lead my ship, howling insults at one another's math skills and academic integrity.

"Don't listen to either of them, *dominus*!" shouts a woman in that slow accent. She falls to her knees. "My name is Virga xe Sedierta. I have studied the physics of astral drift in the Midnight School—far superior to the Observatory. I hold, among others, a doctorate on dark matter and gravitational lensing. Let me guide your vessel, *dominus*. To decide in favor of another would be specious and worse: illogical!"

These Blues should have used their logic and seen that I look only at the woman who does not kneel like the rest of them. Orion, the first to speak, still stands, shoulders square, long neck unbent. Her dialect is lowborn, sharper, and more worldly than the dreamy lingo of these academics. Likely from the dock city of Phobos or the String Docks near the Academy's Can. If she really is a Docker who didn't go to the Observatory or the Midnight School, I wonder about the story of how she came to be on the bridge in the first place.

"What about all that noise?" I ask Orion, gesturing to the Blues.

"They're full of batshit, *dominus*." She taps a slender finger against her temple. "I am not full of batshit." She smiles and nods to the displays where the other torchShips creep closer. "And you're running out of time." I glance to the scanner stations where alerts signal the secretive launch of two leechCraft from the Sovereign's nearby men-of-war and cruisers. "I know I can do this, otherwise I would not have spoken out. *Give me a chance*."

I nod to Sevro and he tosses her the captain's winged star.

"Get us to our fleet."

"Rules of engagement?" she asks me.

"Minimal casualties," I say. "We are good. The Sovereign is the tyrant. That is how this must play."

"Aye, *dominus*."

I watch with Sevro as Orion takes command of my ship and sets orders to rendezvous with Augustus's ships beyond the Rubicon Beacons. The squabbling stops as soon as I appoint Orion. They know their chance has passed, so they slip into their comfortable roles as though they wished they'd never left them. Their blue Sigils look like tridents against their forearms in this dimmed lighting.

There's a curious remoteness to Blues. An island people in the abyss of space, they were designed to survive the long journeys from Luna without mutiny. So they share. They share the same oxygen, the same food, the same bunks, the same routines, the same pits, the same commanders, the same lovers, the same Sects, the same ambitions—to do their job with precision and rise high through merit so that they might honor their Sect.

I open a com channel to the rest of the fleet and the satellites of Luna. They can't stop the signal. Not of this ship. Our arrays are as sophisticated as any in the Sovereign's navy.

"Sons and daughters of Society. This is Darrow au Andromedus of the House Augustus. I bring terrible tidings. Tonight, your Sovereign has broken the Compact of our Society. As my master, ArchGovernor Nero au Augustus, slept under her protection, she made attempt upon his life, the lives of his family, and those of his Praetors and aides. Along with the Bellona, she attempted the illegal and immoral murder of more than thirty Peerless Scarred. She failed.

"In retaliation, I have taken one of her flagships. And I am now besieged, with my life, as well as those of my master and his family, at risk. If we do not fight back, we will die. If we surrender, we will die. I have not vented the ship. Those aboard have seen the merit of my cause and have allied themselves with a family that would resist the power-hungry tyrant Octavia au Lune."

Close enough to the truth.

"Hours ago, our Sovereign told me to betray my house. To betray my vows. Like her father before her, she is drunk on power and now believes herself Empress. She told us to bow, witness now our reply."

I turn the com off.

"Mr. Pelus, as you will," Orion declares. "Let the bastards have it when they come." She activates her own tattoos and sinks into digital speak with the rest of the crew.

The bridge is silent. A second ticks by, another. On the HC, I watch three Grays shoot a Gold in the head. In the hangars, Oranges huddle to the side as Golds lead warColors against the downed stork. Then Ragnar arrives in the hangar, and the Oranges rally around him, as do armed Reds, who've followed him from the halls. Many die. Something furious grips these Colors. And though they die, I feel the flickering of rebellion as I give them permission to do what they've wanted to do their entire lives. It's there, even if you never see it till the end—that spark of individuality, of freedom. The door of the stork pops open and Mustang charges out with my Howlers to aid the lowColors and Ragnar, though even the Telemanuses keep their distance from the monstrous man.

Beyond my vessel, the enemy ships finally show their menace. The scanners swell with red. Enemies, leechCraft freshly spilt from the bellies of the armada around us, streak through space to find our hull. They aim to take us by storm.

Orion opens broadsides.

"It's so beautiful," Sevro murmurs. I stand in silence. Railgun payloads slam through leechCraft, shearing away metal and men, only to carry on and smash into the hulls and shields of the same men-of-war that launched the leechCraft.

My newly appointed captain paces the command plank, arms crossed. My five-kilometer war vessel begins a roll, cycling through her banks of railguns as they hurl death into the face of the Sovereign's fleet. Orion half turns to face me, smirking for all to see.

"Now, about carving that path, *dominus.*"

She orders the engines to pound blackmatter. We shoot forward through the remains of two men-of-war.

My bridge is silent but for the buzz of technical orders. Missiles flash in concert beyond our hull. We deploy our flak screens, as the enemy has now deployed theirs, rendering missiles worthless. An aura of light surrounds us like a no-man's-land. Railgun ordnance smashes into our hull, though we do not feel the reverberations here on the bridge. Our equipment does not spark. Wiring does not fall from overhead compartments. This ship is the pinnacle of seven hundred years of design.

Sevro nudges me. "We might just gorywell make it."

The armada around us is massive. Beyond massive. It was brought here to make the gathered lords and all their fleets out past the Rubicon Beacons tremble, and still it is not half the combined fleet. But now that very armada quakes from the inside like a corpulent body as some alien chews its way out of the host.

We make our escape from the armada in quick fashion.

They do not pursue us past the Rubicon Beacons, where we are joined by our small fleet as well as those of the Cordovan, the Telemanuses, the Norvo. I hope more will flock to our banners after today's last surprise.

I examine our wake—naval detritus. Bodies of men and women float behind my vessel. They came out of cracked and punctured ships. Some are still alive but will soon freeze or suffocate. More dead in my path. How many will it take?

I leave Orion the bridge. Sevro and I find our way to the engineering bay, where we have Oranges cut us out of our mangled suits. We rush from there to the hangar, a vast metal depot scattered with ships, equipment, and now broken men. Yellows dart about aiding the wounded and carting them off to the medbay, Grays and Oranges helping carry.

Weed prods several unarmed Golds with his razor. Pebble and Harpy help the Yellows. My eyes search frantically for Mustang. I find her under one of the battered stork's wings, speaking with her father. A long wound mangles her left arm. I don't mention it. They were boarded by a leechCraft, and managed to shear the other off when entering the hangar.

"We've put the bulk of the Sovereign's fleet behind us," I tell Augustus.

"Where is Quinn?" Sevro asks sharply. "Did they get her to the medBay yet?"

Mustang does not answer. Instead, she looks to the ramp of the stork, where Roque descends, carrying Quinn in his arms. She's pale. Long. And lifeless. Sevro does not move. Does not speak. His nostrils flare as a breath catches in his chest, a pitiful sob locked tight in the boy who never cries. He goes numb. Ghostlike. And I reach for him, but he pulls away not in anger, but in confusion, as though he was told the future once, and this reality is not what was promised. He stumbles backward, away from her body, looking around, before turning and fleeing the hangar.

Roque walks past me with Quinn. His face is slack and tired. He wants to say something bitter, but he bites his tongue and just shakes his head at me. He still does not know why I attacked him in his room before the gala. And now this. I've never seen him so broken.

"Look at her," he tells me. "Darrow, look at your friend."

I look at Quinn and feel everything go quiet. Here she is, peaceful in death. Why can we not breathe life back into her? Why can we not simply restart the day? Do everything right. Save the ones we love.

Roque moves away with Quinn toward the hangar's transparent pulse field, which opens into space. He's bent and broken as he walks to the stars to push his lost girl out among them.

I grab the Jackal when I see him exit the stork, demanding to know what happened. She died, he tells me. It's just that. He's tired like the rest of us. He rolls down his sleeves. "I won't apologize. I did my best."

"Of course you did," I say, shaking myself. "Of course."

He asks me where my helmet cam is. I stare at him. "The footage," he says. "Do you even understand what you just did?" He waves around. "Two men took one of the greatest vessels ever built. Golds will flock to our banners. All it takes is my media and your story."

I tell him, absently, almost forgetting the dataRecorder the Sons of Ares put in my tooth to record the bomb blast. It's activated with a clench of my molars. I clenched them as soon as I sat down in the Sovereign's office. I reach inside my mouth and delicately pry it loose of the gums. It is smaller than a hair. The Jackal's eyes light up.

"Where did you get this?" he asks.

"Black market," I say. "Sovereign has damned herself. Use the recording. Make this war a fair fight."

I leave the Jackal there and am about to leave the cleanup to others, when I notice the Oranges and lowColors watching me. I can't simply lead with violence. So I join Pebble and Harpy and lend my aid in helping the wounded to the medbay. The rest of the Howlers help too. And Mustang, and eventually even Victra.

After the last Gray is loaded on a gurney, I stand in the empty hangar. Augustus has gone to the bridge. The Jackal avoids the Telemanuses who accompany him, and instead makes for the communications hub. I'm left alone. Roque is gone. I don't know what to do, where to go.

Blood and scorch marks stain the deck. I look at my hands. These are the consequences of my actions, and I feel so alone. I lean my head against the cold metal wall.

She comes from behind. I don't think she says my name. I'm not sure. I just smell her damp hair as her arms wrap around me. Squeezing tightly.

"I know you're tired," Mustang says quietly. "But Sevro needs you."

"What about Roque?" I ask, turning to face her. So much lingers unsaid between us. So many questions unanswered. So many crimes left unforgiven. So much anger and perhaps still the faint flicker of something more. I feel it as she cups my neck, and lets the strength in her fingers lend itself to me.

"Not now," she says. Roque blames me. And he should. They all should blame me. And it's only going to get worse.

23

||||||||||||||||||||||

TRUST

I find him in a communal washroom. He's earned one of the state-rooms that the others are claiming for the return voyage to Mars, but that's not how he thinks. This is still the boy who hid in the horse. No, I think. Not a boy any longer.

"She cared for you, Sevro."

His arms cross before him, freckled and thin. A towel wraps around his waist, another hangs around his shoulders. Golds don't care about nudity but Sevro always has. He's gained a tattoo since last I saw him. A huge black and gray wolf along his back. The Howlers are his everything. Once they were just a tool to me; now I think of them as something more. But what does that mean, when I use them just the same? He stares at the water running into the drain of the shower. Down and down it spirals.

"In the end, I believe I'll enjoy war," he says. "Gotta toughen my spine a bit. Callous my hands. Bastards tell us it's all roses and glory." He looks up. "Don't you smell the roses, Reaper?"

I sit beside him on the bench. "Did you hear what I said?"

" 'Course I gory heard you. I'm missing an eye, not an ear." He taps his bionic eye with a bony finger. " 'Course I know she cared. But never in the way I wanted. She deserved to live. If any of us ugly little shiteaters deserve it, it was her. There wasn't a cruel bone in her body. Not one. But it didn't matter. It doesn't matter if we're good or we're evil. It's all up to chance."

"It was chance you knew her at all," I say. "Chance that brought her to House Mars."

"No. It was my father," Sevro says. "He drafted her, traded a pick with Juno to get her." He shakes his head. "All because he thought she would temper us, govern our anger. If he hadn't picked her, we wouldn't have met her, and she'd be alive."

"Maybe," I say, thinking of Eo. "But she chose to come here. She chose to follow me. To follow you."

"Just like Pax."

I nod, touching my pegasus.

"It's all piss and shit. Isn't it?" Sevro says. "Doesn't matter how pretty they dress it up. We're still in the game. We're always going to be in a slagging game. Spit on their empire. Spit on this piss and this shit. I came for you because he told me what you are."

I stare at him, unable to understand.

"What do you mean?" I ask with a nervous laugh.

"Turn it on," he says. "I know you brought one. You're thorough, Reaper. Always thorough."

"Why are you acting so—"

"Shut up and turn it on."

I nod and activate the device in my pocket. A jamField deploys. I'm not so prideful as the Sovereign to believe no one could listen in. Sevro stares as me till I shift uncomfortably.

"So what am I?" I ask.

"Even now?" he asks, shaking his head. "You are wound tight. Say the name of the person who sent me."

"Mustang sent you. You told me she brought you in from the Rim. Same with all the Howlers."

"That's right. She did. Took six months to get here from Pluto. But guess who came to me during my layover in Triton. Go on, Reap. Guess."

"Lorn?" His lips curl into a sneer. "Fitchner?"

Sevro spits in my face, right under the eye. "Guess wrong again and I leave you like this." He snaps his fingers. "I will not come back. I will not help you. I will not bleed for you. I will not sacrifice *my friends* for a man who doesn't give enough of a shit about me to put his neck out just once. Trust goes both ways, Darrow. This time you have to take a leap."

He's not bluffing. And I know what I want to say. But how can it be? Sevro is a Gold. A bloodydamn Gold. He heard me say "bloodydamn" to Apollo. He covered it up. Didn't he? Or was that a mistake? Is he trapping me? No. No, if that's true, then the game is already over. Eo's dream has failed. Who is closer to me than he? Who loves me more than this strange, nasty outcast? No one.

So I look him in his dull gold eyes. "Ares sent you."

Silence between us.

A terrible five seconds. Six. Seven. He stands and locks the door before pulling a small black crystal from the pocket of his crumpled pants. "For your breath only."

"A whisperGem . . ."

I take it tenderly, knowing how much it costs, and blow against its surface. My breath makes it wobble, then shatter. Small motes of black rise, drifting up like fireflies out of the grass as dusk settles in deep summer. They coalesce. Floating and forming a rough holo that hovers between Sevro and me. The spiked helmet of Ares.

"My son," he warbles. *"I am sorry. Harmony has betrayed me and initiated a campaign against our principles. I discovered her intended use of you too late. But you were wise. This is why I chose you. Steps are being taken to curb her efforts. Continue with your own. Set Augustus against Bellona and fracture the Pax Solaris."*

I try to ask it a question, but it is a recording. Made sometime after the gala.

"I realize this must be difficult. I have asked too much of you already. But you must carry on. Sow chaos. Weaken them. You have much reason to doubt me. We have not contacted you until now, because you were watched by Pliny, by the Jackal, and by the Sovereign's spies. Troublemakers breed interest. But I have watched you too, and

I am proud. I know Eo would be as well. In case you doubt the verac-ity of this message, a friend would like to say hello."

Ares's helmet fades and Dancer smiles at me. *"Darrow, I want you to know, we're with you. Your family is alive and well. The end is coming, my friend. Soon you'll be with us. Till then, trust the man Ares sent; I recruited him myself. Break the chains."*

The image erodes, blackish light decaying into the air. And I'm left staring at the shower floor.

"You look good for all that surgery," Sevro says. His smile is no less nasty than usual. "Ares sent that cripple to me. The one who sent you to the Institute. Dancer."

He can't say any more because I'm hugging him and crying. I sob and hold on to him, shaking, scaring him. He doesn't move except to pat me on the head. All the weight falls from my shoulders. Someone knows. He knows and he's here. He knows and he came to help me. To *help* me. I can't stop shaking and saying thank you. Eo was right. I was right. "You are my friend," I tremble out like a child. It almost makes him cry seeing me this way.

A true friend.

"Of course," he says haltingly. "But only if you stop blubbering, man. We're still Golds."

I pull back from him, embarrassed, wiping my face on my sleeve. I think I mumble an apology. My vision's bleary. I sniff. He hands me a towel, which I blow my running nose into. He makes a face.

"What?"

"That was for your eyes."

We laugh together and then sit in an awkward silence. In time, I ask him how long he's known. He suspected something since the Insti-tute, he says, where he heard me say "bloodydamn" to Apollo. My voice went all thick, all rusty. Then Dancer showed him the video of my carving.

"Somehow they knew you could trust me, even if you didn't, shit-head. Always been that way. Always will be that way."

"It doesn't . . . *bother* you?" I ask him. "What I am?"

"Bother. That's a tiny-ass word for a gory big thing." He scratches his buzzed head. "A crotch rash bothers me. Bad fish bothers me. En-titled dickweeds bother me. This . . ." He shrugs. "Piss on it. You like my angle more than any other pisshead in the worlds. Figure I'd re-turn the favor, even if I really am bigger than your rusty ass."

I laugh at that. He would have dwarfed my Red self. "You must know what I'm here to do. It isn't just infiltration. It will end with the fall of the Society."

"Rise too high, in mud you lie."

"That's it?" I ask incredulously. "You're on board?"

He snorts. "It took me six months on a torchShip to reach you. Three months from Triton after Dancer showed me the truth. Was I confused? Damn straight. But still I boarded the ship and had three months to reconsider. Still I am here. So I think the time for second-guessing my commitment has passed. Anyway, my Gold 'brethren' have been trying to kill me since I was born." He looks around, un-comfortable even after all we've shared, despite the jamField. "Only people to ever treat me decently are people who don't have a reason to. LowColors. You. I think it's time to return the favor."

"And what of the others?" I ask intensely. "Pebble, Clown?"

"Not my secret to share. Quinn would have understood," he says slowly, fighting back something. "Rest might go along. Thistle won't. Roque won't. Not in a million years. Too in love with their own spe-cies. Don't know about the tall arrogant one."

"Victra. And Mustang?" I ask.

"I don't give love advice, shithead." He stands. "Say, just because I'm a revolutionary doesn't mean I can't get a massage from a Pink, does it? That would suck sack."

"I don't know," I laugh. "I'm still figuring it out, to be honest."

"Slag it. I'm getting one. Back feels bloody broken." His crooked teeth bare themselves as he laughs. "Feels good. That's how I know it's right, Reap. Despite all this *shit*. It feels good in here." He taps his thin chest. "It feels . . . how do you say . . . *bloodydamn* good."

Victra finds me after I've said my goodbyes to Sevro. "Augustus sent me to tell you the Ash Lord's stateroom is yours."

"Augustus is giving me the largest room?"

"Your ship, your spoils, he said. You know how particular he is about order."

"I hope you know the way. I'm already lost."

She motions me along. We walk in silence through the halls. I'm weary, but happy enough knowing Sevro is with me, that Ares still believes in me, and that Dancer is still alive out there. It's a salve on the pain from Quinn's death.

"I suppose you know my family has betrayed the ArchGovernor," she says.

"I'd heard. But you're still with us."

"As I said. I do what I want. Mother doesn't control me, or my accounts, like she does Antonia's." She grins sideways, watching me. "I like you when you're like this."

"Like this?" I can't help but laugh. "What do you mean?"

"I don't know. You seem calm. At ease. Despite what's happened."

"And you seem particularly kind," I say.

"Kind? A quaint fiction. But we both know I'm far from kind."

We walk in silence till we reach the door to my stateroom. I glance back and see Ragnar trailing in the halls behind. If it weren't for the bandages on his body, I wouldn't have seen him at all. I motion him away.

At the door, I search Victra's haughty eyes. "You could have sent a lowColor to tell me I was to be in the stateroom."

"But then I wouldn't get to see you."

"Is that the only reason?" I ask.

She smiles mischievously. "I think I'll keep my secrets." After a moment, she looks up at me. "But I do worry for you."

"For me?" I roll my eyes. "What are you playing at, Victra?"

"Nothing," she says, offended. "You're such a hypocrite, Darrow."

"Me?"

"Remember when Tactus discarded your violin because he was suspicious that you wanted something? Now you treat me the same way. Same as when I came to you in the gardens on Luna. Is it too much to believe I'm your friend and care about you?" She wrinkles her nose. "You're making me emotional, and I hate it."

"I'm sorry," I say. "You're just . . ." I try to find the right words for the tall woman. There aren't any. So I shrug and say, "It's hard knowing you're Antonia's sister. That's the full of it."

"But I'm not her."

"I realize th—"

"Do you?" She reaches out and touches my face. Her lips part searchingly. I remember the feel of them on mine before I launched myself through the spitTube. I let her kiss me then. Even if she is a cold woman, there is something in her heart for me. Different from Eo. Different from Mustang. I move gently away from her hand and shake my head.

"You are a strange man," she says with a soft sigh, all the vulnerability that was in her now gone. Her claws return. She leans back against the wall opposite me, bending a knee and putting a boot on the wall, laughing at me with her eyes. Here's the Victra I know.

"You love women, but you do not enjoy us." Smile lines crease as her lips part slightly. My eyes cannot help but trace the slender contours of her neck, the strength in her slim shoulders, and the rise of her breasts. Her eyes burn into me. "There's much to enjoy. Do you even know how soft my skin is?"

I cough out a laugh. "You're mocking me."

"As ever."

Victra is a schemer. It's her way. But for a moment, she was vulnerable. And seeing that . . . seeing that made all the difference. I kill the sexual tension the best way I know how.

"Good night, sister," I say, and kiss her on the brow.

"Sister? Sister?" She laughs dismissively as I leave. It takes her a moment, but she calls to me.

"Is it because you think me wicked?"

I turn back to her. "Wicked?"

"Is that why you've never wanted me?" She pauses, choosing her words with care. "Because you look down on me?"

"Why would you think that?" I ask gently.

She shrugs and looks around the hall, strangely hesitant. "I don't . . ." She twists her hands, trying to wring out the right words.

She gestures to herself. "This is how I survive, do you understand? It's how my mother taught me. It's what works."

"What do you say we try something new?" I offer, walking back to her. I extend a hand. "Darrow. Contrary to popular rumor, I don't eat glass. I love music, dancing, and I'm very fond of fresh fruit, particularly strawberries."

She snorts a laugh. "So stupid. We're reintroducing ourselves?"

"No armor. Just two people. I'm waiting," I say playfully.

Rolling her eyes, she steps forward, looking either way down the hall. She brings up her hand, fighting back a childish smile. "Victra. I like the way stone smells before rain falls." She makes a face, cheeks flushing red. "And . . . don't laugh. I actually hate the color gold. Green goes better with my complexion."

I cannot sleep. The bodies of those I've left behind float in the darkness with me. I wake a dozen times, flashes of bombs, slashing of swords ripping into my dreams. I earned these sleepless nights. I know that, and that's what makes them all the harder.

I stand and pace my new quarters, wandering its expanse. Six rooms. A small gymnasium. A large bath. A study. All belonging to the man who burned a moon. The father of the Furies. How could I sleep in a room like this? I take the pegasus pendant from my pocket, almost forgetting it's a radium bomb.

Wandering the halls of the ship, ghostlike, I look behind me, wondering if Ragnar follows. I told him to sleep, but I know little of his moods, how he thinks, what he does at night. There is much to learn.

I pass through dimmed halls, past Orange technicians and Blue systems operators, who quiet and bend as I pass through metal halls down to the bowels of the ship, where Golds never tread. The ceilings are lower, meant for the Red workers and Brown janitors. This ship is a city, an island. All the Colors are here. I remember the roster. Thousands of jobs. Millions of moving parts. I examine a maintenance panel. What if the Orange who worked it were to overload the panel?

What would happen? I don't know. I wager few Golds really do. I make a note of it.

I continue on, hunger drawing me to the mess hall. Food could easily be delivered to my rooms, but my valets have not yet been organized. Anyway, I hate being waited on. In the mess hall, I find someone as sleepless as myself sitting at a long metal table.

Mustang.

24

|||||||||||||||||||||||||||

BACON AND EGGS

I slide across from her.

"Can't sleep?" I ask.

She wraps her knuckles against her head. "Lot rattling around." She nods to the clamor of pans back in the kitchens. "The cook's beside himself," she says. "Thinks I need a feast. Told him I just wanted bacon and eggs. Pretty sure he's disregarded everything I said. He babbled something about pheasant. Has this Earthborn accent. Hard to understand."

Moments later, a Brown cook stumbles out from the kitchen, carrying a tray of not only bacon and eggs, but pumpkin waffles, cured ham, cheeses, sausages, fruits, and a dozen other dishes. But no pheasant. His eyes turn the size of the waffles when he sees me. Apologizing for something, he sets the tray down and disappears, only to reappear a minute later with even more food.

"How much do you think we eat?" I ask him.

He just stares at me. "Thank you," Mustang says. He mumbles something inaudible and backs away, bowing.

"I think the Ash Lord was a bit different from us," I say. Mustang pushes the fruit toward me. "Thought you didn't like bacon," I say.

She shrugs. "I had it every morning on Luna." She delicately butters her waffles. "Reminded me of you." She avoids my eyes. "Why can't you sleep?"

"Not much good at it."

"You never were. Except when you have a hole in your stomach. You slept like a baby then."

I laugh. "I think comas don't count."

We talk about anything but the things we should. Innocent and quiet, like two moths dancing around the same flame. "Amazing how big the beds are, even on a starship," Mustang says. "Mine's monstrous. Too big, really."

"Finally! Someone else agrees. Half the time, I sleep on the floor."

"You too?" She shakes her head. "Sometimes I hear noises and sleep in the closet, thinking if someone's coming for me they won't look there."

"I've done that. Really does help."

"Except when the closet is big enough to fit a family of Obsidians. Then it's just as bad." She frowns suddenly. "I wonder if Obsidians cuddle."

"They don't."

Her eyebrows rise. "Have you researched it?"

I finish a handful of strawberries, shrugging as Mustang frowns at my manners. "Obsidians believe in three types of touch. The Touch of Spring. The Touch of Summer. The Touch of Winter. After the Dark Revolt, where the Obsidians rose in arms against the iron ancestors, the Board of Quality Control debated destroying the entire Color. You know how they gave them religion, stole their technology. But what they wished to kill most of all was the incredible kinship the Obsidians then possessed. So they instructed the shaman of the tribes, bought and paid for liars, to warn against touch, saying it weakened the spirit. So now the Obsidians touch one another in sex. They touch each other to prevent death. And they touch each other to kill. No cuddling." I notice her watching me with a small smirk. "But of course you knew all that."

"I did." She smiles. "But sometimes it's nice to remember all that's going on inside you."

"Oh." I look away as she tries to hold my gaze.

"I forgot you can blush!" She watches me for a moment. "You probably don't know this, but one of my dissertations on Luna concentrated on mistakes in the sociological manipulation theorems used by the Board of Quality Control." She cuts a sausage delicately. "I deemed them shortsighted. The chemical sexual sterilization of the Pink genus, for instance, has led to a tragically high suicide rate within the Gardens."

Tragically. Most would have said "inefficient."

"The rigidity of laws maintaining the hierarchy are so strict they'll one day break. Fifty years from now? A hundred? Who knows? There was this one case we studied where a Gold woman fell in love with an Obsidian. They had a blackmarket Carver alter their reproductive organs so his seed was compatible with her eggs. They were found out and both were executed, their Carvers killed. But things like this have happened a hundred times. A thousand. They're just scrubbed from the record books."

"It's terrible," I say.

"And beautiful."

"Beautiful?" I ask, repulsed.

"No one knows of these people," she says. "No one but a handful of Golds with access. The human spirit tries to break free, again and again, not in hate like the Dark Revolt. But for love. They don't mimic each other. They aren't inspired by others who come before them. Each is willing to take the leap, thinking they are the first. That's bravery. And that means it's a part of who we are as people."

Bravery. Would she say that if she knew one of those people sat across from her? Does she live in the world of theories Harmony spoke of? Or could she really understand . . .

"So how long, I wonder," she continues, "till a group like the Sons of Ares finds the records, broadcasts them? They did it with Persephone. The girl who sang. It's only a matter of time." She pauses, squinting at me as I react involuntarily to the mention of Eo. "What's wrong?"

I can't tell her what I'm thinking, so I lie. "Dissertations. Sociology. You and I specialize in very different things. I always wondered what your life was like on Luna."

Mustang eyes me playfully. "Oh? So you thought about me?"

"Maybe."

"Day and night? What is Mustang wearing? What is she dreaming about? What boy is she kiss—?"

She winces at that last part.

"Darrow, I want to explain something."

"You don't have to," I say, waving her off.

"With Cassius it—"

"Mustang, you don't owe me anything. You weren't mine. You aren't mine. You can do what you want when you want with whomever you want." I pause. "Even though he is a gorydamn jackass."

She snorts a laugh. The humor fades as fast as it came. There's pain in her eyes. In her half-opened mouth. Her idle knife and fork hover over her forgotten plate. She looks down and shakes her head.

"I wanted it to be different," she murmers. "You know that."

"Mustang . . ." I rest my hand on her wrist. Despite her strength, it's frail in my hard hands. Frail as the other girl's was when I held her in the deepmines. I couldn't help that girl. And now I feel like I can't help this woman. Would that my hands were meant to build. I would know what to say. What to do. Maybe in another life I would have been that man. In this one, my words, like my hands, are clumsy. All they can do is cut. All they can do is break. "I think I know how you feel—"

Mustang jerks back from me. "How I feel?"

"I didn't mean—" I pause, hearing a noise.

We look over and the cook stands there awkwardly with another tray. He tiptoes forward, sets it down, and then leaves the room, backing away awkwardly.

"Darrow. Shut up and listen." She peers fiercely up at me through the strands of hair that have fallen across her face. "You want to know how I feel? I'll spit it out at you. All my life I've been taught to regard my family over all else.

"What happened with my brother at the Institute . . . when I handed him over to you, that set me against everything I was raised to do. But I thought that you"—She takes a deep breath that wavers at the end—"were a person who earned my loyalty. And I thought that it would be so much more important if I gave it to you in that moment than to Adrius, who has never lifted a finger on my behalf. I knew it was the right thing to do, but it was a repudiation of my father, of all he taught me. Do you even know what that means? He has broken families as easily as other men break sticks. He wields unimaginable power. But more than that. He is the man who taught me to ride horses, to read poems and not just the military histories. The man who stood beside me, letting me raise myself up by my own strength when I fell. The man who couldn't look at me for three years after my mother died. That is the man I rejected for you. No," she corrects herself, "not for you. For living differently, living for more. More than pride.

"At the Institute you and I decided to break the rules, to be decent in a place of horror. So we made an army of loyal friends instead of slaves. We chose to be better. Then you spat in the face of that by leaving to become one of my father's killers." She puts a finger in the air. "No. Don't speak. It's not your turn just because I pause."

She takes her time in gathering her thoughts, pushing away her plate.

"Now, I'm sure you understand that I felt lost. One, because I thought I'd found someone special in you. Two, because I felt you were abandoning the idea that gave us the ability to conquer Olympus. Consider that I was vulnerable. Lonely. And that perhaps I fell into Cassius's bed because I was hurt and needed a salve to my pain. Can you imagine that? You may answer."

I squirm on my cushion. "I suppose."

"Good. Now shove that idea up your ass." Her lips make a hard line. "I am not some frill-wearing tramp. I am a genius. I say this because it is a fact. I am smarter than any person you've ever met, except perhaps my twin. My heart does not make my brain a fool. I sought out a relationship with Cassius for the same reason I let the Sovereign think she was turning me against my father: to protect my family."

She looks down at her food.

"I've always been able to manipulate people. Men, women, it makes no difference. Cassius was a walking wound, Darrow, raw and bloody despite the fact it has been two years since you killed Julian. I saw it in him in a second, and I knew how I could make him love me. I gave him someone who would listen, someone who would fill the void."

The sternness in her voice fades. She looks around as if she could escape the conversation she started. If she stopped, I would be happier for it.

"I made him think he could not live without me. I knew it was the only thing that could keep the rest of my house safe. I knew it was the best weapon I could wield in this game. Yet . . . I felt so cold. So horrible. Like I was the cruel witch snaring Odysseus, making him fall in love, keeping him for my own selfish aims. It seemed so logical. And when he put his arms around me, I felt like I was drowning. Like I was lost, suffocating under the weight of all I'd done, suffocating knowing there was a life ahead of me with someone I did not love.

"Yet it was for family. It was for the people I love even if they don't deserve it. Many have sacrificed more. I could sacrifice that." She shakes her head, the tears that build there mirroring those that well in my own eyes. They fall when she says, "Then you walked in at the gala, and . . . and it was like the ground had broken open to swallow me. I felt like a fraud. A wicked girl who'd contrived a reason to do something stupid." She tries to wipe her eyes. "Can't you see why I did it? I didn't want you to die. I don't want you to die. Not like my brother, Claudius. Not like Pax. I would have done anything to stop it."

"I can stop it."

"You're not invincible, Darrow. I know you think you are. But one day you'll find out you aren't as strong as you think you are, and I'll be alone."

She goes silent as all that has welled up inside her breaks loose. She does not sob. But the tears come. She's the type of woman to be embarrassed by them.

It breaks me to see this.

"You are not wicked," I say as I take her hand in mine. "You are not cruel." She shakes her head, trying to pull away. I take her jaw between the fingers of my right hand and bend her head till her eyes find a home in mine. "And what you do for the people you love cannot be

judged. Do you understand?" I deepen my voice. "Do you understand?"

She nods.

It should not be this way. The Golds have everything, yet they demand sacrifices even from their own. This place is sick. This empire
broken. It eats its kings, its queens, as hungrily as it does the paupers
who mill its earth. But it cannot have this woman as it had the girl I
buried. I will not let it devour her. I will not let it devour my family in
Lykos. I will break it, even if it claims me in the end.

I wipe the tears from her face with my thumb. She is different from
her people. And when she tries to do as they do, it cracks her heart to
the core. Looking at her, I know I was wrong. She is not a distraction.
She does not compromise my mission. She is the point of it all. Yet I
cannot kiss her. Not now when I must break her heart to break this
empire. It would not be fair. I've fallen in love with her, but she's fallen
for my lies.

"You can't trust him," she says quietly.

"Who?" I ask, startled by her sudden words.

"My twin," she whispers as though he sits in the corner of the
room. "He's not a man like you. He's something else. When he looks
at us, when he looks at people, he sees sacks of bone and meat. We
don't really exist to him." I frown as she clutches my hand. "Darrow,
listen to me. He is the monster they don't know how to write stories
about. You cannot trust him."

The way she says it makes me know she understands our pact.

"I don't trust him," I say. "But I need him."

"We can win this war without him," she says.

"I thought you said I wasn't strong enough."

"You're not," she says with a smile. "Not by yourself." She dons
her lopsided grin. "You need me."

If only it were so simple.

I leave Mustang for my rooms soon after. The halls are quiet, and I
feel a shade drifting through some metal realm. I don't know how to
accept her help. Or how I should handle her. Seeing her with Cassius

wounded me more than I'll ever tell her, and part of me knows not all of it could have been a manipulation. He was never a monster; and if he ever becomes one, I know it will be because of me.

The door to my suite hisses open. A hand settles over my shoulder. I turn to see Ragnar's chest. I didn't even hear him. **"Someone breathes inside."**

"Theodora, probably. She's my Pink steward. You'll like her."

"Gold breath."

I nod, not asking how he knows, and take my razor from my arm. It whispers into a sword as I step through. The lights are on, muted. I search the suite's rooms with Ragnar to find the Jackal sitting in my lounge with a sherry. He chuckles at our weapons.

"I do admit, I am quite threatening."

He's wearing a bathrobe and slippers.

I excuse Ragnar. With his wounds, he should be resting. Reluctantly, he trudges out.

"Seems no one sleeps on this ship," I say as I join the Jackal on the couch. "I imagine we have to restructure our arrangement a bit."

"Fond of understatements, aren't you?" He sips the liquor and sighs. "Thought I'd drown in that damn lagoon. I always thought my death would be something grand. Launched into the sun. Beheaded by a political rival. Then when it came . . ." He shudders, looking so very frail and boyish. "It was just a careless coldness. Like the rocks of the Institute falling all around me again in that mine."

He's right, there is no warmth in death. I cried like a child when I thought I was dying after Cassius stabbed me.

"Obviously this changes our strategy, but I don't believe it must change our alliance."

"Nor do I," I agree. "We'll need your spies more than ever. Pliny won't take my ascension lightly. And you're stuck here in your father's court. The Politico will try to remove us both." I make no mention of the Sons of Ares. As I guessed, they were forgotten by all as soon as I tipped that wine onto Cassius's lap.

"Pliny will have to go. But you and I should maintain social distance until then so he doesn't know the threat against him is unified. Better for him to misunderstand our individual resources."

"And so the Telemanuses still talk with me," I say.

"True. They do want me dead."

"As they should."

"I don't begrudge them it. It's just damn inconvenient." He hands me a holoCom from his pocket. "They're synced. I'll be calling my ships to meet us, and I imagine you'll stay here with your new prize. Wouldn't do to have shuttles going back and forth."

I want to ask him about Leto. Why he killed him. But why show a devil you know his strength? It just makes me a threat to him. And I've seen how he deals with threats. Better to play ignorant and make sure I'm always useful.

"War presents us with more opportunities," I say. "Depending on how far we want it to spread . . ."

"I do believe I take your meaning."

"All others will try to suffocate the flames, to preserve what they have. Especially Pliny, and your sister."

"Well, then we must be cleverer."

"She doesn't get hurt. That part of our agreement is static."

"If ever she's wounded, I believe it'll be from you, not me." He might be right. "But I'm on your level: Fan the flames. Spread the war. Win it. Take the spoils."

"I think I know just how to do it. What can your network tell me about the shipyards of Ganymede?"

PART III

CONQUER

When falls the Iron Rain, be brave. Be brave.

—Lorn au Arcos

25

||||||||||||||||||||||||

PRAETORS

"We are undone, that is what the ArchGovernor of Callisto has said." ArchGovernor Nero au Augustus peers around the table to see if we understand the gravity of his words. The aquiline angles of his face catch the ship's warroom lights, hollowing his cheeks and giving him the look of a falcon peering down its beak. "And why should he not? The Core rallies against us. Neptune is in farOrbit—Vespasian's ships will be six months in coming to reinforce us. All this while my own bannermen hide behind their shields in their cities on Mars, sending only their second- and third-born to aid us." He looks at the two far members of the table. "Their feebleness cripples us. And now I sit here in council with my Praetors, my men of arms, and what grand schemes do they devise?"

Run. That's what they say. We fled Luna a month ago. And we've not stopped running since, because the Sovereign was crafty and her forces beat us to Mars.

This is not how I thought it would go. But then again, none of this is my damn fault. Cautious bloody fools surround the ArchGovernor. Golds too frightened to lose all the favor and power they've gained in the past to risk any of it now. Worse, they squeeze me out. Alliances form against me. You can see it in their eyes, in their shoulders. My gain is their loss. Even those who followed my lead on Luna. Even those I saved from certain death. They do the same to the Jackal, and they think it a victory he is not here in this room bickering with them. Their mistake.

I sit ten chairs down from my master at the massive cherry oak table in the warroom of his flagship, the six-kilometer dreadnought *Invictus*. The ceiling is forty meters above us. The room overly grand and imposing. A carved relief of a lion glares out from the center of the table. Over forty places are empty. Trusted advisors gone, having abandoned Augustus like rats from a sinking ship. Those with us are Pliny, Praetor Kavax, his son Daxo, and a half a hundred of Augustus's most powerful Praetors, Legates, and bannermen. They do not glare at me. Nothing so childish. These Golds preside over a billion souls. So they simply ignore me and push doubt into Augustus about my ideas.

"Are we in agreement, then, with the ArchGovernor of Callisto? Are we undone?" Augustus demands.

Before any can answer, the grand doors hiss open, retracting into the marbled walls. Mustang strolls through, tossing an apple hand to hand.

"Apologies for my tardiness!" She beams at her father, approaches him and gives him a too-gracious kiss on his lionhead ring.

"I sent word over an hour ago," Augustus says.

"Oh?" Mustang spares a look at Pliny. "I must have missed it. I only knew you were here because I went looking for my brother to play a game of chess." She laughs at the joke. Only the Telemanuses get it. Sighing, she makes her way to the far end of the table, squeezing Daxo and Kavax on their shoulders as she passes. Kavax greets her with rumbling, warm words. She sits and kicks her military boots up. "Did I miss anything? Of course I didn't. Dithering as always?"

Her father's cheek twitches. "This is not a stable." He eyes her boots. Sighing, she brings her boots down and shines the apple on her black sleeve.

She's one of a very few women in the room. Agrippina au Julii should be here, but it was her betrayal that depleted Augustus's fleet of the numbers he needed to capture Mars quickly. And it was her betrayal that's made Augustus put men on Victra to make sure her loyalty to him is true. It took nearly all of my clout with the man to keep her out of the brig.

We've been chased from the Core worlds here, far beyond the orbital path of Mars. Our asteroid mining operations are seized. Augustus's assets frozen. And his cities, those that did not surrender already to the Sovereign, are besieged. Not to mention there are bounties on our heads. The old men don't like that I have the second-highest bounty behind Augustus.

"Before we were interrupted," Augustus continues, "I believe someone was justifying their pos—" *Snap*. His voice falls away as Mustang takes a loud bite of her apple. She looks around at the annoyed faces. I stifle a laugh.

"My liege." Pliny leans forward. "I'm afraid there is no alternative but to continue our tactical retreat. If things continue in this manner, we will lose. And you, my liege, will be tried for"—*Snap*. He flinches before finishing—"treason." He looks around the table to his bought-and-paid-for allies. "There is but one path available to us."

"Continue to run with our fleet till Vespasian's reinforcements arrive from Neptune," Augustus murmurs. "In six months."

The Politico nods. "Or surrender."

"Would that you had killed Octavia when you had the chance, boy," Kavax says.

"If I had, everyone here would be dead," I reply.

Daxo nods. "He meant no offense. Wistful thinking."

"Why didn't you kill Octavia?" Pliny squints at me skeptically.

"I couldn't have. I was in a room with Aja au Grimmus. Perhaps if you were there, you could have done better, but I'm a mortal man."

The Praetors who know their business laugh.

"Even Lorn au Arcos wouldn't have dared," Augustus mutters. "And I once saw him kill Stained without a razor. Darrow did as he could." He turns his attention on me. "Do you think we should run now as well?"

"It makes you look weak."

"We are weak," Pliny replies. "But this makes him look wise."

"Wise men read books about history, Pliny. Strong men write them."

"Stop quoting Lorn au Arcos!" Pliny snaps.

"I thought you'd be open to all knowledge."

"Your many years of life no doubt make you an authority on innumerable things," Pliny says melodically. "Do recycle more maxims from old warriors so we may learn more of life and wisdom."

"This isn't about me, dear Pliny. So cut the *ad hominems*." I gesture to the ArchGovernor "This is about our liege. This is about his fate."

"How theatrical of you to note, Darrow." Augustus rubs his eyes, tired of our bickering.

"The young can't help but be eager," Pliny continues. "But we must remember, there is no dishonor in prudence, my liege. Six months' delay is a small price to pay for victory." He splays out his long-fingered hands. "In fact, time is our friend. Octavia cannot afford to scour the Solar System for us. Not with the Senate so divided at home. Her grasping hand will be like iron. It will rake along the backs of the other ArchGovernors, and it will not be long before those who follow her begin to chafe at her orders. They will learn why we fight against her; namely that she is not our representative, but is instead an Empress. This will give us time. Which will give us power. Which will give us the ability to sue for profitable peace."

Praetor Kavax slams his fist on the table. "Piss on this."

A titan of a man, he's carved more from rock than flesh. His neck is so thick that I couldn't wrap even my hands around it. Unlike most Golds, he has shaved his head and permitted his beard to grow. It is thick and dyed blood-red. When the lights dim, it glows like a brand in the night. Only three fingers remain on his left hand. They say his son, Daxo, bit them off as a child. Though Daxo always smiles and with his soft voice suggests that it was his younger brother, Pax. The Telemanuses are the only Praetors in the room not beholden, in one way or another, to Pliny. I like Kavax.

"It chafes my balls. This Pixie talk chafes my balls!" Kavax sneers. "We should not be in this position. Give me leave, my liege, and I will take a thousand of my guard to treat with the cowards who did not answer your summons. *Apologies, my darling,*" he whispers to his favorite fox, Sophocles, a red-gold, sharp-eared thing that flinches at the loud sound of its master's voice. Sophocles eats little jelly beans from Kavax's massive palm.

We wait for Kavax's attention to return to his words.

"You were saying, Kavax?" Augustus prods with a quick smile he reserves for his favorites.

"Father." Daxo nudges the larger man.

Kavax looks up, startled. "*Oh.* And when their balls are *ripped* off and made to dangle from their own earlobes, others will remember you are *ruler* of Mars and they will beg to aid you, Nero."

Satisfied, he goes back to feeding Sophocles jelly beans.

"And they will know that we few lords were found loyal," Daxo quickly adds, waving to the Golds around the table, who nod appreciatively. Daxo sucks on a stick of cinnamon. He smiles even more than Pax, though his are half as grand and twice as mischievous. The only frown I've yet seen on his face was when he saw the Jackal at the gala.

That particular grudge will not fade. Nor should it. The Jackal took their Pax. In reply, the Telemanuses demanded his head. In turn, Augustus banished the Jackal from Mars. But now war brings new complications, new necessities. And the Jackal seems to have been forgiven in his father's eyes, if not those of the Telemanuses. I watch them carefully. They are not stupid, despite the guise they enjoy wearing. I only hope they remain ignorant of my alliance with Pax's killer.

"All should be reminded that fealty is not easily cast off," Daxo finishes, his voice astonishingly cordial. "A visit from my father and my sisters would remind other bannermen of their duties to you in times of war." He tilts his head playfully, allowing us to admire the workmanship of the gold angels engraved into his scalp. "It is in the Telemanus nature to leave an impression. Perhaps it would swell our ranks."

"My thunder lords." Augustus smiles. "Ever eager for violence." He traces a finger along the back of his long left hand. "But no. That reminder must wait. Punishment can only be doled out in victory. It would look petty, the sad flailing of a drowning man, considering my fleet is scattered and my legions trapped behind the shields of my cities."

He looks to Pliny and asks how the rest of our trade allies fare. I sneak a glance at Mustang. She notices and raises an eyebrow at me, wondering when we shall begin.

"All our Politicos have been *received*," Pliny says slowly. Today, Pliny wears a very serious coat of black lipstick. "As you know, my Politicos and I conferred after we fled from Luna. And we developed a rather advanced theoretical breakdown of potential alliance shifts—"

"With computers?" Kavax asks with a booming laugh.

"With computers," Pliny continues, irritated. "Simulations were performed by my Green analysts. Of the Galilean Moons—Io, Calisto, Ganymede, and Europa—none will cast their lot with us. Neither in simulation nor actuality."

"Hardly surprising," a hawkish Praetor mutters. "We had the same results from the moons of Saturn."

Pliny continues. "Naturally, they fear the repercussions of choosing the wrong side. The Saturn Governors are a lost cause for now. They see Rhea's corpse in their sky every day. In the Galilean sector, the presence of Lorn au Arcos on Europa is a problem. His . . . isolationist political leanings have proven infectious to the ArchGovernors of Jupiter's moons, particularly since his private army is twice again as large as any of the ArchGovernors'."

"Isolation? More like retirement." Augustus sighs. "Perhaps he has the right of it."

"You would go mad, Father," Mustang says from the end of the table. "No scheming, no plots or stratagems. Just family and time to spend with Adrius and me."

His smile is tight, unreadable. "How well my daughter knows me."

"What worries *me* most," Pliny says, "is that the Galileans, in their own words, doubt the validity of our cause."

"That's because we don't have a cause," I moan, remembering my role. "At least not so far as anyone else cares."

"Explain," the ArchGovernor demands.

"He's getting to it, Father," Mustang says. "Darrow plays for drama."

I make a show of looking around the room. "It's safe to say that the gentle Golds in this room understand human nature. Yes? Even if we did not, what motivates us? A cause? *No*. None of us have a cause. Freedom? Liberty? Justice?" I roll my eyes. "Hardly. What do we care that the Sovereign acts like an Empress? What do we care about the Compact and the liberties it extends Golds? Nothing.

"This is about power. It is always about power. We fight her because we attached ourselves to a star, the ArchGovernor. But the star falls, fades . . ."

Kavax half rises from his seat. "Don't insult your lord as if—"

"As if he's what? A fool? He's not, so come off it. The Bellona take Mars. They will get the contracts, the government positions. We will be pushed to the fringe, dead or irrelevant." My voice plays with the audience. "Power is the only thing of worth in this world. Consider Tactus au Rath—a loyal ally of mine for three years. But as soon as my star began to fall, he stole from me and departed out the back door. A thief in the night.

"How many empty seats are here that were filled before Luna? So many men and women who would have bled for Augustus. So many men and women who would have given their eyes for him when he sat on his dais in Agea. Now . . ."

I dust off my hands.

"We are losing. To run is to wither and die. If we want to rise again, draw the Galileans to our cause, marshal the Governors of Saturn to our banners, then we show them we are not powerless. Show them we drip with power. We are arbiters of life and death. We, not the Bellona, are the House of Mars."

Pliny begins to say something, but Augustus motions him to be quiet.

"What would you propose?"

"The Galilean families are soft for Luna for one reason. Commerce. Ganymede has her shipyards. Calisto is little more than a factory of Grays and Obsidians for the Society's armies. Europa is an oceanworld of banking and deep-sea mining and vacation homes. Io is the breadbasket to any world along Jupiter's orbital path. They depend too much on commerce with the Core to run to our side. And even the basest child knows what happened when the Ash Lord descended upon Rhea." The Praetors nod along. "So we must impress them. We must terrify them so that they know our power can touch them at any time and they cannot risk alienating us."

"How?" Augustus asks. They're all on the hook now.

I set my razor on the table so they know what business I propose. "We take their ships. We take their children. We take them as allies as the Spartans took their wives. By force, in the night."

Silence forms around me. Then comes the uproar. Pliny lets his Praetors slash at the idea. His energy he spends whispering in Augustus's ear. I glance at Mustang, but she watches the others, gauging them.

"Boasts." The ArchGovernor quiets the room and readdresses me. "I've not heard a plan."

"One plan. Two parts."

I touch a datapad, and the holo the Jackal's agents gave me expands over the table to show Ganymede. The moon shines bright with blues and greens from its oceans and forests, brilliant against the marbled white and orange of Jupiter's vaporous surface. Gray shipyards ring the moon. I zoom in so that they stretch across and above the table. I list the ships registered, highlighting one in particular. "Ganymede has a moonBreaker."

Whistles from around the table. "A moonBreaker?" someone whispers.

"Is this information reliable?" Augustus asks.

I nod. "Very." My fingers twitch, rotating the image of the docks. In the shadow of an orbital dock floats a ship like my *Pax,* but newer, larger. Black as night, and eight kilometers in length. "The Sovereign herself commissioned it as a present for her grandson."

Kavax nearly drools at the sight of the monster of a ship. "What a loving woman."

"Assuming this is not contrived." Pliny inspects the holo. "How did you come upon the information?"

"Little birds whisper into my ears too."

"Don't be coy. It is important."

"My sources are mine, just as yours are your own, Pliny."

"So you want to steal the moonBreaker from Ganymede?" Pliny asks. "That's an act of war."

I chuckle. "No. You misunderstand. I want to steal all of the ships."

26

||||||||||||||||||||||||

PUPPET MASTER

Pliny glances worriedly at Augustus. "Do this, and this war does not end till one side is ash."

"It's already that way . . . ," Kavax begins.

"This is different," Pliny crows. "It expands the scope."

"My father is right," Daxo declares. "We are already in open rebellion."

Pliny slaps his hand down. "This is *different*. This declares war on the Society, not the Bellona, not the Sovereign as a singular person. Ganymede has not harmed us. This will fracture everything."

Augustus sits quietly, his cold eyes staring at the moonBreaker on the holo. Without looking at me, he asks, "You said there were two parts to this plan. What is the second?"

I change the holo. The Academy replaces the shipyards. Ships ring its dull gray surface. Asteroids rotate in the backdrop.

"Those ships are ancient," a balding Praetor named Licenus says before I can begin. "Useless in a fight. Is your plan to steal them too?"

"No, Praetor Licenus. My plan is to steal the students." I add another visual. Mars's Institute joins the Academy. Then another Institute, Venus's. Then Earth's two Institutes. Then the Galilean Institutes and Saturn's. Then more till nearly a dozen images float in the air. "I want to steal all of the students. Not to fight. But to ransom."

"Goryhell." Mustang bursts out laughing. "Are you insane, Darrow?"

Augustus frowns. "Virginia, control yourself."

"I am under control, Father. Your attack dog isn't."

"You forget your place."

"And you forget how Claudius looked, dead on the ground. Leto too. Do you want that for the rest of us?" She regrets the words as soon as they leave her lips.

"Shut your mouth, girl." Augustus shudders with wrath. His bony fingers clutch the edge of the table till it creaks. "You've been unhinged since you let that Bellona boy between your legs. Walking in here like a Pixie pomp. Eating that apple like a child. Stop being a sideshow whore and live up to your name."

"Like your remaining son?" she asks.

He takes a long, calming breath. "You will be quiet or you will leave."

Mustang grinds her teeth together, but stays uncharacteristically silent. Pliny's lips curl in a rather pleased smile.

"Don't blame her, my goodmen, if she's already tired of war," Pliny says, softly placing a knife in a wounded enemy. "After so many nocturnal summits spent engaging in horizontal diplomacy with the Bellona, her stamina isn't what it used to be."

Kavax lunges at Pliny. Daxo pulls him back just in time. But it's Mustang who is first to speak over the uproar.

"I can defend my own honor, my goodman. But from Pliny, such insults are to be expected After all, I would be bitter too if my wife bent over backward to make sure so many of your young mercenaries learned how to properly sheathe their swords."

Pliny stares angrily at her as she rises, continuing, "I left Mars to pursue knowledge in the Sovereign's court. I did not abandon my family, as so many of you have suggested. And I'm not sorry I left and missed conversations such as this. For you goodmen seem good only at one thing, and that is bickering. Yet you quickly come to agreement upon me as an item of ridicule. Curious. Is it because you see me as a threat to your power? Or is it simply because I'm a woman?" She peers at the few scattered women around the table. "If that is the case, you forget yourselves. This Society was founded by men and *women* based on merit.

"The dear Politico Pliny is right, however: I would have avoided this war. In fact, I tried. Why else do you think I allowed Cassius au Bellona to court me? But war is here. And I will protect my family again from all threats, those from without and from within."

Augustus lets slip the smallest, barest of smiles, a twin to the first. His love is the most conditional I've ever seen. How quickly he can call his daughter a whore, then smile as she reclaims what power she lost in the room. Suddenly, she matters.

"Then what do you think of my plan?" I ask.

"I think it is dangerous. It spreads the war without ensuring our benefit. It is immoral and sets dangerous precedent. But then again, war is inherently immoral. So we must simply decide how far we want to go."

"You know Octavia better than I," I say. "How far will she go?"

Mustang is quiet for a moment. "If we have a victory and sue for peace either from a position of strength or weakness, she will accept the overture. . . ."

"You see!" Pliny beams.

Mustang isn't finished. "She will suggest a neutral location. And on that day when we go to make peace, she will do everything in her power to kill all of us."

Pliny looks back and forth between us, realizing how easily he's been played.

"So there is no going back? Win or die?" I ask flatly.

"Indeed, Darrow," she says with a smile. "Win or die."

"It seems you've been outmaneuvered, Pliny. We move forward with Darrow's plan." Augustus stands. "Tomorrow, Praetor Licenus will take command of this vessel and its fleet and lead the Sovereign's fleet on a chase, while I take a small strike group of corvettes and frigates to the Gas Giants. With them, *I* will raid the shipyards of Ganymede."

"I will go with you, my liege!" Kavax booms. His fox jumps off his lap at the noise to tremble under the table.

"No."

Kavax's face falls. "No? But, Nero . . . the defenses there—battle stations, destroyers, torchShips—they will shred any force of corvettes you bring." His large hands gesture imploringly. "Let us do this for you."

"You forget who I am, my friend."

"Apologies, I did not mean . . ."

Augustus waves the apology away and turns to Mustang. "Daughter, you will take what elements of the fleet you need to execute the second portion of Darrow's plan."

Watching Pliny now is like watching a child try to hold on to a handful of sand. He doesn't understand the course things have taken. But he's not fool enough to make his play now. He will wait in the grass like the snake he is.

The ArchGovernor turns to me. "Darrow, what did you say to me before you shed Cassius's blood?"

"I said that you should be King of Mars."

"My friends." Augustus sets his thin hands down on the table, fingers rigid. "Darrow has demonstrated powers none of you possess. He predicts what I want. I want to be king. Make me so. Dismissed."

The room empties. I wait with Augustus. He wants a private word.

Mustang brushes close to me as she passes, winking playfully.

"Nice speech," I mutter.

"Nice plan."

She squeezes my hand and then she is gone.

"In league again," Augustus observes. He gestures me to close the door. I sit near him. The hard lines of his face deepen as he stares into my eyes. From a distance, the lines are invisible. But this close, they are the things that make his face. Loss gives a man lines like this, reminding me, This is the man you do not anger. The man you do not owe.

"We can do away with righteous indignation before it finds a place on your tongue." He steeples his fingers, examining the manicured cuticles. "The question is simple, and you will answer it: Are you a demokrat?"

I had not expected this. I try not to look around nervously.

"No, my liege. I am no demokrat."

"Not a Reformer? Not someone who wants to alter our Compact to create a more fair, more decent society?"

"Man is organized properly now," I say, pausing, "except for a few notable exceptions."

"Pliny?"

"Pliny."

"You each have your gifts. And you would do well not to question my judgment in keeping him close."

"Yes, my liege. But I am no more a demokrat than you are a Lune."

He does not smile as I intended. Instead, he presses a button and the speech I used to win over the *Pax* comes on the speakers. An HC holo shows the faces of different Colors.

"Watch their expressions." He watches mine as he cycles through a series of video clips from different parts of the ship as the crew listens to the speech I gave before they rose against their Gold commanders. "Do you see that? That right there. The spark? Do you?"

"I see it."

"That is hope." The man who killed my wife waits for my face to give me away. Good luck with that. "Hope."

"Are you saying I made a mistake?" I ask.

He recalls old words. "Hateful to me as the gates of Hades is that man who hides one thing in his heart and speaks another."

"My heart has always been laid bare."

"So you say." His lips part slightly, hissing the words. "But as terrorists spread lies over the net, as bombings rack our cities, as the lowColors rumble with displeasure, as we begin a war despite the termites in our foundation, you say *this*."

"Any chaos is—"

"Shut your mouth. Do you know what would happen if the other Governors thought us Reformers? If the other houses looked at mine as a bastion of equality and demokracy?" He points to a glass. "Our potential allies." He brushes the glass off the table, letting it shatter.

Points to another. "Our lives." It falls and shatters too. "It is bad enough my daughter had the ear of the Reformer bloc on Luna. You cannot *seem* political. Stay a warrior. Stay simple. Do you understand?"

What if the lowColors rally to us? I want to ask, but he would have his Obsidians kill me where I stand.

"I understand."

"Good." Augustus looks at his hands, twisting the ring there. Hesitancy creeps over him. "Can I trust you?"

"In what way?"

A scornful laugh bursts from his mouth. "Most would say yes without thinking."

"Most men are liars."

"Can I trust you with power autonomous from my own?" He scratches his jaw idly. "That is when many leave their lords. It is when hunger fills their eyes. The Romans learned this time and again. It is why they did not let generals cross the Rubicon with their armies without the permission of the Senate. Men with armies soon begin to realize how strong they are. And they always know that their particular strength is not forever. It must be used with haste, before their army leaves them. But hasty decisions can ruin empires. My son, for instance, must never be allowed such power."

"He has his businesses."

"That is a slow power. Cleverly done on his part, if unfit for my name. Slow power can grind away any stagnant enemy. But fast power, one that can travel where you go, do what you wish it to as effectively as a hammer hitting a nail, that is the power that lops off heads and steals crowns. Can I trust you with it?"

"You must. I am the only man who can go to Lorn."

Surprise flashes in his eyes; he is unused to having his machinations guessed. He buries the surprise quickly, unwilling to give credit where credit is due. "You knew already."

"You wish me to approach Lorn, ask for his help, because he taught me the razor."

"And because he loves you."

I blink dumbly. "I'm not sure that's the word."

"He had four sons. Three died in front of him. The last Lysander's father, in an accident, as you know. I believe you remind him of them, though you're in fact more capable and less moral, which is to your advantage. But as much as he loves you, Lorn hates me."

"He hates Octavia more, my liege."

"Still. It won't be easy to convince him to join us."

"Then I won't give him a choice."

27

IIIIIIIIIIIIIIIIIIIIIIIII

JELLY BEANS

The Telemanuses wait for me in the hall. Kavax takes me into a hug that cracks my back. Daxo nods his head. I'm left feeling dazed between the two of them. It is the first time I've spoken to either without violence afoot. Truth be told, I've avoided them for shame of what I let happen to Pax.

"My boy only ever lost to you," Kavax says. "Little Pax. If he was to fall to a knee, it is no shame to have fallen in friendship. I only wish he could have taken Olympus with you. That would have been a sight."

"I would have liked to have seen him take Proctor Jupiter's armor."

Daxo grins. "I was Jupiter House myself. Primus till I lost to Karnus au Bellona."

"Then I believe we have a mutual enemy."

"Besides the scheming little bastard that killed my baby brother?" Daxo asks softly. "We have many shared enemies, Andromedus."

Kavax scoops up his fox. It licks his neck and peers fiercely at me before it nuzzles into his thick red beard. It has a white chest, black legs, and dark russet fur covering the rest of its body. Thicker and hardier than a normal fox, and weighing nearly thirty-five kilograms, it really is more wolflike in size.

"Foxes are beautiful creatures," Kavax says, stroking the beast.

Daxo nods. "Mischievous. Omnivorous. Resistant to poaching. Monogamous. Very special, and able to expand their hunting grounds even in the territory of wolves." He looks up at me darkly. "But because of a damn quirk of nature, foxes fare poorly against jackals. We asked Augustus to banish Adrius. For a time, he was, yet now he returns to the fleet."

"A crime," I say.

They nod.

Daxo sets a hand on my shoulder. "The girls—my sisters and mother, I mean—wanted you to know that we do not hold you accountable for Pax's death. We loved that little boy, and we know you only ever mean him honors. We know you named your ship for him. And will not forget it. Once friends, always friends. That is our family's way."

Kavax nods to every word his remaining son says. He tosses his fox a handful of jelly beans.

"So if you need us," Daxo suggests, nodding to the warroom, "you need merely ask, and the House Telemanus will lend itself to your cause."

"You mean that?" I ask.

"It would have made my Pax happy," older Kavax rumbles.

I clasp his hand and try my luck. "You'll forgive me my manners, but I need you now."

Great eyebrows arch as the two behemoths share a look of surprise. "Investigate, Sophocles! Investigate," Kavax says excitedly. The large fox at his legs slips forward warily to investigate me, sniffing my knees, peering at my shoes and hands. It weaves through my legs in its search. Then it pounces on me, putting forepaws on my hips and digging its snout into my pocket. Sophocles resurfaces with two jelly beans, chewing contentedly.

"Magic!" Kavax booms, clapping me on the shoulder. "Sophocles has discovered a propitious sign of approval, by magic! What a good omen! Daxo, my son. Summon your sisters and mother. The Reaper calls. House Telemanus must answer!"

"The girls were visiting Neptune, Father. They'll be a few months."

"Well, then *we* must answer."

"Couldn't agree with you more, Father."

"I'll have instructions within the hour," I say.

"Great anticipation!" Kavax thumps away. "We await them with great anticipation." He roars compliments at passing Oranges, terrifying them with his wide-grinning approval. Daxo and I watch on.

"Does he really believe in magic?" I ask.

"He says gnomes steal ear wax from him at night. Mother thinks he's been hit too many times on the head." Daxo backs away, following his father. But he can't hide his clever smile as he pops a jelly bean into his mouth, and I see where the ones in my pocket came from. "I say he just lives in a more entertaining world than we do. Call on us soon, Reaper. Father is eager."

After meeting over holo with the Jackal to bring him up to speed on my plan and adjusting it according to a few of his recommendations, I have Orion set a course for Europa. It will take two weeks. Roque joins me on the bridge, watching the skeleton crew of Blues. He doesn't speak. Yet it's the first time he's sought me out since we left Luna. It's a weight hanging over my head.

"I'm sorr—" I begin.

"I don't want to talk about Quinn," he says quietly. "I know you wanted this war. Engineered it instead of trusting me to buy your contract and protect you. What I don't know is why you drugged me."

"I wanted to protect you. Because I knew I would need you after the gala, and I couldn't risk your safety."

"What about what I need?" he asks. "You don't have the right to make choices for me because you're afraid it might interrupt your plans. Friends don't do that."

"You're right. It was wrong of me." I nod slowly, meaning it.

"Wrong to stick a needle in my neck?"

246 | PIERCE BROWN

"Beyond wrong. But know the intent was good, even if the idea and execution were as stupid as they come. If I have to get on my knees . . ."

"There's an image." I know he's joking, but his face does not laugh or smile as he turns and walks away.

28

|||||||||||||||||||||||||||

THE STORMSONS

"You come to me at the head of a storm," my friend says, gray beard blowing sideways in the wind as he looks at the waves far beneath. "Did you know there are boys here on this ocean world who take skiffs into gales worse than this? Lads from the dregs of the Grays, Reds, even Browns. Their bravery is a mad, crazed sort." He points out from the balcony with a heavy finger to the roiling black water, where waves crest ten meters high. "They call them stormsons."

The gravity here is maddening. Everything floats. At 0.136 of Earth's gravity, every step I take must be measured, controlled, else I'll burst upward fifteen feet and have to wait to flutter back down. A fight here would be like a ballet underwater. I wear gravBoots just to move comfortably.

The old man watches the ocean world move around his island. He is as he always told me to be—a stone amid the waves; wet, yet unimpressed by all that swirls about him. Saltwater spray drips from his beard. Burnished gold eyes blink against the storm's bitter wind.

"When you are in the salt, you feel like every gale is the world ender. Every wave the greatest that has been. These boys ride the gales in rapture at their own glory. But every now and then, a true storm rises. It shatters their masts and rips the hair from their heads. They do not last long till the sea swallows them whole. But their mothers have wept their deaths long before, as I wept for yours the first day we met."

He stares at me intensely, mouth pinched behind his thick beard.

"I never told you, but I was not raised in a palace or in a city like many of the Peerless you know. My father thought there to be two evils in the world. Technology and culture. He was a hard man. A killer, like the rest of them. But his hardness was found not in what he could do, but in what he wouldn't do, in his restraint. In the pleasures he denied himself, and his sons. He lived to a hundred and sixty-three without the help of cell rejuvenation. Somehow he lived through eight Iron Rains. But still he never valued life, because he took it too often. He was not a man to be happy."

I watch the former Rage Knight, Lorn au Arcos, lean over the balcony of his castle. It is a limestone fortress set amid a sea ninety kilometers deep. Modern lines shape the place. It is not medieval, but a meld of past and present—glass and steel making hard angles with the stone island—so like the man I respect above all other Golds of his generation.

Like him, this castle is a harsh place when the storms come. But when the storms fade, sunshine will bathe this place, shining through her glass walls, glinting off her steel supports. Children will run its ten-kilometer length, through its gardens, along its walls, down to the harbor. Wind will tickle their hair, and all that Lorn will hear from his library is the crying of gulls, the crash of the sea, and the laughter of his grandchildren and their mothers, whom he guards in place of his dead sons. The only one missing is little Lysander.

If all Golds were like him, Reds would still toil beneath the Earth, but he would have them know their purpose. It doesn't make him good, but it makes him true.

He's thick and broad and shorter than I. He lets his empty whiskey tumbler go and permits the wind to swoop it sideways. It falls and the sea swallows it whole. "They say you can hear the dead stormsons whooping in the wind," he mutters. "I say it's the crying of their mothers."

"Storms of court have a way of drawing people back in," I say.

He laughs a derisive laugh, one that scorns the idea that I would know anything about the storms of court, anything about the winds that blow.

I came to him in secret, flying with a single ship, my five-kilometer destroyer *Pax*. I told my master he would not help us. But I held on to hope he would *want* to help me. Yet now that I see Lorn au Arcos again in the knotted flesh, I'm reminded of the nature of the man, and I worry. He knows my captains and lieutenants are listening through the com unit in my ear. I paid him respects and showed it to him so that he would not assume our conversation to be a private one.

"After more than a century of living, my body does not yet betray me." One would think him to be in his midsixties, at first glance. Only his scars truly age him. The one on his neck, like a smile, was given to him four decades ago by a Stained in the Moon Kings' Rebellion, when the Governors of Jupiter's moons thought to make their own kingdoms after Octavia deposed her father as Sovereign. The one that claims part of his nose came from the Ash Lord, when they dueled as youths. "You've heard the expression 'The duty of the son is the glory of the father'?"

"I have said it myself."

He grunts. "I have lived it. I have lost many for my own glory. I have set my ship into the storm on purpose. Each time with women and children in tow." He lets the waves speak for a moment. They crash on the rocks and then pull backward, slurping as they go, drawing things to the sea they call Discordia.

"It is not right to live so long, I think. My great-granddaughter was born last night. I still have the smell of blood on my fingers." He holds them out—like tree roots, crooked and calloused from the holding of weapons. They tremble slightly. "These took her from the darkness to the light, from warmth to the cold, and cut the cord themselves. It would be a fine world if that was the last flesh they cut."

He relaxes his hands and sets them on the cold stone. I wonder what Mustang would say to this man. Seeing them face-to-face would be like watching fire trying to catch on stone. She balked at my plan in public, but then again, that was all our design. Plans within plans within plans.

"To think about what hands feel," Lorn mutters. "These have felt the lifeblood of my sons as their hearts pumped it out of their bodies. They've felt the cold of a razor's hilt as they stole the dreams of youth. They've worn the love of a girl and a woman and then felt those heartbeats fade to silence. All for my glory. All because I chose to ride the sea. All because I do not die easily as most." He frowns. "Hands, I think, were not meant to feel so much."

"Mine have felt more than I'd wish," I say. I feel the *snap* go through them that I felt at Eo's hanging. The texture of her hair. I remember the warmth of Pax's blood. The chill of Lea's pale face in the cold morning after Antonia butchered her. The grainy red smear of haemanthus blossoms. Mustang's bare hip as we lay by the fire.

"You are young still. When you're white-haired, you'll have felt even more."

"Some men don't grow old." No Helldiver does.

"No. Some don't." He pokes Augustus's lion's badge on my dark uniform. "And lions do not live so long as griffins. We can fly away from things, you see." He brandishes his own family ring and flaps his arms foolishly, drawing a smile from me. He wears it along with his House Mars ring. "You were a pegasus once, were you not?"

"It was the symbol . . . *is* the symbol of Andromedus." My false Gold family. But the symbol reminds me of Eo. She pointed out the Andromeda Galaxy to me before she died. It means so much and so little all at once.

"There's honor in staying what you were," he says.

"Sometimes we have to change. Not all of us are born rich as you."

"Let us go find Icarus in the forest." He mentioned him often on Mars, but I've never seen Lorn's favorite pet. "Carolina conspired with Vincent to make him a new toy. I think you'll appreciate it."

"Where are your children? I'd love to see them again."

"East wing till you leave."

"I'm that dangerous?"

He does not answer.

I follow my friend in off the balcony just as one of Europa's clouds spits blue lightning across the dark sky. Her oceans buck and heave as great swells of water slither and seep along the white walls, as if the world of oceans conspired to swallow the man-made island. Despite all this, the castle and the raging storm still seem so small when I see how Jupiter consumes the night sky behind the clouds—a textured gas giant staring down at us like the head of some great marble god.

As we walk through the stone villa, Lorn happily greets every servant we pass. He sees people, not Colors. Most have been with him for years. I should have studied with him. But then I would have ended up here, a better man, but unable to change anything so many months' journey from the Core.

Children's toys litter the halls. His family is here—dozens of loved ones he brought together after he left public life. Most live scattered in the southern archipelagoes in the warmer waters near the equator. Hurricanes forced them north this month to take refuge with Grandfather Lorn. Seems the storm followed them.

He pushes open a grand glass gate, leading me into the center of his citadel. Here, he keeps himself a forest, one several acres large and open to the air. The walls stretch around the forest, closing it off from the vicious waves. Lorn's standards whip high in the air—a roaring purple griffin on a field of snow white. Rain falls on the trees, hissing into their needles until he activates a pulseBubble. Then the rain sizzles on its roof and folds up in thick clouds of vapor. He walks ahead of me, and I linger, taking small black spikes no longer than my fingernails from a hidden pouch in my sleeve. I scatter them through the moss just outside the door.

"You came to me in a stolen vessel of war asking for my ships and my men. Why?" Lorn asks, looking back curiously. I speed up my gait and drop a few more spikes when he turns again. I'm waiting for him to mention Lysander.

"Because half of Mars is still held by forces loyal to the Bellona and the Sovereign. To free Mars from them, we need your ships and your men. Once we have them, the Moon Lords and the ArchGovernors of the Rim will come to our aid against the Core."

"So you need me to aid you in your treason?"

"Is it treason for a dog to bite its master's hand when the master tries to kill it?" I ask.

"Terrible metaphor." He stops, peers around the forest, searching. "Ah." We set off again.

"The point is: I need your help."

He spits on the mossy ground and motions me to follow him up a hillside. My boots crack a water-sodden log. "Why should I care about you?"

"Because you trained me."

"I also trained Aja au Grimmus."

"For some reason, I think you like me more than her."

"And why's that?"

"I have a sense of humor."

He laughs. "Aja can be funny."

"Surely you're joking."

"You meet a man, you know him. You meet a woman, she knows you." He laughs to himself about some memory. "Might be easier thinking her some terror in the night. But she's flesh and blood. She has friends. She has family. And she thinks you a threat to them."

"Yet she's the one who killed my friend."

"Yes. I heard. You had the child. Clever tactic." He squints back at the razor curled around my arm. "Does everyone wear their razor like a fool now?"

"It's the fashion."

"It's meant to be looped on the hip. You'll cut your arm off by accident." He sighs. "Your generation . . . So arrogant. Changing things for no reason. I wonder, arrogant boy, did you think that if you rode in here with your stolen ship that I, a man of a century, would follow you to battle? That I would put in danger all my servants, all my family, all I love, for you? Someone who rejected me when I asked him to join my house?"

I ignore his bitterness. "You left the Society for a reason, Lorn. Can you remember why?"

"To avoid loud fools."

"I think you left because you thought the Society sick. Because it was not worth sacrificing for anymore."

"Stop barking at me, puppy."

"So I'm right."

"No. You're not right." He wheels angrily. "I left the Society not because it is sick, but because it is dead. The Society was created to instill order. Men were made to sacrifice so that humanity endured. They were given Colors, lives limited and ordered so that we could destroy the timeless cycle of our race—prosperity to greed to war. Gold was meant to shepherd the other Colors, not devour them. Now we are trapped again in that cycle, the very thing we endeavored to avoid. So the Society? The beautiful sum of all human enterprise? It's been dead and rotting for hundreds of years, and those who fight over it are but vultures and maggots."

"So it wasn't Brutus's death." I speak of his youngest son who was married to Octavia au Lune's deceased daughter.

"That was an accident."

"A convenient accident," I say. "There are rumors that Octavia's daughter was organizing a coup against her mother."

"I don't entertain rumors," he says darkly.

"If you help me, I can give you your grandson back."

"Lysander has been raised so long ago with poison in his ear that now it's in his blood. He is not my kin."

"You're not that cold. Lorn, I've met the boy. He's more like you than her. He isn't wicked. Fight for him."

Lorn stares quietly at the rain falling against the pulseShield.

"You fight a tyrant to replace her with a tyrant," he says wearily. "This is the same game I have seen a hundred times. Do you even know who you serve?"

"I have a feeling you're about to tell me."

"I'll not stop being your teacher just because you've stopped listening. Sit. I don't want Icarus to be bothered by this damn story." He sits on a large stone and instructs me to take a place opposite him. I do. He hunches forward and plays with the thick House Mars ring on his finger.

"House Augustus was always strong, I'm sure you know that. Even when Mars was little more than a mine for helium-3. They bribed or killed their way into owning most of the governmental contracts. And as their pockets swelled, so did their influence. They became, along with several other families—including the Bellona and my own—the lords of Mars. There was one family of greater power, however, named Cylus. They controlled the ArchGovernorship and were favored by the Senate and the sitting Sovereign.

"When your master, then simply called Nero, was seven, his father found himself in dispute with Julius au Bellona, Cassius's grandfather. Nero's father attempted to have the Browns who served the Bellona poison the entire family at supper. The plan failed. A housewar began.

"Nero's father summoned his bannermen and led them against the Bellona and the ArchGovernor Cylus, who had declared his forces for Julius au Bellona. The sitting Sovereign did not intervene, and instead allowed the two families to go to war. Eventually, Nero's father found himself besieged in Agea when his fleet was destroyed and captured around Phobos.

"Cylus put House Augustus to death, sparing only young Nero from punishment. He was allowed to live so that an aged family that had partaken in the Conquering did not disappear from history. It is said that ArchGovernor Cylus even gave young Nero grapes to quench his thirst because there was no water as the city burned around them. After that, he raised him in his own court.

"Twenty years later, Nero, who had always been considered an honorable and honest man, much unlike his wicked father, asked for Iona au Bellona's hand in marriage. She was the youngest and favorite daughter of old Julius."

He stares up at water droplets falling from the needles of overhanging evergreens. "I knew her well. My sons were her playmates. I knew Nero too. I liked him, even if he was a little cold as a child.

"With hopes of mending the lingering wounds of past generations and making Mars strong and unified, ArchGovernor Cylus agreed. Bellona married Augustus.

"It was a beautiful wedding. I attended, representing the Sovereign as the Rage Knight. And I had a wonderful time of it. I'd never seen Iona so happy as she was in that stern young man's arms. But that night, when the Bellona family returned to their estate with the rest of their family, a package arrived. Inside, old Julius found his daughter's head. Grapes stuffed in Iona's mouth along with two wedding rings.

"He summoned his daughters and sons, including Cassius's father, and flew to the Citadel to ask for justice from ArchGovernor Cylus, as he had twenty years prior when the Augustuses first rose up.

"But instead of his old friend, he found young Nero on the Arch-Governor's throne, backed by Praetorians and two Olympic Knights. I was among them, having been told that Cylus was a threat to the Society by my Sovereign. I did as I was commanded. The House of Cylus was wiped out and stricken from record.

"I found out later, Nero contrived an agreement with the daughter of the sitting Sovereign. You know her as Octavia au Lune. Younger then, she convinced her father to give Nero the throne of Mars and his revenge; in return, she earned Nero's support when she led the faction that overthrew and killed her father five years later. That is the man you started a war for."

"I didn't know this," I say quietly.

"History is written by the victors."

Lorn looks at me and the lines on his face seem to deepen. "I don't want to go to war, Darrow. In my time, I have seen a moon burn, because one man would not bow. I have led a million warriors shot from warships to invade a planet. You cannot begin to understand the horror of it. You think only of how beautiful it will be. But they are men. They are women. They have families. And they die by the thousands. And you will be helpless to protect even the best of your friends.

"Ah!" He points uphill. "There's Icarus."

Rain drips from the pines as we push through the lower tree boughs to find Icarus, Lorn's pet griffin, sleeping in a great bed of moss on a high promontory inside the small forest. Icarus's paws curl into his body. His wings curve around him as he sleeps—iridescent and glittering with droplets of water. His great eagle's head is nearly larger than I, one of his eyes half the size of my skull. The Carvers made him well.

"He looks peaceful when he sleeps," Lorn says.

"He's bigger than any I've seen," I say, unable to conceal the awe in my voice.

"You've not been to the pole of Mars or Earth, then."

"No. Where did you buy him?"

"Martian Carvers made him for my family. Damn that fashionable Zanzibar twit. Icarus is of the same genus as the beasts in the high aeries in Mars's north pole. The ones they use to terrify Obsidians into believing magic is real." He strokes the sleeping giant. "Are you still in love with the ArchGovernor's daughter?" He glances back at me hopefully. "Is that why you do this? I heard about her and the Bellona."

"It isn't about what happened between her and Cassius."

"No?" He sighs. "I could have understood that, at least. You were sloppy in that, you should know. The Irenicus Folly would have done him in three moves."

"I wasn't sloppy. I was making a show."

"Sloppy. Violets are showmen. Did I train you to be a showman?"

I move past him to pet Icarus. "So you do care about me."

He does not answer me for a spell, and it's then that I know the moment I've dreaded most is nearly upon us. "In another life, you would have been one of my sons, Darrow. I would have found you earlier, before whatever happened that filled you with this rage. I would not have raised you to be a great man. There is no peace for great men. I would have had you be a decent one. I would have given you the quiet strength to grow old with the woman you love. Now all I can give you is a chance. *Icarus,*" he booms.

His griffin stirs by his side, its amber eye showing me my reflection. The ground shudders as the creature moves, uprooting a tree as easily as I'd pull a hair.

I move back from the beast, unsure of Lorn's intentions.

"What is going on?" I ask Lorn.

"Look to your ship." He points upward in the night. Through a break in the clouds, we can see my long ship glittering in orbit. She's no longer alone. Ten torchShips come for her now, slipping around the cover of Europa's equator to capture the *Pax.*

"A Praetorian death squad waits for you inside my home, Darrow. Aja au Grimmus leads them. They will take you, chain you, and bring you before the Sovereign."

"You betrayed me?" I ask.

"No. They arrived days ago. They threatened. What could I do? Kellan au Bellona leads their fleet. It will destroy or capture your ship. I can't stop that. But I do not want you to die. So Icarus will take you to an island where I have hidden a ship for you. Use it to escape."

"Will they hurt your family if I escape?"

"They may try," he growls. "That is the consequence of your decision and mine."

He stands with his back to the sea.

"I want to fade in peace. So please, leave and never return, Darrow."

He gestures to Icarus and I see a thin saddle upon the beast—the new toy of which he spoke. But I do not need to flee. I shake my head for what is about to happen.

"I'm sorry, my friend. But I cannot allow that."

"Allow?" he asks, turning.

"You will join us in this war." My razor uncoils. "Whether you like it or not." I speak into my com, telling the Howlers to prepare to rise and the Titans to bring the ships around.

The blood drains from his face and he looks at the beast emblazoned upon my tunic. "A lion after all."

29

||||||||||||||||||||||||

OLD MAN'S WRATH

I prepared the trap before I even left the fleet. All secrets find themselves whispered into Pliny's ears and he would wish for nothing more than my timely demise, particularly after I provoked him in the ArchGovernor's meeting. So he did his work. He schemed and plotted and found himself an ally against the big bad Darrow au Andromedus in the Sovereign herself, a fact that I will be happy to share with Augustus as soon as possible.

The Sovereign's ships hid themselves among the ruins of a derelict space station that was once used as a base of terraforming operations. Kellan au Bellona was smart, but predictable. My larger secondary force—a detachment of Telemanus ships—which I hid behind another smaller moon's mass, will ambush the Bellona force in sixty seconds, slingshotting around the other side of the moon by using its gravity to gain velocity. With Roque in command, I'll have ten Bellona ships to add to my personal armada by day's end.

"You knew," Lorn accuses me quietly, his thick hand gripping my uniform at the neck and shaking me. "You knew." And he knows what this means for him. It is not simply my victory. It is his defeat. One way or another, he must ally himself. And I've made it easy for him to pick a side.

"'If you're a fox, play the hare.' Isn't what you taught me? But it will look like *you* knew I set a trap for her. That you slipped news of her trap to me." I touch his shoulder as he releases me. "I am sorry, friend. Truly. But you are part of this war."

His jaw works, but he says nothing.

"The Sovereign will send her Praetorians again to Europa once I have left," I say. "Only this time they'll come for you and yours. Their black-and-purple ships will shell you from orbit till your islands and your cities on the archipelagoes and mainland and the rising mountains in the south are made of glass and swallowed by the seas. The waters will weep over your shattered towers, and of your house, there will be nothing but crypts in the deep. Unless we win."

His eyes seek in me something to give him time. But instead he sees only what made him take me under his wing from the start—himself. Most men would give anything to see that, but here and now, he wishes to see anything else.

"I put my family at risk to help you escape. I took you in, taught you. And you betray me like the others. Like Aja."

"You look for pity? You let me come here, Lorn. You would have consigned my friends above to torture and death even as you gave me a path to escape. But my friends will not be prisoners."

I point upward to the fiery gashes in the night sky as my secondary force rockets around Europa.

"Hate me, but fight at my side," I tell Arcos. "Only then will your family survive." I put a hand out for my former teacher. He pulls out his razor.

"I should kill you."

"Can I come and shoot the geezer?" Sevro asks over the com.

"Hold," I tell him.

"You forget." Lorn pulls his own datapad from his pocket. "I could have my fleet destroy yours, boy."

"Not before mine takes the Sovereign's."

"But she would know then where House Arcos stands. She would know that you tricked me. That my house is not part of this."

"Then do it," I tell Lorn. "Launch your ships if you think my cause evil. Put me down if you think me a monster." I step forward, close to him. "But you know the heart that beats inside. Choose me. Or choose that darkness." I nod down the hill of the forest garden to where we entered the place. Twelve Obsidian Praetorians file through the same glass door we used. Huge men and women in black-and-purple armor, skull helms. Only one Stained—this one thinner than the others, like a winter asp standing on its tail. His armor is white and splashed with colors like blood.

They are less than fifty meters away. With them, shorter than the rest, but more glorious, is the Protean Knight in her golden gear. Her razor shimmers with the colors of a nebula, and her armor writhes like the waves that batter the white walls of Lorn's island. Aja peers up to the night sky, where she sees my ambush unfolding. She lets her helmet recoil into her armor.

"And then the traitors were two," she calls. "House Arcos has embraced treason as well. Lorn. You stand with the lions?"

"The House Arcos stands apart," Lorn calls back.

"Apart?" Quinn's killer frowns and tilts her head so I can see the dueling scars on the right of her neck. Her cat eyes scan the woods for signs of a trap. "There is no such thing."

"I was as deceived as you, Aja!" Lorn calls. "Darrow knew you were here. I don't know how. But I am not your enemy. I want only to be left alone."

"That was never a choice!" Aja calls. "You know this better than anyone. You are with us or you are against us, Lorn."

"Aja. No. I have no part in this! None!"

"The strong always have a part," I mutter.

"I will not have my hand forced." He cuts me with a wrathful stare. "I have no quarrel with either of you. I am a man of peace now."

"Then why is your blade out?" Aja smiles. "Do what you know. Come down and speak, teacher. We should not shout! Isn't that what you said when I used to raise my voice in anger?" She eyes the griffin that now growls beside us. It's larger than four horses. I wonder what those talons would do against their armor.

"Her ships are lost," I whisper to Lorn. "What would Octavia have her do?"

"Kill us. For spite."

I lower my voice. "Then you have no choice."

"So it would seem."

Aja watches me kneel to the ground and gather dirt in my hand. She has studied me. She knows what this must mean. And she must wonder what plan I have. Why I've come alone. If I really set an ambush in the sky, wouldn't I set one below? I'm about to shout something to her when another figure steps through the gate to join Aja. He's rangy. Darker skin than mine. A smirk on his bored, patrician face. Tactus. All in Praetorian armor. He slinks forward, a shadow of purple and black, eyeing the sky apprehensively before beaming me a lopsided smile.

"Speaking of traitors," I shout. "Hello, Tactus. Pretty armor."

"Reaper, my goodman!" Tactus bellows, and throws up the crux. "Where's Sevro?" He leans in to tell Aja something. Aja straightens and looks around again at the trees. Her men condense in defensive formation. Tactus warns them of my tricks. They know something is awry. Their aegis shields activate, glittering over arms.

Lorn closes his eyes and lifts his left hand into the air, feeling the whipping of the storm's wind. "Leave Aja to me. You'll have better luck against the Stained."

"No. They're all mine. *Sevro, rise.*"

The Howlers emerge from the sea beyond the castle. Water drips from them as they fly silently over the hundred-meter-high walls, armor glistening like black beetle shells. A golden lion has been painted on each breastplate. The gold winks as lightning flashes. They land silently around us.

"*My* stormsons," I say to Lorn. Twenty new recruits have come from the families of the Howlers and the Telemanus ranks. Sevro held tryouts. I hear it was a bloody bit of fun. Snakes, alcohol, and mushrooms were involved. That's all they let me know.

"Goblin! Why are you always hiding?" Tactus calls. His voice is all jest, but he looks to the sky anxiously again. "Least it's better than a horse's belly this time."

Sevro pulls out his skinning knife, the one he used to take scalps with Harpy years ago. It's a curved customer. He taps it on his groin and points to Tactus. His eyes flick to Aja.

"You killed a Howler, Aja," he says. "Wrong play."

As I expected, the appearance of the Howlers reassures Aja and Tactus. This makes sense to them: I had soldiers hidden. Now I do not. A battle to the death. Honor. Pride. One force against another. The Obsidian Praetorians begin to keen their terrible throat song. All those men want is the glorious end. To join their relatives in the laughing halls of Valhalla with their blades in hand. They step forward on Aja's command. The deadliest men and women in the Solar System, a Stained among them.

And I take a page from Evey's book.

Ensuring Aja is clear, I detonate the landmine spikes I dropped on the ground as Lorn and I strolled into this forest. Only Tactus is quick enough. He grabs Aja from behind and jerks her back, hard—so hard in the lowGrav that both of them tumble in through the door just as the first explosion rips the salt air.

The explosions are tiered. First comes a concussion that disables pulseShields and scatters the Praetorians into the air. Then comes a gravPit, which pulls them back toward the source of the explosion like a vacuum collecting flies; and then comes the third—pure kinetics—to destroy armor and bone and flesh, blowing the warriors outward, into the air, scattering their pieces in the low gravity like breath scatters the seeds of a dandelion. Limbs float gently down. Blood beads and spatters the ground. The explosion breaks the bubble roof overhead and rain again drifts down on the garden to extinguish the fires and thin the blood that leaks into the two dozen bomb craters. Only three Praetorians survive. They're in poor shape.

"*Do not let her escape.*" Roque's voice sears my ears. He watches my holofeed from the ships above.

My Howlers have not yet moved.

Lorn's furious with me, saying something about honor.

"What?" I sneer. "You think I fight fair?"

"Darrow . . . ," Sevro hisses as I wait. "Darrow . . ."

"Hold."

"She's getting away!" Roque's voice frightens me. It drips with spite I didn't know he had. *"Darrow!"*

I growl at him to pay attention to his part of the battle.

"Darrow . . . ," Sevro begs. "Long enough."

Lorn watches, perhaps beginning to understand.

I snap my fingers. "Hunt."

The Howlers surge forward like loosed wolves to finish what the bomb started. They dispatch the remaining Praetorians. Sevro shouts Tactus's name amid the howling as they tear into the castle searching for him and Aja.

"Darrow, what are you playing at?" Roque asks me over the com. I let the holo of his face appear in the corner of my helmet's HUD display. His jaw muscles flicker. *"If Quinn's killer escapes . . ."*

"Lock that up," I tell Roque as I see reports of one of our torch-Ships taking massive damage. He's distracted. "Men are dying up there. Focus on your own job." I shut off the link.

Harpy's image appears on my display. *"Seahorse is under."*

"Good. And Tactus?"

"No sign."

"Copy." I close the connection.

"Aja spooked into the sea. But no sign of Tactus," Sevro says to me several minutes later as the Howlers scour the inside of the castle, going room to room. "He's hiding. Unless he teleported." He spits at that bit of science fiction. "Ask the geezer where they are."

A dark worry slithers into my brain. I turn to Lorn. "What would Lune have them do if they could not kill you and me? If she thought someone expendable, what would she order them to do?"

He stands there for a moment in the rain. Then his face goes pale. "The children . . ." Arcos pushes past me, running through the bomb's carnage to the shattered glass door. "They're going to kill my grandchildren!" he shouts back.

"Where are the children?" I ask Sevro.

"What children? We found none."

Cursing, I chase Arcos.

"I hid them," he says over his shoulder to me as he sprints down the castle's hall. He's fast for an old man, but the gravity slows us till we start using our hands on the walls and ceiling, using gravBoots to take the long halls. We launch around corner after corner. And when he touches the head of a stone griffin and a steel wall falls away to reveal a hidden passage, I smell blood. Two corpses lie on the other side of the passage. One Gray, one Obsidian. I push past Arcos and fly ahead, pulling myself down a series of stairs via handholds in the ceiling till I find myself before two doors. I open one. Just a storeroom. I open another and let my razor slither into my hand.

"Tactus," I say slowly.

His back is to me. Three Obsidian bodies lie around him, their blood making a pool about his shoes. His razor coils in his hand, hardening as he stands with his head lowered in a room of children and women. Blood slithers down the mercurial blade.

When I came, Arcos hid the children from me here—some Gold, some Silver, some Pink and Brown. Tactus could kill half of them with a lazy swing of his razor before we reach them.

"Tactus, remember *your* brothers," I say to him, looking at the children.

"My brothers are shits." He laughs coarsely, voice sounding strange. "Said I should get out of your shadow. Mother calls me the Mighty Servant. Did you know that?"

Children sob in the corner. One buries her face in her mother's lap. The women are not armed. These are not warriors like Victra and Mustang. A Brown nursemaid covers a Gold child's eyes. I hear Arcos in the tunnel behind me.

"Lune's orders are wrong," I say to Tactus.

"She asked me if I could fill your place, *Reaper,*" Tactus says quietly. "Said she didn't think I could. Said I was so long in your shadow that she didn't know if I would ever be more than an echo of you. I told her I could do anything you could do."

"Tactus, she is evil."

"Is she?" He spits blood on the ground, still not facing me. "They say the same thing about you. They wonder who you think you are to do what you do. To challenge the men and women you challenge. They wonder what right you have."

"We all have a right to challenge. That's the point."

"The point. Was there a point?" he asks. "I was never told. You took me for granted. Never telling me anything." Just as I'm doing with Roque. "Always whispering with others. Dismissing me like I'm a fool. You're just like her. . . ."

"Your mother?"

He says nothing. Arcos edges in beside me. I put a hand out to stop him.

"Would you kill them, if Augustus told you to?" Tactus asks me, turning slightly.

"No," I say. "I'd rather die."

"I didn't think so. She was right. I am the Mighty Servant."

I open my hands to him. "I don't know what I'm to do now, Tactus."

"That's a first." He laughs bitterly, voice slurring slightly.

"Hardly. I didn't know what to do when I whipped you," I say. "At the Institute. I didn't want to lose you from my army because of your talents. But I couldn't *not* punish you."

"Talents. Talents. *Talents*. Then that's the difference between us," Tactus's voice thickens further. "Because if it had been my army, I would have killed your arrogant ass." He turns more and I see the hints of the ruin the bomb's made of his face.

"You know what happens if you kill any of them?"

He nods to me, then to the Rage Knight, as if saying it'll be either one or the other that does him. "I'm not sorry I took Lysander, you know."

"I don't think you're ever sorry for much."

"Not sorry." He chuckles and dips a toe in the blood surrounding him. "But I think I shouldn't have done it. I was testing you at the Institute. But . . . I wanted to see what you'd do. If you were worth following."

"Was I?"

"You know that answer."

"Am I still?"

He nods. "Always," saying it so pathetically that it feels like my heart has been pulled into my throat. He's a traitor, a liar, a cheat. Yet I see a friend. I want to fix him and make him whole. What am I doing? I have to put him down. But I've done that before with Titus. That cycle erodes us. Death begets death begets death, and ever more.

"What if I let you live?" I ask suddenly, drawing a confused, frantic glance from Tactus. Of course he doesn't understand forgiveness. "What if I let you come back?"

"What?"

"What if I forgave you?"

"You're lying." He turns more and I see the full measure of what the bomb did to him. His nose is crooked, broken. The rest looks like a cherry stripped of its skin. My friend . . .

"I'm not lying." I did not put my faith in Tactus once, and I lost him. Now I will. I'll take the same leap I ask him to take. I step forward. "I know there's good in you. I saw your face when those children were killed at the gala. You're not a monster. Come back to me. You would be one of my lieutenants again, Tactus. I would give you a legion to lead when we take Mars. You'll carry one of my standards. But you can't wear that ugly armor."

"It is uncomfortable," he wheezes with a slight smile. "But Sevro, Roque, Victra . . ."

"They miss you," I lie. "Drop your razor and come back to my army. I promise you will be safe." The razor dips in his hand. One of the children spares a smile at his younger siblings, a hopeful smile. "Just leave the children alone, and all is forgiven."

I mean it. Deep in my heart, I mean it.

"We all make mistakes," he says.

"We all make mistakes. Just come back. I won't hurt you." I drop my own razor. "Neither will Arcos." I stare at Arcos till he nods his weathered head in complicity.

"I want to come home," Tactus murmurs quietly, pain in his voice. "I want to come home."

"Then come home."

Tactus's razor clatters to the floor and he falls to a knee in front of me. He's rasping from pain. Relief floods the room. The children start crying again from the tortuous shift from death to life. The caretakers hug their charges, tears making lines on their faces. I go forward to Tactus and motion him upward to clasp my arm. He wraps me in a frantic hug and sobs into me. Body shaking, bloody features painting my armor.

"I'm sorry," he says a dozen times. He's weeping hard into my shoulder, clasping tight. His face is such a ruin. And I hug him. Exhaustion fills me. His sadness is like a weight that nearly drives me to tears. Yet I'm buoyed by the strange feelings of having him back, standing with me, gripping me. It is a humbling thing knowing someone cannot live without you, knowing that though they've betrayed you, they wish for nothing but absolution. And as he clenches my back, I wrap my arms around his armor and try not to cry myself. Even the cruel feel pain. And even the cruel can change. I hope this changes him. He could do so much, if only he would learn.

In so many ways, he is the embodiment of his race. And so if Tactus can change, Gold can change. They must be broken, but then they must be given a chance. I think that's what Eo would have wanted in the end.

When at last his sobs are done and we part, he stands at my side, loyal as a puppy, looking to me subtly for signs of affection. His hands tremble from the pain of his wounds, yet he watches in silence with Arcos and me as the children, high and low alike, file upward out of the hidden bunker with their caretakers. Pebble comes down to giddily tell us Roque is wrapping up the space engagement. Seeing Tactus's wounds, she pales. I tell her to fetch a Yellow.

Soon Lorn, Tactus, and I are left alone in the basement.

Lorn looks over to us. "Now that the children are gone, consequences." His hands flash faster than a hummingbird's wings. An ion-Dagger appears, lurches forward four times into Tactus's armpit, where the armor is the weakest. I rush to stop Lorn, but it's already done. He twists like he's wringing a towel, severing the artery, an old man killing a young one. Tactus's ruined face wrenches with pain; and he gasps, as though he knew justice would finally find him in the end.

Lorn leaves. And I hold my friend as he dies, his eyes fading to some distant place, where perhaps he'll find that peace Roque always wished for him.

30

||||||||||||||||||||||||

GATHERING STORM

"How long till we reach the rendezvous?" I ask Orion on the command deck. Except for our attendants, we are alone in front of the viewports of the *Pax,* watching my ships cross through space. The newest additions to our fledgling armada are painted white and carry Lorn's angry-faced purple griffin. With them fly the black and blue and silver warships captured from Kellan au Bellona above Europa. Oranges and Reds crawl over the exteriors of the metal monsters, mending the holes made by leechCraft and preparing them for the siege of Mars.

"Three days till Hildas Station. The other ships will have beaten us there, *dominus.*"

Kavax and Daxo approach from behind. I turn to them and gesture out the repaired windows to the ten ships of Kellan au Bellona.

"Thank you for the presents," I say.

"Your plan, your spoils," Kavax declares.

"With us taking a percentage, naturally," Daxo adds, smooth as ever, raising his swirling golden eyebrows. "Fifty percent finder's fee." I glance at him with amusement. "Well, thirty percent, because Pax liked you."

"Ten percent!" Kavax booms.

I cock my head. "You're a poor negotiator, Praetor."

He shrugs amiably and points in joy to jelly beans on the ground. He tosses Sophocles down, encouraging him to vanquish them all.

"Twenty." Daxo splays his hands, movements always seeming to belong to a thinner, more bookish man. "That is fair, no? We lost a hundred and sixty house Grays and thirteen Obsidians."

"Then thirty percent to compensate you. For friends."

"Three ships! What a haggle!" Kavax proclaims. "What a haggle. Sometimes a man needs a good haggle." He claps me on the back, making the joints crack again. "If only we had caught Aja. That'd be a spoil to divide!"

"She fled into the sea, unfortunately." I gesture to Ragnar, who stands at the edge of the bridge. "Heard he did well." Pale and tall, he continues looking at me from behind his beard and runic tattoos, appearing as devoid of emotions as Kavax and Daxo are full of them.

"The leader of his boarding party was killed. So were the lieutenants. Lots of heads smashed. They ran into some of Kellan's friends," Kavax says dourly as he rummages through his pockets for his impatient fox, who clawed at his leg for more jelly beans. *"I don't have any more, my little prince."* He smiles up at me hopefully. "Do you have any jelly beans?"

"No. Sorry."

"Ragnar there took command. Did himself well," Daxo says.

"Took command?" I ask.

Kavax explains. "There was a kill squad of Peerless. Half a dozen Bellona blade dancers, real noble boys, carved up all our Golds and most of the Obsidians. The Stained there collected the surviving Grays and a few Obsidians and managed to get the ship."

"Any of these blade dancers survive?"

"No."

Ragnar looks at the ground again, as if expecting a reprimand.

"Well done, my goodman," I say instead.

Both Kavax and Daxo squint at the familiarity.

Worth it to see Ragnar surprise me with a smile. A broad, yellow-toothed grin.

"Do you think he could do more?" I ask.

Daxo hesitates. "What do you mean?"

"Could he lead absent a Gold?"

Daxo and Kavax share a worried glance. "What would be the benefit in that?" Daxo asks.

"I could send him places I could not send Golds."

"There is no such place." Kavax crosses his arms. I go too far.

I smile to placate them. "Of course. Just a theory. The mind wanders from time to time." I clap Kavax on the shoulder and they depart together for their own ship.

"You overstepped," Orion says.

"I beg your pardon?"

"You have ears."

I look down, searching the pale blue tattoos on her dark skin as if the math there holds the key to understanding her mind. "You're observant for a Blue."

"Because I know how the world works outside my digital sync? Comes from working the docks, *dominus*. When you're at the bottom, you have to notice everything."

"Which docks?" I ask.

"Phobos. Father was a Docker, born outside the Sects. Died when I was small. A young girl has to be on her toes if she wants to grow big in the Hive dock cities. It's the only way to beat the monsters."

"It's not the only way," I say.

"No?" she asks, surprised.

"You can always become a monster too."

Orion turns from the viewport to look up at me. Fierce intelligence burns behind her arctic eyes. "And there's the beauty of space. A billion paths to choose."

I'm spared from replying when the comBlue calls from the pit.

"*Dominus,* we've an assault shuttle inbound. It's Virginia au Augustus."

31

||||||||||||||||||||

COUP

"Father is captured," she says to me as she storms down the ramp from her smoking ship. She's flanked by several Obsidian bodyguards in battle-scarred armor. A dozen Grays exit the shuttle behind them. Sun-hwa from Luna at their head. They're all lurcher mercenaries, plain and dangerous. The Jackal's hunters. Sevro eyes them warily.

Around us, hundreds of ripWings and a dozen storks sit parked in the bay—large enough a place to swallow all of Lykos's Common and her townships. Oranges clamor about the craft, preparing maintenance checks before the eventual invasion of Mars.

I greet Mustang with my own coterie—Lorn, Sevro, the Howlers, Victra, and Ragnar. Roque did not respond to my summons. I want to rush forward to embrace Mustang, but she's in a rage. Spittle flying out of her mouth. Dark circles ringing angry eyes. Exhaustion pulls at her face.

"Pliny has begun a coup. He arrested my brother. My aunt is dead, and her children murdered along with six of our Praetors. More than twenty of my father's bannermen have sworn new oaths of fealty. And we've lost control of the fleet."

I ask Mustang if she's injured.

"Injured?" She sneers the word. "As if that could matter. They killed my men. We came upon the Academy in stealth, and as soon as I launched my leechCraft toward the space station and the training ships, a Bellona fleet emerged from behind an asteroid and destroyed every one of my leechCraft. Ten thousand men. Dead. They didn't have to do it. They had enough guns on us that we could do nothing but surrender. It was merciless."

"Sounds like Karnus," I guess.

She nods. "And Pliny. They didn't lead the Bellona on a goose chase. They led them straight into my operation."

"Why didn't Pliny just kill you?" Sevro asks.

"A man like Pliny craves legitimacy," Lorn says from my side, nodding in greeting to Mustang. If she thinks his presence here strange, she doesn't let on. "It's his nature. He came to you beforehand, didn't he?"

Mustang shares a disgusted look with my mentor.

"The Pixie had me put under guard in my quarters as he took my captured fleet to Hildas. During the journey, he came to me and showed me the holo footage of my father's failed raid on Ganymede." She shudders in anger. "And he said that though my house had fallen to ruin, he would not see my bloodline ended. The Sovereign and he had come to an arrangement. If he could provide her with peace, then she would provide him with position, legitimacy, and a prize of his choosing. So he batted his pretty lashes at me as my father's ships burned on the holo and said he would divorce his wife and allow me the honor of taking his hand in marriage."

I say nothing. The Howlers rumble discontentedly.

"And your response?" Victra asks.

Mustang ignores her. "He said he always had his eye on me." She reaches into her pocket, pulls something out, and drops it onto the floor. "So I took one of his."

Sevro cackles with Harpy. Lorn makes a sound of disapproval. Like he has any ground to stand on in matters of cruelty.

"It is good to see you again, Rage Knight," Mustang says. "I'm sorry you were drawn into this. But we need you now more than ever."

"I'm beginning to see that."

"Where's your brother?" I ask Mustang, looking up from the eye.

"Captured. There's more that should be said." She glances at the Oranges and the Grays in the hangar. "In private."

"Of course. We'll continue in the warroom—" I begin.

"In due time, Darrow." Grandfatherly concern spreads across Lorn's face as he turns to Mustang. "My lady, you've been through a trial. Perhaps you should find rest and we could—"

The Howlers and I back away from Lorn.

"Rest?" Mustang's voice rises. "Why would I need rest?"

"My mistake," Lorn says politely.

"Theodora," I call. She slips forward. "Coffee, stims, and food in the warroom. Enough for ten." I remember the two Telemanuses. "Make it twenty."

She laughs accidentally. "Yes, *dominus*." Theodora steps aside to call her staff.

Mustang jerks her head at her ship. "Just going to let it sit there?"

"Chief!" I call to the Orange in charge of the hangar deck. Grease stains his beard. He saunters up, wiping burly hands on his orange greasers. "Put that ship out the airlock."

"It can be salvaged," the Orange says.

I look to Mustang. "Did you escape, or did they let you escape?"

"I don't know. My brother was the one who saved me. His own ship was caught helping mine escape."

The Jackal is full of surprises.

"What if there is a bomb in it?" Sevro asks, staring at the ship uncomfortably.

"It won't be a bomb," I say.

"Pliny wants me still, and he wants Darrow for the Sovereign. But more so, he wants your fleet, Darrow. When it didn't show up at Hildas, he must have realized that you'd been warned or that you were waiting for a code confirmation that he didn't know."

"And he figured if anyone would know where I was, it'd be you."

"So tracking me is how he will find this fleet," Mustang says.

Lorn looks back and forth at us. "When did you two discuss this?"

"Just now," Mustang says, confused at the question.

Sevro claps Lorn on the shoulder. "Don't worry. You're not senile. They're just odd."

Lorn stares at Sevro's dirty hand. The fingerless glove is covered with mashed potatoes and brown gravy. Sevro's broad smile fades and he sheepishly withdraws his hand.

I turn back to the Orange. "Put it out the airlock. Fastlike." He seems hesitant. Keeps rolling onto the balls of his feet. "Unless you've a better idea?"

He scratches his head, looking worried with all the Gold faces staring at him. The deckhands watch the exchange furtively.

"Out with it," Sevro barks.

"Sure. Well, I could put it out the lock, *dominus*. Or, I mean, I could find the scanners and the radiated material, if they went that route. We got some clever nuts and bolts here. Could find 'em out, and I could put 'em all in a long-range scout, no problem. Might do nice to let Pliny's hounds go barking in the wrong direction, yeah?"

"What is your name and world?" I ask.

"*Dominus* . . . uh." He blinks heavily. "Cyther's my name. Luna. Three girls. Wife works in the Center for Automotive Development, so we have—"

I cut him off. "Do this right and we'll bring them to Mars and put them up on the Citadel staff, Cyther. You have ten minutes."

"Yes, Sir!" He wheels to his men excitedly.

I lead Mustang and my coterie to the lifts.

"Pliny said he killed you," she whispers as we walk.

"Aja and a Bellona fleet waited for us, like we thought they would." I grin sideways at her, then pull up my datapad. "Orion, take command of the fleet. I want us far from this sector before we have more company. Sevro, summon the Telemanuses. I want them in the . . . Sevro?" I look around for him. He's loitering around Pliny's eyeball some twenty meters back. We turn to look at him and he shuffles his feet awkwardly.

"Can I . . ." He gestures to it.

"What?" Mustang asks.

"Can I have it?"

Mustang squints at him. "All yours."

He scoops up the eyeball and jams it into his pocket, grinning merrily. He runs to catch up. "Collecting the set, hopefully."

32

||||||||||||||||||||||||||

DIE YOUNG

Mustang insisted on seeing Tactus before the meeting. Theodora guides us. We find Roque sitting by his body in the ship's medBay. The way he sits with his hands clasped together, you'd think Tactus might still have a chance at life. Perhaps in some other world where men like Lorn don't exist.

"He's been here since Europa," Theodora says quietly.

"You didn't tell me he was down here," I say.

"He asked me not to."

"You're *my* servant, Theodora."

"And he's your friend, *dominus*."

Mustang nudges me. "Stop being an ass, can't you see she's as exhausted as he is?"

I look at Theodora. Mustang's right. "You should get some sleep, Theodora."

"A prime idea, I think, *dominus*. Always lovely to see you, *domina*," Theodora says to Mustang before shooting me a cross look. "Master has been rather moody in your absence."

Mustang watches Theodora glide out. "You were lucky with her." She gently touches Roque's shoulder. His eyes flutter open.

"Virginia."

They grew close in the year we all spent in the Citadel together. Neither could ever get me to join them at the opera. It's not that I wasn't interested in the music. Lorn simply demanded time.

She squeezes his hand. "How are you?"

"Better than Tactus." He glances at me. I wager he'd say more if I weren't here. He sees Mustang's state of disarray, brow creasing in worry. "What went wrong?"

Once we tell him, he gently runs a hand through his wavy hair. "Well, that is bad. I never thought Pliny would ever be so thoroughly bold."

"We're meeting in ten to discuss plans," I say.

Roque ignores me. "I'm sorry about your father and brother, Virginia."

"They're still alive, I hope." She looks to Tactus and her face quiets. "I'm sorry about Tactus."

"He went as he lived," Roque says. "Only wish he could have lived longer."

"You think he would have changed?" Mustang asks.

"He was always our friend," Roque says. "It was our responsibility to help him try. Even if it was like hugging a flame." He looks at me momentarily.

"You know I didn't want him to die," I say. "I wanted him to come back with us."

"Just as you wanted to catch Aja?" Roque says, snorting at my expression.

"I told you why I did that."

"Naturally. She kills our friend. She kills *Quinn,* but we let her walk away for the grander scheme. Everything costs something, Darrow. Perhaps you'll soon tire of making your friends pay."

"That's not fair," Mustang says quickly. "You know it's not."

"What I know is we're running out of friends," Roque replies. "Not all of us are as tough as *the Reaper.* Not all of us want to be warriors."

Of course Roque thinks this life is a choice of mine. His own childhood was one of leisure and reading, spent going back and forth between his family estate in New Thebes and the highlands of Mars. His parents didn't believe in enhanced learning uploads, so they hired Violets and Whites to teach him pedagogically—walking and talking in peaceful pastures and beside still lakes.

"Tactus didn't sell the violin," Roque says after a moment.

"The one Darrow gave him?"

"Yes. The Stradivarian. He sold it, then felt so guilty he didn't let the sale finalize with the auction house. Made them cancel the order. He was practicing in private, shaking off some of the rust. Said he wanted to surprise you with a sonata, Darrow."

The heaviness in me deepens. Tactus was always my friend. He just got lost in trying to be the man his family wanted him to be, when all along his friends loved the man he already was. Mustang puts a hand on my lower back, knowing what I'm thinking. Roque leans down now to kiss Tactus once on the cheek and to give him a benediction.

"Better to go into that other world in the full glory of some passion than to fade and wither with age. Live fast. Die young, my wayward friend."

Roque walks away, leaving Mustang and me alone with Tactus.

"You have to fix that," she says of Roque. "Fix it before you've lost him."

"I know," I say. "Soon as I fix a hundred other things."

We sit in the warroom in full council around a grand wooden table. Coffee cups and trays of food litter it. Mustang sits at my side, boots up on the table, as ever, while she explains what went wrong with her father's mission. Kavax leans forward precariously in his seat, terrified at the idea of Augustus suffering defeat. He wrings his hands nervously, so distressed that Daxo takes Sophocles from his lap and hands him to an uncomfortable Victra. Mustang's voice fills the room and the holo Pliny gave her comes to life above the table. A brigade of corvettes rockets silently through space toward the famed shipyards of Ganymede that ring the industrial moon of mottled green, blue, and swirling white.

"He dispatched a lurcher squad of Grays concealed in the belly of two tankers. They disabled three of the defensive platform's nuclear reactors. Then my father came in hard with his ripWings and corvettes, as is his way—burning engines and dropping munitions before curling back around.

"It was a treasure trove—some seventeen destroyers and four dreadnoughts in dry dock, most near or at completion. Supposing the ships to be manned by skeleton crews, he boarded them simultaneously. He even commanded the leechCraft that boarded the moonBreaker with his two Stained. But the ships were not manned by skeleton crews. There were no crews at all. Instead, they were loaded with Praetorians, Gray lurcher squads. And Olympic Knights."

"And he . . . *surrendered*?" Kavax asks in panic.

Mustang laughs. "My father? He nearly cut his way free. He killed the Hearth Knight, then he ran into some of our old friends."

The holo shows Augustus flowing through twelve Grays, like a man wading through stalks of high, dry grass. His razor sings and shrieks, sparking against the walls, sliding through men and armor till he meets another man in armor the shade of flame. The Hearth Knight. There's a flurry of tight lunges and then red mist. A head thumps to the ground. Then two men appear. One in a sun-crested helm, the other Fitchner in his wolfhead helm. Together, the men kill the Stained and put Augustus bleeding on the ground.

Lorn looks over at me. "Lady . . . Mustang, who was the man in the sun-crested armor?"

She's silent.

"That's the armor of the Morning Knight," I answer. "Cassius. They must have mended his arm. Or given him a new one."

Mustang continues. "Julii ships were also there." She looks at Victra. "They finished my father's forces off."

Sevro glares at Victra, taking Sophocles from her as though she couldn't even be trusted with the fox. "Do you feel awkward? You should."

"We've been over this," Victra says, sounding quite bored with the accusations. "My mother was threatened by the Sovereign. She's not political. She cares about money and little else."

"So she doesn't care about loyalty?" Mustang asks. "Interesting."

"Pfah. Agrippina's a wicked bitch," Kavax grumbles. "Always has been."

"Careful, large one," Victra warns. "She's still my mother."

Kavax crosses his burly arms. "Apologies. That she is your mother."

"And how do we know you're not in collusion with them, Victra?" Daxo asks softly. "Perhaps you spy? Perhaps you wait. How do you trust her loyalty, Darrow? She could easily have sent word. . . ."

Mustang looks at me. "I was wondering that myself."

"Why do I trust you, Daxo, or you, Kavax?" I ask. "Either of you would be in prime shape, earn pardons, earn more territories and monies if you delivered my head to the Sovereign."

"And your heart to Cassius's mother," Sevro reminds me.

"Thank you, Sevro."

"Here to help!" He grabs a drumstick off the table's spread and feeds it to Sophocles. Considering, he takes a bite himself, saying something quietly to the fox.

"I trust Victra for the same reason I trust any of you—friendship," I say, managing to look away from Sevro.

"Friendship. Ha." Mustang sets her coffee cup down loudly. "I'll be blunt. I don't trust a Julii farther than I could throw one."

"That's because you're intimidated by me, little girl."

Mustang sits up straighter. " 'Little'?"

"I have a decade on you, darling. One day you'll look back at yourself and laugh. Was I really so foolish, so simple? Additionally, you're not very tall. So I'll call you little."

"I don't cat-fight," Mustang says coldly. "I don't trust you because I don't know you. All I know is your mother's reputation is not apolitical. She's a schemer. A briber. My father knew it. I know it. You know it."

"Yes, to a degree my mother is a schemer. And so am I and so are you, but if there's one thing I am not, it is a liar. I've never told a lie, and never will. Unlike some people." The arch of eyebrows makes it quite clear what she means.

"Bad apples spawn bad seeds, Darrow," Daxo warns. "Put your feelings aside on this one. She was raised by a dangerous woman.

There's no need to mistreat her, but we can't have her in this council. I would encourage you to place her in quarters till this is over."

"Yes." Kavax raps the table with his knotted knuckles. "Agreed. Bad seeds."

"I can't believe you lured me into this mess, Darrow," Lorn mutters. He looks out of place here. Too old, too gray to be party to squabbling. "Can't even trust your own council."

"Grumpy. Low blood sugar perhaps?" Sevro tosses him the half-gnawed drumstick. Lorn lets it flop against the table, unimpressed by the display.

"We would hear your wisdom, Arcos," Kavax says respectfully.

"I would listen to your councillors, Darrow." Lorn pops his knotted fingers. "I've got scars older than them, but they aren't completely naïve. Better safe than sorry. Confine Victra to her quarters."

"You don't even know me, Arcos!" Victra protests, finally pulled out of her chair. You see the warrior in her now, flaring just beneath the cultured calm. "This is an affront to me. I was fighting with Darrow when you were still cowering in your floating castle pretending it's A.D. 1200."

"Time does not prove one's loyalty." Lorn scoffs and runs a finger along a scar on his forearm. "Scars do."

"You took those fighting for the Sovereign. You were her sword. How much blood did you draw for her? How many men did you watch burn at the side of the Ash Lord?"

"Do not speak of Rhea to me, girl."

Victra's teeth glimmer in a cruel smile. "So there is a Rage Knight beneath the wrinkles and moth-bitten rags."

Lorn surveys her, seeing the wrathfulness of youth in her, and he looks to me, as if to wonder just what sort of man brings Golds like Tactus and Victra to his side. Does he even know me? his eyes ask. No, he's realizing. Of course not.

"*Honor in the first. Honor in the last.* Those are my family words. Whereas you . . . young lady, well, the name Julii does not exactly lift one to nobler purpose, does it? You're just traders."

"My name has nothing to do with who I am."

"Snakes beget snakes," Lorn replies, not even looking at her now. "Your mother was a snake. She begat you. Ergo, you are a snake. And what do snakes do, my dear? They slither. They wait, coldblooded, cruel in the grass, and then they bite."

"We could ransom her," Sevro says. "Threaten to kill her unless Agrippina joins us or at least stops pissing all over our plans."

"You're a sinister little shit, aren't you?" Victra asks.

"I'm Gold, bitch. What'd you expect? Warm milk and cookies just because I'm pocket-sized?"

Roque clears his throat, drawing eyes.

"It seems we are being unfair, hypocritical even," he observes. "All here know my family is full of politicians. Some of you might even think I come from noble blood and noble seed. But we Fabii are a dishonest breed. Mother's a Senator who lines her pockets with agricultural funds and lowColor medical subsidies so that she can live in more homes than her mother did. My paternal grandfather poisoned his own nephew over a Violet starlet a quarter his age, who ended up stabbing him and blinding herself when she discovered he killed the nephew, her lover. But that's nothing next to my great-great-uncle, who fed servants to lampreys because he read Emperor Tiberius pioneered the strange passion. Yet here I am, spawn of all that sin, and I wager no one here questions my loyalty.

"Why, then, do we doubt Victra's? She has remained steadfast to Darrow since the Academy. None of you were there. None of you know anything about it, so I insist you shut your mouths. Even when her mother demanded she abandon Darrow and Augustus, she stayed. Even when the Praetorians came to kill us on Luna, she stayed. Now she is here, when we are little more than a ragtag coalition of bandits, and you question her. *You disgust me.* It makes me sad to be among you bickerers. So if another man or woman questions her loyalty, I will lose faith in this fellowship. And I will leave."

Victra's smile for him is like a sunrise, creeping, slow, then blindingly bright. It disappears slower than I thought it might have. The warmth in her surprises Roque as well, and his fair cheeks are quick to flush.

"I am not my mother," Victra announces. "Or my sister. My ships are mine. My men are mine." Her wide-set eyes are cool, almost sleepy, but they flash as she leans forward now. "Trust me, and you will find reward. But all that matters is what Darrow thinks."

All eyes turn to me and my silence. In truth, I was not thinking about Victra, but about Tactus and wondering how easily he could tell that I kept him at arm's length. When I showed him love at first and he rejected the violin, I grew embarrassed and hurt. So I pulled back. Better if I had been true to how I felt and stayed the course. His walls would have broken. He never would have left. He could still be here. I'll not make the same mistake again, least of all to Victra. I reached out to her in the hall, and I will do so in this company.

"Chance made us Golds," I say. "We could have been born any other Color. Chance put us in our families. But we choose our friends. Victra chose me. I chose her, like I chose all of you. And if we cannot trust our friends"—I look to Roque plaintively, seeking absolution in his eyes—"then what's the point in breathing?"

I look back to Victra. Her eyes say a thousand things, and the Jackal's words come back to me as he lay burned on his bed from the bomb. Victra loves me. Could it really be so simple? She does all these things not for the Julii way of gain and profit, but for that simple human emotion. I wonder, could I ever love her? No. No, in another world, Mustang would never be a warrior, would never be cruel. In any world, Victra would always be this. Always a warrior, like Eo really. Always too wild and full of fire to find peace in anything else.

Mustang notices something pass between Victra and me.

"Then it's settled," Mustang says. "Back to the matter at hand. Pliny waits now with the main fleet. There, he has brought all of my father's bannermen to compose a document of formal surrender to the Sovereign and a restructuring of Mars. The deal, as far as I understand it, will make him the head of his own house. He, along with the Julii and the Bellona, will be the powers on Mars. Once the peace is agreed upon, it will be sealed with the execution of my father in the courtyard of our Citadel in Agea." Mustang looks around the table, letting gravity build behind her words. "If we do not rescue my father, this war is done. The Moon Lords will not come to our aid. In fact, they will send ships against us. Vespasian's forces from Neptune will turn around. We will be alone against the entire Society. And we will die."

"Good. That makes things simple," I say. "We take back our fleet, then we take back Mars. Any ideas?"

33

‖‖‖‖‖‖‖‖‖‖‖‖‖‖‖‖‖‖‖

A DANCE

I sleep with a dream of the past. My hand curled in the tendrils of her hair. About us the vale lay quiet in slumber. Even the children did not yet stir. The birds rested on knotted limbs in the pinewood nearby, and I heard nothing but her breath and the crackling of the old fire. The bed smelled of her. No scent of flowers or perfume. Just the earthy musk of her skin, of the oils in the hair around my hands, of her hot breath as it warmed my cheek. Her hair was of our planet. It was wild like mine, dirty like mine, red like mine. A bird outside croons loudly. Incessantly. Louder. Louder.

And I wake hearing someone at my door.

Kicking aside sweaty sheets, I sit up on the edge of the mattress. "Visual." A holo appears of Mustang in the hall. I rise instinctively to let her in, but when I reach the door, I pause. We have our plan. There's nothing left to discuss at this hour. Nothing from which any good could come.

I watch her on the holo. Shifting foot to foot, something in her hands. If I let her in . . . it'll just cost us both in the end. I've already hurt Roque. Already killed Quinn and Tactus and Pax. Bringing her close now would be selfish. At the very best, she survives this war and she learns the truth about me. I back away from the door.

"Darrow, stop being an ass and let me in."

My hand choses for me.

Her hair is wet and loose, her uniform replaced by a black kimono. How fragile she seems next to Ragnar, who lurks in the hall.

"Told you," she says to Ragnar. To me she says, "Knew you'd be awake. Ragnar here was being stubborn. Said you needed to sleep. And he wouldn't take the food I brought him."

"Do you need something?" I ask, more coldly than I intended.

Her feet make a show of shuffling nervously. "I'm . . . afraid of the dark." She pushes past me. Ragnar watches this, eyes giving nothing away.

"I told you to go to bed, Ragnar."

He does not move.

"Ragnar, if I'm not safe here, I'm not safe anywhere. Go to bed."

"I sleep with my eyes open, *dominus*."

"Really?"

"Yes."

"Well, do it in your bunk, Stained. That's an order," I say, hating the master's words as soon as they come from my mouth.

Reluctantly, he nods his head and slips silently down the hall. I watch him go as the door hisses closed. I turn to find Mustang inspecting my suite. It's more wood and stone than metal, the walls carved and worked with woodland scenes. Strange the efforts these people go to in order to make themselves feel part of history and not a piece of the future.

"Sevro must be pissed he's not the only one lurking behind you anymore."

"Sevro's grown up a bit since you last saw him. He even sleeps in beds."

She laughs at that. "Well, Ragnar was so adamant I go away that I thought you might have company."

"You know I don't use Pinks."

"It's big," she says of the suite. "Six rooms for little old you. Aren't you going to offer me something to drink?"

"Would you—"

"No, thank you." She tells the room's controls to play music. Mozart. "But you don't really like music, do you?"

"Not this sort. It's . . . stuffy."

"Stuffy? Mozart was a rebel, a brigand of monolithic genius! A breaker of all that was stuffy."

I shrug. "Maybe. But then the stuffy people got ahold of him."

"You're such a hayseed sometimes. I thought that Theodora would have managed to feed you some culture. So what do you like, then?" She runs her hands along a carving of an elk leading its herd. "Not that electronic madness the Howlers thump their heads to, I hope. Makes sense that the Greens came up with that . . . it's like listening to a robot having a seizure."

"Have much experience with robots?" I ask as she moves around the Victory Armor in a room off to the side of the entry hall. The Sovereign gave it to the Ash Lord when he burned Rhea. Mustang's fingers play over the frost-hued metal.

"Father's Oranges and Greens had a few robots in their engineering labs. Ancient, rusted things that Father had refurbished and put in the museums." She laughs to herself. "He used to take me there back when I wore dresses and Mother was still alive. Absolutely detested the things. I remember Mother laughing about his paranoia, especially when Adrius tried restarting one of the combat models from Eurasia. Father was convinced that robots would have overthrown man and now rule the Solar System if Earth's empires had never been destroyed."

I snort out a laugh.

"What?" she asks.

"I'm just . . ." I snicker quietly. "I'm trying to imagine the great ArchGovernor Augustus having nightmares of robots." A louder bout of laughter seizes me. "Does he suppose they'd want more oil? More vacation time?"

Mustang watches me, amused. "Are you all right?"

"I'm fine." My laughter fades. I hold my stomach. "I'm fine." I can't stop grinning. "Is he afraid of aliens too?"

"I never asked him." She taps the armor. "But they're out there, you know."

I stare at her. "That's not in the archives."

"Oh, no no. I mean we've never found any. But the Drake-Roddenberry equation suggests the mathematic probability is $N = R^* \times fp \times ne \times fl \times fi \times fc \times L$. Where R^* is the average rate of star formation in our galaxy, where fp is the fraction of those stars that have planets . . . You're not even listening anymore."

"What do you suppose they would think of us?" I ask. "Of man?"

"I suppose they would think we're beautiful, strange, and inexplicably horrible to one another." She points down a hall. "Is that the training room?" She flips off her slippers and walks away down a marble hall, casting a look back at me over her shoulder. I follow. Lights come mutedly to life as we pass. She slips ahead faster than I care to follow. I find her moments later in the center of the circular training room. The white mat is soft under my feet. Carvings line the wooden walls. "The House of Grimmus is an old one," she says, pointing to a frieze of a man in armor. "You can see the Ash Lord's first ancestor there. Seneca au Grimmus, the first Gold to touch land in the Iron Rain that took the American eastern seaboard after one of Cassius's ancestors, forget his name, broke through the Atlantic Fleet. Then there is Vitalia au Grimmus, the Great Witch, right there." She turns to me. "Do you even know the history of the things you try to break?"

"It was Scipio au Bellona who defeated the Atlantic Fleet."

"Was it?" she asks.

"I've studied the history," I say. "Just as well as you."

"But you stand apart from it, don't you?" She paces around me. "You always have. Like you're an outsider looking in. It was growing up away from all this on your parents' asteroid mine that did the trick, wasn't it? That's why you can ask a question like 'What would aliens think of us?' "

"You're just as much an outsider as I am. I've read your dissertations."

"You have?" She's surprised.

"Believe it or not, I can read too." I shake my head. "It's like everyone forgets I only missed one question on the Institute's slangsmarts test."

"Ew. You missed a question?" She wrinkles her nose as she picks a practice razor from a bench. "I suppose that's why you weren't in Minerva."

"How did Pax manage to get picked by House Minerva, by the way? I've always wondered . . . he wasn't exactly a scholar."

"How did Roque end up in Mars?" she replies with a shrug. "Each of us have hidden depths. Now, Pax wasn't as bright as Daxo is, but wisdom is found in the heart, not the head. Pax taught me that." She smiles distantly. "The one grace my father gave me after my mother died was letting me visit the Telemanus estate. He kept Adrius and me apart to make assassination of his heirs more difficult. I was lucky to be near them. Though if I hadn't been, maybe Pax wouldn't have been quite so loyal. Maybe he wouldn't have asked to be in Minerva. Maybe he'd be alive. Sorry . . ." Shaking away the sadness, she looks back to me with a tight smile. "What did you think of my dissertations?"

"Which one?"

"Surprise me."

"'The Insects of Specialization.'" *Snap.* A practice razor slaps into my arm, stinging the flesh. I yelp in surprise. "What the hell?"

Mustang stands there looking innocent, swishing the practice blade back and forth. "I was making sure you were paying attention."

"Paying attention? I was answering your question!"

She shrugs. "All right. Perhaps I just wanted to hit you." She lashes at me again.

I dodge. "Why?"

"No reason in particular." She swings. I dodge. "But they say even a fool learns something once it hits him."

"Don't quote"—she slashes, I twist aside—"Homer . . . to me."

"Why is that dissertation your favorite?" she asks coolly, swinging at me again. The practice razor has no edge, but it is as hard as a wooden cane. I leave my feet, twisting sideways out of the way like a Lykos tumbler.

"Because . . ." I dodge another.

"When you're on your heels, you're a liar. On your toes, you spit truth." She swings again. "Now spit." She hits my kneecap. I roll away, trying to reach the other practice razors, but she keeps me from them with a flurry of swings. "Spit!"

"I liked it"—I jump backward—"because you said 'Specialization makes us limited, simple insects; a fact . . . from . . . which Gold is not immune.'"

She stops attacking and stares accusatorially, and I realize I've fallen into a trap.

"If you agree with that, then why do you insist on making yourself only a warrior?"

"It's what I am."

"It's what you are?" she laughs. "You who trust Victra. A Julii. You who trusted Tactus. You who let an Orange give strategic recommendations. You who gives command of your ship to a Docker and keeps an entourage of bronzies?" She wags a finger at me. "Don't be a hypocrite now, Darrow au Andromedus. If you're going to tell everyone else they can choose their destiny, then you damn well better do the same."

She's too smart to lie to. That's why I'm so ill at ease around her when she asks me questions, when she probes things I can't explain. There's no explainable motivation to so many of my actions if I am really an Andromedus who grew up in my Gold parents' asteroid mining colony. My history is hollow to her. My drive confusing . . . if I was born a Gold. This must all look like ambition, like bloodlust. And without Eo, it would be.

"That look," Mustang says, taking a step back from me. "Where do you go when you look at me like that?" The color slips from her face, retreating into her as her smile slackens. "Is it Victra?"

"Victra?" I almost laugh. "No."

"Then her. The girl you lost."

I say nothing.

She's never pried. She's never asked about Eo, not when we shared time together after the Institute when I was a rising lancer. Not when we rode horses at her family's estate or walked through the gardens or dove in the coral reefs. I thought she must have forgotten I whispered the name of another girl as I lay with her in the Institute's snows. How stupid of me. How could she forget? How could it not linger there inside her, forcing her to wonder, as she lay with her head on my chest listening to my heart beat, if it didn't belong to another girl, a dead girl.

"Silence isn't the answer right now, Darrow." After a moment, she leaves me alone in the room. Sounds from her feet fade. The Mozart disappears.

I chase after her, reaching her before she finds the door to the hall. I grab her wrist. She flings me off.

"Stop it!"

I reel back, startled.

"Why do you do this?" she asks. "Why do you pull me back if you're just going to push me away?" Her fists ball like she wants to strike me. "It's not fair. Do you understand that? I'm not like you . . . I can't just . . . I can't just shut off like you do."

"I don't shut off."

"You shut me off. After that speech about Victra . . . about the importance of friends . . ." She snaps her fingers in front of my face. "You can still cut me away like *that*. You care and then you don't. Maybe that's why he likes you so much."

"He?"

"My father."

"He doesn't like me."

"How could he not? You are him."

I back away from her and find rest on the edge of the bed. "I'm not like your father."

"I know," she says, releasing some of her anger. "That's not fair to you. But you will become him if you follow this path alone." She puts her hand on the door controls. "So ask me to stay."

How can I let her? If she gives me her heart, I'll break it. My lie is too great to build a love upon. When she discovers what I am, she will reject me. Even if she could survive that, I would not. I look at my hands as if the answer is there.

"Darrow. Ask me to stay."

When I look up, she is gone.

34

||||||||||||||||||||||

BLOOD BROTHERS

Lorn's scouts capture the camel vessel as it brings foodstuffs to Pliny's fleet gathered around Hildas Station, a star-shaped hub of trade and communications on the fringes of the asteroid belt between the orbits of Mars and Jupiter. For fifteen hours, I hide with Roque, Victra, Sevro, the Howlers, the Telemanuses, Lorn, Mustang, and Ragnar among boxes and crates of vacuum-sealed protofiber meals. Ragnar crushed the first box he sat on, sending meals scattering everywhere, before he left the humid cargo bay for the subzero freezer unit.

Sevro cuts open a half dozen of the meals and nibbles throughout the journey, sharing with the Telemanuses and his Howlers while Roque sits speaking with Victra in the corner. Mustang leans against Daxo, sharing stories with Kavax about Pax. She avoids my gaze.

I tried apologizing before we boarded the ship, but she cut me off fastlike. "Nothing to apologize about. We're adults. Let's not sulk and bicker like children. There's things to be done."

The words grow colder as I roll them over and over again through my mind.

Lorn nudges me with his boot. "Try to be less obvious, boy. You're staring."

"It's complicated."

"Love and war. Same coin. Different sides. I'm too wrinkled for either."

"Maybe war will breathe some life into your old bones."

"Well, I tried love last month." He leans close. "Didn't work like it used to."

"Too honest, Lorn." I can't help but laugh.

He grunts and adjusts himself on the boxes, groaning audibly as something pops in his back. "So that's the reason for all this. Helping poor old man Lorn get his fix of war." His anger has not yet dissipated, nor do I expect it to. "Let me return the favor to you. The key today will be tact. The Praetors, Legates, and bannermen you attempt to woo are not fools. And they do not suffer fools. Pliny has given them valid argument. He's aligned their interests with his. You must counter with the same."

"Pliny is a leech," I say. "A liar as much as you're an honest man."

"And that makes him dangerous. Liars make the best promises." Lorn plays with his griffin ring, no doubt thinking of the beast and of the grandchildren on his ships in the fleet. He brought his whole household off Europa, three million men and women of all Colors. "I could not leave them," he told me when I noted the size of his fleet as we left that water moon. "Octavia would come and burn the home while we're away." So they left their floating cities and set to the stars. The civilians will separate from my fleet soon, hiding in the infinite black space between the planets. His three surviving daughters-in-law will guide them.

"And Pliny has the power of the Sovereign behind him," Lorn continues. "It will be difficult to dissuade them. Speaking of the Sovereign . . . I noticed that you have something of hers."

"The *Pax*?"

"No. Smaller. Though not much smaller. The Stained that was here."

"Ragnar?"

"If that's its name," Lorn says.

"*His* name," I say. "He was meant to be a gift to the Julii for betraying Augustus."

"Saw it in the Citadel's arena once—scary as some of the creatures that hide in Europa's seas."

"He might be an Obsidian, but he's still a man."

"Biologically, maybe. But he's bred for one thing. Don't forget that."

"You treat your own servants kindly. I expect you to treat mine the same."

"I treat people kindly. Pinks, Browns, Reds are people. Your *Ragnar* is a weapon."

"He chose me. Tools don't choose."

"Have it your way, but know the consequences." Lorn shrugs and mutters something further under his breath.

"Say what you want to say."

"You will fall to ruin because you believe that exceptions to the rule make new rules. That an evil man can shed the trappings of wickedness just because you want him to. Men do not change. That is why I killed the Rath boy. Learn the lesson now, so you don't have to learn it with a knife in your back later. The Colors exist for a reason. Reputations exist for a reason."

For the first time, he seems small and old to me. It's not his wrinkles. It's what he says. He is a relic. Thoughts like his belong to the age I am trying to destroy. He can't help what he believes. He's not seen what I've seen. He's not come from where I've been. He had no Eo to push him, no Dancer to guide him, no Mustang to give him hope. He grew up in a Society where love and trust are as scarce as grass in the Helion waste. But he's always wanted both. He's like a man planting seeds, watching them grow into trees, only for his neighbors to cut them down. It will be different this time. And if all goes well, I will give him back a grandson.

"You taught me once, Lorn. I'm a better man for it. But now it's my turn to teach you. Men can change. Sometimes they have to fall. Sometimes they have to leap." I pat his knee and gain my feet. "Before you die, you'll realize it was a mistake to kill Tactus, because you never gave him the chance to believe he was a good man."

I find Ragnar lying on the ground in the freezer unit, at home in the bitter chill. His shirt is off, so I see the frightening angles of his tattooed body. Runes everywhere. *Protection* over his back. *Malice* over hands. *Mother* over his throat. *Father* over his feet. *Sister* behind his ears. The mysterious skull marks of *Stained* upon his face.

"Ragnar," I say, sitting. "Not much for company, are you?"

He shakes his head, the white ponytail curls on the floor. Eyes like stains of pitch stare at me, measuring. Second eyes, tattoos on the backs of his eyelids, are strange, pupils like those of a dragon or a snake, so that when he blinks, his animal soul sees into the world around.

I sit watching him, wondering how to say what I want to say. Obsidians are the most alien of the Colors.

"By offering me stains, you are bound to me. What does that mean to you?"

"It means I obey."

"Unconditionally?" He does not answer. "If I asked you to kill your sister or your brother?"

"Are you asking me this?"

"It is a hypothetical." He does not understand the notion when I explain it.

"Why plan?" he asks. **"You plan. You decide. I do or I do not, there is no plan."** He considers his next words carefully. **"Mortals who plan die a thousand times. We who obey die but once."**

"What is it that you want?" I ask. He doesn't stir. "I'm speaking to you, Stained."

"Want." He chuckles. **"What is *want?*"** The derision in his voice comes from a deeper place than our godless realm. He's alien here, because we grow his kind in worlds of ice and monsters and ancient gods. We get what we pay for. **"You name it, so you think I know it. Want."**

"Don't play games with me and I won't play them with you, Ragnar." I wait a long moment. "Must I repeat myself?"

"Gold plans. Gold wants," he rumbles slowly. Time between each sentence. "Wanting is your heartbeat. We of the Allmother do not want. We obey."

"On your knees?" He says nothing in reply, so I continue. "You once wore shackles, Ragnar. Now the shackles don't weigh you down. So . . . what do you want?" He doesn't respond. Is it petulance? "Surely you want something."

"You struck off the shackles of others and seek to bind me with the shackles like your own. Your *wants*. Your *dreams*. I do not want." He says it again. "I do not dream. I am *Stained*. Destined by Allmother Death to deliver her promise." His face shows me nothing, but I feel petulance in the man. "Did you not know?"

I examine him warily. "You make yourself look dumber than you really are."

"Good." He sits up swiftly, before I even have time to move back. Bloodydamn, he's fast. He takes out a knife and very quickly cuts his palm. "When I offered stains, I bound myself to you. Forever. Till nothing."

I know this is their way. And I know what horrors he went through to gain the title of Stained. He is not a man of half oaths or half measures. To be an Obsidian is to know misery. To be a Stained is to be misery. And it is to angle themselves one way in life—to serve their Golden gods, like myself, if they are so lucky. We take their strong. We leave their weak. We send Violets with tech to make lightning shows on hillsides. We sow famine, then descend with food. We send plagues, then bless them with Yellows to heal their sick and cure their blind. We have Carvers seed monsters in their oceans and griffins and dragons in their mountains. And when we are displeased, we destroy their cities with bombardments from orbit. We make ourselves their gods. And then we bring them into our world to serve our greedy aims. We want. They obey. How could Ragnar ever be what I need him to be?

"What if I wanted you to be free?"

He flinches back. Eyes expressing a deep fear. "Freedom drowns."

"Then learn to swim." I set a hand on his massive shoulder. Muscles like rocks beneath the skin. "One brother to the other."

"We are not brothers, Sunborn," he says, his voice wavering. "You are master. Do you not understand? I obey. You command."

I tell him he chose me for his master. I did not take him, as he thinks. And it was he, not I, who commanded the assault team that took Kellan au Bellona's ship. He did that. There was no Gold to guide him. No Gold to make him a leader. But that alone is not enough. What would Eo say to him? What would Dancer say?

"Our Color is the same," I tell him. He doesn't understand, so I cut my finger. Red blood comes out and I smear this on the black Sigils that mark his Color on his hands. Then I take his blood and smear it over the gold on the back of my hands.

"Brothers. All water. All flesh. All made from and bound for the dirt."

"I do not understand," he says fearfully, actually scooting back and away from me till I have him cornered like a little child. "We are not the same. You are from the sun."

"I am not. I was born six inches from the dirt. Ragnar Volarus, I release you from my service, whether you like it or not. I will not let you be bound. I will not let you be led. You stay in this icebox till you are man enough to decide what you want. You shoot yourself in the head. You freeze yourself to death. Go ahead. But whatever you do, it will be because *you* chose to do it. Perhaps you'll choose to follow me. Perhaps you'll choose to kill me. Whatever it is you decide, you must decide for yourself."

He stares at me, eyes wide with terror.

"Why?" he rumbles. "Why do you shame me? In all the worlds, no man would reject a Stained. I *choose* to offer myself and you spit on me. What have I done?"

"When you offer yourself, you offer your brothers and sisters and people into slavery as well."

"You do not know." Ragnar seethes. "We live to serve. If we do not, Gold will end us. We will be no more. I have seen fire rain from the sky."

Centuries ago, in the Dark Revolt, the Golds killed more than nine-tenths of his Color. Exterminated them like culling a population of predators. That is the only history they know. The one we give them. Fear.

"The history of men is kept from you, Ragnar. The Golds teach you that you have always been slaves. That Obsidians exist to serve, to kill. But there was a time before Gold where man was free."

"Every man?" he asks.

"Every man. Every woman. You were not born to serve Gold."

"No," he rumbles. "**You tempt me. You bait me. I have seen this before. I have seen false words meant to trick. The true words are known to me, to us. Our mothers teach them. 'Fear and serve the men of Gold. Or they will come with iron from the sky. Gold will treat you with fire of the Sunborn. For they are not bound by love. Not bound by fear. Not bound to earth, but to sky and sun. Fear and serve the men of Gold.'**"

"I do not serve them."

"**Because you are one of them.**"

"What if I told you I was not?"

He stares at me. No answer. No movement. Nothing. Just confusion. And so I tell him. I tell him in that freezer what Dancer told me in the penthouse. We have been deceived. "I had a wife," I tell him. "They took her from me. They hanged her. They made me pull her feet so that her neck would break and she would not suffer. I killed myself after that, burying her, letting them win. Letting them hang me. I drowned in grief." I tell him how the Sons came for me. "And Ares gave me a second chance, the same chance you now have to rise.

"For seven hundred years we have been enslaved, Ragnar. Your people. My people. We have languished in darkness. But there will come a day when we walk in the light. It will not come from their mercy. It will not come by fate. It will come when brave hearts rise and choose to break the chains, to live for more. You must choose for yourself. Will you choose the hard path? Will you choose to be my friend? Will you rise with me? Or will you go as all who have gone before, never knowing what might have been?"

I leave after that. I do not swear him to silence. I do not demand an answer. Dancer demanded none from me. I had to make the choice. If I had not, if I had been forced into service, then I would have given up a thousand times. Slaves do not have the bravery of free men. That is why Golds lie to lowReds and make them think they are brave. That is why they lie to Obsidians and make them think it is an honor to serve gods. Easier than the truth. Yet it takes only one truth to bring a kingdom of lies crashing down.

Ragnar must join me, because Red alone will not be enough.

35

||||||||||||||||||||||||

TEATIME

Our disguise in the camel ship holds as we approach the fleet around Hildas Station, aiming for what was once Augustus's flagship, now Pliny's. *Invictus*. RipWings fly silently past us, requesting clearance codes. Our pilot sends the codes and we are escorted to join a procession of supply ships that funnel into the *Invictus*'s hangar, like caravan traders lining up outside the grand gates of some desert citadel. Guns track us as we taxi.

We land with a thud. The pilot pops open the aft bay doors and I and mine hop from the ship down to the hangar's floor. Instead of greeting Brown haulers like she might have expected, the Orange Docker looks up from her datapad to see a war party in full armored panoply. Armed to the teeth. Without hesitation, she sits down, wanting no part of this.

Sevro laughs and pats her on the head. "Wiser than Gold."

A circus of ships fills the bay. Lights glow down from the high ceiling. Oranges and Reds scuttle about. Welding torches sizzle against hulls. Men and women shout at one another. My fellows follow me, walking through the hangar toward the lifts where we can access the rest of the ship.

And as we walk, silence spreads like wildfire. Welding torches cease to sizzle. Men no longer call out. They simply stare. I stalk forward in the front with Lorn. Mustang and Kavax au Telemanus flank us. Roque follows with Sevro and Daxo. Victra comes next with the Howlers. And then behind them all, like some sort of pale, giant shepherd, comes Ragnar.

He chose to join us from the freezer. We exchange a look, and in one nod, I know I have a new general for the rebellion. I swell with confidence.

Not a soul protests our movement, though by our attire they know we do not come for peaceful talks. My armor is black. Carved with roaring lions. A thin pulseShield flickers over it. On my left arm, my aegis activates, its opaque blue surface drinking in the light. My white razor slithers on my arm. Our boots make the sound of hail on the metal decks. I dispatch Pebble to have her Green squads crash the ship's communications system.

A Copper sees us and makes a deal of playing with his datapad. Ragnar slips up to him, touches his shoulder hard enough to push the man to his knees. "**No.**"

We enter the lift and the guts of the ship without a shot being fired. We take the lift to the deck one above the command level. The lift doors open, bringing us face-to-face with a squad of Gray marines.

"Captain, you're to accompany Virginia au Augustus to the engineering bay," I say to the Gray. His eyes appreciate the gravity of the situation; after barely a hesitation, he salutes. His confused men fall in behind Mustang and the Telemanuses as they head off at a trot.

The ship alarm begins to wail.

The Howlers go to the engines and life support systems as my own force continues three decks up, heading not for the command deck, where Pliny will be hosting his new allies, but for the brig. Roque, Victra, Lorn, Sevro, and Ragnar slip in through the doors, subduing the guards before I even enter.

The prisoners, some forty Peerless Augustus Loyalists, are imprisoned in small duroglass cells. Sevro walks past each, freeing the men and women inside with a datakey as he goes.

"Thank the Reaper," he says to each, repeating it four times to a towering old Peerless woman till she finally realizes she's not getting out till she plays his little game. They each roll their eyes and say thank you. "What a good, abnormally tall and decrepit Peerless you are. Excellent," Sevro says, and lets the woman out. "Lorn! I found a possible bedmate." He pauses as he comes before the Jackal's glass cage.

"What do I spy with my little eye?" Sevro happily crows. "Wait! I have two again!"

"Let me out," the Jackal replies flatly. "I'm not playing your game, Goblin."

"Thank the Reaper. And the name's Sevro. You know that."

The Jackal rolls his eyes. "Thank you, Reaper."

"Bow like a good servant."

"No."

"Just let him out," Lorn grumbles.

"He has to play my game!" Sevro says. "Shithead isn't getting out till he plays nice. I'll give him a riddle instead. What do I have in my pocket?"

I grow tired of the game, so behind his back, I point to my eye.

"An eyeball," the Jackal says.

"Gorydammit, who told him?"

Roque takes the key from Sevro's hand and scans it over the cell's console. The Jackal joins us. "Grow up, Sevro," Roque mutters.

"The hell is your problem?" Sevro asks. "We need to take our time anyway. Can't let me have a little bit of fun?"

We take our time so Pliny can fear our actions. He must suspect the loyalty of most of the crew. But no doubt he has a contingent of bought-and-paid-for soldiers on board. Mercenaries, most likely. He'll hide behind them like a shield.

"Where's your father?" I ask the Jackal.

"I don't know," he says. "I don't believe he's on the ship. My sister make it to you safely?"

"She found us."

"Good," he says, turning quickly to acknowledge Lorn. "A pleasure, Arcos. My father forbade me from reading your exploits as a child. Still, I managed. Tales of Old Stoneside kept me up late into the night."

"As did your performance at the Institute," Lorn replies with a small smile for me. "I was afraid to close my eyes after seeing your campaign."

The Jackal chuckles. "Seems your mission was a success on Europa, Darrow."

"They sprang the trap as we hoped. And Aja escaped."

"Then let's go fix this problem and get on with our war."

Roque looks back and forth between us, perhaps noting the familiarity with which we speak. Yet another thing I never told him. The gulf grows.

We meet Mustang in the lowColor galley during lunch hours. Hundreds of Orange deckhands and electricians mingle with the Red factory workers and Brown janitors. The buzz of conversation and the clatter of plastic trays on metal tables falters as soon as Ragnar enters the galley. Dead silence except an overexcited Brown janitor who screams at the top of his lungs. His comrades quickly cover his mouth.

Ragnar walks to the center of the room and moves one of the tables without waiting for the lowColors to get up. Pulling it free of its metal bolts, he drags it screeching across the metal floor, lowColors still sitting on the attached benches. They stay motionless, eyes huge and terrified and utterly confused at the sight of my cadre of fifty Golds.

The Telemanuses follow Ragnar, carrying between father and son a circular metal device one meter thick, two meters in diameter—the purpose of their trip to the engineering bay. Their arms are covered by armor, but the veins of their necks bulge under its weight. Mustang guides them, looking at her datapad. "Here," she says. They drop it where she points. The Grays follow, carrying a huge battery unit, which they set on top of a nearby table.

"Howlers, make some noise," I say into my com.

"Pardon me. Excuse me. Sorry," Pebble says, waving her pudgy little hands. She takes a cable from the battery unit and attaches it to the disc.

There's a crackle as the ship's speakers activate. *"Pliny,"* a voice calls sweetly. I look around for Sevro and see him at a terminal with two of the Greens.

"Sevro!" Mustang and I snap.

He holds up a finger for us to wait.

"He's on the com," one of the Greens jabbers out sincerely. "Just a sec."

"Dear Pliny," Sevro sings over the com.

> *If your heart beats like a drum,*
> *and your leg's a little wet,*
> *it's 'cause the Reaper's come*
> *to collect a little debt.*

He sings this three times until Ragnar throws a table into the console. Sparks shower out. Sevro looks up slowly at the table hanging over his head. It missed by inches. He wheels around. "What the gory-pissandshit is your damage, you overreacting mountain troll!"

"**Rhyming . . . nnnngh.**" Ragnar makes an uncomfortable groaning sound.

"You found him," Mustang mutters as we share a look.

"Which one?" I ask as Sevro curses the Stained out in every compound manner he knows. Adding the crux for good measure.

"**You squawk like a . . . like a chicken,**" Ragnar says in reply.

"He can't insult me," Sevro says, aghast. He looks at me. "Control him."

I wash my hands of it.

"If I may suggest continuing," Lorn says.

"Right. Serious faces, everyone." Helmets slide from armor to cover our skulls. I see thermal readings, power levels in the digital display. "Prime it," I tell Mustang.

She activates the leechCraft thermal drill. It's meant to burrow through the outer hull of a ship and create a breach large enough for a boarding party to pour through. So carving through the floor of a ship is nothing. And we're only one deck above the command rooms. I jump atop the drill.

Momentum is everything to a Helldiver, to military endeavors, to life. Keep moving and dare someone to get in your path.

"You know what I said earlier?" Lorn asks me.

"About tact?" I ask.

He grins evilly behind his beard. "Slag tact. Terrify them."

I look at Mustang. "Burn."

She presses a button. The drill glows red. Heat radiates up into me. Spreads along the floor. LowColors flow away, abandoning their food, fleeing the room as the floor sags and melts like sand pouring down an hourglass. The drill falls through the dripping deck into the command room beneath with me riding on its back. A Helldiver again, if only for a moment.

It slams into the middle of Augustus's great wooden table, sheaving through and impacting like a meteor into the marble floor, still melting. I cut the power cable with my razor and rise amid the smoke and steam and leaping flames as the table catches fire.

A hundred Golds of the Society stare up at me. Praetors, Legates, Judiciars, and knights of powerful houses stand with their razors drawn. All once loyal to Augustus. All now under Pliny's thumb. Going with the wind, as they say.

And there he is, at the head of the long table, his face fast paling. Beautiful, clever Pliny. One eye left, the other sporting a temporary bionic replacement. At his right sits one of the Sovereign's Furies, the Politico, Moira. Compared with Aja, she's a puffy pastry of a woman. But her sweet smile is half again as sinister as her sister's razor. Beside her is an Olympic Knight, the Storm Knight from the Japanese Isles of Earth.

"*My goodmen!*" I bellow through the voice amplifier in my helmet. "*I have come for Pliny.*" I jump down from the drill, helmet rippling back into my armor so they can see my face. I walk toward him. My friends follow through the hole. Arcos first. Then Mustang and Sevro.

"You said he was dead!" someone to my left snarls, razor half pulled.

"Lorn au Arcos?" murmurs another. His name rips through the place as Sevro and Roque secure the doors leading into the room.

"And KAVAX AU TELEMANUS!" Kavax booms wildly as he lands. Guess Pax had to learn it somewhere.

"The Reaper is not dead," Mustang says, hopping down from the drill. "Nor am I. Nor is my brother. And we have come to reclaim what belongs to our father."

These Peerless don't know what to do.

"Liars!" Pliny cries. "You betrayed the ArchGovernor. Seize the traitors!"

Lorn makes a simple proclamation. "If anyone comes within two meters of Darrow, I kill *everyone* in this room."

They don't seem eager to call his bluff. The men I walk between jump backward. Lorn's reputation carves a hole for me straight to Pliny. I don't break pace.

"Pliny," I say. "We must speak."

"Kill him!" Pliny screams. "Kill the Reaper."

A young man lurches forward and dies as his neighbor stabs him in the back. The neighbor looks fearfully to Lorn.

"Two point three meters," Lorn says. "Close."

"Kill him!" Pliny shouts futilely. "He's just boy!"

I speak quietly, but all can hear.

"Pliny au Velocitor, you are a traitor to ArchGovenor Nero au Augustus. You have conspired to destroy his house, to forcibly marry his daughter, to kill his son, and betray him to the Sovereign, who has set herself against him. Your master raised you up, and you tried to tear him down. You have betrayed his trust all for personal gain. Worst of all, you have failed."

"Stop him!" Pliny screams now, wildly gesticulating at me. "Moira!"

Moira whispers to the Storm Knight, and both step to the side.

"You're supposed to be dead," Pliny mutters. "Aja said she would kill you on Europa."

"And who do *you* know that can kill me?" I say, that ridiculous Gold rage building in my voice so that it might impress all these hungry souls. "The Jackal failed. Antonia au Severus-Julii failed. Proctors Apollo and Jupiter failed. Cassius au Bellona failed. Karnus failed. Cagney failed. Aja au Grimmus and her Praetorians failed."

The hangman failed. The mines and pitvipers failed. "And now you fail."

That's when I slip forward, faster than a striking pitviper, and slap him across the face. He pitches sideways out of his seat like a leaf battered by the wind, careening into a Gold who stood to the side. She spits on him and moves for me.

"You are a worm who thought himself a serpent just because you slither. But your power was not real, Pliny. It was all a dream. Time now to wake."

Pliny scrambles to his feet, pushing himself away from me. His carefully combed hair is a mess, and redness swells on his right cheek. I spin him around and slap him again, harder. He's startled. Doesn't know what to do. He was not taken from his bed during his first day at the Institute and beaten by Obsidians. He did not ride upon the snow-crusted beaches at the head of an armored column. He did not starve. So now all he can do is scramble and cry.

I seize him with my hands, raise him high into the air. But I hurt him no more. I will not demean the moment with cruelty like Karnus or Titus would. My condescension is my weapon. I set Pliny back in the ArchGovernor's chair. I buff his dragonfly pin. Straighten his hair like a kindly mother. Pat him on his tear-stained cheek and extend my hand, which bears my House Mars ring.

He kisses it without me asking.

"Goodbye, Pliny. I leave you to your friends."

I walk away, the eyes of all these Peerless following me, abandoning Pliny. I hear a slurping sound and do not turn, because I know what razors sound like when they kill. They didn't even wait. Pliny is forgotten.

These Peerless thump their chests in salute to me. The monsters. They go with the wind, chasing power. But they don't realize power doesn't shift. Power is resolute. It is the mountain, not the wind. To shift so easily is to lose trust. And trust is what has kept me alive. Trust in my friends, and their trust in me.

The Sovereign knows this. It is why she keeps her Furies close. They would die for her, as my friends would die for me. Because in the end, what does all the power in all the worlds matter if your closest friends can betray you? The Sovereign's father learned that when his daughter took his head. Pliny learned at the price of his life. I forgot it, distanced myself from my friends, and nearly lost everything because of it when Tactus felt as overshadowed and alienated with me as he did with his brothers. It is why I started fresh with Victra, why I told Ragnar the truth, why I must make amends with Lorn and Roque.

Trust is why Red will have a chance. We are a people bound by song and dance and families and kinship. These people are allies only because they think they must be.

I look at them now and I know they are so stern and so rigid that they will break and shatter against one another, not because of me, but because of what they are.

I float on my gravBoots, pausing to say, "Tell all who will hear, the Reaper sails to Mars. And he calls for an Iron Rain."

36

||||||||||||||||||||||||||

LORD OF WAR

"Power is the crown that eats the head," the Jackal said to me as we planned the invasion. He spoke in reference to Octavia. But the truth reaches further than that. These Golds have had power for so long. Look how they act. Look what they want. They jump at the chance for war. They come from near, from far, ships racing to join my armada as they learn that I have called for an Iron Rain, the first in twenty years. I used the Jackal to spread the news, along with footage of Pliny's fall. Many of them are second sons and daughters, who will not inherit their parents' estates. Warmongers, duelists, the glory-hungry. And each bring their attendants of Grays and Obsidians. The worlds of the Society wait with bated breath to see what happens today. If we lose, the Sovereign rules on. If we win— complete civil war. No world can stand apart.

Legions marshal within my ship as my armada gathers around the dock moon of Phobos. I carry my razor curved as a slingBlade; crooked and cruel, it is my scepter. My iron House Mars ring tightens as I flex my hand and stare through the viewports. The pegasus bounces against my chest.

I cannot see my enemy—Bellona and much of the Sovereign's local fleets—but they lie between me and my planet. The Sovereign's ancient Ash Lord comes fast from the Core to aid with his Scepter Armada, but he is still a week away. He cannot help the Bellona today.

My Blues watch me, and my generals—of Victra au Julii's personal fleet, who abandoned her mother's forces, of House Arcos, of the House Telemanus, and the bannermen of Augustus.

Mars is green and blue and pocked with shielded cities. White caps mark her poles. Blue oceans stretch along her equator. Fields of grass along with thick forests coat her surface. Clouds swirl about her, a cotton shift to hide her sparkling shielded cities. And there are guns. Great stations in the deserts, around the cities, where shipkilling railguns point to the sky.

My thoughts dip below the surface of the planet. I wonder what my mother is doing now. Is she making breakfast? Do they know what comes? Will they even feel it when we do?

My fingers don't tremble even on the brink of battle. My breath is even. I was born to a family of Helldivers. I was born to a bloodline of dust and toil, born to serve the Golds. I was born to this velocity.

Yet I am terrified. Mickey carved me to be a god of war. But why do I feel like such a boy standing in silly armor? Why do I want to be five years old again, before my father died, sharing the bed with Kieran, listening to him talk in his sleep?

I turn to the sea of Gold faces.

This race—what a beautiful monster. They carry all of humanity's strengths, except one. Empathy. They can change. I know that. Perhaps not now, perhaps not in four generations. But it begins today, the end of their Golden Age. Shatter the Bellona, weaken Gold. Drive the civil war to Luna itself and destroy the Sovereign. Then Ares will rise.

I don't want to be here. I want to be home, with her, with my child who never was.

But can't be. I feel the tide inside me go out, baring old wounds. *This is for you,* I tell her. For the world you should have lived in.

And so I return my part, feeding these wolves.

"In the fading days of autumn," I say, voice loud and bold, "the Reds who mine the bedrock of Mars wear masks of happy ghouls to celebrate the dead claimed by the red soil, to honor their memories and subdue their spirits. We Aureate took those masks and made them our own. We gave them the faces of legend and myth to remind ourselves that there is no evil, no good. No gods. No demons. There is only man. There is only this world. Death comes for us all. But how will we shout into the wind? How will we be remembered?" I pull off one of my gloves and cut my palm very shallowly. I clench my fist till the blood coats my skin, and then press my hand to my face. "Make your blood proud long after death claims you."

There's the stomp of feet. Just one.

"Luna is the new Earth. It rules us and makes us bow and scrape. Our sacrifice means its gain. Again, the weak hold back the strong. After today, when we take the Thousand Cities of Mars, our ranks will swell. The Galilean Lords will swear for us. The Governors of Saturn will bow to us. Neptune will come with her ships and we will cut off the leech that is Octavia au Lune."

And make a tyrant king. It makes so much sense to them. I don't know how. A tyrant for a tyrant. How do they find inspiration from this? Men always have.

Another stomp.

"Every moment today will be captured by the holoCams we've given you." Like it was at the Institute and when I took the *Pax*. The Jackal's idea. "Each moment will be remembered. If you win glory, it will be spread across the HCs of every world. If you shame yourself or your family, it will not fade with your death." I look to Ragnar, as though he were my headsman. Lorn rolls his eyes at the dramatic flair. "We will remember."

Stomp.

"The cities are to be taken. The Golds who will not bend, killed. The lowColors protected. We will not collapse the mines. We will not rape her cities and despoil her verdant grounds. We are to capture the bounty of Mars. We do not want to take her corpse. She is home to many of you, so harm only the pest that destroys her from within. And when the glory of the day is over—when you wipe the blood from your sword and give the cloth to your sons and daughters, so they will remember you were party to one of the greatest battles since the Fall of Earth— remember, you have made your own destiny. It was not given to you by the Sovereign. It was not given to you by a governor. *You* took it like our ancestors took the worlds. We are the Second Conquerors."

Now there's the roar. I hate how my body shivers at the idea of glory. There's something deep in man that hungers for this. But I think it weakness, not strength, to abandon decency for that strange darker spirit.

I look at the Jackal to the side of the bridge. He has little importance on this day. He has done his work bringing all these men and women here. He has muddled communications and sown false information, leading much of the Sovereign's aid to the Bellona scattered chasing false rumors of elements of my fleet sneaking off to attack Luna. A ploy only. My forces are all here.

"Quite the puppet master you play," the Jackal whispers to me as we wait for the Whites to enter the bridge behind the waiting Golds. Sevro scoots closer to me, as if to remind the Jackal of his place.

"You made most of the strings. I never thanked you," I say quietly back to him.

His plain face wrinkles with distaste. "Must we become sentimental?"

"You helped Mustang escape. That's why Pliny caught you." He never mentioned it, never boasted or used it as leverage. It was the simple act of a brother helping a sister. I shrug. "And you tried your damnedest to save Quinn. Maybe you're a better man than you know."

He laughs that barking laugh of his. "Doubtful. But tomorrow, a traitor will be king, and an Empress shall be traitor, so maybe wicked men can be virtuous."

I look out the viewport. "Are your satellites ready?"

"For the virus?" He nods. "My Greens will shut down all communications as soon as you give the word. For fifteen minutes, it will be quiet as death, for everyone. Their global and regional defensive units won't have surveillance or sensors. Time enough to shatter most of the static positions." He looks at his feet, as though suddenly self-conscious. "Save my father if you can."

Sevro shifts, annoyed at our whispering.

"I will."

I'd rather Augustus rot forever in a hole in the ground. But I need him once Mars is taken. Despite what I can do, I'm not a Governor or a king. I need his legitimacy, as Theodora reminded me last night. Without it, I'm just an arm with a razor.

"And you're sure about Agea?" he asks. "About the prize? Otherwise it's reckless."

"One hundred percent," I reply.

"Good. Good. Prime luck, then, Reaper." He moves away.

"Replacing me already?" Sevro snorts, watching him go.

"He's got one hand. You've got one eye. I have a type."

The ceremonies continue. Two hundred Golds bend their knees as the Whites walk through their ranks. I try to think it a stupid, solemn thing, all these men and women with their pompous silence and their attention to tradition. But this is the history of mankind in the making. And there is a nobility to the moment.

Armor glints against the artificial light. Ethereal Whites wander through the ranks, virgin maidens barefoot in snow-white cloaks, with daggers of iron and laurels of gold. Child Whites carry the triangular golden standards—a scepter, a sword, and a scroll crowned with a laurel. I feel hands on my shoulders.

I feel their weight.

They say this is the way the Old Conquerors went to battle, with virgins of White wounding them with iron. They touch our brows with the laurel and cut our left palms with the iron as they whisper softly in our ears:

"My son, my daughter, now that you bleed, you shall know no fear, no defeat, only victory. Your cowardice seeps from you. Your rage burns bright. Rise, warrior of Gold, and take with you your Color's might."

Then each warrior smears the handprint of blood across his face and across the top of his demonfaced helm. One by one we stand in silence. Each Gold represents ten legions. This is the storm that will fall on Mars in a torrent of metal. Millions of Golds, Grays, and Obsidians.

"We do not fight a planet. We fight men and women. Cut off their heads and see their armies crumble," Lorn reminds us all.

The assembly of warriors stands, faces now smeared with blood, and together we recite the names of our chief enemies. "Karnus au Bellona, Aja au Grimmus, Imperator Tiberius au Bellona, Scipia au Falthe, Octavia au Lune, Agrippina au Julii, and Cassius au Bellona. These are wanted lives."

In the halls of my enemy, they will recite my name, and the names of my friends. He who kills the Reaper will have bounty and renown. Individual hunters and killgroups will scan our com signals, searching for me. And in packs they will descend, some for single battle. Others for the sly kill of a sniper's bullet. Some will not even participate in the battle for Mars. They are Gray mercenaries. Freed Obsidian bounty hunters. Knights of Venus and Mercury here only for my head, using their family assets, family soldiers, to help them privately stalk me and make their own glory. The Jackal intercepted a communiqué that three of the Olympic Knights are here. They all will have watched me, studied my recordings, my victories, my defeats. And they will know my nature, the nature of my Howlers. But I will not know them.

Let them come make their introductions.

I'm more interested in meeting Cassius. At least that's what I told Lorn. But he knows that's not true. A deep shame burns in me for how I yelled like a monster at his family. I beat him fairly, but I didn't have to like it as much as I did. Sometimes I wonder if he were raised a Red and I a Gold if he wouldn't have ended up a better man than I am now, and I a worse man than he ever could be.

For some reason I think I could have been capable of great evil. Maybe that's the guilt. Maybe that's the fear of a life where I never knew Eo. I don't know. Or maybe it's the fear of knowing how easily I fall to pride.

My warriors disperse back to their own family vessels. I watch out the viewport as half a hundred shuttles streak away to the great armada we've assembled. Though they know we're here now, our enemies did not expect us to come to Mars so quickly.

I turn my attention to my remaining commanders. Orion will lead the *Pax* and Roque will lead the fleet in conjunction with Victra. I approve of their plan. The rest of my inner circle lingers, except for Mustang, who goes ahead to the hangars.

I reach up slightly to thump both of the Telemanuses on their shoulders. "Pax would have looked brilliant this day." Sophocles curls around Kavax's ankles.

"My brother always looked brilliant," Daxo says warmly. "Silly, shouting, trying to be like Father. But brilliant nonetheless. We'll kill Tiberius au Bellona, don't you worry."

"Do I look worried?"

Both Titans nod their giant heads. Kavax has gone into his battle quiet. He cannot speak except to mumble, so Daxo continues to speak for him. "Take care of yourself, Reaper." He spares a look back at the Jackal. "We know it's a marriage of necessity, but don't trust him."

"You know I don't."

"Do not trust him," Daxo repeats.

"I trust only friends." We say our goodbyes.

Orion's brow is wrinkled in thought. I ask her if anything is the matter as she leans over the scanner display. She's assessing the enemy disposition in the sync. "They noticed us come into orbit an hour ago. We were vulnerable while filtering in, but they remained in defensive formation over Agea."

"It is odd," Roque agrees. "They cede much of the planet without a fight. Perhaps it'd be better to orient your drop to the south. . . ."

"I want Agea," I say coldly.

"We'll be shooting you into the thick, brother. The capital can wait. Seize the other cities and we can take it without assault. Why such a wild rush?"

"If we take the capital, the other cities fall."

"And many men die."

"It is war, Roque. Trust me on this one."

"It's your war." Roque salutes. After catching a glare from Victra, he pulls me close. "Fare thee well, Primus." He kisses both my cheeks, surprising me.

"It's been a long road," I say carefully.

"And we've miles to go before we sleep."

"My brother." I clasp the back of his neck and bring his forehead to mine. "I'm sorry. I'm so sorry." I shake my head. "For Quinn. For Lea. For the gala. For a thousand slights I've laid upon you. You've been my dearest friend." Pulling back, I avoid his eyes. "I should have said it earlier. But I was afraid."

"In what world should you be afraid of me?" he asks.

I shake my head. "Forgive me, for everything."

"We'll make amends later." He claps my shoulder. "Prime luck."

I leave him. Lorn and I draw up just outside the bridge, where our paths diverge into different halls. He's shaved for war, and he wears his old Rage Knight armor. He looks brilliant but smells terrible. These old knights are like the Howlers. Superstitious and unwilling to wash their gear for fear of washing away whatever luck kept them alive thus far.

"I've received communiqués from many old friends," Lorn says. "They side with Bellona."

"All old men and women?"

"The old have weathered many seasons of the young." There's a twinkle in his eye. "But they ask me about you. They ask if the boy warlord is really four meters tall. Is he really followed by a wolfpack? Is he a worldbreaker?"

"And what do you say?"

"I said you are five meters tall, you're followed by a midget and a giant, and you eat glass with your eggs." We share a laugh. "I don't like that you brought me here. I don't believe you're being the man you want to be. If you survive this and I don't, be better than the man who tricked his friend."

A dull ache grows behind my eyes. It's a plea he makes. Not for me to feel guilty, but because he truly cares. I should be better. I want to be. I *am* being better in the end. But with the means to reach that end . . . am I just like all the other lost souls? Am I just another Harmony? Another Titus?

"I promise," I say, meaning it even as I intend to hurt him again and again.

"Good. Good." He pops his leathery neck. "So after Agea, you take the northern hemisphere. I'll take the southern. And we meet back here for whiskey. Deal, my goodman?"

I nod, but still he does not separate.

He stares at me for a moment and glances down, unable to meet my gaze. Emotion thickens his voice. "Each time I returned to my wife, I told her that her boys died well." He fidgets with his ring. "There's no such thing."

"Achilles died well."

"No. Achilles let his pride and rage consume him, and in the end, an arrow shot by a Pixie took him in the foot. There's much to live for besides this. Hopefully you'll grow old enough to realize that Achilles was a gorydamn fool. And we're fools all the more for not realizing he wasn't Homer's hero. He was warning. I feel like men once knew that." His fingers tap his razor. "It's a cycle. Death begets death begets death. It's been my life. I—I don't think I should have killed the boy. Your friend."

"Why do you say that?"

"Because I see the way the rest of them look at you. I think they'd do anything for you because you believe in them."

I move suddenly, leaning down to kiss him on his weathered cheek the way Reds kiss fathers and uncles. "Tactus wouldn't have blamed you. And neither do I. You've another grandson to raise. Maybe you can teach him the peace you couldn't teach me. So do us a favor, don't die, old man."

"Ha," the grizzled lord laughs, falsely at first. Then more forcefully as he turns on a heel. "Ha! They've yet to make a man who can kill Old Stonesides!" His old knights, craggy men and women, flank him, not one younger than seventy, but I recognize all their faces from the histories of the Moon Rebellion and other great wars. Their friends and former comrades wait for us on Mars.

I leave for the hangars, saying a quick farewell to Victra. She calls me back. I feel Roque watching us. She looks about to say something. The red sun of her black armor weeps blood. Black warpaint streaks diagonally across her face. Eyes burning out of it, yet they are vulnerable, gentle as they search mine for a reflection of what she feels.

"After today, the name Julii will mean more than money," I say. Her plan will turn the tide of the space battle.

"I don't care about that." Her fingers touch my breastplate and I see her lips sliding sharply into that wicked smile of hers. "If you die, I want your last thought to be how great a mistake it was to spend all those nights alone in your stateroom at the Academy." She flicks my armor, making a pinging noise. "What a beautiful mess we could have made of each other."

Theodora waits for me in the hall, giving me a look.

"Oh, shut up."

"She would have eaten you up and spit you out, *dominus*."

"Why aren't you in the staterooms where it's safe?"

"It's not safe anywhere." Theodora motions me to bend my head. She puts a small red flower clip, the sort a young girl would wear, into my hair. "All knights need their tokens," she says, tearing up. "Don't be too much a hero. You're too clever to die in a stupid battle."

She leaves, squeezing Ragnar's forearm as she passes. I didn't know they were familiar. Ragnar follows along, hanging back like a hesitant shadow as Sevro and I speak on the way to the hangars.

"So it is done?" I ask Sevro.

He shrugs. "I sent it."

"You spoke to *him*?"

"A holoNet dropCache," he says. "I send a message. They get it. Hopefully."

"You mean you don't know if they got it?"

"How should I know? I said I sent it. Followed protocol."

I curse quietly. He whistles that damn tune he sang Pliny. I swat at him. We turn a corner and pass six dozen Gray special ops troopers heading for the tubes at a jog. Six Obsidians follow behind them, opening their palms to Ragnar and me as signs of respect.

"You see what they were wearing? SlingBlades on their armor." Sevro smirks over at me. "It spreads."

"Have you thought about what happens if your father is down there?" I ask.

"No," he says, losing his smile. "No, I haven't."

37

||||||||||||||||||||||

WAR

The forward hangar bay is massive. A giant cave in the belly of my ship crawling with men and women of all Colors. Six hundred meters in length. Along its left side are hundreds of spitTubes. Each row is accessed by a network of giant causeways where men in starShells can walk. Thousands stand ready to disperse, grouped according to legion.

The alarm for battle stations warbles throughout the ship. Orion's voice rasps over the intercom. Beyond the hull, Roque, now the youngest Imperator in a hundred years, will be breaking our armada into fleets to engage the Bellona over Mars. Squadrons of ripWings and wasps pour forth. Blues flying to their deaths. Gold squad leaders in their midst. All to carve a hole large enough for the leechCraft to swarm onto the enemy hulls. Some Praetors hoard their soldiers to fight off enemy waves that make it aboard their ships. Others launch full attacks. It's a gamble either way. Can't think of it. Victra, Roque, and Orion have that responsibility. I have my own.

I pause, looking out at the hangar. "What if Ares isn't real?" I ask Sevro quietly.

"What the hell you talking about?" Sevro asks.

"What if it's just a Gold trick? Someone pulling strings to make Society go the way they need it to go. What if it's all a lie?"

Sevro looks at me for a long moment, then he hops up on a banister and howls at the top of his lungs down at the hangar bay.

The bay howls back.

It comes from Grays. It comes from Obsidians, from Oranges. It comes from Reds working on tubes. And it comes from the Golds who requested transfer to my ship.

"That's no lie."

And that's when I see the standards of the legions fall, replaced with something new. Gone are the pyramids of the society. Gone are the laurel and the scepter and the sword and the scroll. Gone is Augustus's lion. Instead, the high golden standards that the legions carry to battle are peaked with wolves and slingBlades.

These legions are mine.

I feel something buzzing in those around me. A sort of physical fanaticism. It did not buzz in the Golds quite like this. The Golds love me because of the victory and glory I bring. These other Colors love me for something far different, something far more potent. Any other conquering Gold would have vented the ship, but I did not, because they chose me instead of the Golds who once were their masters. I gave them that choice.

Sevro grips my arm. "Do you understand that you must fight differently today?"

"I get it, Sevro." I try to shake off his hand.

"You don't." He pulls me to look at him and shoos Ragnar back. "Every move you make today will be recorded and broadcast to every part of the Solar System. This battle is to make the fleet *yours*." His voice drops to a harsh whisper. "The Sons will spread it. Jackal will spread it. House Augustus will spread it. Act like a god, get followed like a god. Register?"

"Win or lose, this is still Augustus's fleet," I say.

"Not if he's dead."

I assigned Sevro to infiltrate the Citadel in Agea where the Arch-Governor is being held captive. But I did not tell him to kill Augustus.

"You're not going to kill him," I say with authority. "I forbid it. It is . . ."

"Necessary. You don't need his *legitimacy*. Haven't you figured us out yet? Here you get what you take, no matter the right of it." He spits on the ground. "You are twenty years old. If you win Mars, Darrow, you become a living god. And so when you reveal what you really are . . . you transcend Color. Do I register?"

Sevro has grown wiser since we first met. No doubt about that. But I fear he thinks too much of me. Apollo thought he was a god. Augustus thinks he is. A god is not what I should be. A god is something to serve, something to worship. I've never wanted that. Eo never wanted that. Sevro will have to learn. This is about freedom. Yet it seems like everyone just wants to follow.

Mustang oversees the troop operations today. She floats through the air with Milia, the horsefaced Gold we adopted at the Institute. Nearer me saunters an ambling, pitiless Gold with a familiar face. I laugh and point him out to Sevro, who curses poignantly.

"Proctor Jupiter?" I call to the man. "Darling, could that really be you?"

"Who else would it be, you uppity brat?" Jupiter comes before me. He's tall. Careless in the eyes. Hair bound tight. Half a foot taller than I, he's a sinful, hedonistic beast of a man with an arrogant streak a kilometer long, and it is clear that he and Ragnar are two misunderstandings away from opening each other up. He eyes the razor wrapped around my forearm, and I see his is worn in the same new fashion. "I heard you're the one responsible for the new style." He holds up his arm. "I do approve. Bold as a naked prick in an ant nest."

"Limping still?" Sevro asks.

"Shut up, Goblin," Jupiter sneers.

"Daddy dearest had a little duel with Proctor Jupiter here to win the Rage Knight post." Sevro smiles. "Old man sliced him up the same place I did. Right in the ass."

"That slippery slag Fitchner is . . . tricky." Jupiter nods grudgingly. "Very, very tricky. I have been helping the lady," Jupiter rumbles on, gesturing to Mustang.

"How so?" I ask.

"Most of the Augustus cities are on communication interdict. Can't get a word out or in. I'm the emissary to those still loyal. Sneak in. Sneak out. Been doing it for weeks now and sending word to remote dropCaches and the other loyal cities. A whole war's been going on here with her agents and her brother's while you were out stitching together a fleet. It's been nasty, my goodman."

"So what can you tell me?" I ask.

"Well, Daddy Bellona commands the house fleet against your friends. Cassius and Karnus have been allocated to ground operations inside Agea. I am going to help you find them and kill them." Jupiter raises his large eyebrows, as though telling us how tedious he finds the chore. "That is the point—kill the Bellona family members and all their allies will suddenly wonder why they're fighting—isn't it?" He winks at Sevro. "Next best thing to pounding that Luneborn Sovereign's head in."

"You sure all Bellona are in Agea?"

Jupiter nods grudgingly. "Last we saw. That was a couple days ago, though, after they brought Augustus down in chains." He airily holds up a finger. "And there was a peculiar series of heavy shuttles that landed last night."

I wave a hand, ignoring mention of the shuttles. He squints at me, but I tell him to shut up and get behind me as I meet Mustang and her entourage.

"Everything is prepared," she says. "We're awaiting launch orders." She wrinkles her nose as if smelling something foul. "Sevro, do watch Jupiter. He tends to shit where he eats."

Jupiter yawns. "Pleasure working with you too."

"Milia, lovely seeing you washed," I say.

"Reaper." She nods and smiles, an ugly thing on her face. "Still playing with scythes? Warms the heart."

"You've a heart?" Sevro chuckles.

She examines his height. "A full-sized one." She pauses. "I saw Pollux just yesterday, on the other side, however. Been sneaking in and out with Jupiter here. You've arranged us all a little reunion. I heard about Tactus. He was a bastard."

True enough. I glance at my datapad. We'll be at the launch coordinates in five. My team disperses. Mustang lingers, face thoughtful.

"What's what?" I ask. "Worrying about me already?"

"A little," she confides, coming close enough for me to smell the scent of her. "But it's my father. What if they kill him before we even make landfall?"

"They won't kill him. They'll need him as a bargaining chip. Or if they've lost, they'll spare him and hope we do the same for all the Bellona family members. You don't kill men as important as him."

I reach for her hand to comfort her, but she pulls it away, turning from me. "We have a planet to invade."

I watch her go, shouting orders to her men.

38

||||||||||||||||||||||

THE IRON RAIN

All I see is metal. I'm one of a thousand in the honeycomb of spitTubes. Beyond the metal tube, a battle rages. I feel nothing. Not the shudder of the *Pax*. Not the missiles as they range through space to bring silent death. Just the throbbing of my heart. Mickey told me it was the strongest he'd seen in a Red, courtesy of the pitviper poison that traced my veins when I was young. It makes my hands shake now as it gallops in my chest. Fear rides in me. Fear of so many things. Fear of letting down my friends, of losing my friends. Of telling my friends the truth about what I am. Fear of being unequal to the task before me. Fear caused by doubt—in myself, in my plans for the rebellion. Fear of death. Fear of being lost in the darkness of space beyond the hull. Fear of failing Eo, my people, myself. But chiefly, fear of hot metal.

Chatter comes over the coms. Perfunctory. The plan is in motion, and I'm nothing but a cog now. The battle is too large for me to take part in all of it. I wanted to lead the *Pax* from her bridge so I could watch the enemy ships fall to my fleet. But Orion and Roque are better than I am in space.

I wanted to be in the leechCraft carrying the boarding parties through the breach into enemy hulls; I wanted to storm bridges, repel invaders from my own ship, bounce from destroyer to dreadnought, making them mine. But I will not capture Imperator Bellona. The Titans will do that. In the end, my enemies dictate where I go. I chase the grand prize.

A prize that has been my target since after I left Luna.

My true pegasus pendant is cool against my chest. Eo's hair lies within. *Focus on that.* On the way her hair moved. Drifting on deep-mine winds. *Focus there.* Thinking of her, I am beset with guilt. I like this life. No matter my reluctance to play the Gold, no matter the sorrowful excuses I make, part of me is like them. Perhaps I was born to be of two Colors.

Slag that. Man wasn't born to be any Color. Our rulers decided to relegate us to Colors. And they were wrong.

"Audentes fortuna juvat, darlings," Sevro says over a private com-line. I burst out laughing at the Latin.

"More 'Fortune favors the bold' crap? Why not just say *carpe diem?*"

"Because it's tradition to say . . ."

"Do you boys always flirt like this before battle? It is adorable," Victra adds.

"You should have seen them at the Institute, love at first howl," Mustang laughs.

"I saw the clips! What a lovely couple."

I hear the smile in Mustang's voice. *"They even wore matching garments. Stylish, weren't they, Roque? And smelly."*

"I certainly took no notice."

"Why not?"

"Sevro scared the piss out of me. I wasn't looking at what he was wearing," Roque replies, drawing laughs. *"I thought he'd been bitten by a squirrel and contracted rabies somehow."*

"Roque?" Sevro calls sweetly.

"Sevro."

"Hello."

"*Hello?*"

"*Next time I see you, I'm going to bite you.*"

"*I must go.*" Roque's light laughter fades. "*We're engaging the main enemy element.*"

"*What are you going to do, bore them to death with a light poetry reading?*" Sevro again.

"*You're a pricklick,*" Roque declares playfully. "*May the Furies guide your swords and the Fates bring you home. Till then, my love is with you all.*"

The profession of love startles the Golds. Roque's com clicks off and we can hear him on the main frequency giving orders to attack an enemy destroyer.

"*What a Pixie,*" Sevro mutters, but even a child could catch the tremor in his voice. He's afraid.

"*Hic sunt leones,*" I say to my friends. "Be brave. Be brave and I'll see you on the other side."

"*Hic sunt leones,*" they echo, not for Augustus, but because we wish we were brave as lions.

One by one, we say our goodbyes. Before I can stop myself, I hail Mustang's private frequency. It takes her twenty seconds to answer. "*What is it?*" Hesitation haunts her voice.

"Stay alive," I say.

A pause. Emotion? Annoyance?

"*You too.*"

She closes the com link. Soon the gears begin to whir and click as I'm loaded into the firing mechanism of the tube.

I've acted this whole time like I know what's coming. Like I know what the Iron Rain is. But it looms before me like some dark, slavering beast. A mystery, though I've seen its face. I've seen the virtual reality experientials and HC clips. I know what it is the way a child knows flying from watching a bird.

"*Deployment coordinates reached.*" Roque's voice fills the ears of every Gold in the fleet. "*Let fall the Rain.*"

The whine of the magnetic charge in the tube fills me. I slide forward into the chamber, bracing myself, looking down so I don't snap my neck. Then it fires and I am claimed by velocity and battle as my stomach fills my throat with bile. I rip through the magnetic stream, out of the ship's tube into swarming chaos.

Fire and lightning rule space. Behemoths of metal belch missiles back and forth, silently pounding one another with all the weapons of man. The silence of it, so eerie, so strange. Great veils of flak explode around the ships, cloaking them in fury, almost like raw cotton tossed into the wind. RipWings and wasps buzz at one another, pissing streams of gunfire. They nip and slice at carapaces of metal, fighting in a dense giant cloud. In little packs they slip from their chaotic fights, spiraling silently toward clusters of leechCraft as the destroyers and carriers launch their troop transports across space in undulating waves. It's a game of boarding parties. Over, under, and through the curtains of flak the leeches go, seeking a hull to clamber onto so they can pump their deadly cargo into the belly of crucial ships, like flies dropping larvae into open wounds. All flown by Blues raised to do only this one thing. Bellona craft pass those of Augustus, waves overlapping, breaking on one another.

All in silence.

Missiles leap toward the leeches, wracking hulls with detonations. No flames save where ships are punctured, leaking oxygen flames like harpooned whales of Old Earth would gout blood. Railgun discharges streak through space, tearing through multiple leeches and smaller fighters at the same time, rending holes in the ranks. Ships rupture forth men and women as both sides target engines, hoping to cripple and capture instead of destroy. Amid the blue and silver enemy fleet, the massive *Warchild* shatters corvettes and torchShips like a cyclops wading through sheep—club swinging pendulous and slow.

I hold my breath as Victra's destroyer, shielded by two others, slips towards the *Warchild*. She's strafed by railguns, and men-of-war garland her with missile fire. The Bellona must warrant she's too close to capture, because they open another salvo into her softened belly. Yet amid the fire she suffers, the corvette births out a desperate burst of forty leechCraft. Nearly ten times her normal complement. We carved her hollow to fit in the additional troop carriers. That is the war party of the Telemanuses.

Victra's ship cuts away from the *Warchild,* recklessly plunging into the Bellona formation where her mother's flotilla of ships bearing the bleeding sun support the Bellona eagles. Victra springs her second surprise.

Her mother switches sides, betraying the Bellona as Victra promised the Jackal and me. Her mother's ships unload more than two hundred leeches amid the core of the Bellona fleet. It is chaos.

My Titans land on the hull of the enemy flagship, and soon the *Warchild* is festooned with leeches. Good luck, Titans.

Bellona-friendly leechCraft redirect toward the *Warchild* to lend aid to the battle that'll clutter her halls with smoke and blood. Rip-Wings zip past, shooting the landed leeches, trying to skin them off before they dump their men into the *Warchild*'s body. It is an elegant dance of action and reaction and reaction and reaction.

I carry on my trajectory, unable to alter it. To my left and right streak thousands of Golds and Obsidians in armored starShells, Grays in hivepods of twelve each. A rain of men and metal. Amid our current fly large storks packed with more Obsidians and Grays. Once we make landfall and secure the beachheads, the massed legions will slip out of the dreadnoughts and carriers on landing craft and pour out behind us.

Despite what the Bellona and their allies think, they cannot stop us from landing men—the orbit around the planet is too large. That is why holding the cities is of such importance. They are island fortresses. The only realistic way of seizing them is making landfall and slipping under the two-hundred-meter gap between their disc-shaped shields and the ground. That requires men on the surface. Millions of men in coordinated assault.

We will establish a hundred beachheads, and then our battle will begin in earnest. In the chaos, missiles streak for our starShells. Friendly capital ships deploy screens of flak behind us, and wasps cover our flanks. Enemy wasps manage to swoop in from the sides, strafing us. Dozens in the rain die around me, their armor folding back like burning paper. I hate this. I want to scream. Some do and we have to cut off their coms.

There is nothing I can do. Pray I don't die. Pray my friends don't die. But pray to what? The Golds have no God. We Reds have an Old

Man in the Vale. But he does not help us in this life. He merely waits to shepherd and guard us in the next.

My heart rattles in my chest. Hyperventilating. Tearing out of my own skin. I feel like a boy. I want the comfort of home. Mother's soup, the touch of her stern hand, the love that blossomed in me whenever I managed to make her smile. Anything to feel the joy of realizing Eo loved me. I long for the cold, quiet nights before love when it was only lust and hunger, where we would kiss in secret, hearts fluttering, like two little birds realizing they might build a nest together after all. That was what life was supposed to be. Family. First loves. Not falling through atmosphere where killers care for nothing more than to fill your body with hot metal before moving on to kill your friends.

My mind flees even as my body acts.

The planet grows and grows till it is a swollen colossus that consumes my vision. I do not know who is dead, who is alive. My display is too busy. We hit the atmosphere and sound roars back. Halos of color cocoon my trembling form. To my left and right, the falling soldiers look like raging lightning bugs jerked out of some Carver's fantasy. I admire one to my left, the bronze sun is behind him as he falls, silhouetting him, immortalizing him in that singular moment—one I know I shall never forget—so that he looks like a Miltonian angel falling with wrath and glory. His exoskeleton sheds its friction armor, as Lucifer might have shed the fetters of heaven, feathers of flame peeling off, fluttering behind. Then a missile slashes the sky and high-grade explosives christen him mortal once again.

The moment we clear the atmosphere, surface gunfire screams up at us, carving holes through our falling swarm. Like a beehive struck, we activate our gravBoots and fracture into a thousand different squadrons, each trying to follow its own coordinates. Enemy rip-Wings followed us into the atmosphere, but here we're more maneuverable, and we kill the big fighters with ease. I swoop in on one from behind with the Howlers hot on my tail, and slash it with my razor. I fly off as it spirals down through the clouds into the ocean below.

Antiaircraft fire screams up at us through the clouds and kills the Gold to my right—a Howler, though I don't know which till I look at my datapad. Daria the Harpy is dead. Just like that. No sacrifice to save another. No howl of rage at the end. No noble gesture. No emotion. The loyal girl who wore belts of scalps at the Institute, who held Rotback and Screwface in thrall to her strange devices, is gone.

A stab of panic goes through me and I dive through the clouds with the rest of my legion's vanguard. We streak low over the ocean, where two waterships spit up fire. Sevro sends two missiles slithering through the air; they detonate, turning into a dozen micro missiles, which become another dozen each. They detonate like corn kernels over fire.

War is chaos. It always has been. But technology makes it worse. It changes the fear. At the Institute, I feared men. I feared what Titus and the Jackal could do to me. You see death coming there and can at least struggle against it. Here you don't have such luxury. Modern war is fearing the air, the shadows, fearing the silence. Death will come and I won't even see it.

I slam down on a snow-covered mountain. Clouds of vapor rise as I melt a hole in the white from the heat of my red-hot suit. The rest of my squad lands around me, finding safe harbor on the ground. Roaring down, meteor men from metal monsters. *Thump. Thump. Thump.* And the fog of war rises.

"Landfall," I snarl.

Sevro falls to a knee, pops open his helmet, and pukes into the snow. Others join him. Ugly Screwface gasps in sadness. Rotback grips his shoulder. Clown stands guard over them, his red-painted Mohawk sideways on his head. Harpy doesn't exist anymore. I didn't know it would be like this. I thought I knew horror. I didn't. More men died in the last minute than I've ever even known. Lorn's fear of war quakes through me.

This is war. Chaos. Chance. Death.

Sevro nods to me, wiping puke from his mouth. Jupiter helps him stand. Strangely, Sevro lets him. I look for Mustang's signature on my helmet's datapad. She's alive with the main element of my force, but we've been separated. I'm with a dozen Golds and forty Obsidians specially trained in hi-tech military equipment.

"Exos off," I bark at the Obsidians. "Omega, guard the perimeter."

We shed our clunky exo thermal armor to reveal the more agile starShells beneath. I order helmets up. Metal demon and animal faces replace those of friends.

But there's beauty in this moment. In the half seconds where Golds and Obsidians nod to one another to pass on comfort before going about their tasks, finding solace in the cocoon of duty, in companionship, like I did in the mines.

I gather Sevro to me along with the Howlers. Ragnar, separated from his legion, stands in my shadow. We landed on the day-side of the planet. It looks like a meteor shower as the second wave of starShells pierces the atmosphere, leaving trails of black smoke across the fire-scarred blue sky. Hundreds of ground cannons still shoot at the swarm that spreads from horizon to horizon, but slowly those gunstreams thin as the guns are targeted from space or eliminated by squads like us on the ground. My squad is three hundred kilometers from where we need to be. How did that happen?

I call Mustang over the coms. She's fifty kilometers closer to the designated drop zone on some other mountain. Her force is nearer four hundred men.

"Looks like we're the idiots," Sevro says.

We go down the mountainside. We do not fly. Instead, we skip. In the Academy they taught us to think of it like skipping a rock over the surface of the water. We could fly in our gravBoots, but flying makes you a target to missiles and anti-aircraft, not to mention enemy hunting parties. So we jump fifty meters into the air, then use our gravBoots to jerk us back toward the ground.

Missile fire comes from a nearby peak. Sevro and his squad deal with it, skipping over thousand-meter ravines, skimming up the side of a steep rock façade as Ragnar and I press forward. A dull *thump* echoes over the mountain range as they rid us of the missile turret. The Howlers link up with us at the end of the mountain range. We perch on the side of a cliff, where low clouds gather. To the left, about twenty kilometers off, rise the towers of distant whitewashed Thessalonica, perched on the craggy coastline of the clear Thermic Sea. Tactus's home. I feel a pang of sadness.

We press north. I watch the towers fade, till they're nothing but glinting metal against the coast of that weirdly calm water. Explosions rumble in the distance. I feel the weight of a hand fall on my armored shoulder.

"Just like after we took Olympus." Sevro grins, looking down from a new mountain's peak at the land that lies open before us.

"Except everyone has gravBoots here." I check our coordinates in my helmet's HUD. The invasion continues above us. Enemy gunships, rarer now, flit across the sky. One targets us. It roars through a cloud and chews up the ground with chainguns. We take cover in a ravine. Snow kicks up around us. Then a missile slithers out and collapses a rock onto my legs in the explosion, pinning me down. Pebble and Clown stand over my body, shielding me.

"Ragnar!" I shout. "Kill it!"

I don't see what he does, but the sound is tremendous as the gunship smokes and spins from the air, teetering toward the ground, and then disappears in a cloud of shrapnel.

"Your legs?" Sevro asks frantically.

They pull the rocks off me. Gears groan and electrical components whir.

"Still work."

We descend the snowy mountain range into rugged Martian plains. A mass of heavy infantry like us moves to our left. Their transponders label them ours. But far off to the right, about thirty kilometers out, where the ground swells into subtropical highlands, a Bellona column skips forward—maybe three hundred in separate parties.

"Cracked one of our com sigs," a Green communications director in space relays over a new signal. *"They're hunting you, Icarus."* My secondary call sign.

"Here's when we learn who is winning the heavens," I say. Sevro directs a tracking laser on the enemy squad, just as they set one on us. Theirs bobs on the ground in front of us like a frantic fly. We scatter, Sevro and I flying away together, and then a rain of fire descends on our enemy from two trajectories. At the same moment, Sevro IDs a drone deploying cluster missiles at us. He tags it, and a railgun from nearby Thessalonica fires a projectile that leaves a streak of blue fire across the horizon. The drone disappears in a blossom of red. This is the multi-madness of hi-tech war.

We make our way to Mustang's coordinates, sensors and eyes peeled for the death that hides in the mountains. It stalks the plains. It secretes itself in woods of towering godTrees and in the waters of infant seas.

A great lake stretches far to our left, while a dormant volcano so gradual in its incline that it seems little more than a snow-capped hill broods to our right. I soar higher along the spine of the mountain range we traverse to gain vantage over the surroundings. Periodic topographical data flickers onto my datapad as drones broadcast data, are shot from the sky, then replaced.

It is quiet inside my suit. I cannot hear the wind that whistles around me at this great height. A stormcloud, one of Mars's dramatic thunderheads, rolls in from the distant lake. When it hits the forest below the mountain, the rains come and lightning slashes the sky. Atop the craggy peak, snow swirls, melting against my suit.

I catch movement on a peak nearby. I hold off on discharging my weapon when I see it's no Bellona, but a carved beast. I magnify my vision and see the griffin clinging to the edge of a huge nest set into a narrow stone defile atop the peak, watching in wonder as men fly across her valley below. What a world these Golds have built.

My men rejoin me on the next peak over, pausing a moment to check the powercells in our starShells. They won't last all day. Mustang's group slams into the ground around us, causing snow to scatter as four hundred starShelled killers add their strength to ours. She bumps fists with me.

"Icarus?" a voice crackles in my ear. "Icarus, do you read me?"

"Roque, I read. What's what?"

"Icarus . . . urgent . . . on . . . read me?" His signal breaks up as lightning slashes overhead. Jamming devices from both sides already molest the airwaves. "Dar . . . ead . . . me . . . in Agea."

"Roque? Roque?" I know the plan for the battle above, but the tone of his voice worries me.

"Coms are all scattered," I tell Mustang.

"*Local frequencies are fine. It's the jammers and storm.*" Rain splatters over her armor.

Sevro points up. "*Gonna have to get your ass above it to hear.*" Above, a ship is struck by lightning. Her systems fail and she plummets before reactivating, only to collide with a passing ripWing.

"Oh, goryhell." I give Ragnar and Jupiter orders to push forward of the mountain range and secure the northern valley for our main force of Gray legions. While we besiege other cities to divert Bellona attention, to me Agea is all that matters. A million men will go at her walls. The Stained opens his hand to me in salute and then jumps off the mountain peak with Jupiter and a hundred Obsidian warriors.

Mustang and Sevro wait below as I rip up through the lightning-laced clouds with several of my bodyguards. Past the clouds, I float in relative peace, hailing Roque.

"*Icarus!*" he shouts into the com. "*She's here. She's not on Luna or with the main Societal fleet! We just found out. Kavax's men found Praetorians on board the* Warchild . . . *she's here! She came in secret without her fleet; we caught her.*"

"Roque. Slow down. What are you saying?"

"*Darrow, the Sovereign is on Mars. Her shuttle is trapped behind the shields on Agea. She is trapped.*"

"Roque. I already know. She's why I want Agea."

39

|||||||||||||||||||||||

AT THE WALL

He doesn't ask how I knew. Later I'll tell him that I let Aja escape from Europa so we could track her back to the Sovereign via my bomb's radiation signature. She's Octavia's personal killer. Of course she would return to her side. I've told no one but Mustang, the Jackal, and Sevro. I couldn't risk it spreading, especially with how Roque's been acting.

He hangs up the com without another word, bitterness evident.

The vanguard of my force, Ragnar's men, have made landfall in the valley ahead. I see the fat ships descending, then disappearing into the ground where the Valles Marineris stretches kilometers beneath. We have our Blues in space lay fire down on Agea itself. The deluge heats the shield, causing it to pulse opaque. We'll be coming at her at ground level along the bottom of the hundred-kilometer-wide canyon from the north and south, just through the two-hundred-meter gap her shields must maintain above soil to avoid creating seismic disturbances.

I hop off the mountain peak at the head of my bodyguard. Sevro and Mustang accompany me as we jump to another peak, then skip through the lower foothills, taking fire as we go.

The Sovereign is the key to this war, the key to fracturing this Society so the Sons of Ares can rise. With her captured, the Society itself will wonder in confusion if it even exists without Octavia atop its throne. Senators and governors will try to seize power. There will be a dozen local wars, fracturing manpower and cohesion.

Beneath me, a world of bounty lounges along the bottom of the vast canyon—lakes and streams, waist-high grasses, trees blooming with flowers and Spartan pines growing at odd angles from the kilometers-high canyon walls despite the steep declivity. Above all this, the great floating mountain, Olympus, reigns. I glimpse the quiet castles and see deer running in the vale of Mars. But I see no children along the great rivers, no boys and girls in armor. Only memories and muddied earth. The students have already been collected. How strange that must have been—fighting for their lives with medieval weapons, only to be scooped up by dropships as invaders came from space.

We meet with Jupiter and Ragnar on one of floating Olympus's white spires. There are dead men in the halls, on the slopes.

"They used it as a base," Jupiter says cheerily. "Your Stained disagreed with their presumptuousness. I like the beast!" Our men secure the section of the Valles Marineris set aside for the Institute, far east of Agea in the upper arm of the grand canyon. I watch out the window as hundreds of friendly dropships descend on the staging ground, depositing more than three hundred thousand men in thirty minutes. A Gold runs out of each lowered ramp, always the first onto enemy soil.

"No resistance," I say quietly, my starShell helm popped. I look at Mustang uneasily.

She wipes blonde hair from her eyes. "The longer we're dug in, they harder we are to dislodge. Why are they waiting?"

"Want to cluster us up like a bunch of grapes before stomping," Sevro guesses. "Atomics?"

"Silly children." Jupiter goes through the pockets of one of the dead men. "That's why we have Grays. Let them be stomped. They will lubricate our passage."

"No atomics," Mustang says. "Sensors would have picked them up from a hundred clicks away." She looks out over the land. "They're waiting because they don't have enough men to contest our passage through the valley. Or we've caught them flat-footed, which is doubtful. Or they deployed too many men to halt Lorn's advance. Or they've created choke points in the valley. Or they marshal them around the Citadel. Or there's a trap ahead."

Her mind is a machine.

"There's a trap," she says after a moment. "But they are over-relying upon it to stall us while they reallocate men and matériel." She snorts in contempt. "Static defenses without massive mobile support haven't been relevant since the Maginot Line."

"But they know we don't want to waste the city or the populace," I say.

"They know that." Mustang adjusts her datapad, examining the map. "Which shrinks our flexibility in tactics."

"Total war is easier," Jupiter grumbles. "Let's use the Grays to lubricate our passage, then drop bombs at the walls under the shields. Entry gained."

"It takes a day to break a city, then fifty years to rebuild," Mustang snaps. "You want to sign up to oversee the reconstruction?"

"Do I look like a builder?" Jupiter asks.

"The passage to Agea is eighty kilometers wide on average, seven-kilometer-high walls on either side, all farming and agriculture for the city. Bellona likely littered the place with mines. If they had time. We didn't exactly tell them we were coming." Did they have time?

Mustang motions me to the side.

I walk with her away from the rest of my command staff, who roll their eyes at one another. The airy palace halls should remind me of past victory, but all I feel is steep melancholy being here. So many memories. So many lost friends, I think when I see Grays landing near Minerva castle where Pax and I once dueled.

"It's eighty kilometers to the walls from here," she says. "We could make the dash as planned. Just because they didn't contest our landing doesn't mean there's something nefarious afoot." She sees the hesitation in my eyes. "We are here for my father just as much as we're here for the Sovereign. We have to move with pace."

"You're afraid Lorn is going to kill him if he breaks through the southern city walls first," I guess. "Aren't you."

"You know their history."

"I do."

"And do you trust Lorn not to finish an old grudge?"

"Lorn isn't a murderer."

"No. He hurts men who deserve it, like Tactus. My father deserves it as much as any man. So we must hurry. And you must tell the rest of them about the Sovereign."

"Roque found out. Praetorians on the *Warchild*."

We walk back and I address my small council.

"You know we come here for Augustus, but there's a second reason we press on Agea. The Sovereign is here."

"No shit?" Clown mutters.

Rotback scratches his head. "Goryhell."

"In the Citadel?" Pebble asks, excitedly nudging anxious Weed with her knee.

"In all probability. We traced Aja here. Residual radiation from the bomb we hit Aja with on Europa. The other assaults are designed to draw manpower away from Agea so that we will have a chance to break through her walls and capture Octavia before her Ash Lord arrives with the full might of her armada." And if the Sons have done their part as Ares promised, we should be able to get into the city without fighting through a hundred thousand armored men and women.

"Is Cassius in the city?" Sevro asks.

Mustang nods. "We think so."

Sevro smiles.

"If you come upon Cassius, do not engage him," I say. "Nor Karnus, nor Aja."

"You'd have us run?" Clown asks, insulted.

"I'd have you live," I say. "The prize is the Sovereign. Don't be distracted by revenge, or pride. If we seize her, we are the new power in the Solar System, my friends."

The Howlers share wolfish grins. Sevro squares his shoulders.

"So let's stop picking our butts."

"Couldn't have said it better myself."

Friendly ripWings roar overhead to clear out enemy forces along our path.

With all our powers marshaled, we move through the green canyon. No creeping column. We go fast. Speederbikes have more pace than starShells. Those Grays and the ones on spiders tear ahead after the ripWings and heavily armored dropships that will deposit men even closer to the wall. Flashes ahead indicate they've detonated mines or the mine killers have done their job. No way to tell. The canyon here is narrowing. Verdant canyon walls tower hugely in the distance to either side, colossal and unreal, like the terrain of a greater, larger race than man. I can't see all my force in so vast a place, just the tip of the spear. We come after the fast-moving Grays, a skipping column of dreadful knights in starShells of black. The deluge of rain falls even harder. Behind us roll tanks and the infantry columns in their hover skiffs, lightly armored vehicles that can carry a hundred men in a flatbed. They'll deposit them a kilometer from the walls. Lorn's attack from the south will be much similar.

"Drones!" Sevro shouts through the com. A cloud of metal rises toward us from a small depot in the canyon wall to the east. The Howlers streak after the threat, their guns ripping holes in the air. Still, dronefire shreds a squad of flying Obsidians. They plummet to the ground, bodies unrecognizable. We skim over buildings now. Small towns. Resorts. Estates. Granaries. We find ourselves over a lake. See our shadows as lightning flashes above, silhouetting us.

I see the defensive wall now. It falls over the horizon like an iron curtain. Ninety kilometers across, at this stage of the canyon, and nearly two hundred meters high, it nips the lower edge of the shield. Lakes and rivers don't find their terminus here, but instead run beneath the wall through a thick network of durosteel bars that are strong as a ship's hull. It would take a hundred men ten hours to drill their way through those bars.

Most cities do not have walls so massive. They cost too much. Agea and Corinth are alone in the quality of their fortifications. We could have come through the tunnels that wend through the belly of Mars and connect every city with their mines, but I didn't want to. There are tactics I must save. And there is an example I must set.

Assaults like this are not protracted things. I've seen the histories. They are wild and manic. Technology against static objects always wins, so long as the besieger's resolve never runs dry. Once upon a time, castles were nearly impossible to take through direct assault on a capable garrison without the price of Pyrrhic victory. So field armies laid siege and starved defenders into submission. Now, no one has the patience.

Agea is a city of twenty million souls, but how many of those will give a lick who wins today? There is no difference between the rule of the Bellona and the rule of the Augustus. Coppers and Silvers will care. But the Reds, the Browns, the Pinks will just watch another master take the chains.

Now they'll see ships fill the sky. Bombs rupture the air. And they will huddle in their public tenements and fear faceless marauders. Since the dawn of man, the taking of a city has been echoed by the screams of rape, theft, and drunken horror. Peerless Scarred do not partake in such savagery. It is not profitable nor in keeping with their tastes. But if one takes a city by force, it is the belief of the Golds that the city and all those therein are now property of the conqueror. If you are strong enough, you deserve the spoils. Some spare the spoils. Some give them to the wolves, feeding cities to their Obsidian and Gray armies as reward for blood spilled.

If I can protect this city of Agea, if I can show them that there is a better breed of man, then just maybe I'll win Agea's heart. Capture it. Protect it. Be loved by those in it as I'm loved by my army. But first I must crack her open.

All along the vast defensive wall, fire ripples over steel. Like tiny flowers fast blooming upon the ninety-kilometer-wide sheer gray wall. Two feint assaults are led to my left and my right. The ripWings there fire railguns, sliding sideways as they pump munitions at the wall. Return fire from the turrets on the walls causes my eardrums to shiver and hum. I want to clutch Mustang's hand. A nod from her stills the terror in me. But only just.

Grays in combat armor rush forward like so many ants. Rocket teams deploy and soon send slithering death into the defenders. It is too much to absorb, like the space battle above, layers upon layers of activity and counteractivity. Except this has sound.

Mines rip holes in my force. Bellona kill squads slip out of the wall a hundred meters up, flying out in glory—banners waving, gold glistening. Their shields shimmer as they're lanced by weapon fire. I see an eagle banner amid the Bellona, and ready to set myself against it, thinking it must be Cassius, but Mustang grabs my arm.

"The plan!" Mustang reminds me, pointing to the river. *"We'll all die against that wall. The plan."*

Hard to remember. Hard to remember all this chaos is a distraction. What matters is the river and the work done in the night by the Sons. If they did it. The river slithers under the wall. One hundred meters wide, and more deep, it already carries corpses toward the city.

I dive into the water. Feel the tension as the current slows, then speeds my path. Fish scatter before us. Odd not feeling the chill. The Howlers move like torpedoes beside me. Then Ragnar is with us along with his group of Obsidians. Jupiter too, all splashing down under water. Mustang is closest to me. I scan the river ahead through the murk we kicked up and find Ares's gift.

There. A hundred meters deep, I see it. If there's one thing Reds can do, it's drill. And the Sons spent the night preparing to give us passage into the city. My men will think some elite lurcher squad was sent here before the armada. They will not question how the huge grates were cut, or how the sensors meant to detect damage to the grating were fooled.

"Once more unto the breach," I murmur, as if Roque, Victra, or Tactus could hear me. I activate my gravBoots and move forward.

The passage is narrow as it curls beneath the wall near the bottom of the riverbed. We travel two abreast. So I take the best fighter with me, Ragnar, as we move first through the underwater passage. My com crackles with news of the battle above. We're losing at the wall.

Ragnar and I clear the tunnel together. I half expected a Bellona ambush, but none comes. The Sons did their job well. We wait on the opposite side of the wall, still submerged, one hundred meters down at the bottom of the riverbed. The rest of my cadre join Ragnar and me—Mustang, Sevro, and the remaining Howlers. Fifty more Golds and three times that many Obsidians and Grays.

I speak into my com when we've all gathered at the bottom of the river. "You know your orders."

Sevro bumps armored fists with me. Mustang does the same. Ragnar salutes with his fist balled and against his heart. Jupiter yawns into his com. Clown, Pebble, and Weed rile up the Howlers, stirring silt at the bottom of the river. The seconds tick by. My razor is looped about my arm. PulseFist in my left hand. Feel the thump of my heart and the chill of the pendant on my chest. Hear the crackle of chaos outside. My Helldiver hands ball. My eyes close. Sevro sends up a probe to see if the riverbank is safe.

I'm to find the Sovereign.

Ragnar is to open the gates.

Mustang is to lower the shield so Roque can send reinforcements and we can take the city in one fell swoop. I don't want her to leave me, but I can trust no one else with the task.

Trust. I must trust that she will live, trust that her Obsidians will protect her, and that she will protect herself. There's a weight pressing down on my heart, a fear that she will not come back. It feels like she's already falling into darkness. If she dies, she'll die believing a lie. I promise myself I'll tell her if we survive this. She deserves that much.

Stay alive. Stay alive. All of you, stay alive.

Mustang departs, moving farther downriver, following it for kilometers till she reaches the park near the generators. I watch her go and flounder for something to hold on to, someone to pray to. My father is with me, and so is Eo. I feel them in the beating of my heart.

I close my eyes.

Sevro gathers the probe he sent above and tells me that we are clear, just a girl playing in the mud above us.

"Fight for each other," I say over the com to those at my side in the riverbed. "Or me." We activate our gravBoots and soar through the water, bursting through the surface of the river like inky monsters, our black starShells dripping as we fly up over the riverbank, muddy from rain that fell before the shields were raised to protect the city.

Beneath us, a single unarmored Brown girl stands, ankle deep in the mud. I stare at her from behind my terrible black helm. She should be hiding with her family, not out in a besieged city. Something is wrong.

When she sees us, she snatches from a basket a small globe device. Lightning slashes the sky. Her best dress gathers mud on the hem, turning an even deeper brown.

"Shoot her!" Sevro snarls.

I knock his hand aside. A tree explodes instead. And as I look high above where, on the wall, far out of range of the probe Sevro sent up, and far beyond the limits of the EMP globe the girl carries, perch Bellona knights and their Obsidian retinue. Waiting.

The girl presses a button on the globe.

And that's when we begin to die.

PART IV

|||||||||||||||||||||||||||||||

RUIN

Rise so high, in mud you lie.

—Karnus au Bellona

40

|||||||||||||||||||||||||

MUD

The EMP detonates. Sounds like a giant child gasping when pricked by a needle. Our electronics die. Our gravBoots sputter. StarShell synapses fail, causing the massive metal suits to be gripped by gravity. We plummet down. Most fall into the mud of the riverbank. I splash into the water. Sinking. Sinking. Ears popping. Down and down till I lodge into the mud of the river bottom. Hitting hard. Legs buckling under the weight of my starShell. Fall on my back. Can't see my men. Only saw shapes moving over the surface of the water as I fell. Now too deep to see anything except how the river darkens with blood. Occasional lightning flashes silhouette fast-sinking bodies.

I can't move. My starShell is too heavy. I lie like a turtle, half stuck in mud at the bottom of the river. Confused. Fear rides in me. It happened so fast. Can't even look to my left or my right to see who is with me. My com is dead. If it weren't, I'd probably hear screams, curses.

This starShell brought me from space to land. A life raft, a personal castle in the middle of a war. Now it's my coffin.

Heart thudding. Want to scream.

Hyperventilating. Terror traps itself in my chest, tensing me, making me swallow the air, eating it as though it'll give me power to move. Slow down. Slow down. Think. *Think.* Two bodies sink near me. Heavy in their armor, they fall fast to join the others on the bottom. No grace in death, spilling blood as they go. When the killers finish with those stuck in the mud of the riverbank, they'll come for us down here. But they don't need to. I slow my breathing. Limited oxygen left in the suit. Recycler offline.

Cassius knew my plan. It had to have been him. Or was I betrayed?

I told no one but the Sons and Sevro and Mustang. None of them could have ratted. He just knew. That bloody bastard. If I could surrender, I would. I'd save the lives of those with me. But I don't have a com.

I jerk my body around, trying to push myself off my back. But I'm too lodged in the mud, and my suit is more than one ton of metal. I can't shed the weight. Can't get the starShell off. I need the electronics for that. I push up with my arms. Nothing. The mud swallows me. Mustang got away. I think. I hope. Will she know we're down here?

I look for Sevro, for Ragnar, my Howlers. Dark shapes around me. I'm dizzy. Slow the bloodydamn breathing. Slow. *Think.* They won't even bother coming to kill me. I'll die at the bottom of the river, staring up at the surface as one by one, my friends fall down to join me. So alone. Sevro. Ragnar. Pebble. Weed. Clown. They're dead. Dying. Watching the same thing as me. Or maybe they're on the bank as the Bellona walk among the paralyzed suits of armor, killing at will. I want to cry at my impotence.

Stop. Do something. Move.

"Rise so high, in mud you lie." It echoes in memory.

This is the third time they've left me in the muck and mire to die. I grit my teeth till I feel enamel crumble off as I put all my strength into moving my right arm. Slowly, so slowly, it makes an exodus from the sucking pressure of the mud. But it is all that's freed. I won't be able to get off my back. I'm too sunken in. Too heavy in the shell. Then I see it. When the EMP blast detonated, it shut down the electrical synapses, which means the suit froze, but the razor still works, and there it is like a white python around my arm.

It will save your life for the price of a limb. Those are the words they told me when they put the slingBlade in my hand as a boy. Salvation is sacrifice. The razor's impulse is chemical. Its switch will respond to me. It will straighten. But around my arm . . . I have to be fast.

Taking a breath, I close my eyes, feeling the toggle against my suit's thumb. I have to be faster than a licking flame. Faster than a pitviper. I flick the switch on.

The razor tightens as it straightens, slicing through metal like a knife through pudding.

Flick the switch off. It stops as it bites through muscle, but not through bone. I yelp at the terrible pain in my forearm. Water rushes through the shredded arm to cool the burning wound.

Then I feel terror. Water. I just opened my suit to water. Idiot. Soon it'll fill. I can already feel it slithering up my neck on the inside. In minutes, two or three, I'll drown. I work my bloody forearm arm free of the shredded metal carapace and slide the slack razor off so it floats like a tentacle. Then I activate it again. It forms into a deadly question mark and I angle it toward the other gauntlet.

My suit's filled with water in the torso now. The air is thin. Each breath brings more stars behind my eyes. A sensation of lightness as blood seeps from the wounds on my arm. I can survive a long time holding my breath. But I hyperventilated and now I'm sucking in carbon dioxide. But then my other hand is free of the suit gauntlet. Bare and pale in the weird, dark light. Gentle clouds of blood plume from it.

If I were not made a Helldiver, I would die in this riverbed. As it is, I skin off my starShell and the armor beneath. It is my dexterity that saves me. I cannot move my head because of the weight of the helmet. Cannot see where I cut. My skin and the pain it registers serve as my eyes. Inch by inch, I remove myself from the starShell. Inch by inch, I drag the deadly blade along my body. Shedding my blood and the shell into the water. Parting the exoskeleton. I'm like a locust slipping from its dead husk. Very delicately, I remove the helmet, cutting it off at the neck. I hold my breath, and just nick my throat.

A scratch. So close to the jugular.

My legs are the last part of me I free. I sit up, the broken bits of my suit scratching at my skin, and jerk my right leg out of the hewn metal. I'm alive and wounded in the cold, dark river. Helmet off. Holding my breath as spots bloom across my vision. Now I'm able to see the sunken field of men around me at the bottom of the riverbed. I swim over to the largest one and see Ragnar's closed eyes behind his starShell's faceplate. Tears trickle from them. His lungs are large, but there can't be much oxygen left in that suit. He can move better than I could, because of his great strength. But no armored man could swim in this water.

I did not think he could cry. Yet now he weeps, silently. Not great, dramatic tears. These are different, calm. And when he opens his eyes, I see something else in him. Some dormant part of his soul ignites. He was dead, had given in to his fate. Yet here I float in shredded black tactical cloth, bloody, looking positively deranged, but free of my shell. I'm his dark hope. I start cutting, even though my own lungs are screaming. I need him. I can't search for Sevro. There's no time. And I cannot surface just to be killed on sight.

I operate on him like a proper Carver, till he wrenches himself free of his exoskeleton. Others have seen what we're doing. But we cannot help them yet. They must hold on.

Ragnar and I kick our way through the rough current toward the surface. Lungs starving. Ragnar's pale, tattooed body moves through the water with a grace I can't match. I didn't realize Obsidians were such swimmers. Makes sense for one born near the ice floes.

We're near the surface when my mind loses to my body. Ten feet from the surface, I inhale water.

Darkness.

Feel mud between my fingers. Something moves through my chest. Water. I vomit it, hack it out into a rough hand clutched close to my mouth, quieting me. I keep puking through the fingers. Then feel an explosion of pleasure as I gasp finally for air. Beautiful air. Hand still covering my mouth. And for a moment, there is nothing. Just the pure orgasm of life into my lungs. The full rush of oxygen on empty, aching organs. And suddenly the sound of distant warfare swells. And the groans of men. We're in a field of corpses. The wall towers high overhead. The river runs fast at our feet. It's been minutes since the EMP, but it seems the day has passed and left us behind.

Ragnar dragged me into the mud between two dead Obsidians. Two Bellona Golds, six Obsidians, and six Grays walk along the dark riverbank, finishing those who lie helpless. We're lucky the rest have quit the slaughter to return to the fight at the wall. Cassius will have led them away. That means he didn't know it was me here, but he was well aware of the hole made by the Sons, at least. For me, he would have stayed. Lucky I didn't carry the banner Clown and Weed made for me. Double lucky I didn't let them wear their wolfcloaks.

This mud is a graveyard. My soldiers are half buried. Some try to rise in the heavy, dead armor, only to slip back into the mud or be kicked down by the Golds and mercilessly butchered. Most lie quiet. A field of armored beetles leaking red.

The Grays joke to one another as they go methodically about their task, taking their time on an Obsidian stuck on his back, using force-Pikes to pierce the thick starShell and pin him to the ground like boys tormenting a stranded crab. They finish him eventually with armor-boring bullets called diggers from their rifles.

Ragnar gestures to the mud. Half naked, he and I cake ourselves in the dark, heavy stuff. It cools the tracework lacerations on my body and covers the tattoos on his. I gesture to one of the Gold helmets and mime our survivors' oxygen running out. Ragnar nods. I pull a razor from the body of a dead Gold. I can't tell who. And hand it to Ragnar. It's only ever seen Gold hands. No Praetorian, no Obsidian, not even one of those with badges from the Sovereign herself, has touched this weapon since the Dark Revolt. To touch it means death by starvation. No possibility of reaching Valhalla. Only hunger and cold and the end. But our enemies will have pulseShields. No other weapon will do.

Ragnar drops it like it's made of fire. I shove it back into his trembling hands.

"They aren't gods."

Like shadows pulled from the Styx, we slide forward through the graveyard. Our enemies are not in their fighting bands. Easy targets. I scuttle forward on all fours like some horrible spider, hardly rising from the ground to kill two Obsidians before they even turn. Ragnar snaps another's neck and cleaves a second in half, the recoilPlate peeling away. Rising from my hands, I sprint at the tallest of the Obsidians, jump and bury my blade into his body. I land poorly on my wounded arm. I don't even feel the pain. Too much adrenaline. I see the squad of Grays turning, so I fall with the Obsidian's body and roll into the mud, lying in shadow and filth among the other corpses. Their recoilRifles and pulse weapons would rip me to ribbons without my shield and armor. Ragnar's disappeared too. I don't know where.

Time ticks by. How much oxygen could they have left? The Grays hunting us shout something about ghostCloaks. The remaining Obsidian groups with the two Golds. The Grays go through the bodies, finishing my remaining men to flush Ragnar and me out for the Golds and Obsidian. Lea died like this, down in the mud. I won't. Not again.

I rise, not with a scream, not with a howl. Silently. Let the Grays try to see me coming. I am fast. And I'm nearly on them when they open fire. I rip toward them, dodging, weaving, like a loosed balloon. No beauty to my movement. Just frantic terror. I cannot see the bullets. Only feel their closeness. Sense the heat of them ripping past me. Feel the punch as I'm hit in the bicep. Shock through my body. The skin tears as the bullet goes through flesh, tendon, muscle, then out the other side, knicking bone. I grunt. And then I'm upon them, and they make no noise at all.

They missed their window.

Twelve enemies fall to Lorn's *kravat* lessons. Twelve men and women.

The Golds and Obsidian come upon me now. The Golds use their gravBoots. Ragnar rises from the mud and hurls his razor through the air like a spear. The huge Obsidian falls into the mud as Ragnar rushes the two Golds, picking another razor from the ground.

I marvel at his power. He grabs one of the Golds by the foot as they pass in the air. The pulseShield electrocutes him, sending pain lancing through his body. But he just roars, holding on, and with a scream coming not from his throat, but his soul, he slams the Gold down to the ground like he's chopping wood. He somehow manages to rip the boot off. The lean Gold rolls away, shouting, *"Stained!"* to his friend, who comes back to his aid so they face off with Ragnar together.

I run to Ragnar's aid.

"Reaper!" One of the Golds lets his helmet retract into his armor, revealing the haughty face of a Peerless man. Confident in his rank. In his heritage. In his place. His face is all joy. Then it contorts as he sees Ragnar's razor.

"You give the blade of your ancestors to a beast?" He glares hate at Ragnar. Then down at the razor, furious, confused. "Have you no honor?"

I choose not to answer.

"Know who you face, Andromedus," the older Gold rages. "I am Gauis au Carthus of gens Carthii. We built the Columns of Venus. We first sailed the gaps between the Inner and Outer rims and mined the Helsa Cluster."

"This isn't *The Iliad*. Ragnar, kill this fool. We need his gravBoots."

The Gold spits. "You send a dog to do your fighting?"

"I am a *man*!" Ragnar roars louder than the screaming engines of a passing ship. Spittle flying, face ragged with rage. Veins rise in his neck. He howls, rushing forward before I can even raise my blade. He picks up the corpse of the fallen Obsidian and uses it to deflect their razors. He punches Gaius. No weapon. Just his fist. He hits him so hard in the pulseShield that the man falls backward. Then he kills the other, hacking through his defenses with mad fury till he cuts him in half. He kicks the top of the corpse aside and batters down Gaius, who sinks into the dark mud as Ragnar thumps forward and, muscles twitching from having touched the pulseShield, holds the razor to Golden man's throat.

"Yield to me and live," Ragnar rumbles.

Gaius spits, rising to his knees.

"Yield to me as a man yields to another man."

"Never." Gaius's lips curl sourly. He speaks his last words clear and loud, with spite and courage. All that is good and all that is wicked in these extraordinary people. "I am the Peerless Legate Gaius au *Carthus*. I am the sum of humanity. So yield I do not. For a man cannot yield to a dog."

"Then become dirt." Rangar pushes the blade home.

We ferry our men from the bottom of the river. Fast as we can using stolen gravBoots, but not fast enough. Sevro is not dead, but he's close. I find him buried headfirst in the riverbank. He's cursing and spitting when I peel him out with the help of Clown and Pebble.

"The dead?" he asks quietly. "My Howlers?"

"Too many," Clown says thinly.

"Did Mustang get through?"

They all look at me.

"I think so," I say. "But I can't hail her on any coms. We have to hurry either way. If she is alive and she blows the generators so our reinforcements can land, then the shield falls and the Sovereign has a wide window to escape. Right now, she's bottled up."

Sevro nods. Little Pebble gives him a hand up. Small Thistle, hardly coming to Ragnar's solar plexus, sees him with a razor in his hand as he frees another Obsidian from a dead starShell. "Drop that," she snaps.

Ragnar drops it and looks to me in a strange panic. I motion him to wait.

After we go through the suits of those who fell on the riverbank, we know the count, and it is so devastating that Sevro walks away. Weed is dead. Rotback is dead. Harpy died before we hit the ground. And many of the new recruits are dead. Only Thistle, Clown, Screwface, and Pebble are left. Eleven of the original fifty Obsidians remain.

Pebble and Clown touch Weed's face, their matching mohawks flat against their heads as the rain soaks us all. Pebble claws at his chest, her small hands hitting his heart as though that will bring him back. Thistle goes to pull her away as Clown uses mud to straighten Weed's matching mohawk in death. Sevro cannot watch. I go stand beside him.

"I was wrong about war," he says.

"I can't do this without you." After a desperate moment, "Are you with me? *Sevro?*"

He pulls back and wipes snot from his nose, muddying his face. Tears make lines in the mud as he looks up at me, voice cracking like a child's. "Always, Darrow. Always."

41

||||||||||||||||||||||

ACHILLES

There's no time to mourn. My force decimated, we must divide still further. My army outside the city hurls itself at impregnable walls, expecting help from the inside. They've received none. My Legates will be hailing my signal, wondering if I have died. Such a rumor could lose the battle.

I send Ragnar with the remnants of the Obsidians to open one of the wall's gates for my Legates who wait for us with thousands of Grays and Obsidians in reserve.

"I give you no Golds," I tell Ragnar. "Do you understand what that means?"

"I do."

"This can be a beginning," I say quietly. I bend, picking a discarded razor from the sucking mud. "It is a man's duty to choose his own destiny. Choose yours." I extend the razor to him.

Ragnar looks back to the Obsidians. Their armor is battered from extricating them from the suits. And they're caked in mud. Smaller than he. Some lithe and quiet. Others huge and shifting foot to foot with eagerness. All with those black eyes and white hair. They arm themselves with weapons taken from the Grays and Obsidian I killed.

Hardly enough to go around, and they'll be little use if they run into Golds.

Ragnar chooses. He extends a hand. Howlers prepare themselves behind me, Thistle still eyeing him evilly. "I *choose* to follow you," he says. "And I choose to lead them."

I place the razor in his hand.

"Darrow!" Thistle gasps. "What are you doing?"

"Shut up," Sevro snaps.

"He can't do that!" Thistle stomps forward and tries to rip the razor out of Ragnar's hand. He doesn't let go. "Give it up. *Slave*. Give me the blade." She pulls her own razor out. "Give me the blade or I'll cut away the hand that holds it."

"Then I will cut you down, Thistle," Sevro sneers.

"Sevro?" Thistle turns back to him, eyes wide. She looks at me, at the other Howlers who stand quiet, unsure of what just happened. "Have you gone mad? It's not his right. It's ours. He doesn't . . ."

"Deserve it?" Sevro asks. "Who are you to decide that?"

"I'm a Gold!" she shrieks. "Clown, Pebble . . ."

Pebble remains silent. Clown tilts his head. "Darrow, what is this?"

"It's my army," I say. "You remember the Institute. You remember how I bleed for those who follow me. How I do not take the allegiance of slaves. Why now are you surprised by this? Because it is real?"

"It's a slippery slope, is all." Clown looks at the war around us. "Even here."

"You're right. It is." I bend and find another razor cast in the mud. I toss this one to another of the Obsidians, a nasty-looking woman half my size. She holds it like it's a snake, glancing up at me in fear. They are raised believing we are gods. To be given Thor's hammer . . . how would I hold it? Sevro walks through the corpses and finds several more. He tosses these to the Obsidians.

"Don't cut yourselves," he says.

"I'm counting on you. Go," I tell them. They disappear, sprinting into the swelling darkness toward the back side of the colossal wall. I turn to the Howlers. "Is there a problem?" They all shake their heads quickly, except Thistle.

"Thistle?" Sevro asks.

Clown nudges her. And grudgingly she shakes her head. "No problem."

There is. She will not follow me after this. Already I feel my friends turning from me. And they know not even a fraction of the truth. That is a problem for another day.

We must move fast. But we only have one pair of functional gravBoots among us. I give those to Sevro. We try to see if he can lift us like I lifted the Howlers on Olympus, but as we load onto the boots, they sputter and spark. Only able to carry his weight. Damaged somehow in the fighting and the rescue. *Bloodydamn.*

So it will be on foot. And we cannot be slowed.

I point to the recoilPlate of those lucky enough to have it after the starShell amputations. "Armor off."

"What?" Thistle sputters.

"Armor. Off. Except scarabSkin."

"Unarmored against Praetorians?" Thistle howls. "Do you want us *all* to die?"

"We need to move fast. If the shield goes down before we get to the Citadel, the Sovereign will slip away. If we do not capture her, she will have a chance to regroup. She will join her Ash Lord. She will summon all of the Society, and they will come here with ten times our number to crush us. We'll win the battle, lose the war."

"But if we take her . . . ," Sevro growls, coming to my side.

"We're talking about the Sovereign," Clown says. "She'll have Praetorian Olympic Knights . . ."

"And?" Sevro asks. "We have us."

"Six of us." Clown shrugs sheepishly when we stare at him. "I just thought someone should point it out."

"We have fifteen kilometers to cover on foot," I say. They nod. "My pace." Then they exchange worried looks and start taking off their armor. "If you fall behind, find a place to hide." One-third Earth grav. Bodies in prime shape. This will still be hard. Especially with my arm savaged by my own razor.

Sevro saddles up to me as the Howlers strip away their armor. I can hear their terror in the clinking of weapons and armor moved by shaking hands, see it in the frenzied way they then rub mud on their faces to blacken their aspects.

"They've been with you from the beginning, Darrow." Sevro looks around the stormy park, at the distant Citadel and blaze of passing ships. "We're already half the number that took you from Luna. You might have replaced Pax with Ragnar, but you can't replace them. Or me."

"I thought you were with me."

"I'm your conscience. I follow your ass everywhere. So don't be a shithead."

"Registers. On me!" I shout.

Armor shed, we set off silently. Only our razors and scarabSkin with us. Wearing rubber-soled undershoes instead of gravBoots. We go along the river, leaving the wall behind. Sprinting through acres of grassy parks and woods that separate the wall from the city as mechanized war rages in the distance. Ships roar past, making the tree branches shudder and leaves fall. Ground trams flicker far to our right, shuttling soldiers to the front. Explosions plume in the distance. Clouds consume the sky beyond the great shield that overlaps the city. Explosions flash inside the clouds.

Mustang will be nearing the shield generators now, if she's alive.

It is a ragged pace, covering fifteen kilometers at a sprint. My side stabs with pain. Muscles hunger for oxygen. And my right arm aches from the bloody bullet wound in my bicep and the lacerations that bleed along forearm and wrist. I took half a pack of stims, so I can use the arm. The pain doesn't blind. It focuses. Keeps me from thinking of the dead.

When we reach the edge of the woods, we do not stop to rest, but sprint onto the commercial district's paved streets, cutting through buildings that tower over a kilometer up into the sky. We run through deserted lowDistricts, the bazaar where winding corridors lead us through rough streets and graffiti-stained walls. The occasional Brown or Pink or Red will scuttle out of our way or peer at us through windows, from alleys. Even here, in the center of their reign, I see the graffiti of Eo's death. Her hair is ablaze like the wounded fighters that streak across the sky beyond Agea's transparent shields. Someone pukes behind me. They don't stop. The reek of bile travels with us.

Sevro flies back to us and lands beside me. "Platoon of Grays ahead. Go south one block, then cut back to avoid." Then he's gone again. We follow his instructions.

Suddenly there's movement in the sky and we slow to a jog to watch. Pebble takes the opportunity to collapse onto the pavement, chest heaving. High above, but still beneath the shield, a horde of shuttles ferry soldiers from the smaller engagement on the southern wall, where Lorn fights, toward the northern wall where Ragnar and his Obsidians have gone. Dozens of shuttles full of reserves depart their dock in the hangars and ports that lace the seven-kilometer-high rock walls of the Valles Marineris to the east and west. Most of the barracks are there, as are the factories where highReds slave away making armaments and commercial consumer goods. We hide from the craft. Something has happened at the north wall. We take off again. Pebble moans. Thistle gets her up, keeps her in gear.

Sevro rejoins us minutes later, left arm hanging limp at his side. I eye it. He ignores my concern. "Ragnar opened the gorydamn gates." His face splits into a smile. "Twelve of them in the wall's face. Our boys are pouring in. And . . ." He stands there grinning.

"And what?"

"And Ragnar killed the Wind Knight and almost cut down Cassius."

"An Olympic?" Clown gasps.

"Cut him down in front of the entire army. The Obsidians in the army are going absolutely manic."

Then Sevro is off and we push on. A squad of Gray policemen waylay us. We take cover as their gunfire pocks the sidewalks, and then divert to an alleyway to avoid them.

Four kilometers until we reach our destination.

Coughing and gasping, we stumble into the exterior of the Citadel's grounds. We hide in the trees there like some ragged pack of castaway demons. Through the thin copse of woods and past a high wall, the Citadel stands, a network of spires. Not golden, but white laced with red and still decorated with the lion statues of Augustus, though Bellona blue-and-silver banners flap in the breeze overtop a lion weathervane. Their silver eagle seems so proud till Sevro waves down to us from the weathervane and cuts one of the banners free. They didn't expect anyone to penetrate this far.

Aside from its beauty, the Citadel is also a fortress. One I don't want to tangle with. We'd go room to room and, assuming it is not completely empty of soldiers, be overwhelmed, pinned to its expensive red oak walls and killed on its marble floors. It is not shielded, but a network of bunkers lie far beneath it. I was worried that is where the Sovereign would be kept. If she stayed there, this would turn into a siege. It would be days before we dig her out, if we could at all. So I give her a path of escape. It all falls on Mustang's shoulders: the shield must go down at the proper time. Flush her out.

A decorative wall, one that'd usually be nothing more than a hop-skip in gravBoots, bars us from the silent Citadel grounds. All around us is park. Trees. Fountains. White squares where Golds and Silvers would have afternoon tea, now empty. So silent here at the eye of the storm. Sevro flies down to join me.

"Can you lift us over the wall?" I ask.

"Things are almost outta juice," he grumbles. "Let's try." We hug one another and he lifts me into the air, wincing and favoring his left arm. The boots sputter and shiver out sparks. Twice we dip down. Then we're atop the wall. I set down and Sevro dips down again to pick up the next Howler. Moments later, his head appears at the top of the wall for a moment, then vanishes as his gravBoots spark and whine. With one last mechanical pop, the boots give out and Sevro and the Howler fall the ten meters to the ground.

A great boom thunders from across the city. Smoke rises distantly. Mustang did it.

Above, the translucent shield that separated this world from the world of ships fails. It wobbles and, distorting the fires in the city and the lightning above like a corrupted mirror, shatters into prismatic mist. Or one-eighth of it shatters; a flood of pent-up water falls down on that section of the city in great gray sheets.

"It didn't work!" Pebble cries from the other side of the wall.

But it did. One by one, the nexuses that cast the shield overload. It's a chain reaction as great sheets of water from the storm finally fall on Agea. Roque, if he's winning, will launch the reinforcements. The city is as good as taken. And even now, the Sovereign will be extracted from the bunkers by her bodyguards to make an escape from the lost planet. But the shuttle pads are still two kilometers on the other side of the Citadel grounds. This was all supposed to be different. I should be in my armor, a hundred Obsidians behind me, a dozen of my best Golds. Instead, I lead a pack of my friends into a meatgrinder. I need to change the paradigm, but I won't risk them. I glance down the wall at Sevro, who immediately recognizes the look in my eyes.

"No, Darrow," he says. "Think of your mission!" He's begging me, jumping and clawing at the wall as I turn away. "Don't do it, Darrow. *Wait!* They'll kill you!"

I drop over the other side of the wall into the Citadel's gardens.

Some men have threads of life so strong that they fray and snap those around them. Enough friends have paid for my war. This one's on me.

"*DARROW!*" he screams, horrible, desperate. "STOP!"

I run faster than I have in all my life. The Sovereign will not escape me. I did all this to catch her. Take her, break the Society. Take her, and the stage is set. We will rise. We can win. I jump rows of shrubbery, sprint around fountains, tear through rosebushes. Blood leaks down my arm. I do not feel my body. I fly over the earth. SlingBlade in hand.

There.

I round a corner of the Citadel. Past a garden of roses lies a courtyard of white scored black by the engines of personal yachts. Four lonely ships sit in a landing zone that can hold a hundred. All the shuttles are black with a giant gold crescent on their broad chassis, but the thickest of them, one with larger engines and a reinforced hull, is the Sovereign's. The others are decoys, nearly as thick, nearly as armored. In the air, they are indistinguishable.

I've been seen on sensors, no doubt. Gray lurchers are coming for me. Obsidian bodyguards have been loosed from some hidden barracks to kill me. They'll only catch me if I stop. And even as I examine the landing pad, I do not break my stride. Oranges bustle around the black shuttles, prepping them to launch. I'm not too late. But the door from the Citadel is far closer than I to the ship.

They come out in a rush. I don't see her. Just purple capes swirling in the rain and wind. They duck their heads into the gale, look upward at the sky where Iron Rain entry trails glow behind the storm, making the dark clouds look like steel heating slowly in the forge. My Titans come.

The Praetorians hurry, running up a long ramp into the shuttle's belly with the Sovereign. I catch her face as she ducks into the ship's belly. I see Aja among her entourage. And Karnus. And Fitchner, that ugly, traitorous son of a bitch. I run faster. Legs numb with exhaustion. Lungs aching. All I am, I put into this moment. My life in the mines, the hours suffering with Harmony, the horrors at the Institute. All the love I've earned and lost and still wish to live for, I let burn in me.

Half the entourage waits on the pavement, left behind to watch the ship as its lights glow and its engines prime. The decoys mimic its motions. A Bellona Gold turns as I near. His eyes flash wide and I slash him at the run as he lets out a half scream. More turn—women, men, warriors, Politicos, Golds and Silvers I recognize from my days at Augustus's side.

Their realization of my presence comes in waves. The enemy is supposed to be at the gates, not among them, so they flinch in seeing me. And when they gather their wits, I'm already past their armored hands. I dodge a Gray's outstretched grip, snag a small munitions pouch from his waist. I lash backward, hitting flesh.

Shouts. Fumbling for razors. Bullets, pulseblasts, snap past my head. The shuttle's ramp retracts as it begins to rise.

I scream and jump with all the might I've ever had. The hand of my injured right arm grips the ramp's edge. My eyes bug from my head with the strain and pain in my fingers. The ship continues to rise. The roar of the engines fills me, rattling my heart against my ribs. The ramp continues to close. I grunt desperately and jerk myself upward, awkward at the odd angle, but possible in the low gravity. I roll forward into the bay and onto my knees and pant, slingBlade against the floor. The sound of the engines slips away as the door shuts and pressurizes. All I hear is my ragged breath and the rumble of the deadly shuttle as it makes its escape.

I look up.

42

||||||||||||||||||||||||

DEATH OF A GOLD

Six Praetorians in full armor watch me. Karnus is with them. And Aja. And stocky Fitchner, his eyes widening as he sees me. The Sovereign stands in front of her Praetorians, tall but hardly coming to their shoulders.

Blooydamn. I didn't think they'd all still be in the bay.

"Darrow?" Fitchner almost moans.

"What?" Karnus laughs, looking about to see if the others notice how ridiculous a present just fell in their laps. "*What? . . .* Andromedus, *where* did you come from? It looks like Jove himself just shit you out."

I stay on my knees, panting, dripping blood and rain and sweat and mud.

"We can leverage him as a hostage," Fitchner says quickly as the ship rises in the sky.

"No," the Sovereign answers. "Achilles would never have been ransomed, for by being captured, he loses what makes him Achilles." She regards me for a cool moment. I spit phlegm on the ground. "Aja, cut off his head."

Aja paces toward me. "Stupid boy. No friends. No army. No hope."

I chuckle darkly. "Who needs hope when you have a pulseGrenade?" I hold up the munitions I ripped off the Gray's belt. They recoil.

"What do you want, Andromedus?" the Sovereign asks slowly.

"To prove you are not invincible. Land this ship."

Octavia smiles and speaks into her com. "Pilot. Roll."

The pilot does a barrel roll. Without gravBoots I lose my feet, slamming into the ceiling then back to the deck, dropping the grenade. My enemies stay rooted in place. Aja kicks the pulseGrenade out the open hatch. It explodes far beneath.

I look out into the night, where my plan just disappeared.

"Pride." Octavia smiles. "I suppose it makes fools of us all."

I take my time looking back to her, realizing how very stupid I was to think I could control all the variables. And now I've slipped up.

"You won't escape," I say.

"You know I will. Why else would you risk jumping on my shuttle?" She nods to one of the Olympic Knights and a strange, high-pitched warble ripples through the air twice before subsiding. A ghostCloak. Impossibly expensive for a whole ship. My friends won't be coming to rescue me.

Octavia turns to Fitchner. "Rage Knight, have you a nanoCam?" He nods and produces a ring. "Record Aja killing the Reaper."

Fitchner blanches.

"Let me kill him," Karnus begs. "My Sovereign, let me kill him for my family. It's my right."

"Your right?" she asks, surprised. "Your family has lost me Mars. You have no rights."

"He'd be a better prisoner." Fitchner steps toward the Sovereign. "Let me talk to him. He's my student. You would have had him serve you once before, Octavia. Let him recant and do so again. It will show the greatness of your power—that you can forgive even a little piss-eater like this."

The Sovereign turns slowly to look at Fitchner, examining him. And he realizes he's made a mistake. "Aja, hold." She smiles. "I want Fitchner to kill him."

The ugly man just gapes. It's one of the first times I've seen him speechless.

"Kill your student," the Sovereign says. "Or are you not loyal?"

"Of course I am loyal. I've already proven it."

"Then prove it again. Bring me his head."

"There has to be another way."

"He set your son against you," Octavia says. "And you know I do not keep things near to me that I cannot trust. So kill him."

"Yes, my liege." Fitchner's face pinches in concentration. There's a strange swirling of sadness in his bronze eyes. Is it so horrible seeing his prize student die? Or is it that I am Sevro's friend? Or is it worry for Sevro?

"Sevro lives," I tell him. "He survived the Rain."

He nods his thanks and touches his razor. Then he stumbles sideways, shoved aside by Karnus. The huge Bellona charges me. Mouth curved in hate, huge shoulders shelled in armor that shows the greatness of his family. He bellows my name.

He feints high, curves the razor diagonally at me, quick as a snake. I side-flip forward, inside most of the swing, and put my razor through his stomach. I let go the blade and circle around behind him as he collapses to his knees. "Rise so high, in mud you lie," I whisper as I pull my blade out of his back by its sharp end and cut off his head.

A Praetorian runs at me. I throw my razor at him. It takes him in the chest and he falls to the ground. I take my blade from his chest and stumble back from the watching Praetorians.

"Idiots," the Sovereign mutters.

"Should I keep recording this?" Fitchner scratches his head.

The ship shudders again and banks hard before straightening out. My vision wavers and I stumble to my knee. Hand on the deck. Steady myself. I feel the new warmth spilling down my back and stomach. I'll not kneel. Not to her. Not to a tyrant. I stand unsteadily. Karnus missed most of me. But not all. Blood sluices from between my neck and left shoulder where his razor found purchase. It cut through my collarbone. My body sags.

"What a thing." Octavia au Lune's cold eyes survey the wound on my neck. "Imagine this boy shaped in my house, Aja." She shakes her head and stares at me with a complete lack of understanding. She notes my other wounds. My blood. My exhaustion. My youth. Yet I did all this. Two bodies at my feet. A city stormed behind me. More taken all over Mars. My fleet shattering the Bellona's. The Society ready to fracture. She doesn't understand and she never will. But Fitchner seems to. Eyes glassy. Hands clenched.

"You could not shape me," I mumble. Only Reds could. Only family, only love, gave me this strength. But the strength fades now. It's then that Aja rushes forward. We exchange three moves before she knocks my blade aside and punches me so hard in the chest with her fist that I think I'm dead. She slams me against the ceiling like a rag doll. And when she is done, she rejoins the Sovereign and I moan and sink into the pain.

"Bring me his head, Fitchner," the Sovereign commands.

Fitchner looks at me helplessly and puts a hand out, nearly touching her. "We should film his execution for the HC. Propaganda. Full hanging. A state death."

"Fitchner . . ." The Sovereign's eyebrows go up till Fitchner retracts his hand. "Enough." Her jaw muscles work as she thinks. "I want him gone. No more variables. *Now.* Save the head for a pike. We'll film that."

Fitchner's beady eyes swell with sadness. Born the lowest of the Golds, he rose to the top on merit alone. What a man. To think I ever thought him weak.

Here, at the end of things, I know we will win Mars. Augustus will be freed. The war will continue. Gold will weaken. And Red will rebel. Maybe, just maybe, they will rise and find freedom. I've done what Ares asked. I created chaos. The rest will go to other men, women. Eo would be pleased.

I smile softly and feel the weakness in my legs. I am tired. I'm on my knees. When did I get there again? I care not. How very nice it will be to rest in the Vale while others carry out Eo's dream. I just wish I'd seen Mustang before the end. Told her what I am, so at last she'd understand.

"Your boy burned bright. And fast," Aja says to Fitchner from the shadows of my vision. "Keep the head. But you can cast the body to the soil in the Martian way."

Aja reopens the drop ramp. Metal groans. I feel the wind of the

Vale on my face. Feel the chill of mist. The scent of rain. I'm going to sleep. Soon I'll wake beside Eo. I'll wake in our warm bed, my hand tangled in her hair. I'll wake to love and know that in the world before, I did my best.

I'll miss you though, Mustang. More than I've admitted until now.

Fog and shadows are my vision. For a moment, the smell of rust makes me think I'm in the mine. Am I asleep? I hear metal boots. A man walking through the fog. I can't see his face. But something stirs in me. Father? No, not Father. I squint.

"Uncle Narol."

"No. It's Fitchner, boyo."

His voice jerks me violently back into the hold of the ship. Like a fishing hook tearing silk a direction it doesn't wish to go.

"Oh. I'm glad it's you," I say quietly, finding enough strength to lift my heavy head a bit more to look him in his eyes. Tears fill them. He coughs out a laugh. The wind whistles behind me. Not the Vale. Just Mars. Not mist. Just the clouds. The ramp's down so they can push my body out. I told Arcos I was never meant to have gray hair.

My head dips. I spit out some blood in my mouth. I'm nauseous and fading. "Tell Mustang . . . Eo . . . I love them." I yawn so deeply.

"You bloodydamn fool," he says in a low whisper, shaking his head. *"I had it under control."*

"I didn't . . ." I blink through the fog. *"What?"*

"It is me," he says. "It's always been me, boyo."

The fog disappears. I look up at him. I look up at Ares as he dons his Rage Knight helmet and shoots his pulseFist back at the Praetorians, sending them scattering. He tosses back a sonic grenade.

"Fitchner!" the Sovereign roars. "TRAITOR!"

An explosion. Something hits my chest and I'm falling. Tumbling. Flying? Sense cold. Ragged wind biting me. Stomach in my throat. Spinning. Then a rigid arm under mine. Rising. Wind whips past my ears. But there's another sound before the darkness swallows me. Fitchner—Ares—terrorist lord of the underworld, howls like a wolf as he carries me to safe harbor.

43

||||||||||||||||||||

THE SEA

I wake to the smells of the sea. Brine, seaweed, carried on a brisk autumn wind. Gulls cry. One banks and perches on the white-stone sill of the open window. It cocks its head at me and flies away into the morning sunshine. Clouds move distantly across the horizon, promising rain even as early morning dew drips down the open skylight.

She stirs at my side. Her slender body atop the sheets, coiled around my own damaged form. She's clothed. I'm shirtless. Fresh skingrafts mark my body. Glossy things, pink and tender to the touch. Mustang stirs once more, her movement bringing me into my own body. Making me feel the aches and the pains and the comfort of her closeness. I let my eyelids drift shut and I sigh deeply, allowing myself to sink into the soft pleasures of being human. Her breath against my neck. The drumbeat of another heart against my rib cage. Her golden hair tickles my nose as cool wind blows strands into my face. The morning air is young, vital.

I breathe it deep, slipping back into sleep.

Memories of metal shatter the peace.

Screams echo in the black. Friends die.

My eyes burst open for the light, desperate to remind me where I am. Telling me I'm safe. I'm warm. There's no metal here. Only cotton sheets. A bed. A warm girl. Yet the memories are so close. How did I survive?

I fell from the sky with Fitchner.

Ares—a truth that's always been, but seems so new I cannot even grasp it. I woke to a Yellow's tools inside my chest, restarting my heart. Then I woke again to a Carver's scalpel against my skin. Agony and nausea my bedmates. Tides of vision ebbing in, flowing out. Visitors coming and going. I prefer waking to this.

I'm afraid to close my eyes again. Afraid of what I'll see, what I'll wake to find. As a Red child, I shared my small cot with Kieran. Every morning, I'd wake before him and lie there quietly, letting my parents' hushed voices seep under the flimsy door as they started their day. I'd hear Father's shuffling feet. The throat-clearing sound he'd make every morning as he washed sleep from his face. Mother would make him coffee, grinding the cubes she'd trade to the Grays for pitviper eggs or spools of silk stolen from the Webbery.

I wish it was the sound that woke me at the same time every morning. The grinding, the smell. I wish I could say it was how my body knew to return from sleep. But it wasn't the smell of coffee or Mother's tea. It wasn't the morning sigh of water running through pipes or the arthritic creak of rope ladders as the men and women from Lykos Township's nightshift made their way home from the mines and Webbery. It wasn't the weary murmur of those of the dayshift making their way to work from home.

What woke me was the dread of a closing door.

Each morning it would end the same. First, the clay dishes would clink into the metal sink. Then Father's plastic chair would scrape the stone floor. They would stand together at the door, whispering. A silence. I always imagined it was the moment they shared a long kiss. Then at last, it'd be the goodbye. The front door opened, creaking on rusted hinges. And finally, despite all my prayers, it'd close.

I lean close to Mustang and kiss her forehead. Harder than I meant to. She wakes delicately, like a cat stretching itself out of a summer nap. Her eyes don't open, but she nuzzles into my side.

"You're awake," she murmurs. Her lashes flutter and she bolts upright, away from me. "Sorry. Must have fallen asleep." She looks to the chair she'd been sitting in. "On the bed."

"It's fine. Stay. Please." I'd forgotten we're supposed to be cold to each other. "How long has it been?"

"Since the assault? A week." She brushes loose strands of hair from her eyes. "I'm glad you've come back to us."

"Who did we lose?" I ask carefully.

"Lose?" Her hands fidget awkwardly as she lists the casualties. A moment of silence stretches long. The numbers crushing me in my bed. I remember to breathe.

"The Sovereign?"

"Escaped. But not without a nasty wound courtesy of Fitchner."

"Your father?" I ask.

"You don't know?" She smiles awkwardly and sighs a bit too casually, trying to loosen her own tension. She scoots closer on the bed, still taking care not to touch me. "It's going to be tedious catching you up."

"I'm sure you'll manage."

"Father is alive. When the shields fell, several Golds already inside the Citadel led a lurcher squad to rescue him. Turns out my brother has a long reach. So when the Olympic Knights came to take him with Octavia, they left empty-handed.

"The HC channels are calling Roque 'Nelson reincarnate.' He captured more than eighty percent of the Bellona fleet." Her tone darkens. "Which means, as leader of the engagement, he has claim to at least thirty percent of the ships, the rest going to the House Augustus."

"Meaning he has more than I do, technically."

"The pundits are wondering how long his loyalty will last now that—"

"The Jackal is playing his games," I interrupt with a laugh.

"He never stops."

"I don't think Roque will take up arms against me," I say. "Do you?"

She shrugs. "Power creates opportunities. I told you to mend things with him."

"Roque is our ally. He always will be. You know him."

"He's been here as much as Sevro." She smiles slowly. "Fell asleep here last night. I shooed him away earlier. But I wouldn't be doing my job if I pretended he wasn't a potential threat to us."

Us, I note.

"Your job?" I ask. "Which is . . . ?"

"I've appointed myself your chief Politico."

"Have you now?"

"I have. The game of court can be a nasty, duplicitous business. You're much too earnest for it. Like a lamb thinking it an honor to be invited to a banquet thrown in its honor by wolves."

"And what if it's you I need to be protected from?"

"Well." She arches her left eyebrow. "Then I suppose you've already lost."

I laugh and ask about Sevro.

She pretends to look around. "He's not asleep at the foot of the bed? I think he's off with his father. I only returned from visiting Kavax in orbit last night, but Theodora says Sevro departed shortly after dinner with Fitchner. Thought he hated the man."

"He does."

"What's changed?"

I shrug and wonder how long Sevro has known about his father's true identity. Seems impossible he was as blind as I. Was someone lying to me for a change?

"And Lorn?" I ask.

"He's with that harpy, Victra."

"What's wrong with Victra?"

"Aside from the fact that she flirts with everything that moves? Nothing."

"Wait. She flirts with you? Tell me more about that."

"Shut it." Mustang swats at me. But her smile falls just as quick and she pulls her hand back. "Lorn's taken Victra under his wing. Seems he's comfortable allying his family with the Julii. Victra's mother has agreed to the pact. Three of the most powerful houses on Mars united under my family. A triumvirate against the Sovereign. The Governors of the Gas Giants are on their way to Agea for a summit. So too are the Reformers. You were right. We take Mars, we have a chance against Octavia. This isn't just a battle any longer. It's a civil war. And not a pointless one, it seems. Father is making talk of giving the Reformers a chance at the table. That . . . *this* means something."

I remember my conversation with the man. "And you believe him?"

"I do, Darrow." She smiles hopefully. "For the first time in a long time, I really do."

I am not so sure. "What about . . ."

"Cassius?" she guesses quietly. "His father was killed by the Telemanuses, and he fought Ragnar on the wall. All his brothers and sisters are reported dead. But he and his mother are missing."

I note her quiet. "Are you worried he's dead?"

"He is our enemy," she says flatly. "His welfare isn't my concern." She examines my eyes closely. "Are you worried?"

"I don't know." I consider.

"Goryhell. You're so tender sometimes. Do you regret cutting off his arm, too?"

"I regret killing Julian."

"We're all stained by the past." Mustang considers. "You forget I had to kill someone in the Passage too. Every Peerless Scarred you've ever met—Lorn, Sevro, Pebble, Tactus, Octavia, Daxo, we all started there. Often I think there's too much to regret."

Is she talking about us? Am I a regret?

"I want to hate Cassius," I say slowly. "I really do. Even thinking of him makes me want to crush something. Break a window. Or, preferably, his ugly, smug face."

"Ugly?" she asks skeptically.

"So pretty he's ugly."

Mustang laughs at that. "But it's hard to keep the hate going, isn't it?" she asks.

I nod. Hate is what made Cassius's family throw themselves against Augustus's. Look what that brought them. "I pity him. Wherever he is."

"Earlier I told you not to trust my brother," Mustang says, redirecting the conversation. "I meant it. I know you continued your alliance with him. His companies are making you seem like a god. But it has to end. You owe him nothing. Be cordial. Be polite. Don't disrespect him in public. But no more meetings. No more promises. Cut him off. You don't need him anymore. You have me."

This girl. Would that I could introduce her to Mother, to Kieran and Leanna. They'd like her fire. My throat tightens slowly. Eo would like her too.

"I don't have you," I say.

"Darrow . . ."

Something strange twists inside me. Like a tight spring of emotion finally allowed to uncoil. "When I was on the bottom of the river . . . I knew I wouldn't see you again."

She hesitates, wanting to reach for me, but resisting because of all we've said before. "You know you don't have my leave to die," she jokes instead. "Anyway, Sevro and the Howlers would never forgive you if you tried. None of them would. You've so many friends, Darrow. So many who'd run through fire for you."

So many who have been burned. Shuddering, I take a long breath and close my eyes, trying not to let the guilt swallow me. The tears come quietly, trickling out the corners of my eyes.

"Darrow. *Don't cry,*" Mustang whispers, reaching for me now. She scoots closer, holding me. "It's all right. It's all over. We're safe."

The sobs come, racking my chest.

She's wrong. It's not over. All I see behind my eyelids is a world of war. There is no other future for me, for us. Yet how many times have I already been pieced back together? How much longer can all these stitches hold? In the end, will there even be pieces left of me? I can't stop crying. Can't even catch my breath. Heart thundering. Hands shaking. It all comes out of me. Mustang, barely half my weight, holds me with her gentle arms till I'm exhausted and can do nothing but sink back into the bed. In time, my heart slows, finding rhythm to match hers.

We sit that way for what must be an hour. Eventually, she kisses my shoulder, my neck, lips pausing along the jugular as it pulses. I adjust my hands to move her away, but she pushes them to the side and cups my face with a hand.

"Let me in."

I let my hands fall to the bed. Her mouth crafts a warm path to mine. There we share the taste of my tears as her top lip slides between my own and her tongue warms the inside of my mouth. Her hand slides up my neck, nails grazing the skin, till she finds purchase in my hair, tugging slightly at the tangle. Shivers lance my body.

Gone is any semblance of resistance. All the guilt that kept me from betraying Eo with Mustang is swept away in the chaos inside me. All the guilt I have for knowing she is a Gold and I am a Red vanishes. I'm a man, and she's the woman I want.

My hands find Mustang, pulling her body onto mine, shadowing the length of her legs to the swell of her waist. Long-suppressed hunger wakes in me. Filling me with heat, aching for her. All of her. Forget my restraint. Forget my sadness. This is all I need. I won't run. Not this time. Not when I know how close I came to never seeing her again.

I peel apart her clothing with slow force. Under my hands, the fabric is like wet paper. Her skin is smooth, hot marble warmed in the sun. Muscles coil and tense underneath as she arches her back. Hers is a body made for movement, mocking, coiling around mine. I trace my fingers along the curve of her lower back. She pushes into me, pulsing with breath, hips grinding me into the bed.

It may have been a week to her, but for me it was minutes, seconds ago that I kneeled against cold steel warmed by my own blood, waiting for men to cut off my head. This a moment I thought I would never have again as I dug Eo's grave with my own trembling hands. A moment with a woman I want and love. And what is the bloodydamn point of surviving in this cold world if I run from the only warmth it has to offer?

44

||||||||||||||||||||||||

THE POET

I walk slowly down the stone hall with Mustang. Out the windows, guards patrol the estate. They're here to keep us as much as protect us. Rain falls lightly. Laughter drifts out an open door with the smells of coffee and bacon.

"What do you mean I can't be funny?" Roque asks, offended.

"Just that," Daxo says smoothly. "I'm sure you can try, but you're too . . . scholastic."

"Fine then, who was the first carpenter?"

"Is this a joke?" Daxo asks.

"It's intended to be."

"Jesus of Nazareth . . . ?" Daxo guesses. "It is a history joke, yes?"

"Noah?" Pebble tries. Mustang and I pause outside the door, smiling to each other.

"Jesus of Nazareth?" Roque laughs. "You can do better than that."

"If I knew I'd be mocked for guessing, I wouldn't have guessed."

"Pax said you were the smart one," Thistle says. "Disappointing, Daxo. Disappointing."

"Well, in comparison, he probably—" Clown begins before Pebble smacks him upside the head. "Ow!"

"Don't talk shit about Pax," Pebble snaps. "Big man was a sweetie."

"Does no one care about the answer?" Roque asks melodically. "Fine. Fine. I understand. You all think I'm a bore."

"We're dying to know," Thistle snaps. "Do tell."

"Who was the world's first carpenter?" Roque asks again.

"You don't have to start all over!" Pebble moans.

"Well, it works best that way." Roque sighs. "Eve."

"Eve?" Daxo asks.

"Because . . . ," Roque leads. "She made Adam's banana stand?"

A collective moan.

"That's just embarrassing," Pebble says with a sigh. "Never thought I'd miss Tactus."

Then a high-pitched whining laugh springs out of Daxo. Just like Pax. "Eve! Eve, he said. Banana stand. Ahh." It's like the giants have little ridiculous elves inside them just waiting to spring out and cackle. Just takes a lot of provocation.

"I think he broke Daxo." Pebble giggles.

"Does anyone smell that?" Clown asks.

"I smell bacon," Daxo tries. There's a crunch as he bites into a piece.

"No," Clown says. "Smells like a suicidal madman recently risen from the dead after conquering a planet and abandoning his friends to get himself cut to gory ribbons like a slagging fool."

Daxo sniffs. "That's a particular scent."

"Oh, Darrow dear," Clown calls. "Are you lurking behind the door?"

Mustang pushes me out awkwardly.

"You eavesdropping Pixie!" Daxo glides to his feet and pulls me into a surprisingly gentle hug. The golden angels on his bald head glitter in the morning light. "Glad to see you, my friend."

They all greet me in turn. More hugs than I've ever received from Golds. Roque hugs me mechanically. A perfunctory gesture. There is still mending to be done.

I gorge myself on breakfast as my friends banter. We spend the day on the property, whiling away time in conversation and games. It's been so long since I've had either that I've nearly forgotten how to do nothing. Mustang has to kiss my ear and tell me to relax three times before it really sticks. We're in the library listening to music when she sees Roque out the window on the lawn. She nudges me.

"Go."

I find Roque watching a pair of deer eat from a feeder underneath an old elm. He doesn't turn to look at me as I sidle up next to him. It smells like fresh-cut grass. The sea somewhere over the hill.

"It makes sense this is where Mustang grew up," I say. "It's wild and tranquil all at once."

"My home was meant to be in the city," Roque says. "Though I snuck off to the country with my tutors whenever Mother was away. Which was often. She seemed to think there was nothing out here worthwhile. That the business of cities was more important than this. But this is why we fight, isn't it?"

"For land?" I ask.

"For peace, in whatever way we find it." He turns to me. "Isn't that why you fight?"

"Some of us weren't born with peace," I say, gesturing to the deer and the land. "I didn't have this growing up. Anything I have now or will have in the future I have to earn. But you're right. It's why I fight, so I can have this for me and the people I care for."

His eyes search my face. "Fair enough."

"I want to apologize to you, Roque."

"Again?"

"Since the Academy, I've kept you at arm's length. I've taken you for granted. I shouldn't have done that. Not when you've always been so kind to me." He doesn't meet my gaze.

"I didn't mind that it was always about you, Darrow. That was what burned Tactus, but not me. I'm not in love with you like Mustang. I don't worship you like Sevro or the Howlers. I was a true friend. I was someone who saw your light and your dark and accepted both without judgment, without agenda. And what did you do to me? You used me like a man uses a horse. I'm better than that. Quinn was better than that."

"Are you better than this friendship?" I ask quietly, afraid of the answer.

"I think I'm better than you," he says. I step back, wounded. He watches the deer nibble at the grain in the feeder. "I've sat by the bedsides of three friends this year. Quinn, Tactus, and you. Each time I knew I would have gladly switched places with any of you. Would you wish the same?"

"I'd give my life to bring them back," I say, knowing it is a lie. Much as I love these Golds, I have greater responsibilities. Until this is over, it's not my life to give.

He turns from the deer to watch me, eyes warm and sad and carrying so much more weight than they ever should. He's different from me, from Cassius. We called him brother, and he was one better than either of us deserved. "Have you ever wondered why they put me in House Mars? I'm not the typical draft. Most would probably put me in Apollo or Juno."

"Quinn always had that competition in her blood. But you . . . Yes, I've wondered."

"Darrow." I turn to see Sevro standing behind us in uniform. "It's urgent."

"Not now, Sevro."

"Reap, I'm not shitting you," he says.

I look back to Roque. "Go," he says, and walks toward the deer, pulling berries from his pocket.

"Roque," I call to him plaintively.

"Friendships take minutes to make, moments to break, years to repair," he says, turning to glance over his shoulder. "We'll talk again soon."

I watch him go, feeling a small bit of hope warm me. I turn to Sevro and clap his back. "Good to see you. Sorry about—"

"Piss off. I'm not a whiny little bitch like the poet. It's *Ares*. Your friends, the Red, the Pink, and the Violet, have gotten themselves captured."

"By whom?"

"Who do you think? The Jackal."

45

||||||||||||||||||||||

GIFTS

My ship lands in the early morning snowfall of Attica, a south-ern mountain city set on seven peaks. Jagged buildings of steel and glass christen the peaks like icy thorn crowns, now dusted with fresh powder. The red morning sun rises over the mountain range to the east. Bridges link the seven peaks, and the city's lesser wards spill around the roots of the mountains. My shuttle flies over them. Plows melt paths through the snow with pulsing orange blades. Soon, midColor landcars will flow along the avenues. And highColor shuttles will ferry Silvers and Golds to their offices on the mountain peaks. Remote and renowned for its banking, Attica is a prime seat of power. It belongs now to the Jackal.

Under heavy guard by ripWings, I land on a platform surrounded by evergreens. Several lurchers wait there in white tactical gear. A lone Gold stands with them. Victra embraces me with a hug, a white fur pelt pulled tight about her shoulders. Jade earrings clatter in the breeze as the Grays inspect the outside of my ship.

"Victra," I say, holding her back to look at her. She grins devilishly and kisses my cheek, grabbing my butt as she does. I jump in surprise. She laughs merrily.

"Just making sure the pieces are in order. You had us worried, darling. Roque kept me apprised while I was with Lorn."

"Brokering another alliance, I hear."

"Who would have thought, Victra au Julii, the peacemaker."

The Grays notify me that they have orders to search my ship.

"Ragnar," I call. He steps out of the ship's confines, near twice the size of the largest Gray. "Let the mice search the ship. They're looking for . . ."

The Gray spares a glance at Ragnar, swallows. "Bombs, *dominus*."

Victra escorts me into the Jackal's new home—a fortress citadel atop the highest of Attica's peaks. The city stretches far beneath us. Trees line the path from the landing pad to the Citadel. "Adrius took the place soon as the last Bellona ship retreated. Came in with a thousand lurchers and displaced the Bellona allies who owned the place. Took all they had. Emptied their bank accounts. Full-on theft. But that's war." She nods to the west. "Wonderful slopes just a few clicks out. We'll take a few days when this all settles down. You bring Virginia, I'll find myself a man." Nearly my own height, she looks sideways at me. "You do ski, don't you?"

I snort out a laugh. "Never had the time."

We find the Jackal in his living room. Walls and floor are glass. Fire swirls under the floor, licking up in columns near the window. Several minimalist chairs of steel and leather sit on fur rugs. The Jackal is hunched over a holoDisplay, speaking quickly to someone. He motions us to take a seat. On the holo, I glimpse Harmony in a dark room, surrounded by Grays. One is hunched over her, doing something with some device I can't quite see.

We sit by the flames, but a chill goes through me that no fire can dispel.

The Jackal finishes, giving a dataStrip to Sun-hwa before she leaves. He joins us, rubbing the back of his neck.

"So many moving parts." He winces. "Hell, organizing the food shipments alone takes a hundred Coppers. And those odious little shits will spend all day bickering about whether or not a ship should have granola or muesli in its galley. *Both* is an option. Both! How difficult is that, really? It's like they enjoy the spreadsheets and busywork. Mind boggling."

"I keep telling him he should delegate more efficiently," Victra says. So they've been talking too. I'm behind.

"I hate delegating," the Jackal replies. He scratches his head. "At least with numbers and particulars. You two can take all the gory planets you like. Just leave me my bureaucracy, please."

"Kind of you," I laugh. "Just keep me away from food requisition orders." I lean forward. "I hear the fleet will be ready to depart for the Core in two weeks. By the bye, wonderful new home you have."

"I like it," he sighs. "Father is furious I took it for myself, of course. He wanted to give it as a present to one of the Governors of the Gas Giants."

"I think you've earned it," I say. "That and more."

"Exactly." The Jackal makes a tired motion with his lone hand. "I came here as a boy to ski with Mother. I always looked up here and said it'd be mine. Father said you can't have everything you want."

"And you asked, Why not?" Victra says. She's already heard the story.

"Why not?" the Jackal repeats the words fondly. "So if Father wants it back, he'll have to make his own food purchase orders."

We all know it isn't food purchase orders that occupy his time. Not solely.

I accept a cup of tea from a Pink. A small spread of breakfast is placed in front of me. I'm seven hours behind this timezone, but I can't let on how nervous I am.

The Jackal watches me spear a melon with my fork. Who knows what he thinks behind those dirty gold eyes? "So, Darrow, healed and mended in time for the great battle."

"Mending," I say. "No thanks to your media. The HC shows all say I've become immortal since Karnus opened me up."

"It's all part of the game, my goodman. Perception, deception, media!" He slaps his hand on his thigh, though his eyes don't share the mirth. "Give me the word and I can go public with your improved vitality. We'll schedule a press conference. Dress you in armor. My

Violets are building you a proper suit of your own. They've been conspiring with Greens to give you a marvel of form and tech."

"You know I hate the cameras."

"Oh, stop whining. They're why we have half our allies. And why the Sovereign's scrambling like a spider on ice. Her coalition is . . . stressed."

"We'll do it today, then," I say. I look out the window, remembering Roque's words. "I wanted a moment of peace, but . . ." They join me in looking at the falling snow and the distant city beneath. "I suppose we've yet to earn that. Which brings me to why I called this meeting."

"I admit I've been curious," the Jackal says.

"He's been dying to know," Victra corrects.

I nod to Ragnar, who followed Victra and me into the room. He comes forward with two boxes from my ship. "I wanted to give you both gifts. Our alliance has had an . . . interesting beginning. But I want you both to know how committed I am not only to it, but to each of you. I hope you take this to be a sign of my trust."

"Always trust a Stained bearing gifts." Victra chuckles, looking up at Ragnar. "Goryhell, go over there. You're like a tree blocking out the light, Ragnar."

"Ragnar, wait outside," I say.

The Jackal doesn't even look at Ragnar. Physical power bores him.

Snapping her fingers so I bring my attention back to her, Victra unwraps her box to find a small crystal bottle I had Theodora commission from the Carvers on the *Pax* before the siege of Mars.

"Petrichor," I say as she opens the bottle. The room fills with the smell of stone before rain. She thanks me with a scarred hand on my forearm, holding the bottle close to her chest.

"No one remembers that sort of thing. Thank you, Darrow." She sits there for a moment before rising quickly and kissing me on the lips. I would have preferred the cheek.

"My turn." The Jackal unwraps his box with his lone hand. Tearing through the paper with a grin on his face. He opens the leather box beneath and is quiet for a long moment. "Darrow, you shouldn't—"

He's cut short as a high-pitched alarm screams out of the walls.

A Gray lurcher bursts into the room, weapon drawn. Four others accompany her. "*Dominus,* we have a breach in the lower level. We have to escort you to a safer room."

"Who?" the Jackal rasps. Victra and I draw our razors. The Gray is about to answer when the alarms are cut short and replaced by a rising humorless laughter over the speakers. It echoes through the room even as the lighting of the place blacks out. We hurry to the door. A small metal spider clinks onto the window. The glass melts. My vision and hearing vanish. Replaced by a swarming, high-pitched keening. I stumble, stunned by the flash grenade.

Dark shapes fly into the room. Blinking, I glimpse cacodemon masks. Eyes glowing red out of terrible visages. The Sons have come. They shoot the Grays and kick us to the ground. Ragnar storms in from the hall and catches three stunFist blasts to his chest. He goes down like a felled tree. One masked intruder bends over the Jackal. As my hearing returns, I make out that he's screaming for the code to the facility's mainframe. He shoves the muzzle of his scorcher into the Jackal's mouth till the Jackal gives it up.

"Some Gold," rasps a distorted voice.

Behind the mask, I know Sevro would love nothing more than to pull the trigger, and for a moment I think he's going to. But he waits for me as he's supposed to. And on cue, I rise sluggishly, shaking off the results of the flash grenade, and grab one of the intruder's weapons, taking it for myself. I fire at them. They fire at me. Each of us missing on purpose. Then they are gone, back out the window. The Grays lie dead on the ground. Victra bleeds from a shallow head wound and rises to her feet. The Jackal tries to stand, blood dripping from his nose.

Wordlessly, we try the doors to the room. They're locked. The Sons have control of the mainframe now. The Jackal leans his head against the door. Then he rears back and slams it into the metal again, again, again till blood pours down his face. I have to pull him away before he splits his skull. He laughs darkly for a moment before shaking himself.

"Twice," he sneers. "Twice they violate me." An animalistic shudder goes through his body. "I was breaking them. Another day. Maybe two and they would have cracked."

"Who?" Victra asks.

He doesn't answer. I press the question. "Who, Adrius? Who the hell was that?"

"Terrorists. Came for captured Sons," he says impatiently. "One was the Pink bitch who tried to kill us on Luna, Darrow. It wasn't Pliny after all. It was the Sons. Another was one of Ares's right hands. They call her Harmony. A Violet was with them. Making them an army of carved soldiers."

"You had captured Sons of Ares here? When were you going to tell us this?" Victra snarls, standing from checking for the pulse of a dead Gray.

"I wasn't. Not until I knew who Ares was."

"What else are you keeping from us?" I say. "This is a partnership." I kick over a table. "Why the goryhell do you have *me* if not to protect you from things like this?"

"My fault," he says. "My fault." He swallows the blood in his mouth and walks toward the empty window bank, gripping my shoulder as he passes. Wind howls in. "You did protect me. Yet again. Thank you."

I scowl and brood in fine actorly fashion.

"They couldn't have been Reds," I say bitterly. "Couldn't have been Sons. Sons never would have, could have done that. Not to me. Not to Ragnar." I help the Stained from the floor. "They were too organized. They had gravBoots."

"You underestimate them, my friend," the Jackal says. "They can pull triggers too. And they would have pulled them with their muzzles against our heads if you hadn't stopped them."

"How the gorydamn did they get past your security?" Victra asks. "Were there tracking devices? Signal jammers? GravBoot signatures?"

"I don't know," the Jackal says.

Because the Sons held on to my hull wearing ghostCloaks, like little barnacles.

"Who else has come and gone?" I ask.

He looks around as I hoped he might. He calls up his men on a com at his desk. After a moment, he looks back up to us. "Sun-hwa," he whispers. "Her men are dead and she's gone like the wind. She survived the last attack too." Then he laughs. "She betrayed me." And when he sees the money transferred to Sun-hwa's accounts, he'll find all the corroborating evidence he needs to pin the blame on his chief of security. Only thing is, Sun-hwa is loyal as a dog and dead as a doornail in the cargo hold of the shuttle that now tears away from the Jackal's winter citadel carrying Fitchner, Sevro, and my once-captured friends.

I come beside the Jackal as Victra tries the door again. Together we watch the ship disappear beyond the mountains. And I say in a low, menacing voice, "We will kill the rats, together. I promise. All of them."

"After the Sovereign," he says, patting my back. "After the Sovereign."

46

||||||||||||||||||||||||

BROTHERHOOD

I hug Dancer so hard his back cracks. He taps me in panic. I apologize and separate, feeling large as a Telemanus next to him. Outside the garage-turned-makeshift-office, the Sons of Ares warehouse rattles with industry. They brought me in through the side door and had me wait for Dancer among old engines and rusted aerlons.

Dancer pulls back from me and looks up, rusty eyes glittering with tears. Startling to think that I once considered him a handsome man. He's in his forties; old for a Red. Hair shot with gray. Face creased by age and hardship. His right arm still hangs limp. His foot still drags. And his smile still stretches wide enough, baring uneven, imperfect teeth.

"My boy," he says, gripping my shoulder with his left hand. It's stronger than all the rest of him put together. He smells like tobacco. Nails are yellow. "My bloodydamn beautiful little bastard of a boy. You look so bloody grand!" He laughs and laughs again, shaking his head. "There are no words. I'm sorry I couldn't reach you. Sorry I let Harmony use you like that. There are so many things, Darrow."

"Stop." I clap the back of his neck. "We're brothers. No need for apologies. We're bound by blood and past. But please, please don't let it happen again." He nods. "How is my family, do you know?"

"Alive," he says. "Still in the mines. I know. I know. But that's the safest place for them with this war abound. No one wants to blow up Mars's industry. Register?"

He waves me to a seat. "Don't know many Golds, but that Sevro's a nasty little shit. When I delivered his father's instructions to him out on the Rim, I thought he was going to cut me from gob to pucker." He lights a burner, winks at me. "Never met anyone like him."

"He's loyal as they come," I say. "Like you."

"No! I mean he can swear better than any bloodydamn Red."

"Sevro swears?" I smile. "Guess you get used to it. Though he does like saying 'bloody' a hell of a lot now."

"It's a fine word. Rolls off the tongue. Done some research." He puffs up his chest. "Been with us since the first ancestors, you know. The first Golds, the ones with normal eyes and gold uniforms, took most of the early recruits from the poor bastards from the Irish isles after the radiation from London turned the isles into a wasteland. The Golds took the highly skilled migratory workforce and recruited them to be the first Pioneers. Their slang just stuck around, jumbled up a bit. History's fascinating, isn't she?"

"Harmony's been making up her own history," I say.

"That's right. I'm dead!" He shakes his head and lights another burner, flicking the other onto the floor. I pick it up and put it in the wastebasket. "She went her own way about a year after you left. We discovered several Senators were going to be vacationing on the Gorgon Sea. So we showed up to bug their villa to see if we couldn't get any secrets. We didn't. Just lots of . . . depraved shit. And that was that, we thought. But not for Harmony. On the last night, she walked in and killed the Senators and their guests. Then she left us."

"So there was never a lurcher squad that raided your headquarters?"

He shakes his head. "They came because of her. Killed about forty Sons. But she'd already left for Luna. Ares saved us. Came in hard with a mixed pack of Obsidians and Grays. Laid waste to those lurchers, then slipped away before reinforcements came. It's lucky he killed them all. No way they wouldn't know he was a Gold after that. Had our first face-to-face that day. Man's bloodydamn scary."

"Not the word I'd choose." Though maybe it's accurate considering how well he fooled me. "It doesn't bother you that he's a Gold?"

"It doesn't bother him that we're Reds. Ares would die for the cause, Darrow. Shit. He started it. You know why he did?"

I shake my head.

"It's his story." Dancer traces the pitviper bites on his neck. "A man has the right to tell his own story. But his isn't a happy one. Sad as yours. Sad as mine. Strip a man of what he loves, and what is left? Just hate. Just anger. But he was the first to know there could be something more. He found me. He found you. Who the bloodydamn are we to question him?"

The door opens suddenly. We both turn and Mickey limps in. He looks half dead, thin as a reed, paler than before. Without a word, he hobbles over to me and kisses me full on the mouth, his affection desperate and true. Then he starts weeping like a child. Dancer and I don't know what to do, so I just wrap my arms around him and let him cry. He whispers "Thank you" to me a dozen times.

What did they do to him? Never mind. I know the things the Grays are trained in to get information. He says he told them nothing. Still, I have to discover what the Jackal learned from this. What deductions he's made from finding Mickey's lab.

I look over Mickey's head to see Fitchner standing there, smiling sadly. After a long moment, Mickey pulls back. "I tried to warn you, when you came to us on Luna," he says apologetically. "Wanted to say to run. But she would have killed me if I said any more. I was afraid you would believe her over me."

"I would have believed you, Mickey."

"You would have?" He sniffles. "I knew you'd come for me. I said my darling boy was too kind to forget about Mickey, but she spat on me. Said I was a slaver." He hangs his head, sniffing and so vulnerable, drained and nearly mad from what must have been done to him in the Jackal's torture chambers. "She was right. I am. I am wicked. I hurt the girls and boys. I sold them even when I loved them. Of course she was right. Why would you come? Why would you do anything for wicked little Mickey?"

"Because you're my friend." I bring his hands to my lips, kissing them gently as he looks up at me with hopeful eyes. "Weird as you are, wicked as you were. I know you want to be better. You want to live for more. We all do. And there's not a place they could take one of my friends that I would ever abandon them."

It feels good to speak the truth.

"Thank you, my prince," he says quietly. He draws himself up after that, strong enough to turn and walk out of the office. Fitchner closes the door.

"Well, that was emotional."

I nod. This is the man I'd rather be. Not constantly on guard. Not lying through my teeth. I suppose I didn't even know how much affection I felt for Mickey till now. It's not because he helped make me. It's that he's always loved me so much. Even if it was a strange sort of love, it was real. And I do believe he wants to be a man he thinks I would respect. Just like I want to be a man Eo and Mustang would respect. And that's the good sort of love.

"We need to talk, Fitchner," I say. We didn't have a chance earlier. Sevro came to me with Dancer's plan—call a meeting, attach the Sons to my ship, let them infiltrate the building. All I did was suggest Sunhwa as the scapegoat, and let them know Victra was not to be harmed.

"I'll leave you two to it," Dancer says, pushing back his metal chair.

"No, I want you to stay," I say. "I've too many secrets from too many people. I won't have any more between the three of us."

"Learn to count, shithead," Sevro says, coming around a rusted engine block. The cheap metal door to the outside slams behind him. Smells like autumn even in Agea's oil-stained manufacturing district. He hops onto the rusted chassis of an old fighter and sits with his legs dangling. "Hey, look, it's all pricks for once. Let's tell sexist jokes."

Chuckling, I turn to Fitchner. "So you're Ares."

"Man comes out of a coma and he's a genius!" Fitchner barks. He claps his hands, but his eyes stay deadly serious. "Most call me Bronzie. Students call me Proctor. Some call me Rage Knight. The Sovereign calls me traitor. My son calls me shithead. . . ."

"You are a shithead," Sevro chimes in.

". . . My wife called me Fitchner. But the Golds made me Ares."

Before now I would not know what that meant. He is Gold. How could the Golds do anything to him? But now I've peeked behind the curtain. "Why didn't you tell me who you were from the start?"

"And put my life in the hands of a teenager's acting ability?" he cackles. "I think not. If you were found out and they tortured you . . . bad news. I had alternate plans, other irons in the fire. You just happened to be my favorite. But we mustn't be biased."

"Who was your wife?" I ask, already suspecting the answer.

"Full or short story?" he asks.

"Full."

"I was liaising for a terraforming company on Triton," he begins gruffly. "I didn't have a glamorous job like you. No razors. No armor. Just construction management. Contract was leased by a Silver. I was running one of the last Lovelock Engines on their north pole when an eruption from one of that moon's damn geysers caused an earthquake. Cracked the ice crust. Spilled the whole engine into the subterranean sea. Three thousand souls drowned.

"They fished me out of the sea and I spent the next months recovering in the arctic hospital. I was in the highColor wing. We had the good food. Better showers. Newer beds. But the lowColors had the window that looked at the northern lights. And she had the bed beside that window."

He looks up at Sevro. "She was the most beautiful woman I've ever met. And she was pretty to look at too. She lost a leg in the accident. And they weren't going to give her a new one. They could. It's simple bionics. Not cost-effective, said the Coppers. Shittiest Color ever made, I swear on—"

Sevro clears his throat. "We know."

Fitchner throws a piece of trash at Sevro and continues. "When I left, I took her with me. I'd saved up money enough to leave Triton. Couldn't live in the Core. Too expensive. So I chose Mars. We lived just outside New Thebes for a year. We wanted a child more than anything. But our DNA wasn't compatible. So we went to a Carver to see if we couldn't make some magic. We did. Cost me almost everything I owned, but nine months later, this little Goblin squirmed out."

Sevro waves from his perch as he examines the trash to see if it isn't edible.

"Two years later, the Board of Quality Control busted the Carver for some work he did on some Obsidian gladiator and he ratted us out, fastlike, for a reduced sentence. They came to our home when I was away with Sevro. Found my wife, took her in for questioning. Their doctors saw her fallopian tubes had been modified so that she would be compatible to sire a Gold child. Then they disposed of her. Says so right in the records: 'disposed.' Gassed her with achlys-9, put her in an oven, pumped her ash into the sea. They didn't even give her a name, just a number. Not because she was a thief or a murderer or had violated any man's or woman's rights, but because she was a Red who dared love a Gold. My selfish love killed her.

"It wasn't like your wife, Darrow. I didn't watch mine die. I didn't see Golds come into my world and ruin it. Instead I felt the coldness of the system swallow the only thing I lived for. A Copper pressing buttons, filling out a spreadsheet. A Brown twisting a knob to release gas. They killed my wife. But they won't ever think so. She's not a memory in their mind. She's a statistic. It's as if she never existed. Some ghost I loved but no one else ever saw. That's what Society does—spread the blame so there is no villain, so it's futile to even begin to find a villain, to find justice. It's just machinery. Processes. And it rumbles on, inexorable till a whole generation rises that will throw themselves on the gears."

"What was her name?"

"Her name? Why does it matter?" he asks warily.

"Because I want to remember her."

"Bryn," Sevro says from above. "My mother's name was Bryn. She was twenty-two when they killed her." Only a year older than I am now.

"Bryn," I repeat the word and see Fitchner rock slightly on his feet. A shortness of breath.

"So you're half Red," I say to Sevro.

Sevro nods. "Found out couple days ago. Weird as shit, righto?"

"Weird as shit. You'll make a good Ruster."

"I like to think I'm an endangered species."

Dancer rolls a match through his fingers. "We all are."

"You knew about Titus," I say to Fitchner.

"But Dancer didn't. Don't blame him for that. I thought you'd be brothers at the Institute. A natural affection for your own race. But he went dark, and there was no way to reel him in. I met with him—jammer, ghostCloak—like I met with you. But his mind broke under the strain. I didn't want to see you break."

"I did break." I look over at Sevro, Dancer. "I just had friends to piece me back together. Why didn't you tell Titus and me about each other?"

"Then his mistakes would have been yours and yours would have been his. In a storm, you don't tie two boats together. They'll drag each other down." He clears his throat.

"I always knew a Gold couldn't lead this rebellion. It has to be from the bottom up, boyo. Red is about family. More than any other Color, it is about love amid all the horror of our world. If Red rises, they have a chance to bind the worlds together. MidColors won't. Pinks, Browns, can't. Obsidians have failed before. And if they succeeded alone, they'd break the worlds instead of freeing them."

"So what's the plan?" I ask. "I squabbed up your position next to the Sovereign."

"You're hard to manipulate, Darrow, so I'll just cut to it. Augustus is going to adopt you. You're not surprised. . . ."

"It would make sense. He wants to tie my fate to his family. Probably make me marry Mustang. It'll fracture my alliance with the Jackal if I become an heir, though."

"Does the Jackal care about that?" Sevro asks. "Seems like he's abandoned hope of ever gaining approval. Bloody bastard's building his own empire."

"I'll have to see," I say.

Fitchner continues. "Dispose of the Jackal or make him part of the plan, it doesn't matter. Augustus will adopt you as his heir. And he will use you as a Praetor in his armada. And if you defeat the Sovereign, he won't settle for being King of Mars. He'll want to be Sovereign himself. Help him be. And a year into his reign, Sevro will kill him and pin it on a rival, maybe the Jackal. . . ."

My turn to rock on my feet.

"You want me to inherit the empire," I guess. "The entire Society."

I gawk at him. At Dancer. How can they look so serious?

"Yes," Fitchner says. "After he dies, all will look to the strongest. Be the strongest. Win the game of succession and you can be Sovereign just as you were Primus. Just as you are Praetor. It's all games. Except this time we're helping *you* cheat. We will feed you information, guard you against assassination attempts. With me on your side, you will have a spy network even the Jackal and Sovereign cannot rival. We will bribe who we need to bribe and kill who we need to kill."

I sit reflectively looking at my hands. "I thought the lies were nearly over. I want to declare what I am. I want to declare war."

"We can't yet. You know that."

I do, but I don't want to leave these people. "I won't be in the dark again. We will communicate. We will plan. No more gray areas. Do you understand? I can't be alone like before."

"Say yes, Fitchner," Sevro says. "Or I'm not going either."

"We'll communicate every day, if you need. I can't come with you. There's a ghost war being fought that I have to manage. But in my stead, I'll send some of my best agents. You'll have a cabal you can trust. Spies. Assassins. Courtesans. Hackers. All with perfect covers. All willing to die to break the chains. You are no longer alone."

Relief fills me. But there's something I know I can't do. "I have to go back."

"Yes. They'll be wondering where you are," Fitchner agrees.

"No." I say. "I have to go home."

"Home?" Dancer asks. "To Lykos?"

"Why?" Fitchner asks. "What's left for you there?"

"*My family.* It's been four years. I need to see them before this begins." I look each man in the eyes, each so scarred and so wounded in his own way. "You have to understand that. Things are about to break apart in ways we can't predict. We pretend we know what we're doing, pushing these Golds to war. Planning our own. Like we can control it, but we can't. We're just mortals opening Pandora's box. And before everything turns upside down, I need to remember what I'm fighting for. I need to know it's worth it."

"You want their blessing," Dancer says. "Her blessing." He knows my heart better than Fitchner. If I'm to let Augustus adopt me, then I must go home first.

"You can't tell them what you are. They won't understand." Fitchner steps forward, suddenly cautious of my temper. "You know that."

"How much easier would this have all been if you and I had conspired the whole way through?" I say. "Lies breed lies. We have to trust." I look at Sevro. "I'm taking her to Lykos."

"Her?" Dancer asks.

"Mustang," Sevro murmurs.

"No," Fitchner almost yells. "Absolutely not. No. It's not worth the risk. You're set up now. She's in love with you! Don't lose that leverage because of a guilty conscience."

"And what if I love her too?"

"Shit," Fitchner curses. "Shit. Shit. Shit. You're serious? I thought this was part of your gorydamn game. Shit. Boyo, you'll ruin everything. Gorydamn idiot. Shit."

"This *is* everything," I say. "She loves me. I won't use her anymore. I won't leverage her. If I can't trust her, Gold can't change, and Titus and Harmony were right. Hell, the Society is right. You and I know that it's not about our Color; it's about our hearts. Now let's put that to the test."

"And if you're wrong? If she rejects you for them?"

I don't have an answer.

Sevro hops down from his perch. "Then I put a bullet in her head."

47

||||||||||||||||||||||

FREE

The Pot is a piece of shit—a three-hundred-meter-deep nest of metal and concrete humid with the stink of swill and cleaning agent. Once it seemed to tower above Lykos's Common like some lofty castle. But as my ship descends, it's just a dull metal blister in the southern Martian taiga, far removed from the grand cities where men marshal for the great effort against Octavia au Lune.

The Grays inside aren't fit to get paid doing anything but intimidate Reds. To think I once considered the Grays like Ugly Dan crack troops. Sad to see how weak and petty the demons of my youth really were. As though I come from some hollow fantasy past.

They did not know my ship was coming. They don't know why I'm here, nor must I tell them. They just scatter like horseflies as I stalk down my ship's ramp onto the engine-blackened landing pad, Obsidian bodyguards flowing out before me. Ragnar towering behind as I stalk through the metal-grated halls. Any of these Grays will know how to get where I need to go, but I am looking for a familiar face.

"Dan," I ask one of the Brown janitors. "Where is he?"

I burst into one of their common rooms, where a dozen Grays play cards and smoke cigars. A woman notices me, turning her attention from an HC where several talking heads—a Silver, a Violet, and two Greens—debate the political ramifications of Mars's conquest over a montage of my exploits. Her cigar falls out of her mouth. The man sitting at her side slaps the cigar as it falls on his pant leg and catches the fabric.

"Carly, you dumb meat sheath." He flings himself back from the table. "*Goddamn*. The hell is your . . ."

Ugly Dan swivels to see me for the first time in four years. I can feel the hairs on his skin rise as the spring of discipline hidden in his slothful body snaps to attention. There's no recognition in his eyes, no fear, just obedience.

This gives me no catharsis. Dan should have an impudent sneer on his lips, a nasty hyena cast to his aspect. But he's doesn't. He's tame. Obedient. Face pocked from childhood acne. The greasy hair Loran and I teased him for behind his back, now gone. A crater of baldness has replaced it, fringed with shoots of withered gray. He's as scary as a wet dog. This is the man I let kill Eo.

How could I not have stopped him? Was I ever so weak?

"The bubbleGarden," I say to Dan, voice filling the metal common room. "Take me there."

I've already turned on a heel. Ragnar pats his thigh. **"Come, dog."**

It's been four years since I last stood here. Stars twinkle in the gray above as night pulls on its hood. The garden is smaller than I remember. Less filled with color, with sounds. I suppose that's to be expected, being where I've been, seeing what I've seen. There's more trash. More signs of Grays using the place for screwing and drinking. I toe an empty beer can with my shoe. A candy bar wrapper marks the place where Eo and I last lay together.

I remember it a bed of soft grass. But there are weeds now. Maybe there were weeds then and I just didn't notice them. The flowers are wilted, paltry things. I touch one with my finger and feel a sadness pull at me as I peer up through the bubbleRoof to see stars shooting across the sky. I snort. Once they might have been stars. I thought them such when I was younger. But now I know they are the warships that prepare for an assault on Luna. I don't know what I expected. No magic remains here.

Should have left this place perfect in memory. I wonder if Eo is safer there, safe from my eyes. If I saw her now, if I came back, would I be so in love? Would she seem so perfect?

I walk through the garden. It really is barely larger than my suites on the *Pax*. I'm thicker than the trees I walk under. The grass balds near the base of them where the roots rear through the ground.

I find the place I came for. Haemanthus flowers live atop Eo's grave. Dozens. It would seem a miracle if I did not remember the flower bud I set in the grave with her. She's not there any longer. I know that. The Grays would have dug her up and strung her from the Common to rot after they hanged me.

There's a dark irony I'm only just realizing. I came here to ask for her blessing but she's not here. She's fled this cage for the Vale.

So I sit cross-legged, waiting for the sun to set, where once I waited for it to rise. When it does, the day's waning light fills the bubbleGarden with a bloody hue. And then the sun surrenders to the horizon and night draws its star-pierced shroud over Mars.

I laugh at myself.

Ragnar slips from his place at the door.

"I'm fine," I say without turning to him. "She'd laugh at me for coming here."

"Laughter is a gift."

"Sometimes."

I stand and dust my pants, giving the place one last look.

The garden isn't as perfect as it was in memory. And neither was she. She was impatient. She could be spiteful for small reasons. But she was a girl. Not even seventeen. And she gave the most she could, did the best she could with what she had. That's why I will always love her, and it is why I know whether or not she would give her blessing for what I go to do. My heart can't stay here in this cage she herself has fled. It must move on.

48

||||||||||||||||||||||||

THE MAGISTRATE

MineMagistrate Timony au Podginus waits for me flanked with a coterie of Gray mine guards, now wearing their best and brightest uniforms. One carries a platter of cheese, dates, and Podginus's best, and perhaps only, caviar. Ugly Dan is gone.

"Lord Andromedus, is it not?" Podginus croons with that supercilious inflection uppity Coppers favor. He is fatter. His hair thinner. And he sweats like a pig in heat as he fans open his heavily ringed fingers to favor me with a queer bow popular in the HC political dramas. "I was examining the ore compression facilities"—probably a whorehouse in nearby Yorkton, at the edge of the taiga—"when news of your visit came to me. I hurried back as best I could, but still I beg your forgiveness. I wonder, though, may I be so bold as to ask the purpose of your visit?" So he can sell the information to men like Pliny. Coppers rarely mean all that they say. "An inspection is not due for—"

"In polite society, it is considered rude not to introduce yourself, Copper." I talk like a Peerless, not the Pixies he so eagerly emulates.

"My apologies!" he stammers in alarm, sweeping into a bow so deep I fear he might touch his nose to the floor were it not for the cushion of his substantial gut. "I am MineMagistrate Timony au Podginus, your humble servant. And may I say, if it is not too bold"— he's still bowing—"your aspect is grander than I had indeed expected! Not to say that I did not expect you to be broad and tall—the Arch-Governor has only the best of the best in his employ, naturally—but the HC does you the barest justice."

"You may stop bowing."

He straightens self-consciously and peers behind me into the garden, fiendishly seeking the reason someone like me came unannounced to his mine.

"As I know you've no doubt heard from others, the MineMagistrates were overjoyed to hear the planet had been liberated from Bellona control. War, those men may know, but mining? Pfah, amateurs."

"They don't know war either, apparently."

Swallowing, he glances again to my razor and then to the garden.

"A beautiful space, is it not?" he asks. "It reminds me of my time on the Pyrrus River. The tulip blossoms there—oh, the color! Nothing like it, as I'm sure you know. And the trees, aren't they so very like the birches that stretch along the steppes of the Olympus Mons? I stayed there at the Château le Breu." He makes a strange expansive motion with his hands. "I know, I know, but sometimes one must treat oneself. In fact it is where I discovered the most unique sottocenere cheese." He smiles proudly. "They call me Marco Polo, my friends, because I relish travel. It's the culture I seek. Refined company, as you could no doubt guess, is the damnedest thing to find around here. . . ."

I don't know how long he would continue trying to impress me if I didn't look at his men's best uniforms, then at his best rings, and frown.

"Is something the matter?" he asks.

"You're right," I say.

His beady eyes scurry back and forth between his best Grays, searching for signs of the inequity I noticed. It disgusts me how desperate he is to please me. This man stole from my family. He had me whipped. Watched Eo be killed. Hanged my father. He's not wicked. He's just pathetic in his greed.

"I am right about what?" he asks, blinking at me.

"That it is impossible to find refined company in places like this."
My eyes fall so heavily on him I fear he might burst out crying. Seeing
him, seeing Dan, does nothing but fill me with a distant strangeness.
I wanted them to be terrible, hideous monsters. But they aren't. They
are petty men who ruin lives and don't even notice. How many others
are there like them?

In a panic, Podginus waves to the cheese plate.

"Sottocenere, my liege. It's an Italian import with notes of licorice,
winks of nutmeg, a dash of coriander, a sprinkling of cloves, and a
playful but mysterious bit of cinnamon and fennel coated onto the
rind. I'm sure you'll find it to your—"

"I did not come here for cheese."

"No. No. Of course not." He looks around nervously. "If I may beg
to ask, what did you come here for, my liege?"

I begin walking. Podginus hurries to keep up. "Ragnar." I nod to
the titan, who pulls a small datapad from his pocket. Took Pebble less
than an hour to teach him to use it.

**"Your output of helium-3 has decreased by fourteen percent over
the last quarter. Your projections show an expected shortfall of
13,500 kilos for the current fiscal quarter. Praetor Andromedus wishes
you to explain."**

Podginus doesn't know what to do. He looks back and forth between me, the Obsidian, and the datapad. He stammers a response.
"I—I—we have had issues with the populace. Grafitti, illegal pam-
phlets." He addresses me. "You know we were the nucleus of the
Persephone movement. . . ." Ragnar taps him heavily on the shoulder.

"Praetor Andromedus is busy."

"I—I—" Podginus wheels about, in a nightmare he doesn't understand and cannot escape. "I forgot what I was—"

"You were making excuses."

"Making excuses. *Making excuses?* How dare you!" He squares his
shoulders. "There's a current of rebellion running through Mars. Not
a mine has been untouched by dissent. My mine is hardly the exception. There have been killings. Sabotage. And not just from the Sons
of Ares. From the miners themselves!"

Podginus turns to me again, desperately sensing his demise is fast coming, feet struggling to keep up with our long strides.

"My liege, I've gone above and beyond in following the proper method of quelling dissent as laid out in section three, subsection A of the Department of Energy's *Guide to Mine Management*. I have docked their rations, cracked down on enforcement of legal violations, and discredited leading thought-makers by luring them into liaisons of homosexuality. I have even introduced the recommended scenarios from *On Defusing Rebellion*. Over the past six years I've introduced Plague and Cure, Rebellion and Suppression, Natural Disaster, Pitviper Migration, and even considered the Extraplanetary Government Upheaval package!" Panting, he waves imploringly for me to stop. "No man would have done better than I."

"Your position is not in jeopardy," I say.

He shudders with relief. Suddenly his head snaps back. "You wouldn't . . ." He leans forward. "You're considering Quarantine! Aren't you?"

"Why shouldn't I quarantine this mine?" I continue on down the corridor till we reach the landing pad where my ship waits. There, I stop. "As you said, its populace has failed to respond favorably to strategies endorsed by the Department of Energy and the Board of Quality Control. Why not pump the air full of achlys-9 gas and replace the unruly Reds with clans from compliant mines nearer the equator?"

"No!" He actually grabs me. Ragnar doesn't even bother threatening the fat man.

"Choose your words carefully," I say.

"My liege, don't do it." Tears sparkle in his greedy, panicked eyes. "My mine's profits may have decreased, but it is still viable, still functional. A model of how to weather a storm."

"You are its savior," I say, mocking him.

"The Reds here are good miners. The best in all the world. That is why they're wild. But they've calmed now. I've increased their rations of alcohol and increased pheromone circulation in the air units. They're breeding like rabbits. I've also had my Gamma plants tamper with their machinery and maps. They think the mines are drying up. They'll walk on pins and needles, fearing they won't make quota. Then we'll fix the machines, and they'll be filled with fresh purpose. I can even tell them the terraforming is complete and migration will begin in ten years, and that Earth has begun sending immigrants. There are still so many options before we must accede to Quarantine."

I watch the man as he sputters to an end, slumping down, lifeless as a wet shirt on a hanger. Is this all for his own vanity or does he really care for Reds? This was a test to see. Now I can't tell. He might actually care in some strange way. Another monster from my past made human by Society's lash.

"Your mine is safe, for now. Maintain your workforce. Increase rations, beginning tonight. I want happy workers and flush coffers. In my ship you will find provisions. Food and libations. Throw the Reds a feast."

"My liege . . . a feast? Why?"

"Because I said so."

I sit alone in the viewing room, watching the celebration unfold through the glass beneath my feet. Thousands of Reds drink and eat as the young dance around the gallows to "The Ballad of Old Man Hickory." The tables are filled with foods these Reds have never tasted, drinks they've never downed. And though they laugh, though they dance, I cannot find any joy myself. They live in horror, but it's one they know. It's one they can find refuge from. Will there be any refuge left when the Sons of Ares reveal the great lie? It will shatter their way of life. They will be lost in the greatness of the worlds. And they'll be polluted by them. Like I am.

I recognize nearly all of them. Boys I played with, now grown. Girls I once kissed, now with children. Nieces. Nephews. Even my brother, Kieran. I wipe the tears from my eyes, lest someone see.

A boy sweeps a girl into a dance after kissing her cheek. I'll never be like that boy again. My innocence is lost. And Reds will never accept me as one of their own, no matter what future I bring them. I'm not a conquering hero. I'm a necessary evil. I have no place here, but I cannot leave. There are things that must be said. Secrets that must be revealed.

"Still trying to create a cult?" she asks from the door. I turn to see Mustang leaning against the metal frame, hair in a ponytail, high-collared Politico uniform open informally at the neck.

"I suppose I should commission statues next, yes?" I ask.

"Ragnar is scaring the backcountry Grays."

"Good."

"You're so mean to Grays," she laughs. "Something you don't like about them?" She runs a hand through my hair as she comes to sit on the arm of my chair.

"They're too obedient."

"Ah, so that's why you like me." She digs her fingernails lightly into my scalp, teasing. "Statues are a bad idea. Too easy to deface. Vandals could give you a mustache or breasts at their leisure. Risky proposition, breasts."

"Could be worse."

"Well, there's nothing worse than a mustache. Daxo is trying to grow one. I think it's meant to be ironic? I'm not sure." Mustang laughs lightly as she settles in on the metal chair next to me. "His sisters will sort that out."

She looks around at the mine and the Can. "Place is disgusting. I wrote a piece of legislation that the Reformers plan to put through after all this. It'll gut the Department of Energy, restructure the Board of Quality Control"—she looks around the Pot—"change the way this meat shop is run. You see the supply stores in this place? Food enough for seven years, yet they keep maxing out their requisition orders. I took a look at their files. The MineMagistrate's skimming off the top. Likely reselling the supplies on the black market. Lying Copper thought we wouldn't notice. Probably because some Gold or Silver told him they'd grease the right palms to make sure no one ever quibbled. All while he has a malnourished population. Corruption everywhere."

She wrinkles her nose and flicks a piece of flaking paint from her chair.

"Why are we here?" she asks. "Did something happen with my brother?"

"This is the mine where the girl sang the Forbidden Song," I say after a moment. Her eyes open wider as she scans the crowd beneath.

"These poor people."

She watches me, waiting expectantly for what I have to say. But there are no words left. Only something to show. I take her hand and stand. "Come with me."

49

||||||||||||||||||||||||

WHY WE SING

I've never felt fear like this.

Lykos is dark at night. Lights all turned down so the Reds don't go mad from eternal day. Somewhere, the nightshifts weave silks, mine soil. But here in this wide tunnel, there is no motion, no sound except the murmur of HCs showing old terraforming holos and the hum of distant machines. It is cool here, yet I sweat.

Mustang is silent beside me. She has not spoken since we descended in our gravBoots to the Common's floor, ghostCloaks making us nearly invisible to the lingering drunks slumped over tables and sleeping soundly on the gallows steps. I hear the tension in her silence and wonder what she thinks.

My heart runs wild in my chest, so loud Mustang has to hear it as we enter Lambda Township, where I grew from boy to man. The place is smaller. The ceiling lower. Rope bridges and pulley systems like children's toys. The HC that once glowed with Octavia au Lune's face is an ancient relic, pixels missing. Mustang peers around, cloak deactivated. Her eyes dance from bridge to bridge to home like she's seeing something wonderful. It didn't occur to me a Gold would ever find interest in a simple place like this.

I climb the stone steps to the bridge that leads to my old home just like I did as a boy. Only, my limbs are too large now. I forgot I had gravBoots. Mustang doesn't use hers either. She follows behind and dusts off her hands as she makes the landing where the thin metal door to my old family home has been cut into the wall.

"Darrow," she says so quietly, "how do you know where you're going?"

My hands tremble.

"You told me to let you in." I look down at her.

"I did, but . . ."

"How far do you want to go?"

I know she feels what's coming. I wonder how long she's felt it. The strangeness of me. The odd mannerisms. The distant soul.

She looks at her hands, stained red from the dust of the stone stairs. "All the way."

I hand her a holoCube. "If you mean that, press play, and come in when you've finished watching. If you leave, I understand."

"Darrow . . ."

I kiss her one last time, hard. She clutches at my hair, sensing that when we part, something will be different. I find myself pulling back. My hand cups her jaw. Her eyes, closed, begin to flutter open as I step away and turn to the door.

I push it open.

I have to duck to enter. The home is cramped. Quiet. The first floor is the same as I remember. The small metal table has not changed. Nor have the plastic chairs, the small sink, the drying clay dishes, or Mother's prized teakettle that heats on the stove. A new rug covers the floor. It's the work of a novice. Different boots sit where Father used to place his at the base of the stairs, where I used to set mine. Wait. Those are mine. But tattered and worn more than they'd been in my day. Were my feet really so small?

Silence guards the house. All sleep except her.

The teakettle hisses as the water reaches a boil. Soon it begins its breathy murmur. Feet scrape over the stone stairs. I almost run out of the room. But terror roots me to the spot as she comes closer. Closer till she's in the room with me, pausing at that last stair, foot suspended, forgotten. Her eyes find mine. They never leave. Never look at the rest of my Golden form. I panic as she says nothing. A breath. Three. Ten. She doesn't know me. I'm a killer in her house. I shouldn't have come here. She doesn't recognize me. I'm a lost Gold poking his head in out of curiosity. I can leave. Run away now. My mother never has to know what her son has become.

Then she finishes her step and comes toward me. Gliding. It's been four years. She looks twenty older. Lips thin, skin loose and webbed with lines, hair worked through with sooty gray, hands tough as oak and gnarled as ginger roots. When her right hand reaches for my face, I have to kneel. Her eyes still have not left mine. Now they let out tears. The teakettle screams on the stove. She brings her other hand to my face, but it is unable to open and touch like the other. It remains twisted and clenched, like my heart.

"It's you," she says softly, as though I will disappear like a night vision if she says the word too loudly. "It's you." Her voice is different, slurred.

"You know me?" I manage desperately.

"How could I not?" Her smile is twisted, left eyelid sluggish. Life has been less kind to her than to me. She's had a stroke. It breaks me to see her body fail her. To know I wasn't here for her. To know her heart was broken. "I would know you . . . anywhere." She kisses my forehead. "My boy. You're my Darrow."

The tears leave warm paths down my cheeks. I let them linger.

"Mother."

Still on my knees, I throw my arms around her and let the silent tears come. We say nothing for the longest time. Her scent is of grease, rust, and the musty tang of haemanthus. Her lips kiss my hair as they used to. Her hands scratch my back as though she remembers it just as broad as it is now, just as strong.

"I have to take the kettle off," she says. "Before someone wakes and sees you like . . ."

"Of course."

"You have to let go of me."

"Sorry." I do, laughing at myself.

"How . . . ?" she asks me, standing there looking at the Sigils on my hands, shaking her head. "How could this be? You . . . your accent. Everything."

"I was carved. Uncle Narol saved me. I can explain."

She shakes her head, trembling so slightly she must think I can't see it. The kettle shrieks louder. "Take a seat." She turns her back to me and takes the kettle off the stove. She sets out another mug. One from the high shelf. I remember it was my father's. Dust covers the molded clay. She pauses, saying nothing as she cradles it close, slipping into a moment not meant for me, where she remembers those mornings when they would ready for the day together. With a long breath, she drops the loose-leaf tea into the pot and pours hot water after. "Would you like anything else? We have those biscuits you liked."

"No, thank you."

"And I took my portion from the feast tonight. It's delicate Gold food. Did you do that?"

"I'm not a Gold."

"There are beans too. Fresh from Leora's garden. You remember her?"

I spare a look at my datapad. Mustang is gone, heading back to the ship after she watched the holoCube. I feared this. I read a message from Sevro. *"Stop her?"* he asks. Two choices. Let Sevro and Ragnar catch her, and contain her till I can speak with her. Or trust her to make her own decisions. But if I trust her, she could leave, tell her father what I am, and it could all end. Yet she may just need time. I've given her so much to digest. If Ragnar and Sevro capture her prematurely, it may set her against me. Or they may act on their own and kill her.

Cursing silently, I type a quick reply.

"I remember everyone," I say to my mother, looking back up. "I'm still me."

She pauses at that, still facing the stove. When she turns, a lopsided smile crosses her stroke-ravaged face. Her hand fumbles one of the mugs, but swiftly she recovers.

"Got something against the chairs?" she asks sharply, noticing I saw the clumsiness of her hand.

"Other way around, I'm afraid . . ." I hold up the chair. It's better suited for a Gold child than a Peerless Scarred who stands just over seven feet and weighs as much as any three Reds put together. She chuckles that dark chuckle of hers, the one that, as a child, always made me think she'd done something particularly sinister. Gracefully, she folds her legs and sits on the ground. I follow, feeling gangly and clumsy here. She sets the steaming cups between us.

"You don't seem terribly surprised to see me," I say.

"You talk funny now." She pauses so long I wonder if she'll continue. "Narol told me you were alive. Failed to say you'd gone and dipped yourself Gold, though." She sips her tea. "I bet you've got questions."

I laugh. "I thought you'd have more."

"I would. But I know my son." She eyes my Sigils. "I'm more patient. Go on now."

"Narol . . . is he . . . ?"

"Dead? Aye. He's dead."

The breath goes out of me.

"How long?"

"Two years ago." She chuckles. "Fell down a mineshaft with Loran. Never found the bodies."

"Why the hell are you laughing?"

"Your father's brother was always the black sheep of the bunch." She sips her tea. It's still too hot for me. "Suppose it makes sense he'd be as hard to kill as a cockroach. So I'll believe he's dead when I see him in the Vale. Shifty bugger." She speaks slowly, like most Reds. The lisp from the stroke is faint, but always there. "I think he left this place and took Loran with him." The way she says it makes me know she understands there's more beyond the mines. Perhaps she doesn't know the whole truth, but she knows a part. Maybe my uncle and cousin aren't dead. Maybe they left to be with the Sons.

"What of Kieran? Leanna? Dio?"

"Your sister is remarried. Lives with her husband in Gamma Township in the house of his family."

"*Gamma?*" I sneer. "You let her—" I stop as soon as I see the fresh twist in my mother's mouth. I might wear the trappings of a Gold, but I better shut the hell up about her daughter.

"She's got two girls that look more like you than her or any Gamma I've ever seen. And Kieran's well." She smiles to herself. "You'd be right proud of him. Not the sniveling child you might remember squabbling up his chores and talking in his sleep. Man of the house. HeadTalk for the crew after Narol slipped down. Kora, his wife, died in childbirth, though. He took another a few months back."

My poor brother.

"And what of Dio? Eo's parents?"

"Her father is dead. Killed himself not long after you tried the same."

My head sags. "So many deaths."

She touches my knee. "It's the way of it."

"Doesn't make it right."

"It was a hard time after you and Eo left us. But Dio's well. Fact, she's upstairs."

"Upstairs? What do you . . . Did she marry Kieran?"

"Aye. And she's pregnant. I'm hoping for a girl, but with my luck it'll be a boy who wants to dodge pitvipers and steam burns his whole life. If he's got the choice, that is."

"What do you mean?"

"Things are tough. Changed. Mine isn't giving the way it ought. Some of the men are whispering this corner of the world is all used up. And it makes them start fearing—what happens to the miners when there's nothing left to mine? They're hoping the terraforming will catch on before we run through our helium deposits."

"Nothing will happen to you. I promise I will protect this mine. No matter what."

"How?"

"I just will."

"My turn." She eyes me over her tea. "Where you been, child?"

"I . . . I don't even know where to start."

"With Eo's death, I think."

I flinch. My mother was always blunt. Made Kieran cry his way through his childhood. But that bluntness makes calluses out of blisters. So I owe her a reply in kind. I tell her everything, starting with the moments after Eo's death and ending with the promise I made to the ArchGovernor.

Our tea is long gone when I finish.

"That's quite a tale," she says.

"Tale? It's the truth."

"They won't believe you, the rest of them."

"You do, though?"

"I'm your mother." She takes my hand and runs her crooked fingers over the Sigils that run from the back of my hands up my forearms, smirking when she reaches the metal wings embedded on the outside of my forearms. "I never liked Eo," she says quietly.

I twist my head up to look at her.

"Not for you. She could be manipulative. She kept some things from you. . . ."

"I know about the child," I say. "I know what she told Dio on the scaffold."

Mother scoots closer to me, her hands grasping mine and bringing my knuckles to her lips. She never gave much comfort. She's awkward at it now. But I don't mind. Father loved her for the same reason I do. Everything she does, she means. There's no falseness to her. No deception. So when she tells me she loves me, I know she means it with every part of her.

"Eo was not a cruel girl, you know that," she says, pushing back so she can look into my eyes. "She loved you with everything she had. And I loved her for it. But I always feared she'd make you fight her battles. And I always feared how much she loved to fight."

That's not quite the Eo I remember. But I don't find fault with my mother's words. I can't. All eyes see their own way.

"But in the end, Mother, Eo was right about this. About Gold."

"I'm your mother. I don't care about what's right. I care about you, child."

"Someone has to fix all this," I say. "Someone has to break the chains."

"And that someone is you?"

Why is she doubting me? "Yes. It is. I'm not being foolish. I can lead us out of here. Out of slavery."

"To where? To the surface?" She speaks of it familiarly, as if she's known the truth of Mars for years, not minutes. Perhaps she has. "Where we will do what? All we know is the mines. All we know is how to dig, how to harvest silk. If what you say is true and there are hundreds of millions of Reds on Mars, how will there be enough homes for us up there? How will there be enough work? Most won't leave the mines, even if they know. You'll see. They'll just stay miners. And their children will be miners. And their children's children, except the nobility will be lost. Do you think about these things?"

"Of course I do."

"And do you have an answer?"

"No."

"Men." She rubs her right temple. "Your father was one to jump without looking." Her expression tells me what she thinks of that. "Helldivers all think they provide for the clans. No. The women do." She gestures around. "Everything you see, made by a woman. But you know how to shape the world, don't you? Know how it should be."

"No. I don't," I say. "I'm not the one with the answers." Mustang is. Eo was. Mother is. "No one man or woman has all the answers. A thousand, a million bright minds will be needed to answer what you've asked me. That's the point of this. What I can do, what I am *good* at is tearing down the men and women who would keep those minds shackled. That's why I'm here. It's why I exist."

"You've changed," she says.

"I know." I pick dust from the floor and rub it between my palms. The dust looks strange on these hands. "Do you think . . . Is it possible to love two people?"

Before she can answer, feet pad down the stairs.

My mother turns to look.

"*Grandma?*" a small voice says sleepily. "*Grandma, Dunlow isn't in bed.*"

A small child stands on the stairs, nightshirt scraping the floor. One of Kieran's. She's three, maybe four. Born just after I left. Her face is heart-shaped. Red hair thick and rusty as my wife's. Mother looks back to me, worried how she will explain my presence. But I activated my ghostCloak as soon as I heard the noise.

"Oh, he probably snuck out to cause trouble," my mother says.

I squeeze her hand before sliding back from the room toward the door. My time here is at an end, yet I linger. The little girl gingerly steps down the stairs, one foot after another, rubbing sleep from her eyes.

"Who were you talking to?"

"I was praying, child."

"Praying for what?"

"For the soul of a man who loves you very much." Mother touches her nose with a finger.

"Papa?"

"No. Your uncle."

"Uncle Darrow? But he's dead."

Mother picks the girl up in her arms. "The dead can always hear us, my love. Why else do you think we sing? We want them to know that even though they are gone, we can still find joy." Cradling my niece, she turns to look at me as she takes the first step up the stairs. "That's all they'd want for us."

50

|||||||||||||||||||||||

THE DEEP

Mustang is gone. I'd hoped she would come in. But I suspect that was too much to ask. Of course it was. Idiot. I remember thinking this would humanize me in her eyes. Thought meeting my mother would make her weep and realize we're all the same.

The guilt falls fast on me. I handed Mustang the holo of my carving, expecting . . . expecting what? For her to come inside? For her, the daughter of the ArchGovernor of Mars, to sit on my floor with my mother and me? I'm a coward for coming here. I'm a coward for letting the holo speak for me. I didn't want to watch her process learning who I really am. I didn't want to see the betrayal in her eyes. Four years of deception. Four years of lying to the girl who has never been able to trust anyone. Four years and I tell the truth when I'm not even in the bloodydamn room. I'm a coward.

She's gone.

I check my datapad. The radiation tracker Sevro insisted on sticking her with before she came to see me in the Pot's observation room says she is three hundred kilometers away and moving fast. Sevro's ship pursues, awaiting my orders.

Ragnar and Sevro both hail me. I don't answer their calls. They'll want me to give the order to shoot her down. I won't. I can't. Neither understands.

Without Mustang, what is the point to all this?

I wander from the township, down and down into the old mine, trying to forget the present by finding the past. There, I stand alone listening to the call of the deepmines. Wind wails its way through the earth, mournful in its song. My eyes are closed to the black, heels planted in the loose soil, head looking down the maw of darkness that stretches deep into the bowels of my world. This is how we tested our bravery as youths. Standing, waiting, in the deep hollows our ancestors dug in the times before.

I turn my left arm to see the inside of the forearm where the data-pad rests. Hesitating, I hail Mustang's.

It chimes directly behind me.

I freeze. Then a scorcher battery pack whines as it activates, and warm yellow light blossoms behind me, illuminating a swath of the huge tunnel.

"Hands where I can see them." Her voice is so cold I hardly recognize it till it echoes back to me from the tunnel walls. Slowly, I raise my hands. "Turn."

I turn.

Her eyes glow against the lamplight like an owl's. She's ten meters away, higher than I, feet planted on the sloping, loose soil. In one hand, she holds a light. In the other, a scorcher. One that's pointed at my head, finger against the trigger. Her knuckles are all white. Her face is an impassive mask, and behind it, two eyes filled with fathomless sadness.

Sevro was right.

"She'll shoot you in the head, you bloodydamn fool," Sevro sneered at me in the shuttle. Sometimes I think he joined my little crusade so he could have an excuse to curse like a Red. Ragnar stayed silent when I told them my plan.

"Then why'd you back me up with your father?" I asked him.

"Because that's what we do."

"She has to make her own choice."

"And she'll choose you over her race?"

"You did."

"Oh, come off it. I'm not a bloody queen of the Golds, am I?" He held his hand high. "She's been up here her whole life. Air is nice and sweet." He lowered his hand. "I've been kickin' shit since I was born tiny and buttfaced to my lard of a father. Your girl—there isn't a chip on her shoulder. She may spout pretties when the world isn't hard. But when facing the masses who would steal her palace, trample her gardens . . . it'll be a different girl you see then."

"You're a Red," she says now to me.

"I thought you left."

"The tracker left." She flexes her jaw. "Sevro was sneaky. Didn't even notice him doing it. But you. You'd never tell me something like . . . *this* without an insurance policy. I ditched the clothes in the shuttle."

"Why did you come back?"

"No. *No.*" She cuts the air with a gesture. "You answer *my* questions now, Darrow. Is that even your name?"

"My mother named me after her father."

"And you're a Red."

"I was born in the house you stood outside. It was sixteen years before I saw I sky. So yes. I'm a Red."

"I see." She hesitates. "And my father killed your wife."

"Yes. He ordered Eo's death."

"When you sang the song to me in the cave . . . all this was going through your mind? This place, the carving, the plan, was all inside you, all in your memory. This whole other world. This whole other . . . *person.*" She shakes her head, not wanting me to answer that. "Then what happened? *Eo's* husband was hanged. *You* were hanged. How did you escape?"

"Do you know why they hanged me?"

She waits for me to explain.

"When a Red is hanged for crimes of treason, the body may not be buried. It is to decay and rot in front of all as a reminder of what comes of dissent." I jab a thumb at my chest. "I buried my wife, so they hanged me too. Only, my uncle fed me haemanthus oil. It slows the heart to make you appear dead. He cut me down after. Gave me to the Sons."

"And they"—She holds up the holoCube, her face pale in its glow— "did *this* to you."

"I was paler than a Blue. A head shorter than Sevro. Weaker than a Gray. Knew less of the world than a Pink learning arts in the Garden. So they took what was best in me, in my people, and melded it to what was best in yours."

"But . . . it's impossible. The Board of Quality Control has tests," she says, breaking her cool line of inquiry. "Lie detectors, DNA analysis, background checks." She laughs in realization. "*That's* why you came from the Family Andromedus—born to Gold parents who fled debt to try to strike it rich asteroid mining."

"Their ship was lost as they returned after their mines had been bought by Quicksilver."

"So Sons of Ares destroyed their ship, altered the records, and purchased the mines so they could write your story."

"Perhaps." I hadn't put much thought to how Dancer did it. "My friends are resourceful."

"How did you even survive the carving?" she mutters. "It's against physiology. What the Carver did to you . . . *no one* could survive that. The Sigils are connected to the central nervous system. And the implant in your frontal lobe can't be removed without rendering you catatonic."

"My Carver was a unique talent. He managed to find a way to remove two implants, though another Carver did the second."

"Two. There's two of you. *Sevro?*" she guesses. "Is that why you've always been so close?"

"No. It was Titus."

"Titus? The butcher? You were in league with him?"

"Never. I didn't know who he was until after I defeated you. Ares thought we would work together. . . ."

"But Titus was a monster."

"The Golds made him that way."

"And that excuses what he did?"

"Don't act like you know what he went through," I snap.

"I know, Darrow. I don't avert my eyes. I know the policies. I know the conditions your people suffer, but that doesn't excuse the murders, the rapes, the torture he committed."

"It's what we suffer every day. Titus did what he did out of hate. Out of a misguided hope of revenge. In another life, I could have been him."

Mustang searches my eyes. "And why weren't you in this life?"

"My wife." I look up at her. "And you."

"Don't say that." Voice thick with regret. She takes a step back, shaking her head. "You don't have the right to say that."

"Why not? You always wondered what ran beneath the surface of me. Know the deep current."

"Darrow . . ."

"Titus had pain. But that's all he had. I had something more. Eo's dream of a world where our children could be free. But I would have lost it if I never met you." I take a step forward. "You kept me from becoming a monster. Can't you see?" I gesture, trying to encompass my desperation. "I was surrounded by the people who had enslaved mine for hundreds of years. I thought all Golds cruel, selfish murderers. I would have caved to revenge. But then you came . . . and you showed me there was kindness in them. Roque, Sevro, Quinn, Pax, and the Howlers proved it too."

"Proved what exactly?" she asks.

"That this isn't about my people against yours. You aren't Gold. We aren't Red. We're people, Mustang. Each of us can change. Each of us can be what we like. For hundreds of years they've tried to tell us otherwise. They've tried to break us. But they can't. You are that proof. You are not your father's daughter. I see the love in you. I see the joy, the kindness, the impatience, the flaws. They're in me. They were in my wife. They're in all of us because we are human. Your father would have us forget that. Society would have us live by its rules."

I take another step toward her.

"You told me I gave you hope that we could live for more after we won the Institute our way. Then you said I turned my back on that idea when I accepted your father's patronage and went to the Academy. But I never turned my back. Not for one moment." Another step.

"You'll destroy my family, Darrow."

"It is possible."

"They are my family!" she shouts, face collapsing into grief. "My father hanged your wife. He hanged her. How can you even look at me?" She shudders out a breath. "What do you want, Darrow? Tell me. Do you want me to help you kill them? Do you want me to help you destroy *my* people?"

"I don't want that."

"You don't know what you want."

"I don't want genocide."

"You do!" she says. "And why not? After what we've done to your people. After what my father did to *you*." She unbuttons another catch on her jacket as if it will help her breathe through this. The gun shakes in her hand. Finger tenses on the trigger. "How can I live with this? If I don't pull the trigger, millions will die."

"If you pull it, you accept that billions should live as slaves. Imagine all those unborn. If it is not me, someone else will rise. Ten years from now. Fifty. A thousand. We will break the chains, no matter the cost. You cannot stop us. We are the tide. All you can do is pray it is not someone like Titus who rises in my place."

She levels the scorcher at my right eyeball.

"**Pull the trigger, and you die.**" Ragnar speaks like the darkness itself.

"Ragnar, no!" I snap. I can't even see him in the shadows of the tunnel. "Stop! Do not hurt her." He must not have pursued the tracking signal as I told him to. How long has he listened?

"Stay back." Mustang shuffles sideways so her back is to the wall. "Does he know too? Do you know what he is, Ragnar?"

"**The Reaper trusts me.**"

Mustang tosses her light on the ground and pulls free her razor.

"He isn't here to kill you, Mustang."

"What else does a Stained do?"

I hold my hands up. "Ragnar isn't going to do anything. Are you, Ragnar?"

No answer. I swallow hard. Everything is unwinding. "Ragnar, listen to me. . . ."

"You must not die, Reaper. You are too important for the People. Lady Augustus, you have ten breaths left."

"Ragnar, please!" I beg. "Trust me. Please."

Nine.

"I trusted you at the river, my brother. You are not always right. That is the cost of mortality." The voice comes from above. Somewhere near the ceiling of the mine this time. He's not wrong. He put his trust in me during our siege of Agea, and I led them into a trap. Luck preserved me.

Laughing bitterly, Mustang coils her muscles to strike. "See, Darrow? You start this war, it'll be beasts like him who finish it and take their revenge."

Seven.

"This isn't about revenge!" I try to calm myself. "It's about justice. It's about love against an empire built on greed, on cruelty. Remember the Institute. We freed those we were meant to take as slaves. We put our trust in them. That is the lesson. *Trust.*"

Five.

"Darrow," she pleads. "How can you be so foolish?"

Her mind is made up.

Four.

"It never foolish to hope." I strip off my razor, my datapad, and toss them to the ground as I go to my knees. "But if you can't change, no one can. So shoot me dead and let the worlds be as they may."

Three.

"You think too much of me, Darrow."

"Two."

"Let's skip the foreplay, Ragnar." Mustang twirls her razor. Its horrible hum fills the tunnel. "Come at me, dog, and show Darrow what your *kind* lives for."

The silence stretches long.

"One," Mustang growls, stomping out her own lamp. No light, no color but darkness. The silence is deeper than the tunnel. It meanders through the heart of Mars, stretching forever, echoing to places only the lost have ever been.

Ragnar shatters it with his voice.

"I live for my sisters."

There is no scorcher flash. No scream of the razor. No movement. Just the echoing of the words down and down with the fragments of silence.

"I live for my brother."

A light blossoms from Ragnar. He steps forward like some wayward pilgrim, white light glowing along the knuckles of his armor. I see no weapons. Mustang tenses, confused.

"I am and always have been son to the people of the Valkyrie Spires. Born free to Alia Snowsparrow on the wild pole of Mars, north of the Dragon's Spine, south of the Fallen City."

He walks past Mustang, arms at his side.

"Forty-four scars have I earned for Gold since the slavers of the Weeping Sun came from the stars to take my family to the Chain Islands. Seven scars from others of my kind when they placed me in the nagoge, where I was trained."

He kneels at my side.

"One from my mother. Five from the talons of the monster who guards Witch Pass. Six from the woman who taught me to love. One from my first master. Fifteen from men and beasts I fought in an arena for the pleasure of the Ash Lord and his guests. Nine I earned for the Reaper."

The ground sighs under the weight of his knees.

"For Gold, I have buried three sisters. One brother. Two fathers." He pauses in sadness. **"But . . . for them I have never earned a scar."**

Through his armor's pale light, his black eyes burn like witchflames.

"Now, I live for more."

Ragnar closes his eyes, putting himself at the mercy of a Gold. Having faith like I have faith. Like Eo had faith in me. Like Sevro, and Dancer and all the rest.

My eyes meet Mustang's, perhaps for the last time, and I imagine I feel the same as did my ancestors, the first pioneers to Mars, as they looked back across the darkness to Earth. In her I had a home. I had love. And then I poisoned her to me. I know this was always destined to be our end. But still I hope like a desperate child.

"What do you live for?" I ask.

51

||||||||||||||||||||||||

GOLDEN SON

Today is my Triumph.

The day is crisp. Sky robin's-egg blue, stars peeking through the atmosphere. I stand dripping in gold, purple sash across my chest, head naked and waiting for the laurel wreath at the end of the procession. By the end of the day, I will be given a Triumph Mask created by Violets in honor of my victory.

My chariot rumbles under me. Wooden wheels pulled over pavement. Over rose petals. Over haemanthus blossoms. Over a hundred thousand flowers thrown from the open windows of the skyscrapers that stand sentinel to either side of the grand avenue. Hands flourish in the air. Arms reach out. Faces peer down, beaming smiles. So many Colors. They're on the street too, surrounding the parade route. Cheering for the things that went before me, the wonderful floats. The fire breathers. The dancers. The griffins and drakes and zebracores. The few remaining Bellona prisoners. The heads of Imperator Bellona and his brothers and sisters adorn pikes. For all Augustus's personal austerity, he knows the importance of grandeur. RipWings zip overhead. Storks buzz through the air.

But he knows the importance of brutality too. Flies buzz about the heads. And they nip at the four white horses that pull my chariot from the grand boulevard into the white-stoned Field of Mars that stretches before the Citadel's grounds.

I wave to the crowd, holding up my slingBlade. Mania grips them. Fathers hold up their children, pointing to me and telling them that they'll be able to tell their own children that they saw my Triumph in person. They throw fig leaves and cheer wildly, climbing the Field's martial statues and marble obelisks to see me better.

"You are but a mortal," Roque whispers in my ear, riding his horse alongside the chariot, as per tradition.

"And a whorefart," Sevro calls from the other side.

"Yes," Roque agrees solemnly. "That too."

I wish Mustang were here to ride with me. Her quiet strength would make all these eyes easier to bear, all these cheers more pleasant to stomach. Reds applaud in the crowd. They scream and cheer and laugh, perfect victims of the Society's entertainment divisions. They believe the lie of glorious war and glorious Golds. Millions will have relived the holo experience of my fall in the Iron Rain, at least until the EMP knocked my camera out. But Fitchner kept the footage of my slaying of Karnus.

The parade is a dream. A false thing conjured. I flow through it, knowing how little it means. My friends are behind me, at my side. All those I'd call lieutenants. They grin at me. They love me. And I lead them to a hopeful ruin. It all seemed worth it once. But after we take the war to Luna, what then? More lies. More deaths. More impossible schemes.

And what will Mustang do? She has not returned to Agea since she turned and walked away from me in the mines. Fitchner is beside himself with worry. She is an axe above my head. At any moment, she could sign my death. She might already have. Perhaps this is some grand ruse. Perhaps her father already knows.

The Jackal noted her absence from the Citadel when he came last night for the Triumph. I told him we had a fight about their father.

"Not surprising," he said with a sigh. "Just don't let the man come between you two as he came between her and me as children." He clapped my shoulder familiarly and poured us both enough drinks to give me the dull headache that now pulses behind my left eye. I swear to myself I'll never drink again.

Victra rides beside Roque and Lorn, languidly looking around, soaking in the sunshine and festivities. She's brought her mother into the Augustus fold, along with Antonia, who apparently aided in taking Thessalonica from Bellona hands. It's hard to keep track of what side they're on. But Victra, for her part, has been as loyal as anyone. She blows me a kiss.

The Howlers trot behind her, half their original number, though the Telemanuses have promised to bring them fresh recruits. Behind these lieutenants are the dozens of Praetors and Legates who led the army. And behind them walk thousands upon thousands of Grays, who, with embarrassing affection, sing ribald songs at my expense. Behind them come legions of Obsidians. It's a furiously grand affair, not only for me, but because it signifies the beginning of a new era—a Solar System led by Mars, not Luna.

Fitchner is not here. He should be. I look for him at the top of the colossal white stairs that lead to the Citadel grounds. The ArchGovernor and his entourage stand there with dozens of our allies, and a skeletal, bald White who holds my laurel crown.

Leaving my chariot behind, I ascend the stairs, flanked by my lieutenants. Silence claims the plaza. My purple cape catches in the wind behind me. The city smells of roses and horse manure. Augustus steps forward.

"An Iron Rain was called," he proclaims.

"And the call was answered," I reply, amplified words echoing like thunder over the city. A great roar rises from all who fell in the Rain. The White steps forward, face haggard from her many years of giving sentence to criminals. Milky eyes lost in past histories blink with gentle care.

"Son of Mars," her voice warbles dreamily. "Today you wear purple, as did the Etruscan kings of old. You join them in history. You join the men who broke the Empire of the Rising Sun. The women who dashed the Atlantic Alliance into the sea. You are a Conqueror. Accept this laurel as our proclamation of your glory."

She sets it upon my head. Sevro snorts beside me.

The White continues, winding flowery paths with her words, taking the better part of the afternoon, so that it is dusk when her words begin to run their course. I've come to understand why all this spectacle exists. Why all these speeches and monuments. Tradition is the crown of the tyrant. I eye all the Golds in their badges and Sigils and standards, all worn to legitimize corrupt reign, and to alienate the people. Make them feel they watch a species beyond their comprehension. The Jackal seems to read my thoughts, for he rolls his eyes at the farce. The closing words come soon after.

"*Per aspera . . .*" the White warbles, body shaking from effort. Augustus raises his hand and the crystal obelisk commissioned for the siege of Mars rises from its place on the Field via gravLifts in its base. Groaning into place, it floats there fifty meters above the ground, and will continue to float until another Triumph claims its place. Then it will join those others on the ground. Towering tombstones for the million fallen.

"*. . . ad astra!*" the crowd roars.

I remain on the steps as the festival swings into motion below on the Field of Mars. The Golds disperse onto Citadel grounds, heading for our private feast. Augustus watches from my side. Behind us, the bronze sun sets on his city, stretching our shadows over the lowColors below.

"Walk with me," he commands.

We walk, surrounded by bodyguards. Unease spreads through me as I see them cluster tight about us. He's spoken to his daughter. He knows. Of course he knows. I have my razor, no gravBoots. Just ceremonial armor. How many of the Obsidians could I kill before I'm overwhelmed? Not many.

Then I realize where he's taking me and I nearly laugh at myself for being foolish.

The throne room burns with sunlight. Ceiling all of glass, marble columns stretching a hundred meters high. The expanse buzzes with noise. IonSaws, hammers, and the delicate thrum of seven ionScalpels on a lump of onyx twice my height.

"Out," Augustus demands.

The Violets slide from their perches on the onyx and disperse with the Orange masons and Red laborers. Augustus's bodyguards leave us as well. Our boots click against the floor, lonely sounds for such a room.

So he's not going to kill me after all.

"They're making you a throne," I say, going to touch the onyx. I breathe out the tension. A lion's paw takes shape near the base of the throne. To the left, its tail curls around the other side.

"You have broken the law, Darrow," he says behind me. "You gave Obsidians razors. The weapon of our ancestors in the hands of the only Color to ever rise against us."

"Is that all?" I ask in relief. "I did what I needed to do."

"An Olympic Knight was killed by your bodyguard. This is public."

"If Ragnar didn't take the wall, we would have lost, and you, my liege, would be in chains, or executed. You'd know better than I. Ragnar had my warrant."

"My father taught me it is weak to ask others what they think of you," he says, clasping his hands behind his back. "But I must. Do you think I am a cold monster?"

I turn to examine him.

"Without a doubt."

"Honesty." He looks up at the ceiling. "You'd think it would echo differently than all the other horseshit. What I am, Darrow, is a necessity. I am the force that corrects those who err. Tell me, why do you give an Obsidian a razor? Why do you urge lowColors to rise up? Why do you let a Blue run your ship when she should merely take orders and fly it?"

"Because they can do things I cannot."

He nods as if I've proven his point.

"And that is why I exist. I know that Blues can command fleets. I know Obsidians can use technology, lead men. That the quickest Orange could, if given a proper chance, be a fine pilot. Reds could be soldiers, or musicians, or accountants. Some few—very few—Silvers could write novels, I wager. But I know what it would cost us. Order is paramount to our survival.

"Humanity came out of hell, Darrow. Gold did not rise out of chance. We rose out of necessity. Out of chaos, born from a species that devoured its planet instead of investing in the future. Pleasure over all, damn the consequences. The brightest minds enslaved to an economy that demanded toys instead of space exploration or technologies that could revolutionize our race. They created robots, neutering the work ethic of mankind, creating generations of entitled locusts. Countries hoarded their resources, suspicious of one another. There grew to be twenty different factions with nuclear weapons. Twenty—each ruled by greed or zealotry.

"So when we conquered mankind, it wasn't for greed. It wasn't for glory. It was to save our race. It was to still the chaos, to create order, to sharpen mankind to one purpose—ensuring our future. The Colors are the spine of that aim. Allow the hierarchies to shift and the order begins to crumble. Mankind will not aspire to be great. Men will aspire to be great."

"Golds aspire to be great, and we force the Colors to war," I say, taking a perch on the black lion's paw. Augustus has not moved from his place at the center of the floor.

"Yet there are men like me," he replies so sincerely I nearly believe him. "I do not truly fight because I want to be king or Emperor or whatever word you slap above my name in the history texts. The universe does not notice us, Darrow. There is no supreme being waiting to end existence when the last man breathes his final breath. Man will end. That is the fact accepted, but never discussed. And the universe will continue without care.

"I will not let that happen, because I believe in man. I would have us continue forever. I would shepherd us out of the Solar System into alien ones. Seek new life. We are barely in our infancy as a species. But I would make man the immutable fixture in the universe, not just some passing bacteria that flashes and fades with no one to remember. That is why I know there is a proper way to live. Why I believe your young ideas so dangerous."

His mind is vast. Worlds beyond my own. And perhaps for the first time, I really understand how this man can do what he does. There is no morality to him. No goodness. No evil intent when he killed Eo. He believes he is beyond morality. His aspirations are so grand that he has become inhuman in his desperate desire to preserve humanity.

How strange to look at the rigid, cold figure he casts and know all these wild dreams burn inside his head and heart.

"What about all you said? What about the things you've done?" I ask, thinking of his first wife, whose mouth he stuffed with grapes. "You take advice from creatures like Pliny. You bomb innocent civilians, who haven't broken any laws. You embrace a civil war . . . and you say you're trying to save humanity?"

"I do what I need to do to protect the greater good."

To defend himself. To benefit himself. "To protect mankind," I echo.

"Yes."

"Eighteen billion draw breath across this empire. How many would you kill to protect mankind? A billion? Ten?"

"The number doesn't change the necessity."

"Fifteen billion?" I ask. Red, Gold, every part of me is shocked.

"Someone must make these choices," he says. "The rest of our race grows sicker by the day. The Pixies chase pleasure instead of achievement, while the Peerless have grown so hungry for power that our Sovereign is a woman who cut off the head of her own father in order to take his throne. They must be ruled."

"By you."

"By us." His unblinking gaze does not waver. "By us," he repeats. "I treated you poorly, because I feared your brashness, your impudence. But I promised I would make amends, and so I will, because you have shown the capacity for growth, for learning. Become my heir. Not my Praetor. I have enough lords of war. What I need . . . what I *want* is a son."

"You have a son."

"I have a parasite that wants my power. That's all. He has no use for it. No plan once he gains it. He simply hungers as our Society has taught him to hunger." His face shows a flicker of intrigue. "Yet, remarkably, this was his idea. You have his blessing."

I don't doubt I have his blessing. Knowing my ally, I merely wonder what it's going to cost me. He's a businessman. He'll want return on his investment. Especially this investment. He should have told me.

"What about Virginia? You don't need your heir to be male."

"But I want it to be. And I want you for her. A husband fitting her mind."

"You're using me," I say suddenly, seeing through his scheme. "I tie her to you. Especially if we marry. We both know you don't want reform."

Even now Reformers from across the Society flock to Mars to rally behind the man who said he would give them the Senate when he defeats Lune and her allies.

"The Reformers are cancer," he says.

"But you're promising them that you will—"

"Promises were necessary to gain their support. When we have defeated Octavia, I will put the Reformers in prison, or execute them for treason."

"Mustang will never forgive you. She believes you're changing. Whatever conversation you had with her, whatever you promised her, you gave her hope in you."

Maybe she won't forgive either of us.

"You will make her understand once you're part of the family, Darrow. By then, I suspect you'll be married, and she won't abandon you even if she hates me. Our family will stay strong, as we must. But you must always be mine. Answering to me. Not my children."

He takes a step toward me.

"Octavia steers humanity to slow decline. The Reformers, like the Sons of Ares, would slam us into the ground at a thousand kilometers a second. We must protect our species. Help me."

He is a noble man doing what he thinks best for humanity.

Damn him.

We never asked to bow. Who is he to say Reds and Browns toiling to death is for the greater good? Who is he to say Pink children being harvested for rape, Obsidians and Grays for battle, is a necessity? How can he sit there and say that he alone knows what is best for me, for my family? It is not his right. Just as it was not his right to come into my world and take Eo. And if he thinks might makes it his right, then it's my bloodydamn right to cut off his head right now.

Instead I stand and cross the distance between us. Kneeling, I take his hand and kiss his bloodydamn ring. "As you will it, *my liege*."

His hard lips curl into a predatory smile. "Call me Father."

"Try not to look so damn pleased with yourself," Lorn says to me.

We stand amid the white-pathed gardens of the Citadel. A breeze stirs the bells that hang in the trees. It is a simple affair, not like the gross spectacle of Luna. Small tables sit beneath ivy-covered boughs. Pink attendants clear them of the feast. On green grass and white paths, Peerless stand laughing and impressing one another while cradling flutes of champagne. You can sense the Jackal's hand in the planning. He's a tastefully modest creature.

More dignitaries came to the dinner than to the ceremony. So there are many Augustus and I had to greet. They came to us in a line based upon hierarchy, of course. I soon grew tired of glad-handing and sought Lorn near the base of a thin white tree. His arms are crossed, face all stormy and scowling at the champagne in his hand. He tosses it into a shrub.

"I hate this sort of thing too," I say. "Soon as I get my Mask, Augustus wants me to cozy up to some of the Moon Lords. Then it's bed for me." Without Mustang here, there's no real joy to be had.

"Alone it seems. Where is your girl?" He squints around. "Been looking high and low."

"Don't know." Has everyone noticed?

"Ah." He grunts. "Lovers' quarrel? Well, I won't pour advice in your ear except to say, swallow your pride. She's a gem if you can keep her."

If.

"I'm glad you came," I say. "Even if your advice is shit."

He laughs gruffly and nods to the Jackal, who speaks with Roque and several Politicos from Ganymede. "Your friend made it possible. Augustus somehow forgot to invite me, even though my men won him a planet. Manners are so conditional these days. Speaking of, how long do you think I have to stay before it's not rude to leave?"

"It's not even nine. Aren't you presenting the Mask in a few minutes?"

"I was, but it's tedious statecraft. I asked your friend Roque to do it, if that's fine with you. Actually, he asked me. Same difference."

"No. No, that's better actually." It'll be good for Roque to be included as much as possible. There's mending that needs doing. Public displays of friendship are a good place to start.

Lorn props his back against the tree. "My old bones creak at night. I'm going to check on security so I don't have to talk to any of these slippery people." He watches a ripWing pass high overhead.

"Let someone else do that." A Pink hands Lorn the tumbler of whiskey I ordered. His favorite label. He sniffs, subdued. "I only get to see you in armor. Act the proper mentor and stay with me. We have two bottles of the Lagavulin for you."

"Back to your old tricks. Two bottles for an extra two hours of training, wasn't that the deal? Should have charged more. Ha!"

He limps off with his whiskey to play tag with his grandchildren in the trees. I watch the Pink who delivered his drink slip back into the crowd, her movement vaguely familiar.

A woman loops her arm in mine. I turn excitedly only to find Victra. She doesn't notice my disappointment.

"I do hope the Violets put lions instead of a pegasus on your Mask." She laughs at my expression. "Yes, the rumor is already aflight. Darrow au Augustus." She shivers playfully. "The women will come running."

I roll my eyes. "Oh, shut up."

"Make me." She slides her hand along my low back. "It's a shame you already settled down." Nodding to a group of young Peerless from the Gas Giants, she leans close. "But does it mean you can't play?"

"Do you just enjoy trying to make me blush?"

She pulls the laurel wreath from my head and places it on her own, curtsying foolishly. "You've found me out. Where is your little Mustang anyway?"

"Why is everyone so damn curious?"

"Darrow." Roque joins us, holding an ivory box large enough for the Triumph Mask. He's sleek in a black Praetor's uniform, hair slicked back. "I believe we're supposed to gather for the Mask presentation. Do you know where? I'm a bit confused about this whole affair."

Victra frowns. "Citadel staff is still discombobulated. The Bellona had the place for a month. Adrius had to comb through the Pinks for spies. Especially after what happened in Attica. He's got his men everywhere tonight. Oh, hell. It's starting." She sets my laurel wreath back on my head and pulls me toward the clearing where the Golds assemble. Sevro cuts across my path, stopping us.

"Darrow," he says quickly, then, looking to Victra, "move along." She scrunches her face and leaves.

"You like her," I tease. "I can tell."

He ignores me. "He's still not here."

"Fitchner? You call his datapad?"

"Isn't going through. The bastard said he was coming. So if he isn't here, something important must be happening. I should check."

"Check." I grab his arm. "But call Ragnar. And be careful."

"I'm always careful."

It's strange watching him leave. Like watching my shadow depart and realizing its destiny may be separate from mine. Perhaps in the end, he's more important than I. Truly a child of two worlds.

I follow the crowd through the trees. Little lanterns make homes in the branches, bathing the clearing in a warm white glow. There are no Whites present. No formalities here. It's as understated as the Triumph was grand. The crowd parts for me. I walk onto the white cobblestones where Lorn sits with his grandchildren on the edge of a dolphin fountain. Augustus motions me to stand by him near a statue of a blind maiden holding a scale and a sword. It drowns in ivy. The Jackal joins us.

"I hear we're going to be brothers," I tell him.

"Well, who says you can't choose family?" He glances distractedly at his datapad. "Better you than that bastard Cassius."

"Something the matter?" I ask.

"More gorydamn requisition orders." He looks up from his data-pad. "Sorry. All's prime on Mars, my goodman. Just wish my sister were here. You still wouldn't know where she is, would you?"

I shake my head. With each mention, Mustang grows a little more distant. I held out hope she'd appear. Make a grand entrance and I'd know all was well. But some fantasies don't come true.

"Your pardon! My goodmen!" Augustus announces, cutting through the murmur of conversation. "Thank you." He clears his throat and extends a welcome to Mars's many guests, tipping his head to the ArchGoverness of Triton. "Though our glasses sparkle and bellies are full, this night will not last." He peers through his guests, voice firm and dry in the damp air. Fireflies glow among the trees.

"We know that this is only the beginning. War will require much from us. But let us not be so hasty as to pass over a victory such as the one we saw just a few weeks ago. A triumph of will, loyalty, strength.

"All that grandeur of the parade was for them. Quiet moments like these are for us." He taps his facial scar once. "Where we, despite our differences, can nod our heads and raise our glasses to a unique accomplishment of will. It was not done alone. But the Rain was called by one man. So, Darrow au Andromedus, we salute you."

"Hail, Reaper!" Lorn calls, mocking me only slightly.

The glasses rise through the clearing as voices murmur agreement. And they drink. It feels so hollow looking to my left and seeing the Jackal instead of Mustang. To smile feels so false, knowing all this will soon crumble. Victra seems to sense my mood, and so she winks, tilting her glass to me.

Augustus motions Roque, who comes forward with the large ivory box cradled in his arms. He sets the box in my hands and puts one of his atop so I can't yet open it.

"You and I have seen much together." His voice is calm and even. "The night I first met you, you were on the floor of Mars Castle looking at the blood on your hands. Do you remember what I said?"

His other hand touches my right wrist, the tenderness something out of the past, when our hands had fewer calluses, fewer scars.

"Of course. 'If you are thrown into the deep and do not swim, you will drown. So keep swimming,'" I recite. "I'd never forget."

"How far we've come." His eyes survey my face, taking note of its lines, its imperfections. I tilt my head, wondering what he's looking for. "I would have paid a hundred times what your contract was worth to protect you."

"I know, Roque."

"I would have died for you a thousand times more, because you were my friend."

Were. Something in his voice makes me look around. Over his shoulder, I see Victra whisper something humorous to Antonia and their skeletal mother. Lorn serves his grandchildren little plates of cake brought by a short Pink. But it's after the server turns that I freeze inside. He turns haughtily. Ruthlessly. Unlike any Pink ever born. Breaking character only for half a second. I know that turn. I know that man. It's Vixus. It has to be. My eyes dart to the Pink who brought me Lorn's whiskey. *Lilath*. The Jackal's girl who wore bones in her hair. Who allied with the Bellona. They're dressed as Pinks. Golds with fleshMasks. Contacts.

Wolves playing lambs.

I pull back from Roque, about to shout, when I feel his grip tighten, and I realize he was saying goodbye. A needle from his ring pricks my wrist. Gentle, like the kiss he now plants on my cheek.

"And thus go liars, with a *bloodydamn* kiss."

One word shatters a thousand lies.

Face colder than the marble statue behind us, Roque draws back and opens the ivory box's lid. With the gentle creak of silver hinges, my world ends. Augustus gasps in horror at what's inside the box. And a foot away, the Jackal, eyes full of long-dormant hate, smiles at me and cocks his head back like an animal to loose a manic, mocking howl.

A signal of the end.

Victra reaches for her razor. Antonia steps back. Pulls a scorcher from a waiter's tray and fires two rounds into Victra's spine. Two more into her mother's neck before any can move.

"ARCOS!" Augustus screams, whipping out his razor. "TO ARMS!"

"HOWLERS TO ME!" Lorn roars, pushing back his grandchildren. *Protect the Reaper!*

Too late. Even as Lorn stands, Lilath pulls a pulseDagger from under her tray and sweeps it across his throat from behind. Lorn shoves his hand between throat and blade. Four fingers fall to the ground. He angles his body, strains against her, grasping her wrist with his bloody arm. Blade humming. Grunting. Intimate horror as chaos reigns across the clearing.

The poison spreads in me.

I slump to the ground, box in my lap.

Back against the blind statue.

Paralyzed.

The Jackal glides through the midst of this melee, a reptile over ice. He watches stabbing and butchery, and finds Lorn still struggling with Lilath as she tries to cut his throat. Lorn's managed to take a shard of broken glass from the ground and is reaching to stab Lilath's leg, when the Jackal bends, examines Lorn for a moment, and slowly puts a blade into his belly.

"They were wrong. Your side isn't made of stone."

Lorn's face pinches with fear as the Jackal pulls the blade up the old man's body. My razormaster's eyes jump to me, to his grandchildren. He tries to stand, tries one last ounce of fury. Tries to say something. But his body has quit him. He will never see his island again. Never pet his griffin. Never hear his grandchildren laugh or see Lysander, the grandson I promised him. I did this to him. I brought him back from that separate peace he so wanted, but knew he never deserved. And soon his eyes gaze at nothing and the Jackal retrieves his blade and Lilath finishes her work with a slow sawing motion.

I loose a long moan. It's all I can manage. Drool slithers down my throat. Victra crawls toward me, blood leaking from her. Amid all this, Roque stands, a statue, apart.

Pulse weapons warble in the distance. Thunder rips the sky as dark shapes descend, cracking the sound barrier. They come from a stealthed ship. Something snuck in. Where are the patrols?

Obsidians and Praetorians land in the midst of the clearing, thumping down on the stone. They pursue those who fled the killing ground for the gardens, hunting them down with quiet economy. Antonia directs the slaughter, finishing heirs, clipping bloodlines half a millennium old. Taking hostages. Lilath is laughing with Vixus. They peel away electronic fleshMasks and shake free their golden hair. Behind them, Aja lands in splendor, her armor flashing in the lantern light. She surveys the carnage, face dark and content. I hardly notice her, because an old friend lands at her side. Cassius.

"Virginia?" he asks.

"Missing, I fear," the Jackal says.

"Warned?"

"Angered. Lover's spat."

Victra manages to crawl to my ankle. A slick of blood shadows her path from where she was shot to the place where she now curls. Red on her lips. I can't feel her touch.

"I didn't know," she whispers. "Darrow, I didn't know."

Aja bends over Lorn's body, taking his razor from his waist and closing her mentor's eyes forever. He never even drew the weapon. Cassius comes close, stopping at my feet, where he goes to a knee and watches me.

"Can he move, poet?" he asks Roque.

"No. But he can hear."

"You killed my family, Darrow. All of them. Me, Julian, that's one thing. But the children? How could you?" I don't know what he's talking about. "I'll find Sevro. I'll find Mustang. There will be no mercy." He touches the enameled hilt of his razor with his new arm.

"You can't kill him," Roque says from behind him. "You know what he is." Roque puts a hand on Cassius's shoulder. "Cassius, the Sovereign's orders were clear."

"Dissection," Cassius murmurs. He watches me, and it seems that there was never a time when this man called me brother. Never a hope we could ever have been what we are now. Roughly, he takes my hand. I think, for a moment, he is shaking it. But instead, he steals the ring I earned. The iron wolf I killed his brother to possess. My finger is naked without it.

He rises from his bent knee to tower over me, more a beautiful vulture than an eagle. "Julian. Lea. Pax. Quinn. Weed. Harpy. Rotback. Tactus. Lorn. Victra. They deserved better than to die for a slave." With that, he leaves me with Roque.

The world is silent except for sobbing and the sound of sirens. At my side, Victra watches Cassius leave, her life leaking from her. Those clever eyes of hers look up at me, lost.

"We must hurry," Aja drawls in the center of the massacre. "They know we're here. Bring your father and let us go."

The Jackal nods. "A moment, if you please."

Several meters away, Augustus lies pinned to the ground by three waiters. They hoist him up as the Jackal approaches, stepping over Lorn's desecrated body.

"Is the Mask not as you like, Darrow?" he calls to me. "I made it just for you after you revealed your true self to me in Attica."

The Jackal turns to his father. "What do you think, Father? Was this a ploy worthy of your name?"

"You monster." Augustus spits in his face. "What have you done?"

"So you're not proud?" The Jackal wipes the spit away and looks at it. "Damn."

"Stop this. My son, you've ruined us."

"Adrius . . . ," Aja says impatiently. "We must go."

The Jackal steps forward. "So *now* you call me son?" He clucks his tongue scoldingly and straightens his father's jacket. "Was I your son when you put me on a rock for the elements to claim me? Three days. I was a baby. The Board didn't even want an Exposure. But you thought I was so weak, and Claudius so strong. Was he strong when I had Karnus put him in the ground?"

His father's lips tremble. "What?"

"I paid Karnus au Bellona seven million credits and six Pinks to sully Claudius's girl. I knew Claudius's honor would lead him into the ring. Funny thing is . . . it was your money. I asked you for it so I could *invest in my future*. And I did." He frowns. "Father, did you really think a ten-year-old cares about the Silver market? You should have paid better attention."

"You killed Claudius." Augustus's voice breaks under the strain and he sags into the arms of those holding him, shaking from sadness. "You killed my boy."

This would break Mustang's heart.

"*I* am your boy," the Jackal sneers. "I was a *good* son. I *worshipped* you. I feared you. I obeyed you. I learned what you wished me to learn. I went where you wished me to go. I did only as your will commanded. Yet I was not enough."

Augustus shakes his head, drawing back his rage as the Praetorians cuff his hands together with magnetic shackles. His eyes rise to look at the monster he created. "I should have strangled you in your crib."

"Come now, Father . . ."

"You are not my son."

Adrius flinches. With those few words, Augustus releases something. And the small part of Adrius that held out hope to be loved disappears. He shakes off his humanity, leaving only the Jackal.

"*Then farewell hope, and with hope farewell fear. Farewell remorse: all good to me is lost.*" He whispers to some distant, fading part of himself as he lazily lifts the scorcher to his father's forehead. "*Evil, be thou my good.*"

"Stop!" Aja steps forward. "Adrius! In the name of the Sovereign—"

The Jackal shoots his father in the head.

Eo's killer drops to the ground, and I feel hollowness spread over my heart. Death begets death begets death. This is what Dancer warned me about. This is why Mustang said not to trust her brother. This is why my friends will die. Why I will die. Because I cannot match this evil.

Who can?

"You dumb little snake!" Aja shouts. "The Sovereign needed him to talk down the Outer Rim! Gorydammit." She looks to the sky as flame trails blaze across the dark. Someone's coming in hard from the upper atmosphere. Pulse weapon fire flashes across Citadel grounds as Praetorians encounter Augustus's and Lorn's first responders.

"I gave you this prize," the Jackal says, nodding to me. "Do not whine now." He references his datapad and points at the flame trails.

"The Telemanuses are coming. Unless you want to play with them, I suggest we leave."

Cassius agrees. "Lorn and Augustus are dead. This army will wither."

Aja orders her Praetorians to their shuttle. They come to pick me from the ground. Victra's hand on my leg slackens. Her eyes have closed.

"*Roque,*" I murmur through the thickness of the poison. "*Brother . . .*"

"No. *No,*" he says, not a monster, still himself, still quiet and tranquil, if dreadful in his sadness. "You are a son of Red. I a son of Gold. That world where we are brothers is lost." But he comes close, bending, reaching with delicate hands to angle the ivory box in my lap toward my face. "And in this world, the power of Gold will never wane."

I look into the box and my heart shatters.

All that has been, all that was to be, crashes down. Eo's dream falls into darkness. Wherever you are, Sevro, Mustang, Ragnar, do not come back to this world. There's too much pain. Too much sorrow to ever mend it.

I look into the box and see Fitchner's head staring back at me, eyeless, mouth stuffed with grapes. Ares, the one hope we had, the one man who picked me up when I was broken and gave me a chance for something better than revenge, has been butchered. And I know we are undone.

ACKNOWLEDGMENTS

My favorite line from *Lord of the Rings* comes when Frodo has all but given up his quest, and Samwise says to him, "Come, Mr. Frodo . . . I can't carry it for you, but I can carry you."

Writing is a lonely quest at times. You lose the path. You take the mountain pass only to realize you've made a mistake and must double back through a more treacherous route. Often there's no wizard to guide you. No signposts except those you conjure. Everything is up to you, and that can be daunting, at least to me. But though my friends and family may not be able to guide the story, they carry me with their love and friendship, and I'm lucky for it.

I'm also lucky to have found such a fine publishing home as Del Rey. Never once have I felt creatively constrained. Never once have I suspected they've desired anything but the best damn story we can put on paper. David Moench, Joe Scalora, Keith Clayton, Tricia Narwani, Scott Shannon, Dave Stevenson, you're all bloodydamn saints as far as I'm concerned.

Now, as for my editor, Mike Braff. Never was there a greater bullshit detector/Obsidian fanatic in all the worlds. You can thank him for the story's ravaging pace, unabashed killcount, and Kavax's fox, Sophocles. Thank you as well to Hannah Bowman who—along with Liza Dawson and Havis Dawson—took a chance on representing me, and to Jon Cassir for his patience and brilliant shepherding of the film rights.

Thank you also to Joel Phillips for beautiful maps and whiskey nights, Nathan Phillips for being the little brother I never had, Tamara Fernandez for the wisdom far beyond her years, Jarrett Price for making Los Angeles feel like home, Terry Brooks for taking the time to read a young author's first work, Scott Sigler for his generous praise, and Josh Crook for all the plans of mischief over breakfast.

To my parents, I owe you everything. You put a shovel in my hands instead of a video game controller. Digging in the woods was the best education I ever received. I've never met truer, kinder souls. You are the people I wish to be. And to my sister, Blair, thank you for making me wiser by teaching me the unique dangers of landing on a patient woman's bad side, oh, and also for being my ninja assassin.

In the end, I must always credit Aaron Phillips. Without him, there would be no *Red Rising*, no *Golden Son*. A true friend since we met studying abroad in Germany, he has watched me start fifteen books, finish six, and face rejection from agents more than a hundred times over seven years. When things grew dark, he lifted me up and urged me to continue on my quest. It's been a blessing seeing him grow, marry, and become as deep and true a man as Samwise Gamgee ever was.

It's strange thinking I wrote *Red Rising* four years ago above my parents' garage in Seattle. Stranger thinking I suspected only my friends would ever read it. So thank you, readers. Thank you for going on this journey with me. Thank you for letting me live a life as a dreammaker, the only thing I've wanted to do since my father read *The Hobbit* to me as a boy and I realized that the magic of man is in words, in tales, in legends lost and in those still yet to come.

ABOUT THE AUTHOR

PIERCE BROWN is the *New York Times* bestselling author of *Red Rising* and *Golden Son*. While trying to make it as a writer, Brown worked as a manager of social media at a start-up tech company, toiled as a peon on the Disney lot at ABC Studios, did his time as an NBC page, and gave sleep deprivation a new meaning during his stint as an aide on a U.S. Senate campaign. He lives in Los Angeles, where he is at work on his next novel.

pierce-brown.com
@Pierce_Brown
Instagram: PierceBrownOfficial

PIERCE BROWN is available for select readings and lectures. To inquire about a possible appearance, please contact the Penguin Random House Speakers Bureau at 212-572-2013 or speakers@penguinrandomhouse.com.

ABOUT THE TYPE

This book was set in Sabon, a typeface designed by the well-known German typographer Jan Tschichold (1902–74). Sabon's design is based upon the original letter forms of sixteenth-century French type designer Claude Garamond and was created specifically to be used for three sources: foundry type for hand composition, Linotype, and Monotype. Tschichold named his typeface for the famous Frankfurt typefounder Jacques Sabon (c. 1520–80).